JOEL C. ROSENBERG

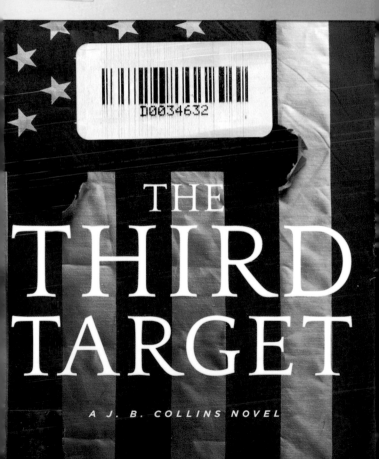

THE THIRD TARGET

A J. B. COLLINS NOVEL

PRAISE FOR
JOEL C. ROSENBERG

"His penetrating knowledge of all things Mideastern—coupled with his intuitive knack for high-stakes intrigue—demand attention."

PORTER GOSS
Former director of the Central Intelligence Agency

"If there were a *Forbes* 400 list of great current novelists, Joel Rosenberg would be among the top ten. . . . One of the most entertaining and intriguing authors of international political thrillers in the country. . . . His novels are un-put-downable."

STEVE FORBES
Editor in chief, *Forbes* magazine

"One of my favorite things: An incredible thriller—it's called *The Third Target* by Joel C. Rosenberg. . . . He's amazing. . . . He writes the greatest thrillers set in the Middle East, with so much knowledge of that part of the world. . . . Fabulous! I've read every book he's ever written!"

KATHIE LEE GIFFORD
NBC's *Today Show*

"Fascinating and compelling . . . way too close to reality for a novel."

MIKE HUCKABEE
Former Arkansas governor

★ ★ ★

THE
THIRD
TARGET

TYNDALE HOUSE PUBLISHERS, INC., CAROL STREAM, ILLINOIS

JOEL C.
ROSENBERG

Visit Tyndale online at www.tyndale.com.

Visit Joel C. Rosenberg's website at www.joelrosenberg.com.

TYNDALE and Tyndale's quill logo are registered trademarks of
Tyndale House Publishers, Inc.

The Third Target

Designed by Dean H. Renninger

Scripture quotations in chapter 51 are taken from *The Living
Bible*, copyright © 1971 by Tyndale House Foundation. Used by
permission of Tyndale House Publishers, Inc., Carol Stream, Illinois
60188. All rights reserved.

Scripture quotations in the dedication and in chapters 46 and 47
are taken from the New American Standard Bible,® copyright ©
1960, 1962, 1963, 1968, 1971, 1972, 1973, 1975, 1977, 1995 by
The Lockman Foundation. Used by permission.

Scripture quotations in chapter 37 are taken from *The Holy
Bible*, English Standard Version® (ESV®), copyright © 2001 by
Crossway, a publishing ministry of Good News Publishers. Used
by permission. All rights reserved.

For information about special discounts for bulk purchases, please
contact Tyndale House Publishers at csresponse@tyndale.com, or
call 1-800-323-9400.

ISBN 978-1-4143-3628-2 (sc)
ISBN 978-1-4964-2327-6 (mass paper)

Printed in the United States of America

23 22 21 20 19 18 17
 7   6   5   4   3   2   1

*To our son Jonah, whose very name reminds us each
and every day that God not only loves Israel, but
also greatly loves her neighbors and her enemies.*

*"You are a gracious and compassionate God,
slow to anger and abundant in lovingkindness,
and one who relents concerning calamity."*

JONAH 4:2

★　★　★

CAST OF CHARACTERS

JOURNALISTS

J. B. Collins—foreign correspondent for the *New York Times*

Allen MacDonald—foreign editor for the *New York Times*

Omar Fayez—Amman-based reporter for the *New York Times*

Abdel Hamid —Beirut-based photographer for the *New York Times*

Alex Brunnell—Jerusalem bureau chief for the *New York Times*

A. B. Collins—former Cairo bureau chief for the Associated Press, and J. B.'s grandfather

AMERICANS

Harrison Taylor—president of the United States

Jack Vaughn—director of the Central Intelligence Agency

Robert Khachigian—former director of the CIA

Arthur Harris—special agent with the Federal Bureau of Investigation

Matthew Collins—J. B.'s older brother

JORDANIANS

King Abdullah II—the monarch of the Hashemite Kingdom of Jordan

Prince Marwan Talal—uncle of the king of Jordan
and a senior advisor

Kamal Jeddeh—director of Jordanian intelligence
(Mukhabarat)

Ali Sa'id—chief of security for the Royal Court

TERRORISTS

Abu Khalif—leader of the Islamic State in Iraq and
al-Sham (ISIS)

Jamal Ramzy—commander of ISIS rebel forces in
Syria and cousin of Abu Khalif

Tariq Baqouba—deputy to Jamal Ramzy

Faisal Baqouba—ISIS terrorist and brother of Tariq

IRAQIS

Hassan Karbouli—Iraqi minister of the interior

Ismail Tikriti—deputy director of Iraqi intelligence

ISRAELIS

Daniel Lavi—Israeli prime minister

Ari Shalit—deputy director of the Mossad

Yael Katzir—Mossad agent

PALESTINIANS

Salim Mansour—president of the Palestinian
Authority

Youssef Kuttab—senior aide to President Mansour

TOP SECRET

PART ONE

July 20, 1951

1

* * *

JERUSALEM

I had never met a king before.

Forty-eight hours earlier, I received a summons from the palace to meet with His Majesty at a certain time in a certain place for an exceedingly rare interview with a foreign journalist. But now I was late, and I was petrified.

Sweat dripped down my face and inside the back of my shirt. As the sun blazed in the eastern sky, the cool of the morning was a distant memory. My freshly starched white collar was rapidly wilting. My crisply knotted azure tie was starting to feel like a noose around my perspiring neck.

I glanced at my gold pocket watch, a graduation present from my father, and the knots in my stomach tightened further. I pulled an already-damp handkerchief from the pocket of my navy-blue pin-striped suit jacket, yet no matter how much I swiped at my brow, I knew it was a losing battle. It wasn't simply the sultry morning air that weighed heavy upon me. It was the nausea-inducing knowledge—indeed, the rapidly increasing certainty—that I was going to be late for this appointment and blow the most important moment of my career.

I had been requesting this interview for the better part of a year and had been repeatedly rebuffed. Then, without warning, I received a telegram from the palace inviting me, A. B. Collins of the Associated Press, to come to Jerusalem and granting me an exclusive interview without limits or preconditions. I cabled my editors back in New York. They were ecstatic. I was ecstatic. For months I had been reading everything I could about this intriguing, if elusive, monarch. I watched every bit of newsreel footage I could scrounge up. I called or met with every expert I could find who knew him or had met him or could give me any tidbit of insight into who he really was, what he wanted, and where he was headed next.

Now the moment had come. I had been instructed to meet His Majesty King Abdullah bin al-Hussein, ruler of the Hashemite Kingdom of Jordan, at the entrance to the Dome of the Rock precisely at noon. That was in less than ten minutes, and at this rate I was never going to make it.

"*Faster, man*—can't you go any faster?" I yelled at my driver.

Leaning forward from the backseat, I pointed through the dust-smudged front window of the cramped little taxi that stank of stale cigarettes. It was an exercise in futility; the answer was pitifully obvious. No, he could not go any faster. It was a Friday. It was the holiest day of the week for the Moslems, and it was fast approaching high noon. Everyone and his cousin were heading to the Al-Aksa Mosque for prayer. It had been this way for twelve centuries, and it would always be thus. No one was going to make an exception—not for a foreigner, not for a Westerner, and certainly not for a reporter.

We were less than a hundred yards from the Damascus Gate, the nearest entrance into the Old City, but traffic was barely moving at all. I surveyed the scene before me and quickly considered my options. Ahead was a classic snapshot of the Orient I had come to know as a foreign correspondent for the Associated Press—a dizzying mélange of vibrant colors and pungent odors and exotic architecture and intriguing faces straight out of central casting. I had seen it in Cairo and Casablanca, in Baghdad and Beirut. Shopkeepers and street vendors who moments before had been brewing coffee and roasting peanuts and hawking everything from spices and kitchen supplies to bottles of Coca-Cola and religious trinkets for the pilgrims were now hurriedly shutting down for the day. Every taxi and truck and private car on the planet seemed to have converged on one traffic circle, their drivers honking their horns and yelling at one another, desperate to get home and then to the mosque. A siren wailed from the south—a police car perhaps, or maybe an ambulance—but it would never get through. A hapless constable sporting a dusty olive-green Royal Jordanian uniform was blowing on a whistle he held in one hand while pointing a wooden club with the other. He shouted commands, but no one paid him much mind.

Bearded, sun-drenched older men, their heads wrapped in white- and black-checkered kaffiyehs, pushed carts of fresh fruits and vegetables as quickly as they could through the filthy, unswept streets while others led goats and camels through tiny gaps in the traffic, back to whatever barns or stables they were usually kept in. Boys in their late teens and young twenties with no jobs and nothing better to do and without fathers or grandfathers in sight seemed in no hurry to get to prayer, taking their last drags on their cigarettes. They stared at giggling packs of young schoolgirls scurrying past with eyes down while older women in long robes and headscarves scowled disapprovingly as they rushed home with boxes of food or pots of water on their heads.

Suddenly the muezzin's haunting call to prayer began to blare from the loudspeakers mounted high up on the minarets. My heart nearly stopped. I was out of time and out of options.

I was going to have to run for it. It was my only chance.

I shouted over the din for my driver to let me out, tossed a few dinars his way, grabbed my leather satchel, donned my black fedora, and raced down the stone steps toward the crush of people flooding through the gate, jostling past the faithful without shame, though I knew my prospects were grim.

I was supposed to meet His Majesty on the Temple Mount, what the Arabs called *"al-Haram ash-Sharif"*—the place of the Noble Sanctuary. After countless phone calls and telegrams from my office in Beirut to the press office in the palace in Amman, it had all been arranged. The most beleaguered and endangered monarch in the entire Moslem world would allow me to shadow him for the day and then sit down with him for his first interview with a Western journalist since a rash of assassinations had set the region on edge.

I couldn't be late. The chief of the Royal Court would never forgive me. He had insisted I get there early. He had promised one of his servants would be waiting. But now they all might be gone by the time I arrived.

I pushed my way through the crowd, a nearly impossible feat, but after considerable difficulty, I finally cleared through the massive stone archway and was inside the Old City. Still ahead of me, however, was a throng of people pressing forward to the mosque.

But I had been here numerous times as a war correspondent in '48 and '49, and I had actually come to know these streets well. I decided to gamble.

Rather than head straight into the *shuq* and up one of the two main streets toward the mosque, already clogged with thousands of worshipers, I moved left, stepped into a pharmacy, and before the owner could even yell at me, I was through the shop and out the back door. Breaking into a full run, I raced through a labyrinthine series of narrow side streets and alleyways, aiming for St. Stephen's Gate—also known as the Lions' Gate—and desperately trying to make up for lost time.

As I neared my destination, however, I found

that everything had come to a standstill. I could finally see the large green wooden doors that were the gateway to the epicenter of the epicenter, the entrance to the thirty-seven-acre plot upon which the third-holiest site in Islam was situated. I was so close now, but no one was moving forward. Not a soul. And soon I saw why.

A contingent of Jordanian soldiers blocked the way. People were yelling, demanding to be let in for prayer. But the grim-faced, heavily armed young men were having none of it. They had their orders, they shouted back. No one could enter until they received the "all clear" sign.

I was stuck, and like the crowd, I was furious. But I knew something they did not. The king was coming. He was heading to the Al-Aksa Mosque for the noon prayers, surrounded by bodyguards who feared for his life, and for good reason.

2

* * *

I set my jaw and pressed forward.

With my press credentials and telegram from the palace in hand, I was certain the soldiers would let me through. But first I had to get to them. The problem was that everyone was pushing forward. Everyone wanted to be at the head of the line. They were shouting at the soldiers to let them get to the mosque on time, and the more resistance they got from the guards, the more infuriated they became.

"Get back!" someone yelled at me.

"Who do you think you are?" another shouted.

Then a burly man with crooked teeth and hatred in his eyes screamed at me, *"Kafir!"*

I recoiled in shock. *Kafir* was an incendiary word. In colloquial Arabic, it technically meant "unbeliever" or "unclean." But on the street it meant "infidel." There were few things worse you could call a man in this part of the world—especially a foreigner—and upon hearing it, I instinctively took several steps back. To be branded a *kafir* was a worst-case scenario. In a crowd already on edge, the term could spark a full-fledged riot, one I would not likely survive. I doubted even the soldiers could guarantee my safety if this crowd turned on me.

There had to be another way. I glanced at my pocket watch again and cursed myself for not having thought my plan through more carefully.

Moving away from the thick of the crowd, I backed into a corner and leaned against a stone wall, watching the raw emotions spiking around me. I could see the young soldiers growing edgy. This had all the makings of a mob. It wouldn't take much for the situation to devolve into violence. The armed military men—the oldest of them no more than nineteen or twenty, I would guess— braced themselves for a fight while I wiped perspiration from my brow. The scorching sun overhead was beating down on us all. The crush of people and the brutal heat began to conspire to make me feel claustrophobic. I couldn't believe what was happening. I wasn't just going to be late; I was actually going to miss this meeting altogether. My career was about to go into the tank. I was beside myself. I had to get out. I had to get some air, something to drink. But there was nothing I could do. Not yet. Not here. All I could do was wait and pray for the winds to shift and my luck to change.

Why hadn't I simply flown to Amman? Why hadn't I met the king's entourage at the palace and traveled with them across the Allenby Bridge, to the meetings they were scheduled to have in Ramallah and Jericho and then on up to Jerusalem? That was their plan. Why hadn't I asked to be part of it?

The reason was simple, though it did me no good now. I had flown from Beirut to Cyprus, and from Cyprus to Tel Aviv, for one simple reason: before I interviewed the king, I wanted to meet with the head of the Mossad.

I had known Reuven Shiloah, the director of Israel's nascent intelligence service, for several years—since before the Mossad had even been created, in fact. I had learned to trust him, and over the years, Reuven had come to trust me, too. Not fully, of course. He was a spy, after all. But he had seen firsthand that I would carefully use his insights but never quote him directly. His perspective was unique and useful for my readers, though I didn't use him as a source often. And I had been helpful to him on numerous occasions as well. He had leaked several important stories to me. I had handled them sensitively, and he had been as pleased as my editors. I was, in effect, a direct pipeline for him to the White House and to members of Congress and, by extension, to other leaders. He had his reasons for feeding me information, and I had mine for accepting it. So over breakfast that morning at a little café in Tel Aviv near the bus station, I asked the Mossad director about the Jordanian king and his situation. The chain-smoking Israeli spy chief had stared at me through his round, gold-rimmed glasses and in hushed tones in a back corner booth confided to me his serious and growing concerns.

"This is a terrible mistake," Reuven said. "He should not be coming."

"Who, the king?" I asked, astonished. "Not come to Jerusalem? Why not?"

"Is it not obvious, Collins?" he asked. "His Majesty is a marked man."

"You're saying he's not safe in Jerusalem, in his own city?" I pressed. "He's not safe anywhere," Reuven replied.

"Do you know of a specific threat?" It's not that I thought he was wrong, but hearing him say it left me deeply unsettled.

"No."

"Then what?"

"I have my gut, my instincts," he said. "The mood is dark, full of rumors and danger. What has happened elsewhere can happen here. As you know, the prime minister of Iran was assassinated just a few months ago."

I nodded. Ali Razmara, Persia's fifty-eighth prime minister, was only forty-nine years old when he was killed. He was the third to have been murdered while in office in recent years.

I pulled a pad out of my bag and began to take notes.

"There were several things notable about Razmara's death," Reuven continued. "He was slain in broad daylight. He was gunned down not by a foreigner but by a fellow Iranian. Indeed, the assailant was a fellow Moslem. And Razmara was walking into a mosque to pray. And Razmara's death was not an isolated incident. Less than two weeks later, Zanganeh was assassinated as well."

He was referring now to Abdol-Hamid Zanganeh, Iran's minister of education.

"Zanganeh was also hit in broad daylight, in this case on the campus of Tehran University," the Mossad director explained. "Very open. Very public. Lots of people. Hard to secure. The weapon was also a pistol. Small. Easily concealed. And who did it? A foreign spy agency? The Brits? The Americans? Us? No. In both cases, the assassins were Moslems, extremists, and locals."

Reuven went on to note that two years earlier someone had tried to assassinate the king of Iran, Shah Mohammad Reza Pahlavi. This too, he reminded me, had happened in broad daylight. In fact, it had happened on the campus of Tehran University, and it too had been the work of an Iranian—not a foreign agent—an Islamic extremist using a pistol. Five bullets had been fired. Four missed their mark. But the fifth did not. Miraculously, it only grazed the king's face, slightly wounding him. But a millimeter's difference would have killed him instantly.

"The assassin posed as a photographer— a member of the press—to get close to the king," the Mossad chief added.

"But that's Iran, not Jordan," I finally said, looking up from my notes. "The situation here is completely different."

"Is it?" he asked. "Certainly there are differences; I grant you that. Iran is ethnically Persian, and Jordan is ethnically Arab. Iran is largely a Shia Moslem nation, while Jordan is predominately Sunni. Iran has oil; Jordan does not. Iran is large and populous, and Jordan is not. But those differences are immaterial. What is important is the pattern."

"What pattern?"

"Iran is a monarchy," Reuven explained. "So is Jordan. The Pahlavi regime is moderate. So are the Hashemites. Iran is pro-British. So is Jordan. Indeed, it was a British colony. What's more, Iran is pro-American. So is Jordan. And though they are quiet about it, Iran under the shah is one of two countries in the region that are on relatively friendly terms with Israel and the Jews. The other is Jordan."

At that, I had to push back. "Now wait a minute—Jordan just fought a war with you. That was only three years ago."

"Things are changing," he said, opening another pack of cigarettes.

"How so?"

There was a long, awkward silence.

"Reuven?"

The Mossad chief glanced around the café. The regulars were starting to fill the place up.

"This is totally off the record," he said finally. "Really, A. B., you cannot use this—agreed?"

"Agreed."

"I have your word?"

"You do," I said.

"I'm serious. You cannot print it under any circumstances. But I'm going to tell you because it's important for you to have some context of who King Abdullah is and what he really wants."

I nodded.

"When I can give you this story, I will," the Mossad chief added. "But we're not there. Not yet."

"I understand, Reuven," I replied. "Really, you have my word. You know me. I won't burn you."

He lit his cigarette and scanned the room again. Then he lowered his voice and leaned toward me. "The king is quietly reaching out."

"To the Mossad?"

"Through us, not to us."

"To whom, then?"

"David Ben-Gurion," he said.

I was stunned. The king of Jordan was reaching out to Israel's aging prime minister?

"Why?" I asked, immediately intrigued.

Again the director scanned the room, making sure no one was listening in on our conversation. Again he lowered his voice, so much so that I could barely hear him and had to lean forward even farther to catch every word over the din of the café.

"His Majesty is probing the possibility of secret peace talks," Reuven confided. "It seems he wants to meet with the PM personally. It's very premature, of course, and all very deniable. But the king seems to be intimating that he wants to make peace with Israel."

I could not hold back my astonishment. "A treaty?"

Reuven shifted in his seat. "Not exactly," he said.

"Too public?" I asked.

He nodded.

"A private 'understanding,' then?" I asked.

"Perhaps," Reuven said, exhaling a lungful of blue smoke. "But even that brings with it great risks. The king knows he's a marked man.

Not by us. We don't have a problem with him. He went to war with us in '48. But we stopped him. We fought him to a standoff, and as far as we're concerned, it's over now. His real problem is the Egyptians and the Syrians and the Iraqis and the Saudis. They hate him. Hate doesn't even begin to describe it. They don't think he's one of them. They don't think he's a team player. They don't think the Hashemite Kingdom is going to be around for long anyway, so they're all gunning for him. They all want him dead, and they're all angling to seize his territory when he collapses."

"So if he opens a back channel with you and comes to an understanding, then maybe it's 'all quiet on the western front' and he can focus his intelligence and security forces elsewhere?" I asked.

"Something like that," Reuven said with a shrug. "Anyway, I don't believe the king wants war with Israel. He certainly doesn't want to annihilate us like the others do. All the evidence says he's not a fanatic. He's a pragmatist. He's someone we can work with. Like the shah."

"But the fanatics want the shah dead," I noted.

Reuven nodded.

"Which is why you're worried someone might try to kill the king—because you think he and the shah are cut from the same cloth," I added.

"It doesn't matter what I think," Reuven demurred. "What matters is what the fanatics think. Which brings us to Monday."

"You mean Riad el-Solh."

"Of course."

I was starting to understand Reuven's concern

now. On Monday, July 16, 1951—just four days earlier—Riad el-Solh, the former prime minister of Lebanon, had been assassinated. Like the shah and the king, el-Solh was a moderate, a pragmatist, and a much-respected regional statesman. His death would have been tragic enough, but he was not murdered in Beirut or in Tehran.

"As you well know, the man was murdered in Amman," Reuven said soberly, his piercing blue eyes flashing with anger. "He was gunned down at Marka Airport, just three kilometers from the palace. He'd been in Jordan visiting with the king, his longtime friend and political ally. Yet he was ruthlessly taken down by a three-man hit team. And I'll give you a scoop. Nobody has this yet. One of the assailants was shot by the police. One committed suicide. But one is still at large."

The implications of that last sentence hit me hard. I just sat there, staring at my cold cup of coffee and untouched plate of eggs and dry toast, trying to make sense of it all. Then Reuven dug in his pocket, plunked down enough lirot to pay for both of our meals, and slipped out the side door without saying another word.

3

★ ★ ★

The crowd around me grew more frantic by the minute.

The time had come. The muezzin's call was over. The faithful were supposed to be in the mosque by now, washed and purified and ready for their noon prayers. But still the soldiers held their ground.

I looked at these young men, barely out of high school, and wondered what they were made of. If they were rushed by this crowd, would they really fire? I wondered. If a disturbance erupted, how quickly would they respond? If someone threatened their ruler, would they really sacrifice their lives to protect him? How well trained, how disciplined were they? How deep did their loyalties to the throne truly run?

We were about to find out.

In mere moments, King Abdullah bin al-Hussein would be arriving just a few hundred steps from where I was standing. Could these young men really protect him? Or was the sixty-nine-year-old monarch truly in grave danger?

Might extremists—perhaps someone in this very crowd—be plotting against him? Abdullah had only formally been on the throne for five years, since May 25, 1946, when the League of Nations granted Jordan its independence at the end of the British Mandate. Was it really possible that some-one—or some group—was plotting to take him down and topple his entire kingdom?

I knew from my conversation with Reuven Shiloah that morning that the Israelis were wor-ried for the king's safety. Surely they were not the only ones. Reuven had said that His Majesty had been strongly urged by his own Jordanian intel-ligence service not to make this trip to Jerusalem. At the very least, they had urged him to reschedule it. But he was not listening. He was his own man. He had business in the Holy City, a city he considered himself personally responsible for, and he would not be deterred. He was, after all, a direct descendant of the prophet Muhammad. His forebearers had been responsible for govern-ing Mecca and Medina for centuries. Now he was the guardian of some of Islam's most revered landmarks. He simply would not cower or shrink away in the face of personal threats, however serious.

That was the king's way. I wasn't sure it was wise, but I had to admit, privately at least, that I wasn't protesting. After all, His Majesty was also being urged by his closest counselors not to speak to the Western press at all—and certainly not to agree to an interview with an American—but he was ignoring this advice too. Clearly he had something to say to the world and had decided to use me to say it, and for this I felt enormously grateful.

I had worked for United Press International and the Associated Press for nearly ten years. I'd interviewed generals and commanders and local officials of all kinds. I had been posted in London, Paris, Bombay, and most recently Beirut. I'd met presidents and prime ministers and heads of state. But I had never even seen a king in the flesh, much less interviewed one, and I confess that the very notion of conversing with a monarch held for me a certain mystique that I cannot put into words.

So this was it. If I didn't do something quickly to get through this crowd and past these guards, I knew I would regret it for the rest of my life.

I scanned the crowd, picked my target, and took my fate into my own hands. Wiping my palms on my trousers, I set my plan into motion. I began pushing aside several old men, then shoved a few teenage boys out of my way, working along the stone wall to my right, toward the soldiers. Immediately, curses came flying back at me thick and fierce, but those I had moved past didn't have a chance. I was over six feet tall and nearly two hundred pounds. So I kept moving toward my target, and with a few more steps I was there. Without warning, I drove my elbow hard into the ribs of the burly young man with crooked teeth who minutes before had called me an infidel. He was probably about twenty-four or twenty-five years old, and I suspected he had far more experience street fighting than I did. But for the moment, at least, I had the advantage. I had a plan, and he was being blindsided.

Infuriated, his eyes flashing with the same rage I had seen before, he took a swing at me with all his might. I knew it was coming, and I ducked in time, so his fist slammed into the stone wall behind me. At that moment, I embedded my right fist in his stomach. He doubled over, and I lunged at his waist, toppling him to the ground, whipping the bloodthirsty crowd around us into a frenzy. It didn't take long for him to recover his wits and flip me over, but as he did, the whistles of the soldiers started blowing. I covered my face with my arms as he landed several blows. But before he could do any real damage, a half-dozen Jordanian guards descended upon us. They beat back the crowd with wooden clubs and soon were beating him, too, until they could pull him off me and clamp handcuffs on him. I received several kicks, one to my back and one to my stomach, and then I too was cuffed. But in the grand scheme, since I was on the bottom of the pile, I actually got the least of it, and when they realized I was not a Jordanian or a Moslem but a Westerner, the captain of the unit—a Captain Rajoub, according to the name on his uniform—looked horrified.

"Who are you?" he demanded while his colleagues aimed their rifles at me.

"I am a reporter," I said in English, scooping my hat off the ground, dusting it off, and replacing it on my perspiration-soaked head as two soldiers rifled through my leather satchel.

"From where?"

"America," I replied.

There was no point in saying I was actually based in Beirut. It would just confuse the matter. And although I was fluent in Arabic, I spoke only in English since the whole point was to distinguish myself from the locals, to be as foreign as possible. *America* was a word I was sure these men knew. They didn't love us. But they had the decency to fear us.

"*Papers!*" the young captain insisted, bristling.

I slowly reached into my suit pocket, careful not to make the boys with the rifles any more nervous than they already were. I pulled out my American passport and my AP credentials and handed them to him. The man opened the passport first, looked at the photo, then looked back at me.

"Andrew?" he asked, his accent thick but his English passable, to my surprise. "Is that your name?"

I nodded.

"Andrew Bradley Collins?"

I nodded again.

"Born September 9, 1920?"

"Yes."

"In Bar . . . Bar . . ."

"Bar Harbor," I said.

"What's that?"

It seemed ridiculous to be discussing my hometown. "It's a little town in Maine."

The man just looked at me. Indeed, the whole crowd was staring at me, and many seemed ready to tear me limb from limb.

"Why are you here?" Captain Rajoub asked.

"I have a telegram," I said, slowly reaching back into my breast pocket and pulling out the crumpled yellow sheet from Western Union. I handed it to the captain and watched as he read it.

Then I saw his eyes widen.

"You are supposed to meet His Majesty?" he asked, incredulous. "You're meeting him here?"

"I'm supposed to—I was trying to get this message to you, sir, but that lunatic there tried to kill me," I said, pointing at the burly man being forcibly restrained by several soldiers from trying to attack me again.

"You're supposed to meet him now?"

"Yes—if you and your boys will let me through."

Genuine fear flashed in the captain's eyes. He and his men had arrested and very nearly shot a man who was supposed to be meeting with the king. For a moment, he was speechless. But only for a moment.

"Right this way, sir," he said at last. "Please, my friend, come—I will take you to His Majesty."

He turned to his dumbfounded men and barked a command in Arabic. Stunned by all that had just occurred, the soldiers immediately cleared a path. Then the captain beckoned me to follow him. I grabbed my satchel from the soldier holding it, straightened my tie, brushed myself off as best I could, and followed the captain onto the Temple Mount.

My desperate plan had worked, and I could hardly believe my eyes.

I was late, but I was in.

4

* * *

I desperately scanned the plaza but did not see him.

Had I missed my chance?

Captain Rajoub told me to follow him closely and not to say a word, and then he set across the plaza at a rather brisk pace. I did what he said, amazed that I was really on the Temple Mount for the first time in my life.

Rising before me was the stunningly beautiful Dome of the Rock. Built in the seventh century and completed around AD 691, it was larger than I'd expected, rising several stories from its stone base. The octagonal structure of the building, covered in exquisite blue-and-green tile work with Islamic decor, was spectacular. And of course the expansive wooden dome, gilded in pure gold, was even more spectacular—and very nearly blinding as well—gleaming majestically in the noonday sun.

Captain Rajoub and I turned the corner and headed for the front door of the mosque, on the south side of the complex, but there was still no sign of the king. I saw several soldiers patrolling the grounds, but not the royal entourage. I was tempted to despair, I'll admit, but I wouldn't allow it—not yet, anyway. Rather, I started asking questions.

"Excuse me," I said in Arabic to a pair of soldiers walking nearby. "I was told to wait here to conduct an interview with His Majesty. Have I missed him?"

Both men looked at me suspiciously, but the captain assured them my story was true and showed them the telegram. What's more, the captain promised them he would stay at my side and make certain I caused no trouble. They glanced at the pistol strapped to the captain's belt and then looked back at me, apparently satisfied.

"No, you have not missed him," the older one replied in reasonably good English. "His Majesty is on his way. Wait over there."

"*Shukran,*" I replied, thanking the men, amazed at my good fortune.

I did my best to look calm, but my heart was racing. *The angels must be looking out for me,* I thought. Somebody up there was.

Perhaps there really was something mystical, even magical, about this spot, I mused while I waited. It was here, the Jews said, that the biblical Abraham nearly sacrificed his son Isaac, until God intervened and saved the day. It was here—on this very spot—that not one but two Jewish Temples had once stood, and where the Jews believed a third Temple would one day be built. That certainly seemed implausible, given that the

Jews hadn't controlled the Old City, let alone the Temple Mount, for more than two thousand years.

Besides, the Moslems would never allow the Jews to build here. After all, they too considered the site sacred. They believed that Muhammad, their Prophet, had arrived here after taking his famed night flight from Mecca on a winged, white horselike creature. Furthermore, they claimed that from this very spot he had been taken up to heaven.

The Christians, meanwhile, believed that not far from here Jesus of Nazareth had been crucified, buried, and resurrected—and that he would return to this very spot at the End of Days to judge his enemies and set up his eternal Kingdom.

I had no idea who was right. I'd never been religious growing up—never cared much about it, I must say. But if there was a God, he had certainly shown me kindness this day.

While I waited, and the soldiers eyed me warily, I tried to get my thoughts in order. What was I supposed to do first when I met the king? Did one shake his hand? Bow down? Kiss his feet? I suddenly realized that I had no idea what the protocol was. No one had told me, and foolishly I had not asked.

I brushed such thoughts aside. There was no reason to be anxious. This man had agreed to meet with me because I had something he wanted: a worldwide audience. He and his advisors had obviously vetted me. They surely had read my dispatches from the region. They must have concluded I was a fair-minded reporter who strove for balance and accuracy. More important, His Majesty clearly had something he wanted to say through me to my readers, to the nations, and to the men who ruled them. But what?

There was something about this particular monarch that intrigued me a great deal. On the face of it, one could argue that King Abdullah didn't matter much to my American readers or even to most Europeans. His kingdom possessed no oil, no gold, no silver, no diamonds or precious minerals. It had no real natural resources to speak of at all, in fact. It had no heavy industry, nothing of substance to export. It had far too little water and precious little arable land. The king ran a tiny, tribal nation of bedouin Arabs who had not exactly distinguished themselves by splitting the atom or curing polio or inventing the wireless or creating the world's tastiest breakfast cereal. This wasn't a nation abounding in Pulitzers or Nobel Prizes. If Jordan was known for anything, it was instability and shifting sands. The nation had gained its independence amid the collapse of the Ottoman Empire. It was first governed by a man who wasn't even born there but rather in Mecca. Then it was overrun in 1948 by hundreds of thousands of Palestinian refugees, most of whom had fled the war with the new state of Israel, though some had been driven out of their homes by the Jews. The Palestinians called the war *"al-Nakbah"*—the "catastrophe," the "disaster"—and they were deeply embittered. How loyal were they to the current king? I couldn't say. But my sources told me officials in London worried about the stability of the throne in Amman. So did officials in Washington.

So beyond a few government officials, who in the U.S. or Great Britain really cared about the fate of Jordan? The AP didn't even have a bureau in Amman. Neither did UPI or the *New York Times* or Reuters. Cairo? Yes. Jerusalem? Of course. Damascus and Beirut? Without question. But not Amman. Didn't that say something? Nevertheless, there was a story here—I was sure of it—and Abdullah was the key.

Suddenly I saw him.

He was approaching from the east, through a grove of trees and an ancient stone archway, flanked by a handful of bodyguards in plainclothes—I counted six—several aides, and a dozen uniformed soldiers, each carrying a submachine gun. The king was dressed entirely in white cotton robes that shimmered in the sunshine, and he wore a white turban. He appeared to be bald, but he sported a well-groomed mustache that connected with a full goatee. As he drew closer, he struck me as more diminutive in stature than I had expected, no more than four or five inches over five feet, if that. But he strode purposefully across the warm stones with a regal bearing, commanding and self-assured. His skin was the color of hot tea with a splash of milk. His eyes were bright and intense, though they never looked at me.

Several minutes behind schedule now, the king headed straight for the ancient mosque. The captain beside me stood ramrod straight and saluted, as did the soldiers nearby. Then I noticed a young boy, no more than fifteen or sixteen years old, dressed in full ceremonial military garb, walking a stride or two behind the king.

"Who is that?" I whispered to the captain.

"That is Prince Hussein, of course," the captain whispered back.

"The king's grandson?" I asked, startled because no one had told me he was coming.

"Who else?"

As the entourage rushed past me, I feared the deal was off and the interview had been forgotten or ignored. But then one of the king's aides caught my eye and motioned me to follow. I quickly complied. As we headed down a flight of steps toward a small crowd of worshipers and well-wishers, the aide moved to my side.

"Mr. Collins, I am Mansour, His Majesty's spokesman," he said in a hushed tone as we walked. "Please forgive us for being late."

"Don't mention it," I said, breathing a sigh of relief. "Is everything okay?"

"Yes, yes—well, it is now," he said. "I confess we had a bit of a scare as the motorcade came over the Mount of Olives. There was a demonstration of some kind—a roadblock, quite unexpected. And as you can imagine, our security detail is on heightened alert."

"Yes, of course," I said, trying to keep pace with him and the others.

"At any rate, our security men were worried for a few minutes, but it all worked out. Everything is all right. I think we should have a good day, and then we will find a time for you and His Majesty to sit down and speak together. He is looking forward to meeting you, and he has confided in me his desire to give you quite a . . . scoop, I believe you call it."

I was elated. This was really happening. Here I was, being escorted into the Al-Aksa Mosque, the third-holiest site in the Islamic religion, right behind one of the descendants of the prophet Muhammad, and I was soon going to speak with him as well.

Ever since my days as a young boy at Phillips Academy in Andover, I'd wanted to be a news correspondent in foreign lands. I cannot explain the obsession. There was no obvious rationale. My classmates certainly did not aspire to be journalists. They wanted to be baseball players and bankers, congressmen and corporate titans. There were no journalists in my family. My father was a tax attorney. My mother was a piano teacher. My father was a good man, kind and generous, but he never traveled outside the United States. He didn't even own a passport. Yet since childhood I harbored an insatiable desire to explore deep jungles and vast deserts and exotic locales of all kinds. My father couldn't stand meeting new people; I lived for it. At Princeton, my father immersed himself in numbers. At Columbia, I immersed myself in history. My father read the King James Bible and the *Wall Street Journal*. I'd had my own subscriptions to *Life* magazine and *National Geographic* since I was eight years old and used to sneak a small transistor radio into my bed at night to listen to the reports of Edward R. Murrow. And here I was, in

Jerusalem—at the Dome of the Rock itself—in the presence of royalty.

A thousand questions flooded my head. Where would I possibly begin? Here was a man who was already eighteen years old when the twentieth century began. Here was a member of the Great Hashemite Dynasty, the son of Sharif Hussein bin Ali, onetime ruler of Mecca of the Hejaz. This king had been schooled in Istanbul at the peak of Turkish power. Later, he had gone back to Arabia and emerged as the esteemed commander of the Great Arab Revolt against the Ottomans. He had been personal friends with T. E. Lawrence, the legendary British colonel who became known as Lawrence of Arabia. Together they had taken the region by storm, organizing the Arab tribes to fight against the Ottomans. And when it was all over and the dust had settled, the Turkish empire had collapsed, and the Hashemite family had been amply rewarded. The Brits carved up the remains of the Turkish fiefdom and gave the Hashemites three territorial gifts: the desert region known as the Arabian Peninsula, the fertile Mesopotamian region that became known as Iraq, and the land on the eastern side of the Jordan River that became known as Transjordan. It was over this last swath of territory that Abdullah now ruled, and as the door to the mosque was opened for us, it finally dawned on me which question I had to ask him first.

5

★ ★ ★

As the king neared the doorway of the mosque, I saw a flicker of movement.

It happened fast, but it seemed odd—out of place.

I looked to my right and saw a man bolt from behind the door and jump from the shadows. He pulled out a small pistol. He aimed it at the monarch's head. The guards didn't react at first. Neither did the king. They were all too stunned, as was I. Then I saw a flash from the barrel and heard the boom—then another—and a third.

Horrified, I watched the entire scene unfold before me as if in slow motion. The king jerked back again and again and finally collapsed to the ground. I turned and saw his grandson lunge forward without a second thought, attacking the shooter. The two men struggled for a moment before I heard another shot. And then the young prince crumpled to the ground, writhing in pain.

A flutter of birds raced for the sky. People screamed and ran for cover. But the shooting didn't stop. For several seconds, the man kept firing, and then he began to run. He was coming straight for me. The king's guards pivoted now and began to return fire. I dropped to the ground and covered my head and face. The Temple Mount had erupted in gunfire at this point. Bullets were whizzing past my head and I was certain these moments were my last.

But a split second later, the assailant crashed to the ground not far from where I was. I didn't know if he had been shot or had simply stumbled. Without thinking, I sprang up and jumped on him. Before I realized what I was doing, I was beating him about the face and head. Soon I could see that he had been shot in multiple places. He was bleeding profusely. But he was not dead—not yet—and I was determined he was not going to run. For the moment I had forgotten I was a journalist. I had forgotten, too, that I was now in the line of fire. I was enraged, and my fists kept raining blows down upon him.

Seconds later, soldiers surrounded us, guns locked and loaded and pointed at both of us.

"Stop—don't move any farther!" they shouted.

Immediately I stopped beating the man. The soldiers yelled at me to put my hands above my head, where they could see them. Then they ordered me to slowly get off the man and step away. I did as I was told and saw two of the king's personal guards running toward us. Before I realized what was happening, someone behind me smashed the back of my skull with what must have been the butt of a rifle. I collapsed to the ground, not far from the assailant. I could feel blood running

down the back of my scalp. My eyes were tearing, and I was in intense pain. But I did not black
out, and as I lay there, I watched a soldier scoop
up the still-smoking pistol lying by the assassin's
side. They checked the man for more weapons but
found none. Then they checked his pulse.

"He's done for," one of the guards said.

I could hardly believe it was true. Dead?
Already? But who was he? What was his story?
Who had sent him? I was seething. This man had
tried to kill a king. He had tried to kill a prince.
He had done so on sacred, holy ground. Why had
he done it? I wanted answers.

A soldier grabbed my arms and tied them
behind my back. Another took my satchel and
patted me down for weapons. As he did, one of
the king's guards was rifling through the assassin's
identification papers and personal effects.

"What's his name?" his partner asked.

"Mustafa," the guard replied. "Mustafa Shukri
Ashshu."

"He's not a Jew?"

"No, his papers say he's a Moslem, sir, a Palestinian."

"You cannot be serious."

"I am, sir."

"Are they forgeries?"

"No, they look real."

"Let me see them."

The guard handed the papers over to his
partner.

"They are real," he said in disbelief. "He lives
right here in the Old City. He's a tailor."

"How old was he, sir?"

"Just twenty-one."

The older guard let fly a slew of obscenities.

"How in the world did he get by all of us?" he fumed.

That, of course, was a question the papers did not shed light on.

Suddenly the two bodyguards turned to me.

"Who are you?" they shouted. *"Where did you come from?"*

Their questions came fast and furious. I explained I was an American, there to meet the king. They pressed for details, and that's when Captain Rajoub came running up, gun in one hand, the telegram from the palace in the other. The guards read the telegram, checked my papers, and conferred with one another. Rajoub confirmed I was telling the truth, and finally the men untied me, pulled me to my feet, gave me my bag and hat, and ordered me to leave.

"But I was expecting to interview His Majesty," I protested.

"You must go. There is nothing for you here," the older guard said. "His Majesty is dead."

I just stared at him, unable to speak. The king was dead? They were confirming this? I don't know why I thought it would be otherwise. I had seen the entire event unfold before me. His Majesty had been shot in the face and chest at point-blank range. But with all that had just happened, it had not yet occurred to me he might actually be dead. Call it denial. Call it the fog of war. Or perhaps I simply still wanted the interview I had been promised. I'd had an appointment. I had made it on time. He was the one who was late. I had been there. I was ready. I had my questions. And now I was being ordered to leave.

A chill rippled through my body. Despite the intense noontime heat, I suddenly felt cold. I was lonely and intensely tired. I knew I was in danger of slipping into shock, and there was a part of me that wanted to succumb to it. I could hear the sirens. Within minutes, doctors and nurses would be arriving. They would take care of me. They would whisk me off to a hospital and pump my body full of drugs and I could sleep and try to forget all this had ever happened. But there was another part of me that forced my legs to straighten, forced myself to stand, and before I realized what was happening, I was walking straight toward the lifeless body of the king, my right hand instinctively pulling a notebook out of the leather satchel hanging from my shoulder.

A crowd of guards and soldiers had surrounded His Majesty, guns drawn, as the young Prince Hussein, weeping over his grandfather, knelt at his side. But it was instantly clear the soldier had been right. The king was dead. His skin was white. His eyes were closed. His white cotton robes were smeared and stained with blood.

I turned to a Moslem cleric of some sort standing nearby, his mouth agape, tears in his eyes, saying nothing.

"Do you have a telephone?" I asked in Arabic, handing him my damp handkerchief. I was surprised by how calm my voice sounded.

"No, no, not in the mosque," he stuttered, accepting my gift and wiping his eyes. "But there is one in the office."

"I must use it to call the palace," I said, choosing for the moment not to identify myself.

"Yes, of course," he said, obviously not thinking about my request clearly or questioning who I was.

As if in a stupor, he led me to a squat outbuilding nearby that housed the administrative offices of the Waqf, the religious institution charged with protecting and maintaining the Islamic holy sites on the Temple Mount. Fumbling with his keys, the cleric opened the door. He led me to his office, showed me the telephone, and explained how to get an operator to place the call to Amman. Then he left me in peace and shut the door behind him.

I picked up the receiver and felt my hand trembling. I took a deep breath and tried in vain to steady my nerves.

"May I help you?" a woman asked at the other end of the scratchy line.

"Operator, I need to make a call to the United States," I said as calmly as I could. "Can you help me with that?"

"Yes, sir, I can," she replied.

I gave her the number and waited for the call to be put through. Finally I was connected to a young woman at the assignment desk in New York. Unwilling to entrust this breaking news to whatever fresh-faced college grad had just answered the phone, I demanded to speak to the international editor, a longtime personal friend, and said it was an emergency.

The woman, however, replied that he was not in, and asked to take a message. *Not in?* I thought. *Why the blast not?* Then I glanced at my pocket watch, and it dawned on me that it was only 12:25 p.m. local time, which meant it was not yet 5:30 in the morning in New York.

"Who's the editor on duty?" I asked.

"Mr. Briggs, sir," the young lady replied.

"Roger Briggs?" I asked, the strain on me beginning to show itself in my speech.

"Yes, sir."

"Well, I need him immediately. Tell him I'm calling from Jerusalem with an urgent exclusive, but it won't hold long."

The wait that followed seemed like an eternity, and the longer it took, the more terrified I became that UPI or the *New York Times* or the *Jerusalem Post* or some Arab paper would scoop me. Surely many had heard the gunshots, and now everyone in Jerusalem was hearing the sirens coming from all directions. I had no idea who was out there in that group of well-wishers. Maybe there had been another reporter. Maybe there had been more than one.

"This is Briggs. Who's this, and what's all the hubbub about? For heaven's sakes, man, you know what time it is?"

"Roger, this is A. B. Collins in Jerusalem."

"A. B., is that really you?"

We had known each other for years.

"Yes, yes, now take this down immediately."

"What did you say?" Briggs asked. The line crackled with static. "Repeat. Say again."

"I said this is A. B. Collins in Jerusalem. Take this down. 'King Abdullah bin al-Hussein of the Hashemite Kingdom of Jordan . . . is dead.'"

TOP SECRET

PART TWO

Present Day

6

★ ★ ★

I had done a lot of crazy things in my life, but nothing as stupid as this.

As I stared out over the roiling waves and countless whitecaps of the Mediterranean below, I couldn't help but think about my grandfather. A. B. Collins was once the Beirut bureau chief for the Associated Press. Long before I was born, he flew this exact route as an American foreign correspondent in the war-torn Middle East. His career was legendary. As a young boy I dreamed of following in his footsteps. As a teenager, I read all his journals. In college I spent hours in the library reading his old dispatches on microfiche. Now here I was, a foreign correspondent for the *New York Times*, wondering if, given all the risks my grandfather had taken, he'd ever done anything quite this foolhardy.

There was still a way out, of course. I could still change my plans. But the truth was I didn't want to. I may never have interviewed a king or witnessed the assassination of a monarch. But I was just as committed to my craft, and I was going in, come what may. That's all there was to it. In six minutes, my Air France flight would touch down in the Lebanese capital. In nineteen minutes, I'd link up with my colleagues. Together we'd drive ninety miles to the border of Syria. And if all went well, by nightfall we'd slip across the border unnoticed and eventually locate one of the world's most feared jihadi commanders.

Jack Vaughn, director of the Central Intelligence Agency, had personally warned me not to do this. So had the head of the Mossad and the chief of Jordanian intelligence, not to mention my mother. My editor, Allen MacDonald, had expressly forbidden me to go. Their rationale was as simple as it was compelling: Jamal Ramzy was a killer.

Born in Jordan. Raised in the Gulf. Went to Afghanistan. Joined the mujahideen. Killed more Russians than any other Arab fighter. Met bin Laden. Became his chief bodyguard. Was in the room when bin Laden created al Qaeda in 1988. Sent to fight in Somalia. Became a top aide to Khalid Sheikh Mohammed, the mastermind of the 9/11 attacks. Personally trained the 9/11 hijackers. Helped plan the bombings of two American embassies in Africa. Helped behead a *Wall Street Journal* reporter in Pakistan. Became a top aide to Ayman al-Zawahiri, the head of al Qaeda after bin Laden was killed, but had a severe falling-out with him over the future of the organization. Teamed up with his barbaric younger cousin Abu Khalif, the head of "al Qaeda in Iraq and the Levant," an ultra-violent breakaway faction of the mother ship. Sent to command a force of rebel fighters in Syria. Ordered to bring back Assad's head on a platter. Literally.

This was the guy I was trying to locate. I knew it was crazy. But I was going anyway.

To my knowledge, Jamal Ramzy had never been photographed or interviewed by a Western reporter. But after nearly a year of my constant e-mails to someone I believed to be Ramzy's lieutenant, he had finally said yes—to the interview, anyway, if not the photograph. If I was communicating with the right person, and if he was being truthful—neither of which, at the moment, I was able to fully verify—the big questions were these: Why would Ramzy talk to anyone? Why now? And why me?

The answers, I believed, were simple: He wanted to be on the front page, top of the fold. He wanted to be the new face of the Radicals for all the world to see. And he knew full well that there was no bigger venue than the *New York Times*, the world's newspaper of record, for which I had been a foreign correspondent for nearly a decade.

As far as timing went, my operating theory was that it was not vanity that was persuading Ramzy to finally respond to my repeated overtures. After all, the Jordanian-born terrorist had lived in the shadows for decades. He had survived all this time by living off the grid, and I suspect he would have been content to remain there if possible rather than risk being obliterated without warning one day by a drone strike, like most of his comrades-in-arms. No, it was unlikely that vanity was driving Ramzy. Rather, I was fairly certain he had something to say at this moment, something he had never said before, and that he was planning on using me to say it.

For the past several weeks, I had been picking up rumors that Ramzy and his rebel forces had captured a cache of chemical weapons in Syria. The Assad regime had supposedly allowed international forces to destroy its remaining weapons of mass destruction, but it was widely believed that at least some stockpiles had been hidden. Now one well-placed American intelligence source told me his agency had picked up frantic radio traffic three weeks earlier between Syrian army forces loyal to Assad saying one of their WMD storage facilities not far from Aleppo had just been overrun. The Syrian forces were desperately calling for air strikes, but while the air support had come, it was too late. Quite separately, another source, this one in a foreign intelligence service, confided to me that a high-ranking Syrian general had just defected to either Turkey or Jordan (he wouldn't say which) and claimed some al Qaeda breakaway faction had seized several tons of chemical weapons south of Aleppo within the last few weeks.

Was it true? I had no idea. All I knew for certain was that nothing of the sort had yet been reported in the Arab press or anywhere in the West. No one at the White House, State, or the Pentagon would confirm or deny my discreet inquiries. Part of this, I suspected, was to prevent the widespread panic that was sure to break out if it became known that one of the world's most dangerous terrorist organizations now had control of some of the world's most dangerous weapons.

Of course, I hadn't raised any of this in my e-mails to my source in Syria. I'd simply repeated my long-standing requests for an interview. But I was increasingly certain this was why Ramzy wanted to talk now, when he had never talked publicly before. He wanted the world to know what he had. He wanted the American people and their president to know. What's more, I had to believe he savored the irony of Ayman al-Zawahiri hearing through an American newspaper that one of his former advisors had hit the mother lode—that an al Qaeda offshoot finally had possession of the very weapons al Qaeda itself had been desperately seeking for nearly two decades.

I hoped I was right. Not that Ramzy had the WMD, mind you, but that he had a story—an important story—he wanted to communicate through me. It was, I suspected, my only hope of survival. After all, this was a man who cut people's throats for sport, Americans' most of all. Only if he really did want to use me to communicate a big story would my colleagues and I be safe.

It was no wonder no one I knew wanted me to head into Syria to track this man down and speak with him face-to-face. Even the colleagues I was about to meet were deeply uncomfortable. I certainly understood why. And I didn't blame them. What we were about to do wasn't normal. But I—and they—were part of "the tribe," part of an elite group, a small cadre of foreign correspondents whose lives were devoted to covering wars and rumors of war, revolutions, chaos, and bloodshed of all kinds. It's what I'd gone to school for, nearly twenty years earlier. It's what I'd been doing for the *New York Daily News* and the Associated Press and the *Times* ever since. I loved it. I lived for it.

Some said it was an addiction. They said people like me were adrenaline junkies. Maybe I was. But that's not the way I thought of it. To me, risk was part of my job, and it was a job my colleagues told me I wasn't half-bad at. I had won an award for covering a Delta Force firefight in Kandahar, Afghanistan, with another *Times* reporter in 2001. And I had even won a Pulitzer for a series of articles I wrote in 2003 when I was embedded with the First Brigade of the U.S. Army's Third Infantry Division as they stormed Baghdad. The awards were gratifying. But I didn't do this to win awards. I did it because I loved it. I did it because I couldn't imagine doing anything else.

Most reporters couldn't wait to get out of Afghanistan or Iraq after the initial invasions and the establishment of the new governments. But I repeatedly requested longer tours. I loved getting to know our boys who suited up for battle every day. I loved interviewing the Iraqis our troops were training and taking into battle. I also loved having beers and trading gossip with the spooks from Langley and MI6 and every other intelligence agency on the planet who had come to play in the Big Game. Most of all, though, I found it absolutely fascinating to slip away from the Green Zone and get out in the hinterland and risk life and limb trying to hook up with one insurgent commander or another to get his story. *All the news that's fit to print, right?* I wasn't there to regurgitate whatever the flacks at State or the Pentagon tried to spoon-feed me. I was there to find the real stories.

So whatever lay ahead, I was absolutely determined to head into Syria. I was going after the story. Not a single person I had confided in approved of what I was doing. But I wanted to think that one would have. I wanted to believe my grandfather would have been proud of me. At least he would have understood what I was doing and why.

A. B. Collins covered the Second World War for United Press International. Then he worked for the Associated Press all over the globe. To be perfectly honest, he was my idol. Maybe it was because of all the stories he used to tell me when I was growing up. That man could really spin a good yarn. I was in awe of the way he had seemed to have met everyone and seen everything. Then again, maybe I simply loved him because of all the ice cream Pop-Pop used to buy my older brother and me whenever he and Grammie Collins came to visit. Or maybe it was because my father had left us when I was only twelve, and I never saw him again—none of us did—and Pop-Pop was the only man I really had in my life growing up. It was he who took me fishing on Eagle Lake and hiking in Acadia National Park. It was he who taught me how to use his collection of rifles and took me on hunting trips all over Maine and even up in Canada. Whatever the reason, I loved the man with every fiber of my being, and for as long as I could remember, I wanted to do what he did, to be what he was. Now here I was, about to touch down in Beirut, a city he had worked in and lived in and loved dearly.

Maybe the olive didn't fall far from the tree.

Then again, my grandfather had lived a long and fruitful life and despite his many adventures had died in his bed, in his sleep, in his old age. At the moment, I had no presumption of meeting such a quiet and peaceful fate.

7

* ★ *

I stared at my hands.

They were trembling. Not much. Not so that anyone else would necessarily notice. But I noticed. It had never happened before.

I unscrewed the top from a bottle of Evian and took several gulps. A flight attendant announced the local time of 6:54 p.m. We had lifted off from Heathrow in London at 10:05 that morning. Air France flight 568 was touching down a minute early. I pulled out my grandfather's gold pocket watch, the one he gave me just before he died. I wound it up and set it. Then I pulled out a pen and my dog-eared passport and began filling out the Lebanese immigration and customs form.

Name: James Bradley Collins
Date of birth: May 3, 1975
City of birth: Bar Harbor, Maine
Nationality: American
Country of residence: United States

City passport was issued: Washington, D.C.
Countries visited before landing in Lebanon:
Turkey, France, Germany, U.K.
Purpose for visit: Business

I filled in my passport number and marked that I had nothing to declare. Then I flipped through the pages of my well-traveled passport from back to front, reading through all the stamps I had acquired over the years—every European capital, every Asian capital, and every capital in the Middle East and North Africa. Except Israel's. I had been in and out of Ben Gurion International Airport near Tel Aviv more times than I could count, of course, but I had always been careful to ask the authorities there to stamp my visa, not my passport, so it didn't prevent me from entering certain Arab countries that would refuse a traveler entry if he had an Israeli stamp in his travel documents.

Before I realized it, I was wincing at the terrible photo of me taken nearly a decade earlier. I was reminded of the old adage: "If you really look as bad as your passport picture, you're too ill to travel." Then again, in some ways the photo was better than the current reality. My eyes were green back then. Now they seemed permanently blood shot. I'd had twenty-twenty vision then. Today I sported prescription eyeglasses in black, semirimless designer frames for which I'd paid more than I care to mention. In the photo, my muddy-brown hair was hideously long and badly in need of a cut. But then again, I actually *had* hair—on my head, at least, though not on my face. Ten years later, I was completely bald (by choice, thank you very much) and sporting a salt-and-pepper mustache and goatee.

As we taxied to the gate, I powered up my phone and checked my e-mails. The first that came up was from my brother. I skipped it and moved on. Most of the rest were a potpourri of updates and questions from colleagues in D.C. and sources I was working around the world, as well as RSS feeds of the latest stories published by the *Times* on the Middle East, national security issues, intelligence matters, and other issues pertaining to my beat. One story was by Alex Brunnell, the *Times* bureau chief in Jerusalem. I scanned it quickly. It was a ridiculously pedestrian piece that focused on why the peace talks between the Israelis and Palestinians had bogged down again and why the White House might soon abandon its effort to strike a comprehensive deal and shift its attention from the Middle East to the Pacific Rim. It was badly sourced and poorly written and contained nothing but conventional wisdom. Everyone knew the talks were going nowhere. Everyone knew President Taylor and his secretary of state had bitten off more than they could chew. This was hardly news. The *Wall Street Journal* had done the same story a month earlier. Everyone else had done it since then. But this was typical of Brunnell. He never seemed to break news, just chase it. Why the suits in Manhattan had given a third-rate hack a byline in the world's most respected newspaper, I would never understand.

The next e-mail, however, sucked the wind out of me.

It was from our publisher, addressed to all of the paper's staff around the world.

> It is with a heavy heart that I write to inform you of the tragic death of Janet Fiorelli, *New York Times* Cairo bureau chief. Janet was working on a story detailing the lingering effects of the Arab Spring in Egypt when she was killed yesterday in a suicide bombing in Cairo. The U.S. State Department is investigating the attack. Janet was a top-rate journalist who was respected and beloved by colleagues and readers alike for her professionalism and kindness, and . . .

I stopped reading. I couldn't believe it. I knew Janet. We were friends. We'd worked together on countless stories. I knew her husband, Tom, and her twins, Michael and Peter. I'd been to their home in Heliopolis a dozen times or more. I read the first sentence of the e-mail again and again. It couldn't be true.

Suddenly we were at the gate. Everyone else got off the plane, but I just sat there, staring out the window.

"Sir, is everything okay?" asked an attractive young flight attendant, trying to be helpful.

No, it wasn't, I wanted to say. But I just nodded and stood, trying to get my bearings.

"Is there anything I can do for you, sir?" she asked.

She had a lovely smile and gentle eyes. I found myself looking at her for a moment too long, then caught myself.

"Sorry; no, I'm good," I said.

I felt numb. I'd had dinner with Tom and Janet in Alexandria only a few weeks earlier. Now she was gone. It seemed impossible.

The flight attendant handed me my black leather jacket and backpack from the overhead bin. I thanked her and deplaned and made my way through the crowds to the baggage claim. I never checked any bags, not anymore, not since Lufthansa lost my luggage back in 2007 while I was on the way to interview the German chancellor. Nevertheless, my editor had told me to meet my colleagues at baggage carousel number three, so that's where I went.

"J. B., my friend, welcome back to Beirut—you look terrible!"

A gargantuan man, swarthy and unshaven, laughed from his belly, his booming voice turning heads in the terminal—not exactly the low profile I was looking for. Then he gave me a bear hug that nearly crushed my spine. I'd told him a hundred times to go a tad lighter, but it was always the same thing.

"Good to see you, too, Omar," I replied, so not in the mood for all his energy. "You ready for this?"

"Ready?" he shot back. "Have you completely

lost your mind? You're a fool, a complete lunatic. You're going to get us all killed one day. You know that, don't you?"

I just stared at him.

"What?" he asked. "What's the matter?"

"You haven't read your e-mails," I said.

"No, what e-mails?"

"You haven't heard about Janet Fiorelli."

His expression changed immediately. "No, why? What has happened?"

I nodded toward the smartphone in his hand. He read the e-mail and I watched as the enthusiasm drained from his face.

Omar Fayez and I had been through a great deal together, and we had lost more than our share of friends and colleagues over the years. Though he was only thirty-two, he had always treated me like I was his younger brother, looking out for me, watching my back. Six feet five inches tall, at least 275 pounds, and in remarkably good shape for his size, Omar looked like an NFL linebacker. But he had a master's from Harvard and a PhD from Oxford in Middle Eastern studies and spoke four languages—Arabic, French, Farsi, and English. Born and raised in Jordan, he'd been a reporter, interpreter, and "fixer" for the *Times* in Jordan and Baghdad for the last six years, much of that time working at my side.

"Let's talk about something else," I said. "I can't process this right now."

Omar nodded.

"How's Hadiya?" I asked, going straight to his favorite topic.

"Like always, my friend, a gift from heaven," Omar replied, his voice now more subdued.

"Glad to hear it."

"She sends you a kiss," he said.

"Give her my love."

"I will."

Then he paused.

"What is it?" I asked.

"Well, I was going to save this for later, but maybe you need to hear it now."

"I can't handle any more bad news just yet," I said.

"No, no, it's good news."

"Oh?"

"Hadiya and I are expecting in March."

I couldn't help but grin. This *was* good news. They had been trying to have children for years without any success, and their marriage had struggled for a time because of it. I gave him a hug and congratulated him. "Good for you, Omar—when we get back, we must celebrate."

"We would like that very much," Omar replied. "God has been so good to us. Hadiya is happier than I have ever seen her."

I had no doubt. But I couldn't help but notice that as he said this, the tone of Omar's voice and his body language changed ever so slightly. He was worried about the task ahead of us, and for the first time, I felt a pang of guilt for taking him into harm's way.

8

* * *

"Where's Abdel?" I asked as I scanned the faces in the crowd.

"He's bringing the car," Omar said. "Come; we must hurry. A storm is rolling in. We need to get moving. We don't have any time to spare."

As we exited the airport, what struck me first was the chill in the air. The sun had long since set. It was mid-November. The winter rains were coming. Dark thunderheads were rolling in over the city. The winds were picking up. Omar was right—a storm was coming, and I needed something warmer than a T-shirt and khakis. I stopped for a moment, dug out a black wool crewneck sweater from my backpack, and put it on along with my leather jacket.

Just then, a silver four-door Renault pulled up to the curb and stopped in front of us. As the trunk popped up, the driver's door opened too, and out jumped a lanky young man with a touch of acne and long, curly, unkempt hair. He wore tattered blue jeans, a dark-green hoodie, and black running shoes. "Mr. Collins, I'm so sorry I'm late," he said with a genuine air of anxiety in his voice. "Please forgive me, sir."

"Don't worry, Abdel; you're not late," I assured him, shaking his hand. "We're a bit early. My flight was on time for once, and I didn't check any bags."

"You are very kind, sir, very kind," he said as he took my backpack and put it in the trunk alongside Omar's luggage and his own. "Please, get inside and get warm, Mr. Collins. I have the heat on for you, plus hot coffee and baklava."

I didn't know Abdel Hamid particularly well. We had worked together just one time, and only briefly at that, but everyone said he was a good kid. I knew for certain he was a phenomenal photographer, and I had asked for him by name to be assigned to me on this project. A Palestinian by birth, he'd grown up in a refugee camp on the outskirts of Beirut. He had no college degree and no formal training as a photographer, but prior to being hired by the *Times*, he had made a name for himself as a freelancer for the work he'd done in Syria, producing some of the most heart-wrenching images of the civil war of anyone in the business. As I got into the backseat, Omar headed around to the other side of the car and got in beside me so we could talk more easily on the three-hour drive ahead of us. And sure enough, waiting for us were two cups of steaming hot coffee.

"Cream and three sugars for you; is that right, Mr. Fayez?" Abdel asked as he got behind the wheel and checked his mirrors.

"It is indeed, Abdel."

"And black for you, Mr. Collins?"

"You got it," I replied. "You're fast becoming my new best friend, Abdel."

"I'm only too happy to help, Mr. Collins."

"Abdel, please, call me J. B.," I told him, patting him on the back. "You say Mr. Collins and I think my grandfather just showed up."

"I would have loved to have met him," Abdel said. "From all I have read, he was a remarkable man and a tremendous journalist."

"That's very kind of you to say, Abdel," I said, touched that he knew anything about my grandfather.

"It is my pleasure, Mr. Collins; thank *you*, sir—you are very kind."

He had completely missed the request that he call me by my first name, but I didn't have the heart to correct him again, so I moved on.

"So look, Abdel, last time I was here was what, July?"

"Yes, late July, Mr. Collins."

"Right, and wasn't there a young lady in your life at the time?"

"Oh yes, Mr. Collins, that's true," he said, clearly surprised. "You mean Fatima. You have a good memory."

"How's that going?" I asked. "As I recall, you were quite taken with her."

"Yes, yes. I was—I *am*."

"How is she these days?"

"Ah yes, she is very well, Mr. Collins," Abdel told me as he wove through evening traffic, heading east toward the city of Zahle. "Thank you for asking. We are very much in love."

"And I understand you have a little news," I said. "Is that right?"

Abdel looked at me in the rearview mirror, startled but not unhappy. "Well, yes, how did you know?"

"I have my sources, Abdel." I smiled. "That is my job, after all, right?"

"Yes, you have always had very good sources," he said, beaming, but then realized that Omar had no idea what we were talking about. "Fatima and I got engaged last week."

"Oh, wow, congratulations!" Omar exclaimed.

"Yes, that's very exciting, Abdel," I added.

"Yes, it is. Thank you both. We are very happy."

"When is the big day?" I asked.

"In a few months—January, probably."

"Very good. And Fatima is still in school, is she not?"

"Yes, she's in her last year."

"At A.U.?"

"Yes, sir."

"What is she studying?"

"Journalism."

"How can you go wrong? Well, bravo, Abdel. I'd love to meet her, and maybe someday she'll end up working for the Gray Lady."

"Oh, she would love that, Mr. Collins. She would love that very much."

Omar turned to me, took a sip of coffee, and asked me about my mom. I knew he was sincere. He was a decent, caring soul, and I loved that about him. But I also knew he was just warming up to the topic he really wanted to discuss: why in the world were we trying to meet Jamal Ramzy?

"Mom's hanging in there," I said, trying my best to be polite.

"And that old house you grew up in—does she still live there?"

"She does, though for the life of me I don't know why."

"Too expensive?"

"Not really. The mortgage is all paid off. But you know, it's big and empty and it's just her. Takes a lot of work to maintain that old place, and with her knee and back trouble . . . Well, anyway, it is what it is."

"And your suggestion that she sell it and move to Florida?"

"Going nowhere, I'm afraid," I conceded. "Doesn't even want to talk about it."

"How is Matthew doing?"

"No comment," I said. "Next question."

Omar looked surprised by my clipped answer. He had once met my older brother at the airport in Amman and seemed to take a liking to him. But to his credit, he quickly shifted gears. "And Laura? How's that all going?"

That wasn't a topic I wanted to discuss either. There was a long, awkward silence as I stared out the window, trying to come up with a suitable yet honest answer as I watched row after row of newly built apartment buildings blur past. "About the same," I said at last, then changed the subject again. "So look, were you able to get anything from the Mukhabarat?"

A few days earlier, as we made plans for this trip, I'd asked Omar to work his sources in the Jordanian intelligence service to see if they would give us anything on Ramzy.

"A little," he said, accepting my discomfort in talking about personal matters and getting to the main topic. "I had coffee with Amir last night. He wouldn't give me much. Told me we were crazy to do this thing, said it simply wasn't worth it."

"He doesn't believe we're going to get to meet with Ramzy."

"No, that's not it," Omar said. "He told me he absolutely thinks we are going to find and meet Ramzy. And that's precisely what worries him."

"What exactly?" I pressed.

"He doesn't want to get on YouTube tomorrow and see the three of us being beheaded."

9

★ ★ ★

Omar, Abdel, and I stashed our rental car in some bushes.

Then we slipped across the border into Syria and hiked for several hours. As we approached the city, we inched our way forward under the cover of predawn darkness. Finally, the three of us lay on our stomachs in the mud in a grassy field trying to figure out our next move.

The crackle of machine-gun fire had grown louder over the past several minutes. Artillery shells were now screaming over our heads. The ear-splitting explosions were becoming more intense. The earth shook violently beneath us, and I realized I was shaking too.

To my left I could see the torched wreckage of a Russian-built T-72 battle tank. To my right, about fifty yards away, was the charred hulk of a school bus. Beyond that, about a hundred yards away, stood the carcass of an old VW van. Behind us lay a deserted playground, complete with slides and balance beams and swings swaying in the

bitter winter wind. But there were no children—
no human presence of any kind, so long as you
ignored the dozens of shallow graves that seemed
to have been dug quite recently.

Clouds scattered and then regathered overhead,
and in the intermittent moonlight I could see row
upon row of bombed-out apartment buildings
ahead of us. There were no lights on in any of
them. No sounds of music or talking or laughter
emanated from their midst. Indeed, there were no
signs of normal life at all as far as the eye could see.

Welcome to Homs.

Once a thriving metropolis, Homs had been
the third-largest city in Syria after Damascus and
Aleppo. More than six hundred thousand people
had, until recently, called this their home. Now
it was fast becoming a ghost town. Most of the
residents had fled for their lives over the past few
years. Some neighborhoods were nearly empty of
living souls. If a ferocious battle between government and rebel forces hadn't just erupted nearby,
I would have had no idea anyone was still left in
the area.

Just why anyone was still fighting over this
wasteland was beyond me. What was the point?
What was left to fight over? Most of the facto-
ries had been blown up. Most of the schools had
been burned down, the Catholic and Orthodox
churches and the mosques, too. The banks had
been looted. All but a handful of stores were
shuttered. There was barely anything to eat. No
running water. No working sewage system. The
airport had been obliterated. Even if you had a

functioning car or truck, you couldn't use it. The gas stations had no petrol. The roads were ripped up or blocked by soldiers or rebels. There was no legitimate way into the city, and only a fool would try to enter. Yet there we were, watching the blaze of rockets and mortars streaking through the sky. We could see tracer bullets slicing through the night.

We couldn't stay put. Forces from one side or the other would be coming soon. We had to keep moving.

Though I tried not to, I couldn't help but think about all my friends who had died covering this miserable war. My *Times* colleague and fellow Pulitzer Prize winner Anthony Shadid had died in Syria. So had Gilles Jacquier, a photojournalist with France Télévisions. And Marie Colvin with the *Sunday Times* of London. The list went on and on. Well over two hundred reporters and photographers had been killed in Syria alone since the start of the civil war. And that didn't even count Janet Fiorelli and all the other journalists who had died covering the Arab Spring or the wars in Afghanistan and Iraq.

I didn't want to be one of them, but I did want this interview. I wanted this exclusive, and I was determined to get it—or get shipped home in a body bag.

I whispered a plan to Omar. He quickly relayed it to Abdel. Then, looking into each man's eyes and making sure we were on the same page, I grabbed my backpack, put it once again over my shoulders, and jumped to my feet and began sprinting toward one of the bombed-out apartment buildings. As soon as I did, however, a machine-gun nest to our right suddenly roared to life. I didn't dare stop. I didn't even dare slow down. If I was going to die, I decided, so be it. I would die on the move, on the hunt for this story, not pinned down in the mud, not cowering in fear or groveling for mercy. I wasn't as fast as I'd been in college. I wasn't as fast as I'd been when this war began. Hate it though I might, I wasn't young anymore, and war correspondence was a young man's game. But I kept moving.

My heart pounded. My lungs desperately sucked in air. My legs burned, but I kept going. As I roared past the back of the bus, I could hear .50-caliber rounds tearing through, but I kept moving. I was terrified—far more so for Omar and Abdel than even for myself, if that were possible—but I didn't dare look back. I had no idea if the guys were still behind me. I hadn't heard any screams or cries, though I'm not sure I would have. My ears were filled with the excruciating roar of explosions and automatic-weapons fire. For all I knew, I was alone. I just hoped it wasn't their time or mine yet.

I broke left and headed for the back door of one of the tenements. As I drew closer, I could see bullets ricocheting off the cinder blocks. The intense roar of the machine-gun fire seemed to increase exponentially. I wondered if two people were firing at us instead of one. Instinctively, I changed direction. Breaking to my right, I could see the VW van just ahead. It had been burnt to a crisp. It had no tires, no windows. It was nothing but a bullet-ridden shell, but it was my only chance, so that's where I headed. As I finally reached it, I wasn't sure I'd stop in time, so I did a Pete Rose, diving headfirst behind the chassis as a hailstorm of bullets slammed into the engine block.

The withering gunfire didn't stop or slow. Dozens of rounds pelted the side of the van. I could hear many more whizzing over my head. I pressed myself as low to the ground as I possibly could and covered my head with my arms. I'd never experienced anything like this. Not in Afghanistan. Not in Iraq. Not covering the revolutions in Egypt or Libya. In the past, I'd usually been on the move with soldiers. I often stuck close to professionals who were heavily armed and trained for battle. On rare occasions, I even traveled with a group of insurgents, but I'd never been alone, in the open, being shot at with no one around me who could shoot back, no weapons, and no way to defend myself.

Almost before I had time to think, Abdel dove in beside me, and Omar right behind him. Abdel was shouting something in Arabic I couldn't quite make out in the cacophony. Omar was breathing as hard as I was. By the way he was shaking, I guessed he was probably just as afraid as I was that his heart was going to explode out of his chest even before he was shredded by bullets and left to bleed to death in an open field. But there was no time to commiserate.

"We can't stay here!" I shouted.

"*Well, we can't keep going,*" Omar shouted back. "*They'll kill us all.*"

"*We should just stay,*" Abdel yelled. "*They have to reload eventually.*"

"*But when they do, we need to move fast,*" I yelled back. "*I'll go first, but don't follow me. We need to break up. Head out in three different directions. Pick a building, each a different one. Then we'll regroup on the front side. Hopefully it will be quieter over there.*"

"*No, no, we need to stay here,*" Abdel shouted at me.

I shook my head vigorously and tried to rally my men. "*If we do, we're dead!*"

No sooner had I spoken the words than there was an ever-so-brief lull. This was it, I thought. We had to move now.

"*Go, go, go!*" I shouted, springing to my feet and running again.

I didn't look back. I couldn't. But sure enough, moments later, the machine-gun nest roared back into business. Bullets pulverized the walls all around me, but somehow I burst through the rear entrance of the building, out of the line of fire, unscathed.

Now, however, I really was alone. I could hear mortars and artillery shells landing close by and moving closer. The explosions grew louder, and I both sensed and felt the already-pummeled and fragile building above me rocking and swaying with every concussion. I began to wonder how much more the structure could take. There was no reason I could think of for anyone to be firing directly at it. But what if a shell or two went astray? What if the building were hit? Might the whole thing come toppling down?

It occurred to me that no one back home had any idea where I was. Allen MacDonald, my editor in Washington, thought I was merely heading up to the Lebanese–Syrian border to interview refugees about the latest battles in the village of Al-Qusayr, since that's all I had told him after he shot down my Ramzy pitch. My mother thought I was going to Beirut to interview a Hezbollah commander. My brother? I hadn't talked to him in years.

Standing in a long, dark hallway, the floor rumbling beneath me, I had absolutely no idea what was in front of me. But I couldn't turn back now. So I stumbled my way down the hallway, groping in the near pitch-dark with one hand, my other hand touching the wall, as shards of broken glass crunched beneath me.

I felt something run across my feet and then something else. I immediately kicked the second one away, but a shudder ran down my spine. What were they? Rats? What exactly was I heading into? My imagination kicked into overdrive.

Just then, in darkness so complete I could no longer see my hand in front of my face, I stumbled over something and crashed to the floor. I had no idea what it was, but it was large and yielding and my hands slid along the floor tiles into something wet and sticky and cold. Repulsed, I wiped my hands on my khakis and felt around for the iPhone in my jacket. I pulled it out, punched in the security code, and clicked on the flashlight app. Instantly, I realized I had landed in a pool of coagulating blood. The fact that it was not yet completely dry made me shudder all over again. I turned and pointed the camera behind me and froze as I stared down into the lifeless eyes of a young boy, no older than fourteen or fifteen, shot at least a dozen times, his white, stiff hands in a death grip around an AK-47.

Click. Click. Click. My journalistic instincts kicked in and I snapped three pictures, then turned away in horror, wondering anew when the senseless killing in this godforsaken country would ever stop.

I pointed the light of the phone toward the end of the hallway and made my way to the front door. But as I reached for the doorknob, I hesitated. I needed to find my colleagues, to be sure. I certainly didn't want to be in this city alone. Nor, I had to imagine, did they. But then again, I had no idea what lay ahead. How in the world were we going to find Jamal Ramzy? For all we knew, he was leading this battle.

Pulse pounding, I again wiped my hands on my pants, then slowly opened the door. What lay before me was a scene from the apocalypse. But Omar and Abdel were nowhere to be found.

10

* * *

The stench of death was thick, revolting, and inescapable.

Everywhere I looked—up and down the street in both directions—I saw mountains of rubble and twisted rebar from half-collapsed buildings, the scorched remains of tanks and trucks and cars and motorcycles, and the ghastly sight of decomposing bodies that even the vultures had rejected. All of it was shrouded in an eerie fog of smoke and ash, bathed in the bluish-silver tint of the moon.

I didn't dare step out of the doorway. I wanted to call out to Omar and Abdel, but I kept my mouth shut. I pressed myself back into the shadows and all but closed the door to the apartment building, keeping it open barely a crack. Then I peered out into the night, scanning for any movement, any signs of friends or enemies. But nothing was moving save the smoke and ash in the winter winds that were now picking up and bringing a frightful chill. As slowly and quietly as I could, I zipped up my jacket and turned the collar up to protect my neck. Then the light began to dim as a curtain of clouds descended upon the moon.

What now? We were not yet at our rendezvous point, though as best I could tell we were getting close. To get to Ramzy, we were supposed to meet up with Tariq Baqouba, one of Ramzy's top lieutenants. Born in the Decapolis region of northern Jordan, Baqouba was, by all accounts, a young but battle-hardened fighter who had distinguished himself killing American Marines and Army Rangers in Iraq before turning his "talents" to the killing fields of Syria. It was his younger brother, Faisal, a former technician for Al Jazeera television, who was my e-mail contact.

Faisal's instructions had been simple: My team and I were to meet him in the remains of the Khaled bin Walid Mosque in a neighborhood several blocks away called al-Khalidiyah. Faisal would then take us to his brother Tariq, who would take us to Jamal Ramzy. I checked my pocket watch. The rendezvous time was just twenty-three minutes away. Yet how could I continue on without Omar and Abdel?

My fears were getting the best of me. Had the fighters manning the machine-gun nests cut my friends down before they had reached safety? Had the jihadists come after them? Had they reached a "safe" building, only to stumble upon armed men inside? Mortar rounds kept exploding. The building kept shaking. I knew it wasn't safe to stay. But I had no idea where to go, unless I headed to the mosque alone. The longer I stayed put, the more questions raced through my thoughts. What if they were injured? What if they were bleeding, dying? Should I go back for them? Of course, I had no idea which buildings they had gone to. Had they split up as I'd told them, or had they stayed together after all?

Feeling dehydrated, I grabbed the water bottle out of the side of my backpack and took a swig. Then, oddly enough, the explosions outside stopped. I had no idea why. Perhaps it was just a lull, but for a few unexpected minutes, there was near silence, broken only by the sporadic crackle of machine-gun fire in the distance . . . and by the ringing in my ears. I began to breathe normally again, but just then I heard a noise behind me. I turned quickly and saw a flash of moonlight pour through the doorway at the other end of a long hallway, though only for a moment. Someone had opened and closed the door. Someone had entered the building. The hair on the back of my neck stood erect. My heart started racing again. Who was it? Was it one of my men? Or someone about to kill me?

I closed the door behind me all the way, careful not to make a sound. I didn't want even the slightest ray of light to fall upon me or make me a target.

Now, however, the hallway was completely black. I was stuck. There was no way forward, and I didn't dare go back.

And now shards of glass were crackling under someone else's feet. Whoever it was, he was moving toward me. Slowly. Step by step. Inching his way forward.

Trying not to panic, I slowly lowered myself

to my knees. Whoever was coming, if they were armed and started firing, I was determined to present as small a target as possible. Then I remembered the AK-47. It was just a few yards away, in the hands of the young boy who likely had been killed merely a few hours earlier at most. I had noticed that the magazine was still in the weapon. I had no idea if there was any ammunition left, but what choice did I have? I did not want to die. Not here. Not yet. On my hands and knees now, I felt around in the dark until I found the cold, stiff corpse. I kept feeling around until my hands came upon the gun.

The crunching of boots on broken glass was getting louder. Whoever was out there, they were getting closer. I was running out of time. Desperate, I pried the boy's stiff fingers from the weapon and pulled it to my side.

Feeling every part of the machine gun in the dark, I tried to make sense of it. I'd never held a Kalashnikov. It wasn't like the shotguns or rifles my grandfather had taught me to use back in Maine. Then again, how different could it really be? The key, I decided, was the safety. It was clear the weapon had one. I could feel the switch. I toggled it up and down. But in the dark I couldn't be sure whether the safety was engaged when the lever was up, or whether it had to be down. There was only one way to find out, of course—aim, squeeze the trigger, and see what happened.

But I hesitated. *I'm a reporter, not a combatant*, I told myself. *I'm not here to kill, but to cover.* This had been my mantra in every conflict I'd ever reported on. Now, however, everything seemed different. Suddenly I wasn't so sure of my ethics. But this was it. I had only a moment. If I didn't shoot now, I might never have the chance. The closer he got, the more likely he was to shoot if I didn't. I crouched down and aimed. I knew if I pulled the trigger and the gun didn't fire, I'd still have time to flick the safety the other direction and pull the trigger again. With the element of surprise, I had the chance to live. But should I take it? What if I was wrong? What if he wasn't alone? What if other armed men were prepared to rush into this hallway and gun me down the moment I fired? If I set down the gun, yes, I might be caught. But in that case, as a journalist, I still might be able to talk my way out. I might be able to persuade this person I was there to help them, to give them a voice to the outside world, and wasn't that my job? If I was caught with a smoking gun in my hand, there would be no mercy. I was sure to be butchered like an animal, whether the footage wound up on YouTube or not.

I heard a rattling behind me, and the door to the street swung open. Instantly the hallway was flooded with moonlight. I pivoted hard, gun in hand, and found myself staring at two silhouettes. I was about to pull the trigger but could barely see. My eyes were desperately trying to adjust, and as they did, I found myself wondering if this was Omar and Abdel. Were they alive? Had they found me? My whole perspective started shifting. But before I could react, a burst of gunfire erupted from over my left shoulder. Stunned, I yelled out but it was too late. The two men standing in the doorway had been hit. They fell to the ground outside, screaming in agony. Horrified, and without thinking, I dropped the gun, jumped to my feet, and ran through the open door to their side. But they were not Omar or Abdel. They weren't anyone I knew. To the contrary, both were in uniform. They were soldiers in the Syrian army. Both held machine guns in their hands. The safeties were off. They had been about to kill me.

One of the men was writhing on the pavement, choking on his own blood. Seconds later, he went limp. The rifle dropped away. He was gone.

The other man had been shot in the face and chest. He was dying a slow, cruel death, and worst of all, he knew it. I stared down at him in the moonlight, sickened but unable to look away. He stared back at me, his eyes wide and filled with terror.

"Help me," he groaned in Arabic.

I stood there for a moment, not knowing what to say.

"Please," he said, his voice barely a whisper.

"I'm so sorry," I said finally.

"I don't want to die. Please, do something."

But I just stood there, frozen. I wanted to help. I really did. But how? I had no medical supplies with me. I wasn't a doctor. I had no training. There was literally nothing I could do, and as soon as he understood, his fear grew all the more.

In all my years covering wars, I had seen my share of battlefield deaths. I'd seen men die in drone strikes and by Hellfire missiles. I'd seen suicide bombers and carpet bombings and sniper shootings. I had seen men die instantly and unaware. One moment they were full of bravado and testosterone, and the next they were gone.

I'd also seen men die in the hands of professionals. I'd seen medics and fellow soldiers fight valiantly to save their friends, racing against time, doing everything humanly possible to save their lives.

But I'd never seen anything like this. This man was about to leave this world and enter the next. He was begging me for help, desperately clinging to life, even as it slipped away. Then his eyes unlocked from mine. He was staring up at the sky now. He had forgotten about me. He seemed to be able to see something I couldn't. He was riveted on it, and it filled him with panic.

"No!" he shrieked. *"No—!"*

Another deafening gunshot pierced the night sky. Then all was quiet. I turned and saw a young boy standing next to me. At least, I assumed he was a boy because of the way he was dressed. But I couldn't actually see his face. He was wearing a black hood, and he was aiming a pistol at the soldier's head. Smoke curled out of the barrel.

And then he turned the pistol on me.

11

★ ★ ★

"Who are you?" he demanded in Arabic, his voice cold and detached.

For a second I was too startled to answer. His head and face were covered by a black hood, but I could see his eyes, and that's what chilled me. They were dark and soulless. There was not a spark of life or hope in them. He had gunned these men down without giving it a thought. He had clearly killed others. Probably many others. And I knew at that moment he would not hesitate to kill me.

"I'm a reporter," I replied in Arabic, my mouth bone-dry.

He said nothing.

"I'm supposed to interview someone."

Still nothing.

"Soon," I added.

The boy just stared through me, this haunted, hunted look in his eyes.

"At the Khaled bin Walid Mosque," I mumbled, not sure why I was still talking.

He obviously couldn't have cared less, and I wondered if he was going to shoot me now.

There was a long stretch of silence. Well, silence in the sense that neither of us was talking. The winds were howling through the concrete canyons and across the barren wasteland of the streets of Homs. A fresh round of gunfire could be heard several streets to the east, the *rat-a-tat-tat* staccato of automatic weapons being fired in short bursts. I heard a stray mortar round or two, but the pitched battle of the last hour appeared to be dying down. Then again, maybe that was wishful thinking.

"The bag—what's in it?" the boy asked at long last, pointing the pistol at my backpack.

Startled, scared, not sure how much to say, I stammered, "Oh, uh, you know, just some stuff. Notebooks, pens, whatever."

"Food?" he asked in a barely audible voice.

"I'm sorry?" I replied, not sure I'd heard him right.

"Do you have any food?" he repeated, only marginally louder now.

"Oh yeah, well, a little—not much—just some apples, some PowerBars, that kind of thing."

"Give it to me," he said.

"Which?"

"All of it—whatever you have."

Was he serious? Didn't he want my wallet, my cash, my credit cards? Then it dawned on me these would do this boy no good. There was no place for him to buy food no matter how much money he had. I took the pack off, set it on the ground, and unzipped the top.

"I haven't eaten anything but a few olives in the past three days," he said as if reading my thoughts.

I stopped what I was doing and looked up. What he said stunned me—not his words but the way he said them. There was no emotion in his voice. None. He wasn't complaining. He wasn't a little kid whining or moaning or asking for sympathy. He was just stating a fact, and come to think of it, I don't think he was even saying it to me. It was almost as if he were saying it to himself. I just happened to be standing there.

As I looked more closely, I saw how loose his trousers were, how they barely hung on his emaciated frame. His gloveless hands, gaunt and bony, looked cold and raw.

Who was this boy? I wondered. What was his name? Where did he live? How did he spend his days? Who looked after him? Did anyone, or was he just roaming the streets at night, gunning down strangers in hopes of finding a little food? I wanted to ask him so many questions. I wanted to write a story about him, put him on the front page of the *Times*.

But he waved the gun at me, hurrying me along. He was growing impatient, and I could sense how dangerous it would be to try to engage in conversation. Whoever he was, he had long since lost his innocence. He had seen too much, done too much, and he didn't want the world to know. His world had contracted. His only aspiration was to survive the night, not tell his story, yet in that cold, dark street I wondered if even his will to live would last much longer.

"Never mind," he said with a sudden urgency. "Just give me the bag."

Again I looked up at him. I could see in his eyes that he meant it. There would be no arguing. No negotiating. And he wasn't going to ask twice. I zipped up the backpack. It wasn't simply filled with notebooks and pens and a bit of food. It also held a brand-new digital camera and telephoto lens and a digital audio recorder, all property of the *Times*. I cautiously took a few steps forward and held it out to the boy. For a moment I wondered if he would look inside and then shoot me for not telling him the full contents. But then I saw he was getting edgy, anxious to get moving, off this street, back into the shadows. I set down the pack and carefully backed up to where I had stood before.

Glancing around in every direction to see if the coast was clear, he reached down, stripped the dead soldiers of their ammo, stuffed the magazines into one of the side pockets of the backpack, slung it over his shoulder, and ran back into the long, dark hallway.

Before I knew it, I was standing all alone in the middle of the rubble-strewn street, just me and two new corpses. I knew I should run. To stand there was to be a target. But I just stared at the two soldiers and the sheer terror in their eyes.

My brother liked to talk about heaven and hell. That's what he'd been trained for. That's what interested him. Until now, I'd honestly never thought much about one or the other. But at that moment, I realized I could not say these men were in a better place. As cruel as their last moments were, was it possible they still existed but now in someplace worse? I didn't want to think this way, and I never had before. I'd never thought much about the afterlife, but to the extent I'd pondered it at all, I had just assumed that when we died, we were all simply snuffed out like a candle. That was it. That's all there was. But now I was haunted by this Syrian's last words. As he was slipping away from this world, he had clearly seen another, and it had terrified him. I'd seen it in his eyes. I'd heard it in his voice. And all of it rattled me.

Forcing myself to turn away, to think about something else, I looked around me. All I saw was carnage and ruin. Ten-, twelve-, fifteen-story apartment buildings were partially collapsed, riddled with bullet holes, devoid of windows, blackened and charred by fire. Not one or two buildings looked this way. They all did. Everything was devastated and abandoned.

This was Syria. This was what the Arab Republic of the Assad years had degenerated into—a concrete jungle of Syrian soldiers and starving, suffering, soul-scarred children rooting around for bits of food, and the decomposing bodies of those who got in their way. Did the world really understand what was happening here? Did it care? Did I? How long had I covered the war like a football match, chalking up wins and losses, with play-by-play and color analysis? How many peace conferences and diplomatic initiatives had I written about from swank five-star hotels in Geneva and Paris, wining and dining with foreign ministers and secretaries of state and defense, all pontificating about the tragedy but never actually doing anything about it? Year after year this nightmare was unfolding, and still the world did nothing definitive to stop it. In Washington, the politicians talked tough. In London and Paris and Berlin and Geneva, it was all the same. But nothing changed. Nothing got better. Not for these two men. Not for this little boy. Not for anyone who had once lived on this street in Homs.

I was witnessing the implosion of an entire country, and for the first time it began to truly dawn on me that if no one stepped in, there might not be a country left in another year or two. Was that really possible? Were we witnessing the utter disintegration of a modern Arab state? Might this nation actually never be put together again?

I'd never thought like this before. I'd certainly never written anything of the sort. But suddenly, standing alone on this street, seeing what I had just seen, I realized I had absolutely no idea what would become of Syria. Perhaps Hezbollah and the Iranian Revolutionary Guards would take it over and turn it into another province of the mullahs in Tehran. Or maybe al Qaeda and the other Sunni rebels would win the day and create a new Afghanistan or Somalia on the borders of Israel, Lebanon, and Jordan. Either way, I couldn't see President Assad and his forces lasting much longer. Honestly, I was stunned that he was still alive after all that had happened so far.

I heard a roar overhead and looked up to see two F-4 Phantoms streaking past. Moments later, two more shot by. Then the bombs started falling. It was the thunderous explosions and massive balls of fire, all just a few blocks to the north, that snapped me out of my foolish introspection. This was neither the time nor the place to muse over the future of Syria. There were far more urgent questions facing me. What was I going to do now? Where was I going to go? Time was fleeting. Faisal Baqouba wasn't going to sit around in that mosque all night. Unless I got moving, I was going to miss him and miss his brother Tariq, and with them the interview that could make my career.

Then again, if I started moving toward the mosque alone, there was a very real chance I wasn't going to make it home alive.

A new round of machine-gun fire erupted, and then sniper fire too. Someone was squeezing off single rounds from a high-caliber rifle. I'd heard it before, but never so close. If I had to guess, I'd have said it was just up the street and around the corner to the north.

I was out of time. I had to get out of there. Stepping over mounds of broken, crumbled concrete blocks, I moved off the street and ducked into the shadows of a doorway.

Someone grabbed me from behind. Before I realized what was happening, he clamped a hand over my mouth. Someone else grabbed my arms and pinned them behind me. I couldn't move, could hardly breathe. They dragged me into a windowless, putrid building. I couldn't see a thing. A surge of adrenaline shot through my system. I wanted to fight back, but I knew someone would slash my throat or put a bullet through my head before I got in my first good hit, so instead I went limp and crashed to the floor.

Immediately I felt the cold steel barrel of a gun jammed into the base of my skull. Someone's boot thrust down hard on my back. Another came down on my neck. My hands were wrenched behind me again. In short order they were bound with rope so tight it cut into my wrists. I felt them start to bleed.

Then someone threw a bag over my head. It was plastic and opaque, a garbage bag probably. It was tied snug around my face and neck. I began to hyperventilate. I kept telling myself to calm down, not to panic, but to no avail. The walls were closing in. I felt claustrophobic. I decided they weren't going to shoot me or they would have done it already. But that could only mean one thing: they were going to behead me. The very thought nearly made my heart stop. Then I felt a needle being jammed into my arm, and time stood still.

12

* * *

When I woke up, I had no idea where I was.

I had no idea how long I'd been unconscious. There was still a garbage bag over my head and tied around my neck, but it had been loosened enough that I could breathe. I was achy and stiff and freezing. My jacket was gone. So was my sweater. All I had on were my T-shirt and boxers.

My arms were still tied behind me. My feet were now bound as well, but my shoes were gone and so were my socks. As best I could tell, I was sitting on a frigid concrete floor, leaning against cold cinder blocks, and I could hear a driving rainstorm and the most intense booms of thunder I had ever experienced.

In the distance, I could also still hear the occasional burst of automatic-weapons fire. I strained to hear anything else, something that might tell me where I was. Soon I heard what sounded like two fighter jets roaring overhead. After a moment, another two flew past, and then I heard repeated explosions. They weren't loud or close—certainly not as close as when we'd first entered the city. But the activity suggested a government offensive was still being waged against a rebel enclave.

I could also hear something flapping in the breeze. At first it sounded like a flag. But then it sounded like sheets of plastic. A terrible draft was coming into whatever room I was in, and occasionally a spray of bitterly cold rain. I didn't hear any windows rattling. Indeed, I hadn't seen much evidence that there was any unshattered glass left in the city. So I concluded I was in a place where plastic bags or sheets of plastic had been fastened over the blown-out windows in a semi-futile effort to keep out the worst of the wind and the rain.

Then I heard heavy footsteps. I don't know how to describe it precisely, but there was something about the tone and pitch of the sounds that made me think someone—or actually several people—were ascending a nearby concrete stairwell. Whoever they were, they clearly wore boots, and the weight suggested they were men. Whether they were regular soldiers or jihadist rebels I had no idea, but I was sure I was not in a bunker or a basement. I was several flights up at least, perhaps in a top-floor apartment or office, doubtless stripped of all carpets and furniture and other amenities.

No one was saying anything, but they were getting closer, and with each step I feared my end was drawing near.

There was so much at that moment that I didn't know. All I knew for sure was that I was not ready to die. There's no other way to put it. I could tell you I was bravely ready to meet my Maker, but that would be a lie. I was petrified.

The footsteps stopped right in front of me.

"What is your name?" a man asked me in English, though his voice bore a thick Arab accent.

I tried to swallow but had no saliva. Suddenly I felt the edge of a blade against my throat, just below my Adam's apple.

"James," I replied, trying to steady my voice. "James Bradley Collins."

"Where are you from?"

The very question struck terror in my heart, but what choice did I have? Would they really hesitate to kill me if I acted Canadian, British, or Australian? Maybe, for a while. But what would happen when they found I was lying to them?

"America."

"What city?"

"Washington."

"What do you do?"

"I'm a reporter."

"For what paper?"

"The *Times*."

"Which one?"

"The *New York Times*."

"Why did you come to Syria?"

Here I hesitated. What was the right answer? Who was holding me? What did they want to hear? My mind rapidly considered a wide range of options. But in my situation, none seemed viable. I didn't have the energy and mental wherewithal to construct a cover story and stick with it through days or weeks of starvation, sleep deprivation, beatings, and whippings. I wasn't in the CIA. I wasn't trained for this.

A simple thought then crossed my mind: *Just tell them the truth—there's nothing to be gained by lying.* But that wasn't necessarily true, I told myself. Lying might buy me time until I could figure a way out of here or until someone could come rescue me, maybe Omar, maybe Abdel. Lying, I thought, just might save me. But before I knew what I was doing, I heard myself saying I had come to do an interview.

"With whom?"

"Ramzy," I said without thinking.

"Jamal Ramzy?" came the reply.

"Yes."

"Why?"

"He invited me."

No one said a word.

"Look in my pocket," I said quickly. "The pocket of my trousers. You'll find a printout of the e-mail."

Did they believe me? Did they care? Were they part of Assad's forces or rebels? And where were Omar and Abdel? Had they already been killed? Had they been captured? Were they being inter-rogated? All the more reason to tell the truth, I decided. My captors very well might know the answer to every question they were asking me.

Thunder crashed around us. The winter rains were coming down even harder now. I thought I heard the rustling of a piece of paper but couldn't be sure. Then the blade was removed from my throat, though I felt it nick me and draw blood. A moment later, the plastic bag was ripped off my head. A flash of lightning momentarily blinded me, but as I got my bearings, I found myself staring up at three men.

Each was well built, muscular, armed to the hilt, and covered in a black wool hood. The one on the left wore a dark-blue sweatshirt, faded blue jeans, and black combat boots. He held a machine gun pointed at me. The one on the right wore a winter parka, green fatigues, and brown boots. He was brandishing a sword, which shimmered in the moonlight. I thought I detected a drop of my blood on its tip. The one in the center seemed the youngest. He wore sneakers, black jeans, and my leather coat. He already had the e-mail in his hand, and when our eyes met, it was he who spoke.

"*As-salamu alaykum*, Mr. Collins. I am Tariq Baqouba. These are Faisal and Ahmed. They are my brothers. Welcome to Homs."

I was stunned yet relieved. I know it sounds strange to say, and I admit that before that night it would never have occurred to me to breathe a sigh of relief in the presence of three proven al Qaeda killers. But I was relieved. Maybe *relieved* isn't the right word, but I cannot think of another. The simple fact was I was glad to still be alive and off the streets. I had not yet missed my appointment, and I was now heading—I hoped—to meet the man for whom I'd come all this way.

"Now, come with me," Tariq ordered.

The man on the right quickly put his sword in its sheath. He untied my feet, pulled me up, and produced a bag that turned out to be filled with my clothes. While his brothers held their weapons on me, he set my hands free long enough for me to put my clothes and shoes back on. They were cold and a bit damp, but under the circumstances I was grateful, especially when I felt my grandfather's watch ticking away in my right front pocket.

I had a thousand questions, starting with where my colleagues were. But I said nothing. My hands were tied again. A machine gun was thrust into my back, and we proceeded down the concrete steps, down five floors to the ground level. Along the way I came to realize we were, in fact, in what was left of the Khaled bin Walid Mosque. It had been shelled and shot up pretty good. But it had not yet collapsed, and I saw signs that people had been here recently. A few sleeping bags in one place. The remains of a campfire in another. Shell casings and cigarette butts were everywhere. It seemed to be a safe house of sorts. I made a mental note of it in case I ever got out of this country alive.

We didn't stay for long. When we reached the ground floor, they led me through the charred remains of the main hall. Then we stepped into another stairwell, where we descended to the basement. They turned on flashlights as we walked down a labyrinth of damp, dripping hallways until we reached a mechanical room of some kind. We entered and they led me past the boiler and some new-looking electrical panels. I couldn't fathom their purpose. The room wasn't that big. What could the panels possibly be powering? But as we turned a corner, I saw an opening in the rear wall.

Feeling the barrel of the machine gun being prodded into my back, urging me to go through the opening, I ducked down and, trying not to lose my balance, crawled through the hole. I found myself crouched in a makeshift tunnel that had been dug under the city. Strangely, though most if not all of the city of Homs was blacked out, the tunnel had power and was reasonably well lit. It was no more than five and a half feet high and at best four feet wide, but it was long. It seemed to go on forever. It reminded me of the smuggling tunnels I'd seen on the Sinai border with Gaza and on the U.S. border with Mexico.

The rebel with the machine gun told me to move faster, and I did as I was told. I hunched over and began to walk. After what I guessed was a good ten or fifteen minutes, we finally reached a ladder and a hole in the ceiling. The tunnel didn't stop there. It kept going and broke off in two directions. But I was directed up the ladder, and with some difficulty since I couldn't use my hands, I eventually made it to the top, where two more hooded thugs, both well armed, grabbed me, pulled me through the hole in the floor, and threw another bag over my head. We walked for another long stretch, down hallways, up and down flights of stairs, and through another tunnel, until finally I was told to stop, sit down on a cold metal stool, and keep my mouth shut. When the bag came off my head, I could barely see at all.

Enormous klieg lights were shining in my face. I was sitting at an old metal table. It reminded me of the kitchen table I'd grown up with. As I squinted, I could see a giant figure sitting across from me.

"Welcome to *ad-Dawla al-Islāmiyya fi al-'Irāq wa-al-Shām*, Mr. Collins," he said in a throaty, almost-gravelly voice, like someone with emphysema or throat cancer. "I am Jamal Ramzy."

13

* * *

The instant Ramzy said his name, the klieg lights shut down.

It took a few moments for my eyes to adjust, but when they did, I saw a gargantuan man—six foot five, three hundred pounds at least, dark-skinned, and masked only by a thick, full, black beard without a touch of gray. He wore a black robe and a black skullcap and had a Kalashnikov and an ammo belt slung over his shoulder. He had small, suspicious brown eyes, which immediately locked onto my own and never wandered, making me even more uncomfortable than I already felt, surrounded as we were by armed men in the signature al Qaeda black hoods. Everyone stared at me as my feet were promptly chained to enormous metal spikes driven into the concrete floor.

We were in a cavernous bunker of some kind. It was as big as a football field, and tall and wide enough to park a jet plane or a few dozen tanks, though at the moment it was empty but for a couple dozen large wooden crates, a few pickup trucks, and some cots. On the metal table before us sat a notebook, several pens, and a digital recorder. I immediately recognized them as my own. Taken aback, I was about to say something when I noticed a smudge on the side of the recorder. It looked like blood. I said nothing. I didn't want to know how they had retrieved my backpack. I didn't want to know what had happened to the boy who had taken it from me.

Even as I looked at him, and he stared back at me, it was still difficult to fully process that I was sitting across from the commander of the Syrian forces of the Islamic State of Iraq and al-Sham, commonly referred to in Western intelligence agencies as ISIS, pronounced "eye-sis." Others called it ISIL—the Islamic State of Iraq and the Levant—while many in the media called it simply the Islamic State. But whatever you called his terrorist organization, Jamal Ramzy was fast becoming one of the most wanted men in the world. The American government had recently marked him a specially designated global terrorist under Executive Order 13224. The State Department had put a $5 million bounty on his head. Yet to my knowledge, no reporter had ever spoken with Ramzy, much less seen him face-to-face. Though he had been mentioned in a handful of articles over the past year, not a single profile had been written on him. Mine, I hoped, would be the first.

"Mr. Collins, you're thinking about the reward," he began, his face expressionless. "I can see it in your eyes. Let me give you a piece of advice. Stop."

I wasn't actually, not really, but just the way he said it made my blood run cold.

"You have thirty minutes," he said after a long pause. "Shall we begin?"

Someone came up behind me and cut the ropes that bound my hands. My wrists were bleeding, but not terribly. They were aching, but I didn't allow that to distract me. I pulled the pocket watch out and set it on the table. Then I reached for the recorder, started it, picked up a pen, and asked my first question.

"Is Jamal Ramzy your real name?"

"Yes."

"When were you born?"

"January 6, 1962."

"Where?"

"Irbid, Jordan."

"Are you Palestinian?"

"You know I am."

I looked up from the notepad. "I don't want to make any assumptions," I said carefully. "I want the facts straight from you."

He just stared at me without blinking. "Yes," he said at last.

"Where is your family originally from?"

"Hebron."

"Was your grandfather killed in the 1948 war?"

"Yes, the Zionists killed him and all my uncles."

"Then your family fled to Jordan?"

"They were ordered to leave."

"By the Jews?"

"No, by the coward Arab leaders who chose to run rather than fight."

This caught me off guard. I suspected it partially explained his apparent preference to spend more time fighting his fellow Arabs than the Jews. It was a thread I wanted to pull on, but there was no time. This was all background information. I needed to get to the real issues, and quickly.

"After high school, your family moved to the Gulf, correct?"

"Yes."

"Bahrain first and Dubai?"

"Yes."

"When were you in Afghanistan?"

"March 1980 to August 1983."

"You were young."

"I serve at the pleasure of Allah."

Now I changed directions. "Why did you change the name of your organization to ISIS?"

"The Islamic State is not my organization," he said. "Allah is our leader. Islam is our path. Jihad is our way. Abu Khalif is our caliph. I am but a servant."

There he was: Abu Khalif, Ramzy's younger cousin, the true leader of ISIS. I had been told by reliable sources that Khalif—not Ramzy—should be my real target. But I was not ready. Not yet. I would have to come back to this.

"Your faction was called al Qaeda in Iraq," I noted. "Now it's the Islamic State of Iraq and al-Sham. Why the change?"

"Again, it is not my faction, Mr. Collins," he said calmly. "Abu Khalif is our leader. And it is the movement of Allah, not our own. At any rate, the original name was given by Ayman al-Zawahiri.

But we no longer serve him. He is a traitor to Islam. Abu Khalif told him to repent. He chose not to. We are no longer responsible for what happens to him. We do not wish to be identified with anything connected to a traitor."

I was about to ask another question, but Ramzy continued.

"Let me be perfectly clear, Mr. Collins. We do not serve al Qaeda. There is no reason to have this in our name. We serve Allah only, and Allah has given us a simple mandate: reestablish the caliphate. We have started in Iraq to bring down the apostate leadership there. But this is about more than just Iraq. Al-Sham, as you must know, is the Levant, the East, the place of the rising sun. This is our focus."

"Beginning with Syria?" I asked.

"Of course," he said. "Assad is a criminal. He has never been a true Muslim. He must be dispatched to the fires of judgment, with his family and all those loyal to him. Assad is a doomed man. But he is just a piece in the puzzle, you might say."

"What are the other pieces?"

"The entire Levant," he said matter-of-factly.

"Again, I don't want to assume anything, and I don't want my readers to assume either," I said. "You've mentioned Iraq and Syria. Do you also plan to take over Lebanon?"

"Of course."

"Turkey?"

"Yes."

"Cyprus?"

"Yes."

"Palestine?"

"Of course."

"Israel?"

"Palestine," he replied.

"I mean the Jewish State of Israel proper," I clarified, adding, "inside the pre-1967 lines."

He stared at me. "*All* of Palestine," he said, his voice rising for the first time.

"Yes, of course," I said. "Just trying to be clear. What about Jordan?"

His eyes narrowed. "How many times must I say it, Mr. Collins?" he said, barely restraining the anger in his voice. "*All* of Palestine."

"Very well," I said. "These are the boundaries of the Islamic kingdom your leadership envisions?"

"The initial boundaries, yes."

I raised my eyebrows. "There's more?"

"This is enough for now."

"So this is a multistage plan?"

"Yes," he said. "We have declared jihad to bring down the blasphemous regime in Baghdad and the equally apostate regime in Damascus. But we will not rest until we bring down every leader, every government, until every man, woman, and child is governed by Sharia law, by the will of the Prophet, peace be upon him."

"At the moment, you are waging war on two fronts—Syria and Iraq. Will there be a third?"

Ramzy paused. I doubted he was authorized to go that far. After all, *that* would be news—ISIS declaring war on a third front.

"Yes," he said at last.

Surprised he was being so candid, I immediately

sought to clarify. "You're going to open a third front?"

"Yes."

"When?"

"Soon."

"How soon?"

"Very."

"Against whom?" I pressed, assuming it was Israel but not wanting to put the words in his mouth. "Who is the third target?"

Ramzy leaned forward in his seat, his eyes dancing. "Anyone who betrays the Palestinian cause, anyone who helps the racist Zionist regime," he said with real emotion in his voice.

"Do you mean the United States?" I asked.

"Anyone who betrays the Palestinian cause will pay dearly," Ramzy replied.

He wasn't being precise, but he wasn't denying that it was the U.S. either, I noted.

"Are you saying ISIS is planning to strike inside the U.S.—on the homeland—at American citizens traveling abroad, at military bases, companies, et cetera?"

"We are about to launch a Third Intifada, Mr. Collins," he said flatly. "But this will be unlike any that has gone before—the scale, the magnitude. You have not seen anything like this. Those who betray the cause of Islam to obtain a false peace with murderers and criminals—they will burn. All of them will burn."

So it was true. I furiously scribbled down every word, terrified the digital recorder might fail. Abu Khalif and Jamal Ramzy and this breakaway al Qaeda faction were about to target the U.S. and Israel, and with them the latest peace process that was reportedly sputtering to a failure like all the others before it.

He was saying ISIS would target those who supported Israel—and no nation was a bigger ally of the Jewish state than the U.S.—but he was also using the term *intifada*. This was an Arab word for "uprising" or "revolution." It literally meant a "shaking off."

The First Intifada had erupted in the West Bank and Gaza in December of 1987. Though it had largely been a popular rebellion using stones and slingshots, burning tires, and Molotov cocktails, the uprising had prompted Israel to respond with mass arrests, tear gas, and shooting at crowds with live ammunition, and later with rubber bullets, all captured by TV crews who broadcast the images into people's homes every night at dinnertime, in the U.S. and around the world. That intifada hadn't won the Palestinians any new rights or freedoms. But it had created a public relations disaster for Israel, making the Jewish State look like the big, bad Goliath staring down the helpless, underdog Palestinian David. That had been the narrative of the international media, anyway, including the *Times*.

The Second Intifada had erupted in September of 2000 after the breakdown of Mideast peace talks at Camp David between President Clinton, Israeli prime minister Ehud Barak, and PLO chairman Yasser Arafat. That time, the Palestinian extremists had unleashed a wave of suicide bombers that struck Israeli buses, cafés, and elementary schools, followed by a barrage of rockets and mortars fired from Gaza at innocent civilians living in southern Israeli towns and villages. The Palestinians had vented their rage at the "Zionist occupation" but this time won little sympathy in the West from mothers and fathers who were horrified by the sight of Jewish children and their parents being blown up by Palestinian bombs and rockets.

"What will this Third Intifada entail?" I asked. "Are we talking about suicide bombers, rockets, IEDs, snipers, kidnappings?"

"I will not say more about this," he said sharply, though I noted he did nothing to deny these were all options. "You will see when it happens."

"Fine, I understand; but just to be clear, are you declaring war on Israel and the United States?"

"No traitor is safe. Allah is watching. Judgment is coming."

14

★ ★ ★

"Mr. Ramzy, I have just a few more questions," I said.

I was still writing as fast as I could, trying to ignore the cramping in my hand.

"Be my guest," he said, leaning back in his chair, suddenly seeming relaxed as if pleased with himself for what he had just told me.

I glanced at the pocket watch and winced. The time was going so quickly. Then I checked the digital recorder. It was still running. Hopefully it was really recording. I took a deep breath, sat up straight, and then leaned forward.

"I have two sources who tell me ISIS now has chemical weapons."

For a moment, Ramzy looked taken aback, but he quickly composed himself. He said nothing.

"My sources say you're planning to use them against Israeli and American targets during Hanukkah and Christmas."

Jamal Ramzy didn't blink. He just stared at me and remained silent.

I stared back, waiting. The man certainly had

a flair for drama, but I had little doubt this was really the news he wanted to make.

"Is there a question there?" he asked finally.

"Are my sources accurate?" I asked point-blank.

"No," he replied. "They are liars."

I was floored. "Liars?"

"You heard me."

I had, but I was not convinced. "Now wait a minute, Mr. Ramzy. Let me be clear about this. I have a very high-ranking source in a Western intelligence agency who has clear proof that you and your forces captured a cache of chemical weapons in north-central Syria three weeks ago, in late October, and that you have transferred these weapons to sites in Lebanon, western Iraq, and the Sinai in preparation for a major attack on Israel, and to sleeper cells in Canada and Mexico in preparation for attacks on the U.S."

"These are all lies."

I pressed on, undeterred. "This source tells me he has personally listened to audio recordings of radio traffic between two Syrian generals. One of them is frantically telling the other that one of their chemical-weapons storage facilities not far from Aleppo had just been overrun. The other is desperately calling for air strikes and ground-troop reinforcements, but the evidence indicates they were too late. Your men got there first and left with truckloads of warheads filled with chemical agents. There is further signals intelligence that your men are developing plans to hit New York, Washington, Los Angeles, and Tel Aviv."

"Your source is misleading you. You should get another."

I had no idea why Ramzy was denying all this, but I forged ahead. "I have another, a source in a different intelligence service in an entirely different country with no connection to the first source," I continued. "He told me that a three-star Syrian general defected to a Muslim country at the end of October. He claimed an al Qaeda faction seized several tons of chemical weapons south of Aleppo within the last few weeks. He gave this Muslim country hard intel—in terms of satellite phone intercepts—indicating this al Qaeda faction is planning to use the chemical weapons against U.S. and Israeli targets during the Christmas holidays."

Now Ramzy leaned forward and smiled. "What can I tell you, Mr. Collins? These are fanciful tales. I wish they were true. I do. But you've been fed a pack of innuendos, deceptions, and disinformation."

"You're denying ISIS has captured chemical weapons?"

"Yes."

"You're denying that you're developing plans to use them in the next few weeks against the U.S. and Israel?"

"You read too many spy thrillers, Mr. Collins."

I was getting exasperated and had to fight to keep my cool. "You just told me you're going to launch a Third Intifada," I reminded him. "You just told me it was going to be unlike any uprising we've seen before. You just told me the Zionists and those who support them will burn."

"That I stand by," he replied.

"Then why not just tell the world the magnitude of the operation you're planning? It'll be front-page tomorrow morning on the biggest newspaper in the world. It'll be picked up by every other news outlet on the planet."

"What I gave you already will be front-page news, will it not, Mr. Collins?" Ramzy pushed back. "ISIS announces a third front, a Third Intifada—won't that be picked up by every media outlet in the world?"

He was right, of course, but I had no intention of giving him the satisfaction of hearing it from me; not before I tried again to get an even bigger story out of him. "It's news," I told him. "But I doubt it will go viral. Not like it would if you confirm ISIS has chemical weapons."

"Sorry to disappoint you, Mr. Collins," Ramzy replied. "And we were getting along so well."

I was baffled. My sources were solid. Unbeknownst to each other, both had let me listen to the tapes in question and had even given me transcripts for my story. Neither source knew I was going to Syria to try to confirm what I had been told. I hadn't even made my plans until after I'd spoken to each of them and had suddenly received the e-mail from Faisal Baqouba about coming to meet Ramzy. This was a major exclusive. I had been sitting on it for more than ten days. It wasn't going to hold much longer.

"Isn't this the story you invited me here to confirm, the chemical weapons?" I pressed.

"No."

"Then why have me come all this way and go through all this trouble, just to tell me what you could have announced in a press release?" I asked again. "Why stop short of giving me the story that would be the shot heard around the world?"

"Time's up," Ramzy said.

That wasn't possible. It couldn't have been thirty minutes. Ramzy was playing with me. But I had to keep my cool as I continued writing out my notes and flexing my aching fingers.

Suddenly he said, "Time to take some pictures."

My pen stopped writing. I looked at him in disbelief, then watched as he snapped his fingers. I turned my head, and in through a side door came Omar and Abdel, surrounded by more men with machine guns.

I couldn't believe it. They were alive. They were safe. They were here. Without thinking, I jumped up from my seat and tried to move toward them but realized—almost too late—that my feet were still chained to the floor. When I noticed several of the guards around us moving their fingers to the triggers of their weapons, I quickly sat down.

My colleagues were brought closer, and I noticed they were in shackles too. They were kept a good ten yards from each other and had a guard on each side. Still, they were smiling and looked no worse for the wear.

One of the guards handed Abdel his Nikon and gave him a few instructions. Then the klieg lights powered back on, creating stunning conditions for a one-of-a-kind portrait of a key terrorist figure the world knew very little about so far.

When all the preparations were complete, Ramzy nodded, and Abdel began snapping away.

Barely a minute later, Ramzy held up his hand and a guard grabbed the camera out of Abdel's hands. The photo shoot was over.

Ramzy walked over to me and handed me my backpack. I wasn't sure I wanted it but knew there was no point in saying so.

"One more thing, if I may?" I asked.

"What is it, Mr. Collins?" Ramzy replied, beginning to sound annoyed.

"I would like to meet Abu Khalif," I said. "Would you introduce me?"

Ramzy didn't bat an eye. "That's not possible."

"Why not?"

"He doesn't speak to reporters."

"Neither do you."

"I made an exception."

"Maybe he will too."

"He won't."

"Is he still in prison in Iraq?"

"This is none of your concern."

"Which prison?"

"You are treading on thin ice here, Mr. Collins."

"But he still runs ISIS, doesn't he?"

"Of course."

"So he's the one who gave the order to launch the Third Intifada, correct?"

"Abu Khalif is our leader."

"So he makes the decisions?"

"That's what leaders do."

"Then why can't I meet him? Why can't I talk to him and get his take on where this region is heading, where ISIS is heading? Just like you, he's got a story to tell, Mr. Ramzy. Let me tell it."

"You do not understand what you're asking," he replied, his eyes narrowing.

"I think I do."

"Oh, but you don't, or you would never have brought it up."

Risking everything, perhaps including my life, I stood and stepped as close to Jamal Ramzy as my shackles would allow. He stiffened but held his ground. In my peripheral vision I could see his guards grow tense. But I didn't care. I leaned in to Ramzy's face and spoke to him man to man.

"Look," I said, "you knew Abu Musab al-Zarqawi. You and Abu Khalif were sent to Iraq by bin Laden and Khalid Sheikh Mohammed to help him establish al Qaeda in Iraq. Zarqawi was the face, but you and Abu Khalif were the brains. It was your ideas, your strategy, your tactics, your money, and your weapons that put Zarqawi on the map, right?"

Ramzy said nothing, but I went on.

"When Zarqawi was killed by that air strike in '06, you and Abu Khalif wanted to take the organization in one direction. Abu Ayyub al-Masri and his forces wanted to go in another. For a time, Masri prevailed. But in the end, you and Abu Khalif outlasted him. Abu Khalif became head of AQI. It was he who brought you in as his chief of operations. It was he who decided to expand the mission, change the name, raise the stakes. It was he who ordered you to build an army strong enough to storm Syria and bring Assad's head back on a platter. And in the end, it was he who broke with bin Laden and later with Zawahiri, and you supported him every step of the way. Am I right?"

Ramzy said nothing, but his eyes told me I was right.

"That must mean Abu Khalif told you to talk to me," I continued. "Why? Because he's about to start a new war, a war that's going to set this region on fire. You don't want to talk to me about the chemical weapons? Fine. I've got two sources. I'll run the story with or without your comment or his. But I'm giving you something no one else can, something money can't buy. I'm giving you and your boss the opportunity of a lifetime, the opportunity to be the new face of al Qaeda, to be the new face of global jihad. Forget your blood feud with Zawahiri. Forget all the men in the caves. Their time has come and gone. Your day has arrived. But I can't do it just by profiling the number two guy. I'm sorry. I can't. I need to talk to the emir. I need to get him on the record. You know it. He knows it. So give me access—exclusive access—before the war begins, before—"

I caught myself just in time. I was about to say, "Before you're both dead." But at the last moment I said, "Before you both go underground forever."

When I was finished, I gave him a little space, a little time, to take the bait. But Jamal Ramzy did not bite.

"We're done here, Mr. Collins," he said through gritted teeth. "But know this: you have made a terrible mistake. You will not write one word about chemical weapons, or you will not live to see it printed. You certainly will not meet Abu Khalif. And you will never presume to lecture me again about what is best for our cause. You are an infidel, Mr. Collins. You and your friends are alive because Abu Khalif chose to keep you alive. You will continue to live until he decides your usefulness to him is over. And when that day comes, he will give me the order, and I *will* kill you—all of you—and believe me, I will take my time and make you suffer."

much was clear, but not much else. I was freezing.
was dripping wet. I was eager to get out of Syria
and back to Beirut. I needed someplace warm and
dry and equipped with Wi-Fi so I could write my
story and get it filed.

So I started counting. Out loud.

I could hear men breathing near me. I assumed
these were Omar and Abdel. I wanted to be certain. I wanted to know they were okay. But we
were not supposed to ask any questions. So I
didn't. I just counted.

When I reached one hundred, I stood there in
silence, the bag still over my head, having no idea
where we were and no idea what to do next.

Finally I tore the bag off my head and held my
breath. No one shot me. No one beat me. We were
alone. Or at least we seemed to be.

We were standing in the stairwell of some
building, and Ramzy's men were gone. Relieved,
I exhaled and tried to start breathing normally.
Then I leaned in and whispered to Omar and
Abdel that they could both take the bags off their
heads but that they should keep quiet and follow
me. They quickly complied and I led them up five
flights of stairs.

As we stepped out onto the roof, we were
immediately greeted by multiple flashes of lightning. We could see jagged, crackling sticks of lightning hitting a nearby radio antenna and then felt
the *boom, boom, boom* of the thunder rattling our
bones.

"What time is it?" Omar asked.

I pulled out my grandfather's pocket watch,

15

* * *

Ramzy's men led us back through the tunnels.

When we emerged aboveground, they put black plastic bags over our heads and led us through the driving rains across one neighborhood after another until they told us to stop.

"Count to one hundred," one of them ordered, his voice seeming to echo a bit.

"Why?" I asked, worried.

"Just do it, and don't ask questions."

I had a lot of questions. Omar, Abdel, and I hadn't been permitted to talk since we left Ramzy's lair, and I was eager to know what my colleagues were thinking. How had they wound up with Tariq Baqouba? What did they make of the ISIS commander? Why did they think he wasn't willing to talk about the chemical weapons? Was he really lying, or was I being misled by more faulty Western intelligence? And what was the deal with Ramzy clamming up about Abu Khalif? Something wasn't right about that, but at the moment I was too scared to figure out what.

The good news was we weren't dead. That

unsure why Ramzy and his thugs had not kept it but grateful nonetheless.

"It's late," I replied. "We'd better keep moving."

The sun would be coming up soon—if it wasn't up already. We wouldn't see it, of course. The ferocious storm slamming western Syria was likely to last for some time. But as dangerous as it was to be caught out on a night like this—in a civil war zone, no less—I knew the only thing worse would be to try to traverse these streets and fields in the full light of day, even a stormy one.

A quick look around revealed we were standing atop one of the least damaged high-rises in the city. It had been hit numerous times, to be sure. There was an enormous crater in the center of the roof, no doubt a direct hit by one of Assad's fighter jets. But overall, the structure seemed sound. We spread out in three directions, looking over the edges and trying to get our bearings. Then we regrouped inside the stairwell.

"I saw the playground we came across last night," Abdel said.

"What about the machine-gun nests?" Omar asked.

"From this height, I could see them too, both of them—they're empty."

"Snipers?"

"I saw no signs of movement," he replied. "Can't make any promises. But with this weather, and with the sun about to come up, I'm guessing they're all gone for the night."

"Would you bet your life on it?" I asked.

"What choice do we have?" he responded.

We all stood there contemplating the question. We weren't out of this thing yet. We had the story—part of it, anyway—but a lot could still go wrong before we were in the clear. Snipers were one concern, but there were others. Mines. Booby traps. Night patrols. Drones. Random twelve-year-olds bearing Kalashnikovs.

"Look, the only question that really matters right now is this: Do you know how to get back to the border?" I asked.

"I think so," Abdel said.

"Good," I said. "Then I want you to lead the way."

Abdel nodded.

"But I want you to do something for me first," I said.

"What's that?"

"Take a picture of my buddy Omar and me on this roof," I explained.

"Sure thing, Mr. Collins," Abdel said. "I'll call it 'The Survivors.'"

Omar put his massive arm around me and chuckled. "I'll call it 'The Lunatics.'"

Abdel snapped a few pictures, then asked if he could take one with me too.

"Of course," I said, and Omar did the honors.

Then I instructed Abdel to use my satellite phone and transmit all his pictures back to the bureau.

Abdel nodded, fished my satphone out of my backpack, grabbed a cord from his own backpack, and digitally transmitted more than a hundred photos he had taken in the past twenty-four hours, including all the ones of Jamal Ramzy. I texted Allen MacDonald, my editor in Washington, telling him that we'd found Ramzy and gotten the interview and were heading back to safety. I knew he would be simultaneously furious with me for going into harm's way without his permission and ecstatic to get the story. But I would have to deal with all that later. Right now, we just needed to get out of there.

We headed down to the first floor, using our cell phones to light the way. When we got to the main level, Abdel motioned for us to follow him down a long hallway, but I grabbed his shirt and held him back.

"Maybe we should . . ." I stopped midsentence.

"Should what?" Abdel asked.

"Find another way," I said.

"Why?" Omar asked. "What other way?"

"I don't know," I confessed. "There's got to be another way out."

"So what?" Omar said. "Let's just go. It's going to be light out there soon."

"No," I said.

"What in the world are you talking about?"

"What can I say?" I half mumbled. "I just have a bad feeling about this."

They looked at me like I was crazy. Both of them. Maybe I was. I couldn't explain it then. I can't explain it now. But I didn't want to go down that hallway. Something wasn't right. I didn't have anything to back it up. It was just a gut feeling, but they were every bit as cold and tired as I was, and they had had enough.

"I mean no disrespect, Mr. Collins; I just want to get home," Abdel said. "I need to call Fatima. She worries about me. You go any way you like. But if it's all the same to you, I'm going this way."

It wasn't all the same to me. Still, I appreciated his humility. Abdel had a kind and decent heart. I knew he wasn't trying to be contrarian or disrespectful. He loved his girl. I got it. I could still remember feeling that way. I'd been married once. It had been a disaster. But even with all the pain, I hadn't forgotten what a good romance felt like. So I nodded, and Abdel left. But I wasn't going to follow him. I poked my head into another room, shining the flashlight on my phone from right to left and back again. It was a large, empty hall that had probably been used as a dining room, I figured, though it had long ago been looted of every furnishing and anything else that was valuable, from the light fixtures to the copper wires and pipes in the walls. Everything had been ripped out. It was all gone.

"You coming with me?" I asked Omar.

"Allen says I have to," he replied.

"What do you mean?"

"He told me to watch your back," Omar replied. "I'm already feeling guilty for having gotten separated from you last night. I don't plan to let that happen again."

"You're a good man, Omar," I told him. "Come on. Let's get out of here."

16

* * *

Omar and I moved through the cavernous hall.

Then we made our way through the gutted kitchen right behind it and then a large but completely empty pantry before we found a back door. It was unsettling to walk through a totally abandoned building knowing it had once—not so long ago—been teeming with boys and girls and women and men trying to make a life in this little corner of the world. Once families had eaten breakfasts, lunches, and dinners here, held birthday parties and wedding receptions, graduation parties and anniversary celebrations here. Once these walls had echoed with laughter and inside jokes and gossip and fights and tears and memories, but now the place was hollow and empty, silent and dark. It was eerie. It felt like one of those early scenes in *Titanic* when Bill Paxton's character—you know, the Jacques Cousteau meets Indiana Jones character who's hunting for the blue diamond—directs that robotic camera through the underwater passageways of the great, sad ship, down long, dark hallways and through ballrooms and stairwells long forgotten, haunted by memories so joyous and so tragic. It was as if Homs had sunk to the bottom of the ocean, and Omar and I had come to navigate our way through its dark and forlorn rooms.

When we got to the back door, we were careful not to go bursting through it. We peered through the jagged shards of what remained of the window, out to the rain and fog. Ahead of us was the large field we had come across the night before—the old VW van, the broken-down school bus, the deserted playground, the charred Russian tank, and all the rest. Ringing the field were dozens of ruined apartment buildings. We looked for Abdel and for any other signs of life, but we saw nothing and no one moving.

"He's probably already made a run for it," Omar said.

"Hope so," I said. "Come on—let's go this way. Stay close, and keep an eye behind us as well."

Omar nodded, and we began. There was no way I was heading across that field again. Maybe the snipers had gone home. Maybe they hadn't. I wasn't taking that chance. Instead, I decided we should work our way around the perimeter. By moving fast and sticking close to the walls of the surrounding buildings, under the cantilevers that jutted out from most of them over a wide side-walk that encircled the park, I hoped we could stay out of the rain and out of the view of any gunmen operating from the buildings on the south side. That's where they had been the night before. We had taken no shots from anyone in the buildings on the north side. If there were snipers in the south-side buildings, we would essentially be underneath them for most of our run, almost impossible to see. If someone did start shooting from the other side of the field, unless they took us out on the first shot, we should be able to quickly duck through doors into abandoned apartments that would hopefully provide us some measure of protection.

It wasn't a great plan, but it was the best I could do on short notice, and once we started running, I was convinced we were home free. But when we were about halfway to our objective, we suddenly caught a glimpse of Abdel. He was running out of one of the buildings on the other side, across the field, toward us. I stopped dead in my tracks. Omar nearly ran me over. We looked at each other and then back at Abdel. It was clear that he hadn't gone ahead of us to the rendezvous point at the border. Rather, he had been waiting for us all along. Now that he saw us, he was apparently afraid of being left behind. But why he would run out into the open was beyond me. Worse, he was yelling for us to stop and waving his arms frantically so that we would see him. My heart almost stopped.

"What in the world is he doing?" Omar whispered. "He's going to get us all killed."

I was glad Omar had said it first. Honestly, I'd have felt guilty saying it out loud. But he was right.

Then it was as if Abdel realized what he was doing. When he had nearly reached the wreckage of the Russian tank, he abruptly stopped running, stopped yelling, stopped waving his arms. He just froze and stood motionless, his hands in the air like he was being robbed.

Lightning flashed. More thunder boomed overhead.

"Now what's he doing?" Omar asked.

I had no idea. I scanned the perimeter and found myself backing slowly into one of the buildings. Omar noticed what I was doing and followed suit. He didn't want to get picked off by a sniper any more than I did. We scanned the room behind us. No one was in there. There were no signs that anyone had been recently. We crouched down and watched to see what Abdel would do next.

More than a minute passed, but Abdel kept standing there.

Why?

Didn't he understand the danger he was in?

Come on, Abdel. Move.

Didn't he remember what we had been through the night before?

You can do it. Just start walking.

I wasn't making a sound, but in my mind I was screaming at him, trying to will him to get going with all the mental energy I could muster. But with every second that passed, I grew more scared. I could barely look.

Come on, Abdel; come on. Think of Fatima. She's counting on you, buddy. She's waiting for you. Come on, just one foot in front of the other.

But Abdel just stood there, looking terrified and confused. My hands were trembling again. I desperately needed something to drink. I reached for my water bottle, but it was gone. I dug through my backpack, but it was not there. Another full minute went by. I couldn't bear it. I actually put my hands over my eyes. I had this palpable fear that a sniper was going to blow Abdel's head off and that would be my last memory of him.

Finally Omar nudged me.

"Maybe we should go out there and get him," he said.

I opened my eyes. "Are you crazy? You want to get killed?"

But Omar persisted. "Something's wrong. Something's out there. Maybe he's found something."

"Then he should bring it here."

"I'll go," Omar said and moved toward the door.

"No way," I responded, grabbing his arm. "You're not going anywhere."

I turned and shouted out the window. *"Abdel! Come on! We can't wait any longer!"*

But Abdel didn't move. I yelled again. I knew I was giving away our position. But I also knew if I didn't, Omar would go racing out there like a fool. *"Abdel!"* I yelled again through the thunder and the rain. *"It'll be okay. Come on. Let's go home!"*

Even from such a distance it was clear how scared he was. He still held his arms high over his head. I had to assume he could see a sniper and was wondering why the guy wasn't pulling the trigger. I was wondering the same thing.

Abdel was soaked to the bone by now. But he still didn't move. And he still hadn't been shot. I had no idea what to do. So I just stared at him and did nothing. Then I saw Abdel's hands slowly beginning to lower. His head began to droop as well. His shoulders slumped forward. He hadn't started walking yet, but something was changing. I could only guess that he knew he had done something terribly foolish, but he also had to know there was no turning back now. If he didn't start walking, he'd never get to us, never get home, never see Fatima. Maybe the sniper was going to let him go.

"That's right, Abdel!" I shouted. *"You can do it!"*

My heart started beating again. Clearly Abdel was steeling himself for what was ahead. I found myself praying God would somehow help him make it across the field without getting shot. I just couldn't bear the thought. There had been too much sadness already.

But then the entire park was rocked by an enormous explosion.

Abdel Mahmoud Hamid disintegrated before our eyes.

He had stepped on a land mine. Now he had just stepped off it. And just like that, he was gone.

PART THREE

17

★ ★ ★

Omar battled his way through rush-hour traffic.

Finally we reached downtown Beirut. Omar took a left past the promenade along St. George Bay. Then he worked his way around the beautiful tree-lined campus of the American University before pulling up to the main entrance of the Mayflower Hotel.

We had driven the entire way from the Syrian border in silence but for the high-speed *whoosh-whoosh* of the windshield wipers, the crackle of lightning, and the bone-rattling claps of thunder in a storm that was only getting worse. Now, as we arrived at the hotel where Abdel had reserved a room for me to do my writing, Omar insisted I go upstairs and get started on my story while he went and broke the terrible news to Abdel's family and to Fatima.

"Absolutely not," I said. "I'm going too."

But Omar would not hear of it. He said he knew I was racked with guilt. He knew I thought it was my fault since I'd taken Abdel into Syria without authorization. But Abdel was a professional, he said. He knew the risks. He could have said no, but he didn't. Abdel loved what he did, and he'd loved being with us.

"Abdel was my responsibility," I protested. "I need to tell the family myself."

But Omar was adamant. "For crying out loud, J. B.," he nearly yelled at me. "You've got a major article to write. ISIS is about to launch a new war against the U.S. and Israel. You have two sources indicating they have chemical weapons. You don't know when the attacks are coming, but the main commander on the ground in Syria says it's soon. That's it. That's all you ought to be thinking about right now. You have to tell the world what you know. Lives are at stake. Hundreds, maybe thousands, of innocent lives. That's why we went there, because you smelled this story, and you were right. Now get it written and get it out. Because if the Ramzy story isn't on the *Times* website by tonight, and isn't on the front page of tomorrow's paper, then Abdel Hamid died in vain. Is that what you want?"

It wasn't, of course.

Omar grabbed my shoulders and looked me in the eye. "I'll be back in a few hours," he said. "Don't do anything stupid while I'm gone."

I knew exactly what he meant. I nodded dutifully. But as he pulled away from the hotel, I had no illusions I was going to be able to keep my promise.

The Mayflower had been a favorite of the international jet-setter crowd since the early 1960s, but this was my first time at the iconic hotel. Heading into the lobby, I checked in at the front desk. As the clerk made a photocopy of my passport and ran my credit card, I picked up one of the hotel's brochures and began leafing through it. I had no desire to think about the story I had to write or any of what we had just been through. All I wanted at that moment was a hot shower, a hearty breakfast, and a large bottle of anything alcoholic. Preferably two. I knew I shouldn't. I knew it was wrong. It had been exactly two years, three months, and four days since I'd had my last drink. But my willpower was shot. I was losing emotional altitude. What I needed just then was to drink heavily and without interruption.

Scanning the brochure, my eye was drawn to the picture of a beautifully appointed British watering hole. *As the quintessential London pub, the Duke of Wellington conveys an air of timeless-ness,* it read. *Built in 1960, it has not changed over the decades. It is a treasure cave of obscure and amus-ing artifacts where you can genuinely enjoy a good pint with friends. Named after the first Duke of Wellington (1769–1852), the pub boasts a relaxed and cozy atmosphere. Every night, a happy mixture of local characters and loyal crowd comes to enjoy the friendly ambience, savory snacks, and fine spirits.*

Perfect, I thought.

The problem was, the pub was closed. It might not open for hours. I didn't have that long.

Bursting into my room, I threw my backpack on the queen-size four-poster bed and headed straight for the minibar. My hands quivered, and

I fumbled with the keys, so it took me a moment to get the blasted thing open.

It was empty. I picked up the phone.

"Room service," a young man at the other end of the line said with a slight British accent. "Would you like some breakfast this morning, Mr. Collins?"

"No; well, yes, but—never mind," I said, practically tripping over my words. "Look, what I need right now is a bottle of Jack Daniel's."

"I'm sorry, sir, but the bar is closed until happy hour."

"Can't you at least fill up my minibar?"

"I'm sorry, sir. We cannot do that until five o'clock."

"But there's nothing in there," I protested. "No Cokes, no water, no candy bars, and certainly no alcohol."

"I'm so sorry, sir. That is our policy."

"Look, I'm paying good money for this room, and I'd like my minibar restocked immediately."

"I do apologize. There's nothing I can do."

I slammed the phone down, then picked it up again and called the front desk. I demanded to speak to the manager. When he came on the line, I let fly like Mussolini from the balcony. After riding out my brief tirade, he told me there was nothing he could do. It was hotel policy not to serve alcohol until five in the afternoon.

"And frankly, sir, even if that were not the case, my staff and I are under strict orders not to serve you any drinks at all, Mr. Collins."

I was rendered speechless for a moment. *Strict orders?*

"Why not?" I finally bellowed. *"Orders from whom?"*

"I'm afraid that is a matter for you and your company, sir," the manager said. "Is there anything else I can help you with today?"

"You're saying the *New York Times* won't let me drink?"

"I'm saying they won't pay for it."

"Fine," I said, finding the loophole. "Then I'll pay for it all personally."

But the manager would not budge. "Again, I'm sorry, sir," he said calmly. "We do a lot of business with the *Times*. Many of your correspondents stay with us. I cannot risk our relationship with this fine client just for you, sir. Now, is there anything else I can do for you?"

I slammed down the phone again. I was seething, and I was more desperate for a drink than any time I could remember.

Then my phone beeped. I had received a text.

It was Omar. **Take a shower. Get writing. And stop harassing the manager.**

Omar knew me far too well.

18

* * *

Two hours later, Omar was still not back.

Avoiding the hotel's public Wi-Fi, I plugged my satphone into my laptop and transmitted my two stories to Allen MacDonald. The first focused on the imminent threat of an ISIS attack against the U.S. and Israel and included the fact that sources in two intelligence services—one Western and one Arab—had evidence that ISIS had recently captured chemical weapons. It occurred to me that Ramzy had threatened my life if I wrote about the chemical weapons, but I dismissed the thought. This story was too important. For balance, I included Ramzy's denial but incorporated extensive details from the material I'd been given on the ISIS coup near Aleppo. The second piece was a full profile of Ramzy, with biographical material and long excerpts from our interview. I also transmitted the digital recording of the interview so Allen could get it transcribed. He would likely run that, too, on one of the jump pages.

I caught a cab for the ten-minute ride to Beirut's Rafic Hariri International Airport, named after the former Lebanese prime minister who was assassinated by a car bomb in 2005, allegedly by Hezbollah operatives who some believed were working at the behest of the Syrian government. It was yet another reminder of the cruel and wanton violence of this crazy part of the world.

On the way, I checked my phone for the latest headlines. One in the *Wall Street Journal* particularly caught my eye:

Palestinian Leaders Warn Israel Must Agree to Divide Jerusalem or Peace Talks "As Good As Dead"

I also sent four texts. The first was to my mom. I let her know I was doing fine and heading back to the States. There was no reason to tell her anything else. She was an avid reader of everything I wrote for the *Times*. She'd know where I'd been soon enough.

The second text was to Robert Khachigian, former director of the Central Intelligence Agency. It was Khachigian, now retired at seventy-three but still very much engaged with the intelligence world, who had first tipped me off that ISIS had captured a cache of chemical weapons. He had pointed me to one source. I had found the other. Khachigian had always been a straight shooter with me, and I had come to trust him implicitly. Indeed, I had just included a quote from him in one of my articles, though not by name. I'd simply referred to "a former senior American intelligence

official" who warned that "it would be a nightmare scenario if ISIS has acquired weapons of mass
destruction, perhaps the most dangerous development of our age." That said, I needed to look him
in the eye and get his take on why Ramzy had
flatly denied it all.

Need 2 talk ASAP, my text said.

The third message was to Ari Shalit, deputy
director of the Mossad. At fifty-seven, Shalit was
one of the most interesting operatives I'd ever met
in the Middle East. Born and raised in Morocco,
he looked and sounded like a full-blooded Arab to
me, though he was actually fully Jewish on both
his mother's and father's sides. He emigrated to
Israel with his family when he was only fourteen,
then joined the IDF and rose to become the commander of Israel's most elite and secretive commando team, known collectively only as the Unit.
Fluent in Hebrew, Arabic, French, and English,
and not bad at Russian, he was quickly snatched up
from the IDF by the Mossad and sent on some of
the most dangerous and highly classified missions
behind enemy lines in the history of the Israeli spy
agency. I had met Shalit quite a few years earlier
when I was trying to track down how the CIA and
Western intel agencies had gone wrong on the Iraq
WMD assessment. I'd used him as an unnamed
source on a few stories about Iran's nuclear program over the years. We'd stayed in touch on and
off, but now I urgently needed his help.

Hearing ISIS has CW, I wrote. **Want to com-
pare notes. Can we talk?**

The fourth text was for Ismail Tikriti, the

forty-seven-year-old deputy director of Iraqi intelligence who, interestingly enough, was neither a Sunni nor Shia Muslim, and not an Arab either. Ethnically he was Chaldean. Religiously he was a Christian. Born and raised in Tikrit, the same town as Saddam Hussein, Ismail came from a military family that had been loyal to Saddam. But after the war, he had been recruited first by the Americans as a translator, then by the newly restructured Ministry of Defense as an operations specialist. He had impressed one supervisor after another and risen through the ranks. We had met while I'd been covering U.S. military operations in his country, beginning with the March 2003 invasion through the insurgency and the withdrawal of all American armed forces from Iraq in December 2011. A brilliant guy who spoke remarkably good English given that he'd never studied outside the country, Ismail Tikriti had his eyes and ears on everything that was happening. More important, he owed me a favor, and I was calling it in.

Found holy grail. Will trade for mtg w/ AK, I wrote, certain he would know I meant Abu Khalif.

With Shalit and Tikriti, I was chumming the waters. I needed both of them to bite to move the story forward. But I had no guarantees.

Once through airport security, I headed up to the terminal's third level, where there was a Japanese seafood restaurant. I'd been there several times. But it was crowded. And I was alone. They said they didn't have a table for one. But after slipping a twenty to one of the waitresses, I finally was offered a seat at the bar.

I hesitated. I was famished and still craved a round of good, stiff drinks. But Omar had been right. I needed to stay sober. I'd made it this far, more than two years without a drink, and I was scared how far I might fall if I didn't stay on the wagon.

"Do you want the seat or not?" the waitress asked when she saw I wasn't following her.

"Sure." I shrugged. "Whatever's available."

The moment I said yes, I knew it was a mistake. Soon I was staring at shelves full of vodka and bourbon and rum and whiskey and all manner of spirits. The aroma of any one of them would have made my mouth water, but with the combination, I was in serious trouble. I felt my forehead break into a light sweat. Not enough that anyone would have noticed unless they were looking carefully. But I knew and winced. I also knew I should get out of there immediately, but I was so hungry, and my flight was leaving soon. If I was going to eat anything, it was going to be here. What choice did I have?

"What'll it be?" said the young bartender, who looked like he was barely out of college, if he had even gone at all.

My name is James Bradley Collins—I'm an alcoholic, I said to myself.

I am powerless over alcohol—my life has become unmanageable.

Only a power greater than myself can restore me to sanity.

"Perrier," I said with all the discipline I could muster, "and some sushi, as quick as you can."

The kid raised his eyebrows as if to ask, *That's it?* But a moment later, he brought back a sushi menu and set a distinctive green bottle of French sparkling water in front of me with a clean glass, a slice of lemon, and a few cubes of ice. I poured half a glass and watched it bubble and fizz. Then I took a long, slow drink and closed my eyes.

One day at a time. One step at a time.

When I opened my eyes, Omar Fayez plunked down in the seat on my right.

"Looks like I found you just in time," he said.

"What are you doing here?" I asked, startled by his presence.

"I'm going back with you," he said, smelling my glass to make sure I had truly ordered Perrier.

"Absolutely not," I protested. "You need to get back to your wife."

"Who do you think told me to fly back with you?" he replied, pulling out his own satphone and hitting speed dial.

"What about Abdel's family?" I pressed.

"All taken care of," he replied. "I can tell you about it on the flight. But right now you've got a call to make."

As soon as he handed me the phone, I winced. I knew full well he had dialed my editor, Allen MacDonald, at his home in McLean, Virginia. It wasn't a call I was planning to make until I was out of Lebanon.

"You haven't talked to him yet, have you?" he said.

"No."

"You have to."

"Not yet."

"Now."

Suddenly Allen was on the line. I sighed and began talking. He was not happy to hear from me for a host of reasons, not the least of which was because it was only five in the morning in the D.C. area.

"You're going to need to rewrite your story," he began.

"Why?"

"You need to take out the references to the WMD."

"Why?" I asked, taken aback. "It's a solid piece."

"But Ramzy denied everything."

"I quoted him," I replied, a bit defensively.

"Why do you think he did that?"

"I'm not entirely sure."

"Did you push him?"

"You heard the interview."

"I did."

"He must not have authorization from Khalif."

"Or maybe ISIS really doesn't have the stuff."

"They do, Allen," I replied. "The story is solid."

"But you wanted him to confirm it. You risked your life, and cost Abdel his, on the premise that he would confirm it."

"I was wrong on that, but—"

He cut me off. "What if you're being set up?"

"By Ramzy?"

"No, by your intel sources."

"I saw the documents, Allen," I protested. "I heard the tapes for myself. I have the transcripts."

"Maybe you saw what someone wanted you to see."

"I have two completely different sources—neither have ever steered me wrong."

"What's to say they weren't coordinating with each other, planting the bait, hoping you'd be hooked by the prospect of a big scoop?"

"These two guys don't even know each other—two different men, two different countries, two different agencies."

"It's not enough," he said. "You need another source, from a third different country."

"Allen, come on," I said. "That's impossible. I'm telling you, the story is solid. It's a huge scoop. And we need to move on it before the *Post* or someone else gets it."

"Forget it, Collins—I'm not going to be set up with another WMD story that turns out to be bogus," he pushed back. "And don't tell me this thing is a 'slam dunk.' Been there, done that. Get a third source and we'll talk. In the meantime, rewrite both pieces ASAP. Take out the references to WMD in the Ramzy profile, and focus on the 'new attacks coming' angle in the ISIS story. That's big enough news for now."

"I'm about to catch a flight home."

"Nonstop?"

"No, I have a layover in Istanbul."

"Rewrite it on the first leg. Retransmit from Istanbul. And I'll need an obit for Abdel by the time you touch down in D.C."

I started to protest that I didn't have the time, that it would be impossible to do the piece justice when I was flying across the Atlantic, but again MacDonald cut me off. He was in no mood for attitude. He said I owed it to Abdel and his family. He was right, of course, which made it all the more painful to hear. I said I'd call him again from Turkey, but I was fuming. I hung up and handed the phone back to Omar.

"I'll do it," Omar said without hesitation as he put the phone back in his briefcase.

"Do what?"

"Abdel's obit," Omar repeated. "I'll write it on the way to Istanbul."

"No, Allen's right," I conceded, ashamed at myself for having resisted the assignment even for a moment.

"Of course he's right that we owe it to Abdel, but he's not right that you can do all this on your own," Omar insisted. "You rewrite the Ramzy piece. I'll write the obit. Now let's order before we run out of time."

"Thanks," I said quietly, unable to look Omar in the eye just then.

"Don't mention it," said the bear of a man sitting beside me. "I've got your back, J. B. Always have."

19

★ ★ ★

Turkish Airlines flight 825 landed in Istanbul at 5:35 p.m. local time.

The moment the flight attendants would let me, I powered up my laptop and satellite phone and transmitted revised copies of the ISIS story and my profile of Jamal Ramzy to D.C. I was still opposed to Allen's decision, but I had no choice. If I didn't do the rewrite, he'd chop up the piece himself, and I definitely didn't want that. At least this way I still had some degree of control over how the piece was phrased.

Then Omar showed me his story on Abdel.

"This is good," I whispered as we taxied to the gate.

Omar said nothing. I quickly glanced at him, sitting next to me in business class. The expression on his face looked as pained as I'd ever seen him. He was a good writer, but this one had clearly taken its toll.

"Really, it's very good," I said. "I'm sending it as is."

With that, I immediately e-mailed the obituary to Allen, then powered up my iPhone and began figuring out how to get us home. After a frustrating fifteen minutes or so on multiple travel websites, I finally came to the annoying realization that there were no direct flights back to Washington that evening from Istanbul. When I tried to route us through Brussels or London or Paris or Frankfurt, I found that there were no late-evening flights to D.C. from any of those hub cities either. Any way we sliced it, we were going to have to spend the night in a hotel and fly out the next day. The best I could do was book us tickets on a Turkish Airlines flight that would depart at 8:10 the following morning for Brussels. We would then change planes and fly United across the Atlantic, touching down at Dulles at 2:45 in the afternoon.

With no other options, I booked the flights, then scanned my e-mails and text messages. There was only one that stood out. It was from Ari Shalit, deputy director of the Mossad, whom I had texted earlier that afternoon. As luck would have it, Shalit would be arriving later that night in Istanbul and was asking me to meet him at midnight in front of the famed Blue Mosque. My mood suddenly improved. The night might not be a complete waste after all.

Omar rented a car and we drove for the Ibrahim Pasha, a four-story hotel in the historic Sultanahmet neighborhood, not far from the Blue Mosque. While I paced in front of a roaring fireplace in the lobby, returning e-mails and scanning headlines, Omar secured two adjoining rooms.

I asked him to clear my minibar of all alcohol. He gave me an "attaboy" slap on the back and took care of it immediately.

We met later in the hotel restaurant, and over a meal of lamb kebabs and rice we speculated about what kind of splash the Ramzy profile and interview would make when it went public in a few hours. We talked about how hard Abdel's fiancée had taken the news of his death and discussed how we could send her some money discreetly, perhaps even anonymously. It seemed the least we could do.

At one point during our meal, Omar asked me why I thought Shalit would want to meet so late, and why in front of the mosque.

"I have no idea," I said. "Why do you ask?"

"I don't know," Omar replied. "Just seems odd. I mean, how did he know we'd even be in Istanbul tonight?"

"Good question."

"Did you say anything in your text?"

"No."

"What did you say?"

"I just asked if we could talk."

"You think he was already planning a trip here, or is he coming just to see you?"

"Does it matter?"

Omar shrugged. "I don't know."

I noticed he wasn't really eating, which wasn't like him. "What is it, Omar?" I asked. "What are you thinking?"

He shook his head. "I'm not really sure," he replied. "Maybe it's nothing. I just . . ."

"What?"

"I just have a strange feeling. But I can't really say why."

We finished dinner feeling a bit unsettled. But then again, we were both exhausted and traumatized by Abdel's death and all we'd experienced in Homs. I decided to go upstairs and take a nap for a few hours. Omar went out jogging.

At precisely 11:30 p.m., the alarm on my iPhone went off. I got up, took a quick shower, and met Omar downstairs. Together we finalized our plan and then headed out to the Blue Mosque.

I went on foot, and Omar shadowed me in the little silver Hyundai compact he'd rented at the airport, keeping a good block or so behind me—close enough to make sure I was okay but not so close that he'd be immediately spotted. It was raining, though not nearly as hard as in Homs. The streets were slick. The air was foggy.

Soon I came to the Sultan Ahmed Mosque, commonly known as the Blue Mosque for the twenty thousand exquisite hand-painted blue ceramic tiles lining its interior walls. It was, of course, locked and closed for the night. But with each of its six minarets and the main dome and its eight secondary domes bathed in the yellow light of high-powered lamps and set against the backdrop of such a stormy night, the entire seventeenth-century structure looked spectacular in the mist, and even with the rain, the dappled reflection in the nearby pool was spectacular as well.

Few people were crazy enough to be out in such weather, but there was a young couple in love making out near the fountain, and a few police officers strolled the grounds. Ari Shalit was nowhere in sight, so I was startled when I heard someone saying my name from the shadows of a small grove of palm trees and even more startled when I realized it was a woman's voice, not that of the man I thought I was to meet.

"Mr. Collins, over here," said the woman, a slim, striking brunette wearing a black faux-silk London Fog trench coat and holding a polka-dot umbrella. "My, my, you're getting soaked. Please, won't you join me?"

"I'm sorry; do I know you?" I asked, genuinely puzzled.

"No, I'm afraid we have not had the pleasure," she said with a warm, alluring smile as she removed a leather glove to shake my hand.

In so doing, she slipped a note into mine and whispered, "Ari sent me."

I looked at her, wondering if that could possibly be true. Did she really know Ari Shalit? Had the Mossad's deputy director really sent her? Why? Why hadn't he come himself? These and a dozen other questions raced through my mind, but before I started asking, I looked down at the note.

J. B.—Sorry I couldn't come in person.
The Old Man needed me. Meet Yael
Katzir. Works on my staff. Expert in CW.
Fully briefed on our conversations. She
can help you.—A. S.

I stared at the note, trying to make sense of it. It certainly sounded like Ari. It was concise, to the point, and consistent with the text message Ari had sent while Omar and I were flying to Istanbul from Beirut.

Meet in front of SAM in I, he'd written. **Midnight. Will carry PDU.—A. S.**

SAM was the Sultan Ahmed Mosque, aka the Blue Mosque.

Did *PDU* mean "polka-dot umbrella"?

The "Old Man" was the nickname Ari called his boss, the Mossad director. Whoever had written the text had certainly known about the chemical weapons angle I'd wanted to discuss. But was all this legit? Had someone hacked his account or accessed his phone somehow? Was this a setup?

I looked at this woman, trying to make sense of her. She was lovely, that was for certain, with a natural, unpretentious beauty that I found instantly attractive. She wore no eye shadow or lipstick or makeup of any kind. She wore no earrings or necklace or bracelets, and her short, well-trimmed nails were not painted. She looked more Arab than Jewish, but then again, so did Ari. Her large brown eyes seemed gentle and relaxed, and they twinkled in the streetlights. Despite the raincoat, I could see she was wearing a black cashmere sweater, well-worn denim jeans, and stylish brown leather boots that went up to her knees. These added a couple of inches to her height, but she was still quite a bit shorter than me. I'm six foot one, so I pegged her at about five-five or five-six. She carried no purse or handbag, just the umbrella, which she kept propped up over our heads to shield us from the drizzle.

She didn't look like an assassin. Then again, no one involved in a honey trap would. But did she really work for the Mossad? Or had she been sent by ISIS? It seemed unlikely that Abu Khalif and Jamal Ramzy were ready to kill me. The story they wanted the world to read hadn't even been published yet. If anyone wanted me dead just now, it would be Khalif's rivals in al Qaeda, not ISIS. But before I could process the questions any further, she leaned toward me, put her warm, soft hands on my face, and kissed me on the lips. I was so caught off guard that I immediately pulled away, but she leaned closer and whispered in my ear.

"You and I are either brother and sister, or we're lovers, Mr. Collins," she explained matter-of-factly. "At this hour, there's no other reason for the police to think we'd be together . . . unless, of course, you want them to think I'm a prostitute . . ."

Her voice trailed off, but she didn't need to finish her point. While prostitution was legal in Turkey, being seen by the police with a *fahişe* could raise all sorts of problems I didn't want to deal with. So I put my arms around her waist, and she pulled me toward her, kissing me even more convincingly this time.

"Nice to meet you, Miss Katzir," I whispered.

"Likewise," she said, raising her eyebrows and seeming to enjoy the game. "Now let's start walking arm in arm, like true lovers."

I did as I was told, still trying to size up the situation.

"Call me Yael," she said quietly.

"Fair enough—call me James," I said, though I had no idea why. Hardly anyone called me James except my mother. Everyone else called me J. B. The guys at the *Times* did. Omar did. Laura had. Everyone did. Why in the world had I just asked her to call me James?

"Very well, James." She smiled. "Is there a place we can talk, you know, privately?"

20

* * *

I had no idea where to take this woman.

Over the years I had been in and out of Istanbul many times, but I didn't really know the city well. I couldn't very well take her back to the hotel, and I could only imagine what Omar must be thinking at the moment. So I suggested we go find an all-night café and get some coffee. She agreed.

That was easier said than done, however. Istanbul, the ancient metropolis straddling the Bosphorus, once named Constantinople, had served as the eastern capital of the Roman Empire, but it wasn't exactly New York or London or even Tel Aviv. It didn't abound with late-night watering holes and all-night restaurants and entertainment. But off we went, looking for one anyway.

We held hands as we walked through the rainy streets. She nestled close to me and laughed and twirled her umbrella and acted like we had been dating for years. It was, I hoped, a solid performance for anyone who didn't know us. But I needed more convincing that she really was who she said she was, so as we walked, I plied her with questions. Her answers were spot-on. She knew detailed elements of my past meetings and conversations with Ari that no one else could have known unless they'd been told by one of the two of us. She was trying to convince me that the deputy director of the Mossad really had sent her, that I really could trust her, that I really could confide in her whatever I had texted Ari was so urgent about my brief trip into Homs, and it was beginning to work.

"Ari says you went into journalism because of your grandfather. Is that true?" she asked as we found ourselves walking along the Sea of Marmara toward the grand Topkapi Palace, once the seat of the sultans who ruled the Ottoman Empire for over four hundred years.

"Actually, it is," I replied.

"A. B. Collins?"

"Right again."

"What did that stand for?"

"Andrew Bradley," I said.

"So you were named after him, right—James Bradley?" she asked.

"As a matter of fact, I was."

"Ari said your grandfather was really rattled when his wife—your grandmother, Betty—passed away in 1980. He never remarried?"

"No."

"They were close."

"Soul mates."

"How long were they married?"

"Thirty-eight years."

"Wow."

"I know."

"Who does that anymore?"

"No one I know."

"My parents divorced when I was fourteen," she said.

"I was twelve."

"Did you live with your mom or dad?"

"My mom."

"In Bar Harbor?"

I nodded.

"And your dad went to Miami Beach?"

I heard the question, but I didn't answer. We kept walking. Suddenly this wasn't so fun anymore. I got it. She knew everything about me. Was she showing off?

"I'm sorry," Yael said after a few moments. "Bad choice of topics."

I shrugged.

"And Ari says Matt is off-limits."

"He is."

"Why?"

"Look, Matt's a good guy, and he's my brother," I said. "We were close when we were young. Not so much anymore."

"Where is he these days?"

"Amman."

"Jordan?"

"Is there another?"

"What's he doing there?"

"I don't know—a sabbatical of some kind."

"What does he do when he's not in Amman?"

"Does it really matter?"

Yael shrugged. "Sorry; I'm not trying to pry."

I sighed and kept walking. "He's a professor," I said at last.

"Where?"

"At a seminary near Boston," I replied. "Can we talk about something else?"

My relationship with Matt was a long story and not one I wanted to get into now.

"How about Laura?" she said.

I stopped dead in my tracks. "You've got to be kidding me."

"Ari said that didn't go well."

"That's none of your business," I said, more coldly than I intended.

Whoever this woman was, I had no intention of talking with her about my ex-wife. It was true Shalit and I had talked about my divorce some at the time. He'd been going through a breakup of his own marriage. I guess we'd sort of compared notes. But this wasn't anything I wanted to discuss now, and certainly not with Yael.

"I'm sorry," she said. "I didn't mean to—"

"It's fine," I lied. "Let's just . . . you know."

Yael had certainly gotten the picture. She took my arm again to maintain our cover, and we kept walking. "Should we talk about Fordow?" she said.

I knew she was referring to the previously secret Iranian nuclear facility near the holy city of Qom that was revealed by Western intelligence agencies to the *Times* and other media in the fall of 2009.

"Ari says you were very helpful when he wanted to leak some details and get world leaders focused on just how much of their nuclear program Iran was hiding."

My mind raced. Was she saying Ari had told her I contributed to the *Times* article on the Fordow facility? Why else would she be mentioning it?

As if answering my unspoken question, Yael surprised me yet again. "'A senior intelligence official said Friday that Western spy agencies had "excellent access" to the site, suggesting human spies had penetrated it,'" she said, looking at me.

She was quoting from the story, from memory. I said nothing.

She continued. "'The official said that "multiple independent sources" had confirmed that it was intended for nuclear use. The intelligence official and other officials declined to be named because they were discussing intelligence matters.'"

Then she added, "Ari said he was one of the 'multiple independent sources' you used to back up the story."

"Why would you think I worked on that story?" I asked. "My byline isn't even on it."

"Ari told me all about it," Yael explained. "He told me how he brought you to Mossad headquarters in Tel Aviv, took you to room E-38, and gave you an ice-cold Mr. Pibb and a plate of hummus and some fresh pita from your favorite restaurant in Abu Ghosh. He showed you satellite photos and let you listen to telephone intercepts and read highly classified reports from agents in the field. And he told me why—so the *Times* would run the story and so the world would know that Iran was hiding key elements of its nuclear program."

Again I stopped dead in my tracks, just a few hundred yards from the palace, and stared into her eyes. She was exactly right, yet I had never told a soul all of these details. I hadn't written these things into my notes. I didn't keep a journal. There was no way she could know any of it—much less all of it—unless Ari Shalit had told her.

I began to breathe easier. She was the real deal. She really did work for the Mossad. She really had been sent to help me. And I guess I had to trust her, as much as I could trust any foreign intelligence agent.

A pair of policemen came walking around the corner. They were on the other side of the boulevard, but when they seemed to take an inordinate interest in the two of us, I leaned forward, put my arms around Yael again, and kissed her on the lips.

For a moment, it seemed as if she had lost her breath. But so had I. Our kiss became so passionate that the policemen kept walking and didn't give us another thought. Yael's plan had worked. We looked like lovers. But it felt so good I wasn't sure if she was still playing a game.

Then again, I wasn't sure I was either.

21

* * *

We finally found a restaurant that was still open.

The owner graciously offered to take our soaking-wet coats and hang them up to dry. Then he showed us to a table in a back corner near the crackling fireplace. A waiter quickly brought us piping-hot chai and some warm bread, and we both began to settle in.

It was a cozy little dive. The place was about half-full, all foreigners. Most were young couples in their twenties and thirties. The problem was they were all drinking beer or cocktails, not tea or coffee. Immediately I felt the cravings I was already battling intensify. Everything in me wanted to begin drinking heavily. The ambience. The aromas. The company, to be sure. And the immense grief that was weighing so heavily upon me.

Yael quickly ordered a glass of a French cabernet, then asked if I'd like to share a bottle. It was tempting beyond measure to say yes. The only reason I could think of to decline was because I wanted something stronger. Over her shoulder I could see shelves behind the bar filled with bottles of Johnnie Walker, Jim Beam, Absolut, and Stolichnaya. All my old friends were whispering my name.

"I'll stick with the tea," I said.

I glanced at Yael to gauge her level of disappointment. Instead, she canceled her cabernet and said she'd stick with the tea as well.

The waiter shrugged and walked away.

"A *tea*-totaler?" Yael asked with a wry grin.

"Recovering alcoholic," I admitted. "If Ari told you anything, he surely told you that."

"He did," she said. "I just wanted to see if it was true."

"Two years, three months, and five days."

"One day at a time." She smiled.

"One day at a time," I sighed.

Just then, I saw Omar walk in, scan the room, and spot me. In another context, I might have cursed him under my breath and found a way to get rid of him. Instead, I stood, introduced him to Yael, and asked him to join us. The fact was I needed a chaperone—and not just to keep me from drinking. It had been a long while since I'd been around anyone as alluring as Yael, and I honestly couldn't remember the last time I'd kissed someone the way she and I had just kissed. I'm not sure I'd realized before that moment how lonely I really was, and it scared me to see how willing I now felt to be swept off my feet by the first beautiful woman who showed me some attention.

"Omar is a good man," I told Yael as we got settled again. "We go way back."

"So I hear," she said, turning to him. "Ari speaks very highly of you."

"Please give him my regards," Omar said.

"I will indeed," she replied.

I tried to take a sip of tea but it needed to cool a bit. So I took a deep breath and got down to business.

"Look, Yael, in a few hours, the *Times* will run a front-page profile of Jamal Ramzy, based in part on the interview I did with him in Homs," I began.

"So your plan worked?" she asked, clearly up to speed.

"It did."

"You were crazy to go there."

"Tell me about it."

"Ari specifically told you not to go," she said.

"Everyone told me not to go."

"But you just couldn't help yourself?"

"A bit of a contrarian, this one," Omar quipped.

"Can only imagine him as a kid," Yael said.

Omar shook his head. "You have no idea."

I didn't play along. "The short version is that Ramzy and Abu Khalif are about to launch a massive series of terrorist attacks," I continued.

"When?" she asked.

"Very soon—that's all he would say."

"Where?"

"All signs point to attacks against my country and yours."

"I'm guessing he didn't draw you a map."

"I'm afraid not."

"What's his plan?"

"He said this was the beginning of a Third

Intifada. He said anyone who helped the Zionists were traitors and would be punished by Allah."

"That's standard jihadist rhetoric," she said. "Why take it seriously?"

"Two reasons," I said. "First, because Ramzy wanted to go on the record and because he wanted to do so with the *Times*. He's never talked to a Western reporter before, certainly not to an American. But he wants people to know. He wants Washington to know. Something big is coming—very big—and when it does, he wants to make sure ISIS gets credit, not Zawahiri and al Qaeda. Now, I realize not every terrorist group signals its intentions ahead of time. But some do. Bin Laden declared war on the U.S. ahead of the 9/11 attacks."

"And the second reason?" Yael asked.

"I believe ISIS has chemical weapons. Ramzy denies it. But I've got two sources from two different intelligence agencies, from two different countries. They're both solid. I'll follow up with both in short order and go back over everything they told me, point by point, to make sure I didn't miss anything. But my editor is feeling edgy. The *Times* has been burned on stuff like this before. He wants me to get a third source—different intel agency, different country. That's why I wanted to meet with Ari. I need to know what you guys know, and I need to know fast. Imagine ISIS with chemical weapons. Imagine how many Israelis and Americans they could kill. And what if they gave this stuff to Hamas and Hezbollah? What if all the rockets you guys have been hit with in recent years were filled with sarin gas? The story that comes out tomorrow doesn't mention chemical weapons. But I need to do a follow-up story immediately."

"And you need our help?"

"Exactly."

It was clear I had her interest, but Yael was keeping her cards close.

"Tell me about Jamal Ramzy," she said. "I'll admit, our files on him are pretty thin. Then I'll help you if I can."

I hesitated, but only for a moment. By this time I was convinced Yael was who she said she was. Talking to her might be as close to talking with Ari Shalit as I was going to get for now. So I dove in.

"The first thing that struck me was how old Jamal is," I began. "I mean, he was born in 1962. That makes him one of the longest-surviving jihadist leaders around. Bin Laden, of course, was born in '57, but he's dead. Zawahiri was born in '51, and he's still kicking, so that makes him the elder statesman within the al Qaeda world. But then Zawahiri isn't in a front-line combat position. Jamal is."

"Another thing that's key is that Jamal and Abu Khalif are related," Omar added. "Jamal is the older cousin by a good seven years. So they're family, but not just any family. A source of mine in Amman told me the family traces its lineage back to Grand Mufti Mohammed Amin al-Husseini."

Yael looked surprised. "The Grand Mufti of Jerusalem?" she asked.

"Exactly," Omar said.

"The one who allied with Hitler and the Nazis during the war?"

"That's the one," Omar confirmed. "These guys aren't simply run-of-the-mill jihadists. They're cut from a certain bolt of cloth. Their hatred of Jews in particular runs exceptionally deep."

"So Jamal decided to follow in the footsteps of Great-Grandpa and went off to fight in Afghanistan?"

"Right—from '80 to '83," I explained. "Then Jamal recruited his younger cousin Abu Khalif to join the mujahideen as a teenager and come fight in Afghanistan from '84 to '86. When the Russians were on the road to defeat, Abu Khalif left the battlefield. He decided to go make some money in the Gulf to support his mother. But Jamal stayed with bin Laden. Jamal was in the room when al Qaeda was born in 1988. In time, he began working with Khalid Sheikh Mohammed, helping to plan terrorist operations. And when Abu Khalif's mother passed away in 1994, Jamal persuaded his cousin to join al Qaeda and serve under KSM."

"Are they headquarters people or field people at this point?" Yael asked.

"Both, and that's what makes them unique— and so dangerous," Omar replied. "They were close to UBL and KSM. They knew the inner workings of al Qaeda. They knew all the top people. But they were also exceptionally proficient both in developing and executing the organization's trade craft. They helped bomb the two American embassies in Tanzania and Nairobi in '98. They were directly involved in training the 9/11 hijackers. In fact, Abu Khalif volunteered to be one of the hijackers, and Jamal supported him, but KSM said no, Khalif was too valuable to him personally. Then, when KSM was captured in Pakistan in '03 and several of his successors were killed in drone strikes, Jamal started working directly for al-Zawahiri as chief of operations."

"How come we've heard so little about Jamal?" Yael asked.

"The Jordanians suggest he kept a very low profile precisely because so many of his predecessors were killed in such short order," Omar said.

"And this is the turning point," I noted. "In 2004, at Jamal's recommendation, UBL and Zawahiri personally met with Abu Khalif. They sent him into Iraq. They told him to create a suicide bombing and kidnapping campaign. They told him to help build al Qaeda in Iraq. Khalif agreed. With Jamal's help, Khalif became a top deputy to Zarqawi. Of course, Zarqawi didn't last long. On June 7, 2006, Zarqawi was killed, and that's when a brutal and bloody internal power struggle began. Abu Khalif wasn't the first choice of bin Laden or Zawahiri to run AQI, but after several other leaders were killed or captured, he emerged as the top dog. He also had the full support of Jamal, who saw his cousin as the better strategist."

"But Abu Khalif wasn't content simply to rape and pillage Iraq," Yael said.

"Hardly," I agreed. "Khalif wanted to expand the mission into Syria. He wanted to topple Assad.

So he renamed his group ISIS, the Islamic State of Iraq and al-Sham. Again, Jamal fully supported his cousin, but bin Laden and Zawahiri were furious. They wanted Khalif to stay focused on Iraq, not get spread too thin. Tensions built within al Qaeda. After U.S. Special Forces took out bin Laden on May 2, 2011, the infighting intensified. Khalif asked Jamal to come with him and command ISIS forces in Syria. Zawahiri went ballistic, but Jamal did it anyway. Zawahiri rebuked the cousins, told them to get out of Syria and change ISIS back to 'al Qaeda in Iraq.'"

"That's when the cousins broke away from Zawahiri once and for all?" Yael asked.

"Exactly," I confirmed. "They think the old man has gone soft. They claim they are the true warriors for Allah. And ISIS is becoming hugely powerful. By early 2012, they had essentially driven U.S. forces out of Iraq. Now they've seized Fallujah. They've seized Mosul. And they've won major battles against Assad's forces in Syria. They've recruited and introduced upwards of thirty thousand foreign fighters into the Syrian theater. They're raising millions from key donors in Saudi Arabia and the Gulf. They're involved in kidnapping, blackmail, extortion, drug smuggling, and drug sales. They see Zawahiri as old news and themselves as the vanguard of the Salafi movement, which they believe is the epitome of true Islam."

"And now?" Yael asked.

"Now, according to Ramzy, they want to open up a new front against the U.S. and Israel, and they want the world to see them eclipsing the old al Qaeda."

"And you think Jamal Ramzy wouldn't have gone on the record with you unless he and his men actually had chemical weapons in their possession?"

"Why else?" I said. "He's never spoken to the media before, never let his photo be taken before."

"You asked him specifically whether ISIS had chemical weapons?"

"I did. I told him I had two sources, from two different intelligence agencies in two different countries. I explained the intel I had personally seen with my own eyes and heard with my own ears."

"And he told you that you don't know what you're talking about."

"Basically, yes," I confirmed.

"He's a liar," Yael said coldly.

I looked at her, then at Omar, then back at Yael.

"You're sure?"

"Absolutely."

"ISIS has chemical weapons?"

"Are we off the record?" she asked.

"Do we have to be?"

"I'm afraid so."

"Then we're off the record," I conceded.

"Then, yes, ISIS has chemical weapons."

"And you can prove it?"

"Of course."

She looked around the room and lowered her voice. "Look, these are the ground rules, and they are sacrosanct," she whispered. "Ari sent me because he wants you to tell the world what ISIS has and how dangerous they've become. They're rapidly eclipsing al Qaeda as the most dangerous terror group on the planet, yet most of the world doesn't really get it. So I can help. But only on the condition that you don't mention the Mossad or any Israeli intelligence agency or operative—not in your article and not to anyone else with whom you discuss what I'm about to tell you. We're clear?"

"Crystal."

She looked at me for a while and then at Omar, who nodded his assent as well.

"We're completely off the record here, and you give me your word?" she pressed. "Both of you?"

We both said yes.

Then she sipped her chai. I sipped mine.

"I don't know who your other sources are, and I won't ask—I don't want to know," Yael began. "But I can tell you for certain that ISIS has captured chemical weapons."

"From where?" I asked, curious to see if her story matched what I had learned.

"A few weeks ago," she began, "Jamal Ramzy's top deputy—a guy named Tariq Baqouba, a real thug, by the way—"

"Yeah, we met him," I broke in. "His brothers, too."

Yael looked surprised but continued. "Anyway, Baqouba and his forces attacked a Syrian military base a few klicks south of Aleppo. At the time, I honestly don't think Baqouba knew it was a storage facility for chemical weapons. After all, it had been widely reported that the U.N. had removed all of Syria's WMD out of the country. But of course that was a lie. The regime had given up a lot, but it was still hoarding plenty. At any rate, radio intercepts suggest the ISIS forces were running low on ammunition. They seemed to have hit this particular base because it had a large ammo storehouse. The firefight that ensued was brutal, one of the fiercest to date. Baqouba's forces seemed taken aback by the strength of the resistance they faced, but rather than back off, they doubled down, probably because they realized they had obviously stumbled onto something valuable. Anyway, they killed off most of the Syrian regulars, and before reinforcements could arrive, Baqouba and his men entered the base and found the WMD stockpiles—sarin nerve gas, to be precise—and the bombs and artillery shells to deliver them."

"How can you be so sure?"

"Drones," she said. "We've been monitoring each of the sites where the Assad regime kept chemical weapons. Again, most of the stockpiles, as you know, were removed under U.N. supervision. But we suspected all along that Assad's people were holding back, not giving the U.N. all they had. So we kept an especially close eye on several of those sites, including the one near Aleppo. We've also been monitoring all radio, phone, and e-mail traffic in the area around these bases. And of course, we have people on the ground, paid informants, and other sources."

So far, everything she said matched precisely what I had learned from the other sources, but it wasn't enough. It was tantalizingly close, but I had to be certain.

"You've personally reviewed all the data?" I asked.

"Yes."

"And?"

"Look," she said, "I was a chemical weapons specialist when I served in the IDF. When Ari recruited me, he put me in a special unit to track chemical WMD in the region. This is what I do."

"And you're certain Jamal's men have these weapons now?"

"There's no question about it," Yael said. "They have them, and they're going to use them. It's a matter of when, not if. And when that happens, it's going to be very, very ugly. Have you ever seen what sarin gas can do?"

22

* * *

I knew that sarin nerve gas had been developed by the Nazis.

What's more, I knew Saddam Hussein had used the stuff against the Kurds in the late eighties, killing some five thousand men, women, and children.

I also remembered that a Japanese cult had used sarin gas in the Tokyo subway system back in the midnineties, killing at least a dozen people and wounding nearly a thousand more.

And Omar and I had covered the sarin attacks on rebel forces by the Syrian regime in the summer of 2013 that had killed more than a thousand people—mostly women and children—and nearly led to military strikes by the U.S., British, and French until all three governments backed out at the last moment. That said, we were both novices on the technicalities of sarin gas, as we readily conceded.

"You have to understand how serious this stuff is," Yael said. "Sarin is among the most toxic and deadly nerve agents. But you can't smell it. You can't taste it. You can't even see it, which makes it all the more dangerous."

She explained that sarin was not a natural substance, but rather a man-made chemical compound, an organophosphate that was similar in many ways to insecticides but, she said, far more lethal.

"Sure, you can fire rockets and mortars and missiles with sarin-filled warheads at an enemy, and you can kill a lot of people," she told us. "You could release it in an aerosol form in a room or in a subway or a mall or a school and kill hundreds or thousands. But it's not just a gas. It can also be a liquid. You could dump barrels of sarin into the water supply—or lace it into the food supply—and you'd kill millions. That's what I worry about. And it's a hideous way to die."

"What happens?" I asked.

"It starts off simple. You get a runny nose. Your eyes start watering and hurting and your vision blurs. But that could be anything. You might not realize how serious it is at first. But then your eyes start dilating. You begin sweating profusely. Soon you're coughing uncontrollably, choking, drooling, possibly foaming at the mouth. You're having trouble breathing. You feel dizzy and nauseated, and then you start vomiting—a little at first, but then again and again until you have nothing left in your system. Then your stomach begins cramping. You have intense abdominal pains. You can't think straight. You're confused and disoriented. Then the convulsions start. If you're lucky, you black out. But more likely you're fully lucid—and filled with terror—as your bodily functions shut down and paralysis sets in, and then you can't breathe, and then you're dead."

I sat there for a few moments, trying to take in what she was saying.

"ISIS with sarin is a worst-case scenario," she said, seeing me process the unthinkable. "An attack like this in my country—or yours—would be catastrophic. You need to write about this. You need to warn people, and fast."

"I agree," I said. "But like I told you, my editor insists I get another source. Will Ari show me what you have?"

"How soon can you come?" she asked.

"To Tel Aviv?"

"Yes," she said. "You wouldn't be allowed to take notes or pictures. You couldn't make copies, and you wouldn't be able to quote anything you hear in your articles or to anyone else you speak with. But since you've already got two other sources, Ari is prepared to show you what we've got and confirm your story based on the intel we've developed."

"Why?"

Yael leaned across the table. "The prime minister has decided Israel needs the world to know who ISIS really is and what they now have," she whispered.

"Yes, but why now?"

"He's concerned the White House isn't taking the ISIS threat seriously enough."

"But if the public knows, maybe they'll light a

fire under Congress, and Congress can light a fire under the president?"

"Something like that."

"So why give the story to me?" I asked.

"Honestly?" she asked as she finished her tea. "Because you already have it, and as you say, time is of the essence. Of course Jamal Ramzy doesn't want to say he's got WMD because that will put every government in the world on heightened alert. But that's exactly why two other governments—and now ours—are giving you the story. We need to make sure everyone knows who ISIS is. We need to make it that much harder for them to operate freely. We have no choice. The attacks could start any day. They've already had the stuff for nearly a month."

"So who do you think is the main target, you or us?" I asked.

"I have no idea, but it's probably us."

"Because you're closer?"

"That, and because of the timing."

"What do you mean?"

"Because the peace process is coming to a head."

"*What?*"

"I mean if we actually strike a final deal with the Palestinians in the next few days, ISIS is going to go ballistic."

I wasn't sure I'd heard her right.

"What are you talking about?" I asked. "I thought the peace process was going nowhere."

"You thought wrong."

"Wait, I don't understand—your prime minister keeps saying the talks are going nowhere, and President Mansour says he's going to walk out of the talks by the end of the month if no progress is made," Omar said, referring to Salim Mansour, the president of the Palestinian Authority. "King Abdullah keeps warning the parties to get serious or a new regional war will break out. If that's all true, it wouldn't seem like Jamal Ramzy and his brethren have much to worry about."

"Actually none of that is true—it's all spin," she said, leaning back in her seat.

"What do you mean by that?" Omar asked.

"Spin," she repeated. "Dissembling. Sleight of hand."

"You're saying the peace talks are moving forward?" he asked.

Yael looked disappointed. "Don't tell me you two have really been buying all this nonsense in the press."

"It comes from the highest officials," I said. "Of course we have."

"Well, stop," she said. "The deal is done."

"What deal?" Omar asked.

"The peace deal," Yael said.

"A full treaty?" I asked.

"Yes."

"How is that possible?"

"Your guess is as good as mine," Yael said. "I'm just telling you what I know. My PM has made major concessions—more than I'm comfortable with, frankly, but that's another story. They don't ask for my opinions on such matters. Anyway, I can't say more about this. I'm definitely not authorized to speak about any of these things. And you can't write about this. Seriously. Nobody knows what I'm telling you right now. But it's important you understand what's motivating Abu Khalif. We don't know where he is—somewhere in Iraq, we think—but we're guessing he knows more about the true state of the peace talks than the *New York Times*. We're also guessing he's about to give orders to kill a whole lot of people to keep this peace treaty from being finalized. Look, James, I'm glad you got your interview with Ramzy. I'm sure it'll be an important story. But don't get distracted. Jamal Ramzy is a supporting character. Abu Khalif is the lead actor. He's the big story. He's the guy you need to talk to, ideally before all hell breaks loose."

"I'm trying," I said. "But I can't find him. No one will tell me where he is. All I know is he's in prison in Iraq. Can you guys help?"

"We don't know any more than you," she said. "If we knew where he was, believe me, he'd be a corpse."

"I assume that's off the record as well." I smiled.

Yael smiled back. "Look, I wish I could give you more specifics, but I can't. But you should hunt him down like you did Ramzy. Find him. Talk to him. See what he says. Then brace yourself for some serious blowback. Because I'm telling you, this is why Abu Khalif is getting ready to strike. He's a barbarian. He's livid at the prospect of the Palestinians cutting a deal with the 'dirty Zionists.' He's enraged that President Mansour is about to legitimize the presence of a single Jew in

'Palestine.' He's hell-bent on doing everything he can to disrupt the peace process, and if that means killing a whole lot of innocent people, then he figures, so be it."

At that, she looked at her watch and stood. "Well, gentlemen, it's been a pleasure, but it's late, and I'm afraid I've got to go," she said. "I fly back to Tel Aviv around noon. If you're smart, you'll come with me."

Omar and I stood as well.

"Thank you, Yael," I said, taking her hand in mine. "It's been a lovely evening."

"Let's do it again soon," she said and then winked at me.

"I'd like that," I replied.

We exchanged numbers. I said I'd call my editor and get back to her as quickly as possible. Then I offered to give her a ride back to the hotel. Given how hard it was now raining, she readily accepted.

"Where's the car?" I asked Omar.

"Just up the street a bit," he said.

"Fine, I'll pay our tab and meet you there," I said, trying to get our waiter's attention to bring the bill.

"And I'll get our coats," Yael said.

As she went to find them and Omar headed out into the pouring rain, I gave the waiter my credit card and pulled out my iPhone. There were twenty-seven new e-mails, none of which were useful, so I sent three of my own.

First, I wrote to Youssef Kuttab, a senior advisor to Palestinian president Salim Mansour.

Y—We need to talk. Hearing rumors
a deal is almost done. Eager to know
more. Can I come see you?—JB

If I was going to Tel Aviv, I figured, I might as
well start working on the next story too.

Next, I wrote to Hassan Karbouli, Iraq's minister of the interior. We'd known each other for
years, and typically he'd been quite helpful, so
long as he wasn't quoted. But he'd gone dark for
the last few weeks, and I was getting desperate. If
anyone could help me track down Abu Khalif, it
was Karbouli.

Hassan—This is my fifth e-mail. Where
are you? Running out of time. Must
ask you directly: where is AK being
held? Just interviewed Jamal Ramzy.
Story to run in tomorrow's paper.
Now need to follow up with AK. Have
gone through all the proper channels,
but no one will help me. Know you're
swamped, but asking for your help.
Thanks.—JB

Finally, I sent a quick note to Prince Marwan
Talal in Amman, an uncle of the Jordanian king
and one of His Majesty's most trusted advisors.
Marwan was getting up in years, but because he
had been around so long, he knew everyone in the
region and had his finger on the pulse of all that
was happening.

Your Royal Highness—I need your help.
Trying to track down AK. Planning a
major attack. Solid sources say he has
WMD. Can we talk soon?—JB

A moment later, Yael came back with our coats.
I finished paying the bill and helped her with her
coat, then put mine on as well. We were about
to leave when she realized she had forgotten her
umbrella.

"I'll be right back," she said.

I offered to get it for her, but she insisted it
was no problem. *So much for chivalry,* I thought.
I waited for her by the front door.

Outside, I could see Omar climbing into the
driver's seat of the rental car up the street. But I
wasn't thinking about Omar. My thoughts were
consumed with Yael Katzir. I could still smell her
perfume. I could still feel her lips on my own.
I pulled her business card out of my pocket and
looked it over. It was a simple card, black and
white, bearing only the initials *YK* and a European
mobile number. No Mossad logo. No mention of
the intelligence agency at all. No address or even
post office box number. For a moment, I wondered if the phone number was even real. Then I
started asking myself whether she was at all interested in me or if she had just been doing her job. If
I asked her to dinner in Tel Aviv, might she accept?
If I asked her to join me for a movie, what would
she say? Omar and Hadiya kept telling me it was
time. I kept telling them I wasn't ready. But maybe

they were right. All I knew for certain was I liked this girl. I wanted to see more of her. The moment wasn't convenient. But when would it ever be?

Yael sidled up beside me with her polka-dot umbrella. She slipped her arm through mine and smiled.

"Ready when you are," she said.

"After you," I replied.

As I opened the door for her, I could hear Omar trying to start the car. He turned the engine over several more times, but to no avail. Suddenly a wave of physical and emotional exhaustion washed over me. Frustration, too. I had neither the time nor the energy to hang out while Omar waited for a tow truck, if that's really what was needed. I wanted to get back to the hotel, type up my notes, take a hot shower, and get to bed.

As we stepped out of the café, I glanced to my left to see if any cabs were coming. Unfortunately, it was now almost three in the morning. The streets were empty. There were no cabs to be found. So I looked back at Omar trying to get the thing started and began wondering how long it would take to call for a taxi.

And that's when the Hyundai erupted in a massive explosion.

PART
FOUR

23

* * *

I woke up screaming, but this was not a nightmare.

Soaked in sweat, my whole body was shivering. I could see Omar inside the car, trying to start the engine. I could feel Yael at my side, her arm in mine. I could feel the heat and force of the massive explosion, the flames shooting into the sky, glass and shards of metal flying in all directions. I could smell burning gasoline, burning flesh. I could hear the ear-piercing boom. It wasn't distant or hazy or detached. It was as if I were still standing on that street, walking out that doorway. It was real, and it was happening again and again and again.

I sat bolt upright in some bed in some dark room illuminated only by the red numbers of a digital alarm clock that read 2:14 a.m. I looked down and found myself dressed only in my underwear. Disoriented, my heart racing, I had no idea where I was or how I'd gotten there. I was breathing so hard I was in danger of hyperventilating.

Dizzy and nauseated, about to vomit, I lay back down in the bed. The pillow was damp with perspiration, so I turned it over and was relieved to find the other side cooler and dry. I kicked off the covers and tried to get comfortable.

Exhausted, I closed my eyes, desperate to regain a sense of equilibrium. But as soon as I tried to fall back asleep, the explosion replayed all over again.

★　★　★

"Good morning, James. Are you awake?"

I heard the voice but could not place it. It was a woman's voice, gentle and comforting, but it also seemed distant and far away. Was it Yael's? Had she survived? Had she found me, come back to rescue me?

Foggy and confused, I tried to open my eyes but my head was pounding terribly. My limbs ached and my breathing was labored.

The woman I saw in the morning light was not Yael. It was a nurse, checking my vital signs and giving me a shot in my left arm.

"Hush," she said. "Don't move. Don't try to get up. It's okay. You're going to be fine."

I passed out again.

★　★　★

The next time I opened my eyes, the digital clock said it was 8:56 p.m.

I squinted through the darkness and then noticed the date in a corner of the display as well. I blinked hard and looked again. That couldn't be right, I thought. But sure enough, the date read November 27.

A shot of adrenaline coursed through my system, and once again I sat straight up in bed in the pitch-black of night. *Four days?* It couldn't be. Or was it five? How had so much time gone by so quickly? Where was Omar? I had a story to file. The deadline had long since passed. Allen had to be furious. I had work to do. Where was my laptop? Where were my notes?

My head still ached, but it no longer felt like it was clamped into a vise, being squeezed without mercy. That was progress, and I would take it.

"Good morning, Mr. Collins," a voice off to my left said.

I turned my head and saw three men standing in my hospital room. One was Turkish, probably in his early thirties, medium height, medium build, jet-black hair, spectacles—a physician of some kind, judging from his white lab coat and the stethoscope around his neck. The other two wore suits. They certainly weren't Turkish. From their manner and their wing-tip shoes, they struck me as Americans, probably from the American embassy or consulate. The younger of these two appeared to be in his late twenties, and it was obvious he was packing heat. He stood near the door. He was security. But it was the older of the two—in his midfifties, I guessed—who was talking.

"You're lucky to be alive," he said.

I wasn't sure that was true, but I said nothing.

"I'm Art Harris," he continued. "I'm a special agent with the FBI."

I nodded.

"Do you know what day it is?"

"The twenty-seventh."

"Do you know the month?"

"November."

"But you read that off the clock radio, correct?"

I nodded again.

"Do you know where you are?"

"Looks like a hospital," I said. "Am I still in Istanbul?"

"You are indeed," Harris said.

But now it was the doctor who spoke as he stepped forward and checked my pulse. "How do you feel, Mr. Collins?"

"I'm fine," I lied. "How soon can I leave?"

"In a few days probably," the doctor said.

"Do I have any broken bones?"

"No," he said. "Fortunately you do not."

"Did I require surgery?"

"Some stitches here and there, but no, surgery wasn't necessary."

"Did I require a blood transfusion?"

"No, nothing like that," he said.

"Then I want to leave today," I said.

"Not quite yet," he replied. "We want to keep you a bit longer for observation. You've been through quite a trauma."

"Perhaps I could have a few minutes alone with Mr. Collins," the man named Harris said.

There was an awkward silence, and then the doctor stepped out of the room, followed by the other FBI agent, who was apparently not there in an investigative capacity. As the door swung open, I noticed two other agents just like him in the hallway.

"Am I under arrest?" I asked.

"Of course not."

"Do you think I did this?"

"No."

"Then why all the suits and guns?"

"Someone's trying to kill you, Mr. Collins," he replied. "My job is to figure out who, and these men have been assigned to protect you."

He handed me a business card. It bore the FBI logo, a local office address, an e-mail address and phone number, and the words *Arthur M. Harris, Special Agent in Charge.*

"What do you remember about the other night?" Harris asked.

I did my best to describe the final moments of watching Omar get into the Hyundai, his efforts to start the car, and the enormous explosion.

"Do you remember being thrown through the plate-glass window of the café?"

I didn't.

"How about the local ambulance crew giving you first aid?"

I shook my head. "I don't remember anything after the explosion until I woke up here."

"What about the woman?" he asked.

"What woman?"

"The woman you and Mr. Fayez were having tea with," Harris said. "The owner says you were leaving the café with her when the bomb went off. We have a description. We have a sketch artist working with several of the witnesses right now. But in all the commotion, she disappeared. I'm hoping you can help us identify her."

My pulse quickened. I wasn't sure what to say.

Was Yael okay? Was she safe? Why had she fled the scene? Didn't she know that would raise suspicions? I supposed she must not have been seriously harmed if she'd had the wherewithal to slip away. Apparently she hadn't turned up in any hospitals or medical clinics in Istanbul, or Harris would have known about it by now. Surely he and his team were canvassing every location. Yael, after all, was either a material witness to a serious crime or a suspect.

Now that I'd had two seconds to think about it, it was clear why she'd fled. She was a senior intelligence agent for the Israeli government, operating in Turkey, which didn't exactly have close working relations with the Israelis at the present time. She didn't want to be interviewed by local Turkish authorities or by the FBI. She didn't want there to be any traces back to the Mossad; that was for sure. So she'd bailed before emergency crews had arrived on the scene. Which meant she didn't want me talking about her.

Still, Harris was a federal agent. I couldn't lie to him. That would be a felony.

"I'm afraid I can't help you," I replied.

"Can't or won't?" Harris asked.

"Look, she's a source—and a confidential one at that," I explained. "She made me promise I wouldn't reveal her identity. I'm sorry."

"Is she American?"

"I really can't say."

"Turkish?"

"Sorry."

"Is she an Arab, Mr. Collins?" Harris pressed. "Someone connected to your trip to Syria?"

"How do you know about that?"

Harris looked confused. "The whole world knows you went to Syria, Mr. Collins," he replied. "You wrote about it on the front page of the *New York Times*."

"The story is already out?"

"What do you mean?" he asked. "Of course it is. It ran several days ago."

Of course it had. I'd been in the hospital four days, which meant the stories on ISIS and Ramzy had already been read by millions around the globe.

I apologized. I was still trying to clear my head and orient myself to all that had happened. But Harris kept pressing.

"What do the initials YK stand for?" he asked.

I was startled but said nothing.

"They were on the business card in your pocket," he explained. "We've tried the phone number. It's local, but it's been disconnected. Imagine that."

"You think my source is trying to kill me?" I asked.

"You tell me."

"It's not possible."

"No?"

"No. She's trying to help me on a very important story."

"About Jamal Ramzy and Abu Khalif?"

"I can't say."

"About ISIS?"

"I told you, I'm not at liberty to tell you anything about her."

"You understand why I'm asking."

"Of course."

"Someone just murdered your colleague," Harris said. "And they were trying to take you out as well."

"And you think she's connected?"

"I don't know what to think, but it's my job to track down every lead," Harris said. "Right now I have a car bombing in Istanbul in front of an all-night café frequented by foreign nationalists. I've got a Jordanian reporter for the *New York Times* dead. I've got an American correspondent for the same newspaper who should be dead but isn't and a mysterious woman who has vanished off the face of the earth. No name. No address. No working phone number. Just the initials YK. See what I'm saying?"

"I do, but I can assure you she's trying to help me, not kill me."

"You've known her a long time?"

"No."

"Months, years?"

"No, we just met here in Istanbul."

"But you're vouching for her?"

"I know her boss. He sent her to meet with me."

"You trust him?"

"I do."

Harris said nothing. He just looked at me, and I could see him trying to decide whether I was telling the truth.

"I'm not the kind of person to go around lying to the FBI," I said in my defense.

"I don't know what kind of person you are," Harris replied.

"I tell the truth for a living," I explained. "All I have in this world is my reputation for explaining events to my readers as accurately as I possibly can. That's something I guard very jealously, Mr. Harris."

He nodded, then pulled out a small notebook and a pen and began jotting something down.

"The reason I'm so concerned, Mr. Collins— the reason I'm asking so many questions—is we have evidence that suggests the bombing was the work of an al Qaeda cell."

"Al Qaeda?"

"Yes."

"Not ISIS."

"No."

"What evidence?" I asked.

"The design of the car bomb was distinctive—very similar to those used by al Qaeda in Afghanistan," Harris said. "The explosives used in the bomb have the exact same chemical composition of a bomb used three weeks ago to kill an American diplomat in Kabul—a case that led to the capture of three al Qaeda operatives, all of whom have since confessed."

"But why would al Qaeda want to kill me?" I asked.

"I was going to ask you the same question."

24

★ ★ ★

The moment Harris left, I powered up my iPhone and called Allen MacDonald.

"Thank God," he said when he heard my voice. "How are you feeling?"

"Fine—just a little shaken up," I said. It wasn't exactly true, but I was feeling increasingly desperate to get back in the game. "But I'm devastated by Omar."

"I know," Allen said. "We're all in shock. First Abdel, and now this. It's hitting everyone hard."

"I'd like to go to the funeral," I said.

"For Omar?"

"Of course."

"In Jordan?"

"Where else?"

"I don't think that's a good idea, J. B."

"Why not?"

"Because the FBI thinks al Qaeda is gunning for you."

"They told you that?"

"Told me, and then demanded I not print it," my editor replied.

"Why not?"

"Obviously they're afraid AQ is going to try again," Allen said. "Didn't they send an agent to talk with you? They said they would."

"Yeah, he just left."

"They think someone working for al Qaeda might have spotted you in the airport in Beirut and tipped off the leadership. They say it's not uncommon."

"But why me?"

"Their working theory at the moment is that AQ got wind of your meeting with Ramzy somehow and wanted to stop you from writing your story elevating ISIS," Allen explained.

"Seems a little petty."

"Maybe," Allen said. "But I don't like the idea of you making yourself a target in Amman. I want you on the next plane back to D.C., first thing tomorrow morning."

"They won't let me leave," I said. "The doctor says he wants to keep me for observation."

"I've already spoken to the chief administrator at the hospital. He'll clear your release so long as I promise to put you in an American hospital for a few more days when you get back."

"No, Allen, I need to go meet another source."

"Where?"

"I can't say—but in the Middle East."

"Absolutely not," he shot back. "Are you crazy?"

"I found another source," I explained. "They're going to confirm the WMD story. It's solid. They have proof. But I need to see it in person."

"You're out of your mind. You know that, don't you?"

"Look, I just need twenty-four hours," I insisted. "I'll turn in this story, and then I'll come back."

"No. I've booked you on a flight back to D.C. that leaves in the morning."

"Allen, all I'm asking for is twenty-four hours."

"The answer is no."

"This story is going to win the Pulitzer."

"Not if you're dead."

"I'll be fine."

"Fine like Abdel? Fine like Omar? Nice try. Get on the plane. Then come straight to the office. We'll regroup. I'll go over your notes and we'll figure out our next moves. End of discussion. And don't try to do an end run around me again, J. B. You went into Syria in direct defiance of my orders. You've gotten two of our guys killed. You make one more move like that, and you're fired. Got it?"

Stung by his vehemence, I said nothing.

"Good," he concluded. "See you tomorrow."

I was angry as I hung up the phone. I didn't need a lecture from my editor on how much danger I was in, but to my way of thinking, the very fact people were trying to kill me only reinforced how important these stories were. There was no way I was going to give up, but at that moment I wasn't sure I was in a position to disregard Allen's explicit directive to come back to D.C. And if I was honest, I had to admit that nothing he had said indicated he was trying to stop me from doing the WMD story. He'd said he was willing to review the evidence I'd gathered and figure out what to do next. But for the moment, he was simply trying to save my life. I appreciated that, and there was a part of me that was grateful. But in the end, what did my life matter when tens or hundreds of thousands of other lives—American and Israeli—hung in the balance?

Looking down at my phone, I was amazed to see there were more than twelve hundred e-mails and two hundred text messages waiting for me, along with a few dozen voice messages. The first wave was from colleagues and friends calling to congratulate me on the Ramzy stories, and TV producers inviting me on their weekend talk shows to discuss Ramzy and the rising threat of al Qaeda and ISIS.

The second wave of messages—and the overwhelming majority, by far—were people checking on me after reading the front-page *Times* story that ran the day after the Ramzy piece, describing the car bombing in Istanbul. There were messages from correspondents and bureau chiefs all over the world. The White House press secretary had called. So had several members of Congress, including the chairmen of both the House and Senate select intelligence committees. There were also messages from a wide range of sources at the Pentagon and the CIA, including Jack Vaughn, the current CIA director, even though he'd specifically warned me not to go. Again, I was grateful and touched by the messages I read and listened to. But I couldn't let myself get bogged down in it all.

I needed time to think, not type e-mails and write thank-you notes and chitchat on the phone.

I sent a quick text message to my mom, letting her know I was all right and that I'd call her when I got back to the States. I deleted a voice-mail message from Matt and an e-mail from Laura. Then I tapped out a generic e-mail thanking everyone for their kind words and assuring them I was okay and would be back on the beat soon. I BCC'd my entire contact list and hit Send, then copied the message and pasted it into all the text messages and hit Send over and over again.

Noticeably absent were any messages from Prince Marwan Talal in Amman or Ismail Tikriti in Baghdad. That bothered me. I'd always been good to both men. We'd helped each other in the past. Why were they ducking me now?

Eventually I came across a text from Robert Khachigian. The onetime director of Central Intelligence had responded to my urgent request for a meeting by saying he'd be happy to meet but was leaving for Asia on Monday.

That was only two days away. **Can we talk by phone?** I wrote back to him. **When's best for you?**

Next I found three e-mails from Youssef Kuttab, senior advisor to the Palestinian chairman. I had e-mailed him about the peace process from the café here in Istanbul just before the explosion. *It is always a pleasure to have coffee with you, my friend,* he wrote in his first response to my inquiry. *Call me when you get into town.* The second was more urgent. *I thought you were coming to Ramallah. Things are getting complicated. We need to sit down*

in person. Where are you? The third read simply:
Just heard the news. No words—are you okay?

"Getting complicated"? What did that mean?
I had no idea, but whatever it was, one thing was
clear: I wasn't going to find out by e-mail or phone.
I was going to have to go to Ramallah and sit with
Kuttab personally, or I wasn't going to hear it at all.

Not sure how to thread that needle just yet,
I focused on two text messages from Hassan
Karbouli, whom I'd been trying to contact about
finding Abu Khalif. His first message, written the
day the Ramzy story was published, read, **Good
to hear from you, my friend. Wish I could help.
Sorry.** I wasn't sure whether to laugh or throw the
phone across the room. Karbouli was the Iraqi
interior minister, for crying out loud. He oversaw
the country's bureau of prisons. If he wanted to
help me, he certainly could. He answered only to
the prime minister and Allah.

If Karbouli's first text message was infuriating,
however, the second was ominous. Dated the day
the car bombing story was reported, it was brief:
Drop AK story. Not safe.

"Not safe"? I wondered. *For whom—for me or
for him?*

Perhaps both.

To be sure, Karbouli had always struck me
as a good man in a tough spot. Born and raised
near Mosul, he was one of the few Sunni Muslims
serving in a predominantly Shia government in
Baghdad. In the past I had always felt I could trust
him. But now I wasn't sure. Was this a warning or
a threat?

Either way, the two messages in combination had me firing on all cylinders. This guy knew exactly where the emir of ISIS was, I realized, and if I could get to Hassan Karbouli, I just might be able to get to Abu Khalif.

25

★ ★ ★

My flight out of Istanbul departed at 8:15 in the morning.

Which meant I had to be at the airport by six.

Which meant I had to be up, showered, and dressed by four thirty.

The three agents Special Agent in Charge Harris had assigned to keep me safe at the hospital graciously offered to drive me to the airport and take me to my gate out of an abundance of caution. They also returned my luggage and briefcase, which I'd left at the Hotel Ibrahim Pasha.

After a grueling mechanical delay, I was finally hurtling down the runway on an Airbus A320 headed for Frankfurt. From there, I'd have a tight connection to catch my flight to Washington Dulles. If all went well, I'd be back on American soil by four o'clock that afternoon, local time.

Then what? I had no idea.

★ ★ ★

There were storms over Frankfurt.

My flight was late and I had to run to get to

my gate on time. But that's when I got an urgent text from Khachigian.

Grave development. Need to meet ASAP.

I wondered if I should stop running and text him back immediately. But I could hear the last call going out for passengers on Lufthansa flight 418 to Washington Dulles International Airport. I was in danger of missing my connection, so I kept running. A few minutes later, I finally made it to the gate and was the last person to board the plane. The moment I found my seat and buckled in, I immediately texted him back.

What's happening?

Five seconds later I got his reply. **Can't explain by text.**

Call?

Too sensitive.

Soon, the text messages between us were flying back and forth.

Topic?

ISIS.

Listening.

Need to meet tonight.

Can't—in Germany, but heading back shortly.

Fine, I'll go to the Post.

What??? Absolutely not.

Can't wait. Story won't hold. I have to get it out. And my trip to Asia has been bumped up. I leave tonight.

Then let's talk now by phone.

No. I can't.

I touch down at Dulles at four. How about dinner?

Sorry. Too late. I'm going to the Post.

Robert, you owe me this.

I don't.

I've done everything you asked. Nearly got myself killed on this story you told me to pursue. Lost two colleagues. Now you're going to the Post???

Suddenly Khachigian wasn't writing back. A minute went by. Then two. I was dying. They were closing the cabin door. A flight attendant was asking me to power down my phone.

You still there? I wrote.

Another minute went by.

Yes, he finally replied.

And?

Thinking.

Hold on the story, please, I insisted. **Meet me at Union Station.**

There was another long pause. A minute. Two. We were beginning to taxi. A second flight attendant was insisting I shut off my phone. Three minutes. Finally, after four minutes my phone chirped with a new incoming text.

Fine. Union Station. Center Café. 7:30 p.m. Don't be late.

26

★ ★ ★

WASHINGTON, D.C.

After repeated weather delays, Lufthansa flight 418 finally landed at Dulles.

As we taxied to the terminal, I pulled out my grandfather's pocket watch. It was now 5:35 Sunday afternoon, a full ninety minutes after our scheduled arrival time.

My nerves were a wreck. I still needed to clear passport control and customs, race home to shower and change before making it to the *Times* bureau at 1627 I Street downtown to meet with Allen for who knew how long, then arrive at Union Station by seven thirty. Otherwise whatever scoop Khachigian was saving for me was going to the *Washington Post*.

With a full flight out of Istanbul, my protective detail hadn't been able to travel with me. But they'd assured me that I'd be met by agents from the D.C. bureau the moment I arrived. As I stepped off the plane, however, there was no one waiting for me. I had no intention of staying around.

Already I was checking flights to Tel Aviv later

that night or the next day at the latest on the working assumption that Allen would see the light and let me go once we'd talked through the evidence I'd gathered so far. At the same time, I knew I needed to call my mom. I needed to let her hear my voice and know for sure I was really okay. She would insist I come up to Maine, but that wasn't going to happen. Not for a while. At least not until I got back from Tel Aviv and Amman. After all, I had to visit with Omar's widow. I had to give her my condolences and tell her what an amazing friend her husband had been to me.

But the truth was, at that moment my thoughts were mostly on Yael. Where was she? Was she safe? Was she okay? I'd already tried the number on her card. Harris was right. It was no longer working. I'd also sent a text message to Ari Shalit asking about her and asking for permission to come see him as soon as possible. So far, I'd heard nothing back.

As I worked my way through the airport, I noticed a crowd gathering around a TV set. When I heard the trademark voice of James Earl Jones saying, "This is CNN Breaking News," I stopped immediately to see what was happening.

"CNN has just learned that Ayman al-Zawahiri, the head of al Qaeda since 2011, is dead," said a female anchor in the Atlanta studios while raw, unedited video of a smoldering crater on a crowded street and the burning wreckage of what appeared to be an SUV played on the screen. "Several sources are telling CNN the al Qaeda leader was killed in a drone strike, but at least one former CIA analyst says the images are more consistent with a car bombing."

I quickly checked the headlines on my phone. Agence France-Presse was quoting an unnamed source inside Pakistani intelligence confirming that Zawahiri and two of his bodyguards had been killed less than an hour earlier as a result of an explosion, but the story offered no further details on how the al Qaeda leader's car had exploded. A quick check of the AP and Reuters wires indicated that neither the Pentagon nor the State Department was commenting, but an unnamed White House source—cited only as a senior aide to President Taylor—said that while U.S. officials were awaiting confirmation from the Pakistani government, they were "cautiously optimistic" that "a great victory over terrorism has been achieved."

Meanwhile, I could hear an analyst on CNN saying, "This could prove to be the beginning of the end of al Qaeda," and adding that under President Taylor's leadership, al Qaeda was being "systematically dismantled."

I hoped it was true. I feared it was not.

Grabbing my briefcase and carry-on luggage, I bought a cup of coffee and a copy of the Sunday editions of both the *New York Times* and the *Washington Post*, hailed a taxi, and gave the driver the address of my apartment in Arlington. As we pulled out of the airport and headed southeast on the toll road toward D.C., the lead headline from the *Post* caught my eye.

**President Warns Israelis, Palestinians
of "Catastrophic Consequences"
if Peace Talks Fail: Aides Say
Administration Will Reconsider
Aid Levels if Deal Not Struck Soon**

Written by the *Post*'s top White House and State Department correspondents, the article was the latest installment in the ongoing media narrative over the past month or so that the Mideast peace talks were floundering, that the parties were not taking the process seriously, and that both sides seemed to be trying to paint the other as the intransigent and irresponsible one. This version added a bit of spice to the stew with the idea that the White House might actually reduce U.S. military aid to Israel, which averaged over $3 billion a year, and might also cut aid to the Palestinians, which averaged about a half billion dollars annually.

The story certainly fit the conventional wisdom inside the Beltway, but was it true? I was now starting to wonder whether just the opposite dynamic was in motion. Yael had insisted that the parties were, in fact, incredibly close to a deal and that the consummation of a comprehensive peace treaty actually made the prospect of a major series of terrorist attacks more likely, not less so. Who was right?

The peace talks were not my beat, per se. I focused primarily on national security and terrorism stories, but obviously the two were related, and the deeper I read into the *Post* story, the more curious, and perhaps more cynical, I became. Was the White House trying to pull off the head fake of the century? With all the carefully timed leaks about how badly things were going, was the administration driving down expectations so that the announcement by the president of a final, comprehensive peace treaty between the Israelis and Palestinians would give him a political bounce of epic proportions?

A text message came in. It was from the senior producer at the *Today Show*. She wanted me on the following morning to discuss my Jamal Ramzy article and the terror attack that had nearly taken my life in Istanbul. She was also interested to know whether I thought the president had ordered the hit on Zawahiri as retaliation for what had happened to Omar and me.

As I checked my other messages, I found interview requests from a dozen other media outlets, from *Good Morning America* to *60 Minutes*. I had no interest in going on any of them. I wasn't a pundit. I was a foreign correspondent. And I didn't plan to spend a second longer on American soil than I absolutely had to.

I dialed my mom. She picked up on the fourth ring. She was ecstatic to hear from me and wanted every detail. I was guarded, not wanting to worry her any further than she must already be, even though I knew she'd been reading all the coverage of the attack on me that she possibly could. She asked me, of course, to come up to Maine that night. I said, of course, that I couldn't.

"When can you get here, honey? You missed Thanksgiving. I didn't celebrate it either. I was too worried about you. But we could celebrate together. I'll make you a big feast."

"Thanks, Mom, but I'm not sure how soon I can get up there. There's an awful lot going on."

"I know, but sweetheart, it's been so long, and I . . . well . . . you know, I miss you."

She sounded so deflated.

"I know, Mom, and I miss you. I'll come visit. I promise. But it looks like I need to go to Tel Aviv and Amman first."

"You're going to Amman?" she asked, seeming to brighten.

"I hope so," I said.

"When?"

"In the next few days."

"Great," she said. "You can see Matty!"

I took a deep breath. "I don't know if I'll have time, Mom. It's not going to be a pleasure trip. It's for work."

"But, James, obviously you can make some time to see your only brother."

"I'll try."

"Good. He wrote to you recently, right?"

"I don't know. Did he?"

"He told me he was going to."

"Maybe he's been busy."

"Maybe you're not reading your mail."

"I was in Syria, Mom, and then someone tried to kill me."

"That's no excuse," she said without a hint of

irony. "You really ought to talk to your brother. You two need each other."

"I'm sure he and Annie are doing just fine without me."

"They are fine, but the fact is they miss you, young man."

"Okay, Mom."

"Really, James, would it kill you to return his notes or to call him now and again? He's your older brother. He loves you and he's worried about you."

"I'd really rather not talk about it."

"That's the understatement of the year."

"Nevertheless . . ." I glanced out the window of the cab. Route 267, the toll road, was now merging with 66. We'd be in Arlington any moment. Which was good. I desperately needed a shower and a change of clothes.

"So, any word from Laura?" my mom suddenly asked.

Every muscle in my body tensed at the very name. "No," I said.

We drove a bit longer.

"Nothing at all?"

"No."

There was no way I was going to tell her I'd just deleted an e-mail from my ex-wife and had no idea what it said.

"I'm sorry, Mom. That chapter is over."

"I'm so sorry, too, Son. Guess I always thought she was the one."

I didn't respond. What was there to say?

"Listen, Mom, I gotta go," I said instead. "I'll call you again tomorrow."

"You promise?"

"I promise."

"Okay. Bye."

She didn't sound like she believed me. I couldn't really blame her. Nevertheless, I said good-bye and hung up. At that moment, though, I realized that rather than exiting into the city of Arlington—toward my apartment—as I'd instructed, the driver was staying on 66. In a moment, we'd be heading out of Virginia and into the District of Columbia. It was not only the exact opposite of where I wanted to go, but given the challenges of D.C. traffic, the error was going to take forever to correct. I was as annoyed as I was confused. I leaned forward and told the driver he was making a mistake.

"I have my orders," he replied.

"What orders?" I asked. "What are you talking about?"

But the driver didn't answer. The car accelerated. The doors of the car abruptly locked as the Plexiglas screen between the front and back seats suddenly closed.

"What in the world are you doing?" I yelled, but still the driver did not answer.

I demanded he turn the car around, but he ignored me. I pulled out my phone to call 911, but now there was no signal. That was impossible, of course. We were heading into the epicenter of the American government. There was plenty of cell coverage to be had. The only possible explanation was that the driver had a device that was jamming my phone. He must have turned it on right after I hung up with my mom.

I looked at him. He briefly glanced at me in the rearview mirror. Furious and becoming frightened now, I demanded he take me home, but even if he could hear me through the Plexiglas, he did not alter his course.

We were not going to Arlington. That much was clear. I had no idea where we were going instead, but given all that had happened in recent days, I found myself fighting panic.

Who was this guy? Who was he working for? And what did they want with me?

Before I knew it, we'd passed the Lincoln Memorial.

We headed east on Constitution Avenue. Then we took a sharp left on Eighteenth Street and started zigzagging through a series of side streets before barreling down a ramp into a dark parking garage, tires squealing like a stunt car's in a movie. Down, down we went, lower and lower into the bowels of the garage, and this guy was driving far faster than was either normal or safe. I was certain we were going to plow into a car coming up in the opposite direction, but no sooner had the thought crossed my mind than he hit the brakes and brought us to an abrupt halt on a deserted level.

The doors automatically unlocked. Immediately both rear passenger doors opened and I became aware that a half-dozen men in dark suits were standing around the taxi. They looked and acted like federal agents, but we were a long way from the Treasury Department and even farther from the Hoover Building.

"Mr. Collins, please step out of the vehicle," one of them said.

"Who are you?" I asked. "What's going on here?"

"Please step out, sir. And follow me."

"Why? To where?"

"Just follow me."

I couldn't decide if I was really in danger. This was Washington, after all, not Syria. In any case, it was clear I didn't have a choice, and by nature I was insatiably curious. They hadn't killed me yet. The deserted level of a downtown parking garage on a Sunday evening seemed as good a place to do it as any. But if that wasn't the objective, what was? It seemed unlikely that Abu Khalif or Jamal Ramzy had an entire group of American-looking thugs operating out of central Washington.

I got out of the cab and followed the agent who was doing all the talking. As I did, the rest stepped behind and around me. We entered a stairwell, but rather than ascend to street level, we went down a flight of stairs. The leader unlocked what appeared at first to be a utility closet but actually led to a tunnel. We stepped through the doorway into the tunnel and proceeded on our way. As we walked, I had a flashback to being taken to see Ramzy, and the farther we went, the more curious I got.

A few minutes later, the point man unlocked and opened another door, and then we were standing in a nondescript vestibule of some sort—white walls, black marble floors, a high ceiling, and a small surveillance camera mounted over the entrance to an elevator, whose door was already open as if waiting for us to arrive. One of the men patted me down and then four of them escorted me into the elevator, and soon we were ascending.

When the door finally opened, I stepped out and couldn't believe where I was.

I was standing in the second-floor private residence of the White House.

27

* * *

The president of the United States stepped forward.

"Welcome to the people's house, Mr. Collins. I'm Harrison Taylor. It's an honor to meet you."

"It's an honor to meet you as well, Mr. President," I said, shaking his hand.

For all my years working in the media, I had never actually met this president. Years before, I had interviewed several of his predecessors, but as a foreign correspondent for the *Times* who spent most of my time abroad, there was no particular reason for me to have met this one. At six feet four inches, he appeared even taller in person than he did on television, and he was certainly a distinguished-looking Southern gentleman. Slender, even lanky, with jet-black hair graying at the temples, a firm jaw, and piercing blue inquisitive eyes, Harrison Taylor was the great-grandson of a famous governor of North Carolina. He himself had made a fortune building a software company in the Research Triangle just outside of Raleigh before selling the company for a half-billion dollars, winning a

Senate seat, and later winning the governorship in a landslide. Now this policy maverick—a fiscal conservative but social liberal—was president of the United States.

But he was in serious political trouble. The U.S. economy was stalled. His immigration reform agenda had likewise stalled in Congress. His foreign policy was in disarray. And his approval ratings were drifting ever downward and were currently in the dangerous midthirties. He had ridden into the Oval Office on a wave of populist sentiment and had benefited from a late-breaking scandal in the Republican nominee's campaign, but more recently he had struggled to find his political sea legs, and I found it striking to see up close how much the last several years in office had worn him.

"Of course, you know Jack here quite well," the president said, turning to Jack Vaughn, the former chairman of the Senate intelligence committee who was now director of the Central Intelligence Agency.

"I do, indeed, Mr. President," I said, shaking Vaughn's hand. "Good to see you, Jack."

"Good to see you, too, J. B.," Vaughn replied. "So glad you're okay."

"Thank you, sir."

"Bet you're wishing now you'd followed my advice, eh?"

"Now, now," the president interjected. "There'll be no 'See, I told you so' speeches in this house, Jack. Not today. This is going to be a friendly conversation. Mr. Collins wasn't exactly expecting this meeting, but I'm grateful he's here. So let's be on our best behavior. Fair enough?"

Jack smiled. We both nodded.

The president led us from the foyer by the elevator to the Yellow Oval Room. I had seen pictures but had never had the privilege of actually standing in the distinctive room before. It was here that Franklin Delano Roosevelt had famously been relaxing when he was told by aides that the Japanese had bombed Pearl Harbor on December 7, 1941. Most of the chief executives who followed Roosevelt tended to allow their First Ladies to use the parlor for their own meetings, but I had read somewhere not long ago that President Taylor liked to use it for more personal and in-depth conversations with visiting heads of state.

The room was certainly less formal, and thus perhaps less intimidating, than the Oval Office. But it was still more exquisite in real life than in any of the pictures I'd seen. The walls were painted a lovely pale yellow, and the couches and chairs were all upholstered with a fabric that was paler still. The room featured a high ceiling, a marble fireplace on the east wall, and two candelabras, one on each end of the mantel. Two large couches faced each other perpendicular to the fireplace. Below our feet was a thick, rich carpet—pale yellow, of course—with an intricate design of flowers and swirls of red and blue and green and a half-dozen other colors.

But what really caught my eye was the door to the Truman Balcony. Ever the politician, as soon as the president saw me admiring it, he marched right over, opened the door, and invited Jack and me to step outside.

A bit embarrassed that I was acting more like a tourist than a hardened, grizzled foreign correspondent, I nevertheless accepted the invitation. I'd seen this view in movies, of course, but it was quite something to be overlooking the South Lawn of the White House, the Washington Monument in the distance, the Potomac River beyond that. It was a stunningly beautiful sight, surely the most beautiful in Washington. What's more, the gleaming green-and-white Marine One helicopter was idling outside.

"We just got back from meetings at Camp David," Jack noted.

"Discussing what?" I asked, fishing for a story.

"You," the president said.

I couldn't help but chuckle, sure he was kidding.

He was not.

"Look, J. B., we need to talk candidly," the president said.

"What about?" I asked warily.

"Your stories on Jamal Ramzy and ISIS," he replied. "They've made a lot of waves in this city. They've got European leaders on edge. I've gotten two calls from Lavi in Jerusalem. He's getting heat from his cabinet. You've created a firestorm."

Vaughn added, "Everyone's trying to figure out what ISIS is up to, what their next moves are, what their next target is."

"Especially now that you've taken out Abu Khalif's chief rival," I noted, hoping to get some insight into the president's decision to assassinate Zawahiri.

"Everything we say here this evening is off the record," the president said. "Is that understood?"

"That would be a shame," I replied. "People are eager for your thoughts on the strike on Zawahiri. Why not go on the record with me right now?"

The president smiled one of those pitifully fake political smiles. "I'm afraid I can't make any news for you on that, Mr. Collins," he said. "I'll make my thoughts known to the American people at the appropriate time. But this is a very delicate moment. And that's why I've asked you here today. So are we agreed all this is off the record?"

What choice did I have? "Of course, Mr. President."

"I have your word?"

"You do."

"Good, now let's go back inside. You survived Homs and Istanbul. I don't want you catching pneumonia outside the White House."

We went back in. The president sat in an ornate wooden armchair near the fireplace. When Jack retired to one of the couches, I took my place on the other, directly across from him. A steward served us all coffee and then stepped out of the room. Two Secret Service agents took up their posts by the doors, but other than that we were alone, and the president turned his attention to me.

"Look, Mr. Collins, things are very sensitive at the moment because . . . well . . . because the Israelis and Palestinians are about to sign a final, comprehensive peace treaty and create a Palestinian state once and for all."

"Good—my sources are telling me the truth," I said, moving quickly, not wanting to let the president box me in. "That's a story I'll be happy to print."

"You already have this?" the president asked, his face not quite incredulous but trending in that direction.

"There are a few more people to talk to, but yes, I'm getting close to running with it," I replied. It wasn't entirely true, but I rationalized that it wasn't a complete lie, either.

"No. You cannot print that yet," the president stated. "The key to success is absolute secrecy."

"I'm sorry, sir; I can't promise that," I noted calmly.

"You have to," he replied. "We agreed this conversation is off the record."

"And it is," I said. "But that doesn't apply to original reporting I'm already doing."

"It absolutely does," the president insisted. "This is a matter of national security."

"And a matter of enormous public interest," I countered.

"Mr. Collins," Vaughn interjected, "you just gave the president of the United States your word that nothing that was said in this conversation was on the record."

"And I will honor my word," I said, doing my best to stay calm. "But I walked in here with sources already telling me the deal was done and the treaty was about to be announced, and I'm sorry—I'm not obligated to ignore information I had before I walked into this room."

The president and CIA director looked like they'd just been hit with a two-by-four.

"J. B., listen to me. A leak at this moment would be devastating," Vaughn said, clearly looking for a way out of the impasse. "But I'll make you a deal."

He glanced at the president, then looked back at me. "We'll leak the final details of the treaty and the behind-the-scenes story of how it came together once everything is ready. We'll give you an exclusive one-day jump on your competitors. You have my word. But you need to sit on this for the moment. The secretary of state is just crossing the t's and dotting the i's with leaders on both sides and with King Abdullah of Jordan. But we need a little more time. A leak, especially right now, could destroy everything."

"How much time do you need?" I asked.

It was a good offer—an excellent one, actually, especially since I was bluffing. I'd gotten a lead on the treaty story from Yael, and I was fairly certain I could get more out of Ari Shalit in the next few days in exchange for doing him the favor of getting the WMD story out. But I didn't have anything else at the moment, and the president and CIA director were offering me an exquisite gift on a silver platter. Why not take it, especially since the peace process was neither my beat nor even of particular interest to me. I wanted the chemical weapons story. I wanted an interview with Abu

Khalif. And to get either or both, I was going to need to stay focused.

Vaughn again looked at the president. "Two weeks, maybe three, tops," he said at last. "Like I said, the negotiators are ironing out final details. But I think we could see a White House signing ceremony before Christmas."

"That's less than a month," I said.

"Exactly. That's why we have to keep a lid on this thing," the president said. "We are engaged in the most delicate, high-stakes high-wire act in the history of modern diplomacy. My predecessors haven't been able to get it done. There was many a night I didn't think I could get it done either. But we're there. So do we have a deal?"

I looked into the president's eyes and then into Vaughn's. Why was this so easy? Why were they giving me so much, so fast? They wanted something else. I decided I'd pocket one story and brace myself for whatever was coming next. "Yes, sir, Mr. President."

"You won't write any stories on the peace treaty until we give you the go-ahead?"

"You'll give me a true exclusive, including the first journalist's look at the treaty itself, and no one else gets the story before me?"

"Yes," the president said.

"Then yes."

We shook hands, and then the president dropped the hammer. "Now, we need to talk about your other story."

"Which one?"

"I understand you're about to run a story that

al Qaeda has captured a cache of Syrian chemical weapons."

"Well, ISIS—not al Qaeda—but yes," I said.

"That's a problem as well."

"How so?"

"It could trigger a wave of panic right at the moment when we're trying to help Arabs and Jews make some very hard, very painful concessions," Vaughn said.

"I'm asking you not to print it," the president said. "Not yet. Not until after the peace treaty is signed, sealed, and delivered. I'm willing to make a deal on that as well, but I really have to insist you not publish anything before the end of the year."

I was floored. The story was basically finished. In less than forty-eight hours, possibly sooner, I'd have my third confirmation. The story was ready to go, and it was going to be huge.

"Well, gentlemen, I appreciate your concerns, but I'm afraid we're going to move forward."

"And risk blowing up this peace deal?"

"Sir, if this deal is the real thing, surely it will have to be strong enough to survive a newspaper story that doesn't fit your 'peace in our times' narrative," I replied. "And anyway, it's ISIS that's going to try to blow up your peace deal, not me."

"It's not just about public relations," the president said. "The larger problem is that the facts aren't there."

"Actually, yes, they are, sir," I responded. "I have confirmation from high-ranking officials in three different governments, including your own."

"It's a mirage."

"With all due respect, it isn't. I've personally seen satellite photos, drone video, listened to phone intercepts, read intercepted e-mails. Believe me, Mr. President, the story is solid."

"I'm afraid that's where you're wrong," the president said. "Jack?"

I looked into President Taylor's eyes. He didn't look angry. He didn't look frustrated with me. Nor did I feel like he was necessarily trying to spin me. In fact, he genuinely looked like he was trying to help me. But the man was a politician and thus, by practice if not by definition, an actor. He knew how to persuade people, and I'd been "handled" by enough people in Washington over the years to have become even more cynical than I was already naturally inclined to be. I turned to Vaughn and braced myself for the pitch.

"Look, J. B., you can't quote either of us on this, but the intel you've been given is, in fact, solid," the CIA director began.

"Solid?" I asked, wondering if I could possibly have just heard him correctly.

"That's right; it's solid."

"Well, isn't that what I just said?"

"Hold on; just listen to me," Vaughn continued. "What you've seen and heard is accurate. I'm sure of that. That's not the problem."

"What is?"

"It's incomplete."

"Meaning what?" I asked, wishing I had a notepad with me.

"Meaning the president and I have seen a lot more intel than you have, and we're not convinced."

"Why not?"

"Because the data doesn't add up."

"Okay, I'm sorry, but I'm not following you, Jack. Stipulate the facts we're talking about so I know we're on the same page." I was sure Vaughn wouldn't take the bait, but I was certainly willing to go fishing anyway.

Vaughn looked at the president, who, to my shock, nodded his assent.

"When you're making sarin gas, you're combining two different chemical precursors," the CIA director explained. "The first is isopropanol. The second is methylphosphonyl difluoride. You don't mix them together until you're ready to kill people. Why?"

"Because you don't want to take an unnecessary risk."

"Exactly. You don't want the whole thing to blow up in your face. So you store the two different chemicals separately—on the same base, but in different buildings. Okay?"

"Okay."

"Now, we know the ISIS rebels hit the Syrian base near Aleppo. We know that historically the base was a storage site for WMD, among other types of weapons. We know that for many years, both chemicals were stored on the base. But that was years ago. We know the rebels removed several hundred crates on trucks and that they sent those trucks to at least five different locations, maybe more. What we don't know is what exactly was in those crates and on those trucks."

I was surprised but pleased to hear Vaughn

confirm this much. I couldn't quote him, of course. But now I knew with even greater certainty that my story—nearly entirely written and waiting on my hard drive—was accurate.

"You think the rebels were carting away office equipment and linens?" I asked.

"I don't know what they were carting away, and neither do you."

"What about all the phone intercepts after the rebels seized the base?"

"What do they actually say?" Vaughn asked. "One rebel tells his commander his men have captured the 'crown jewels.' Another boasts, 'Allah will be most praised.' A third e-mails Jamal Ramzy and says, 'Zionists will suffer.'"

"Right. So why do you think they're so happy?"

"Again, we can't know for sure. The intercepts are intriguing, but they're not proof," Vaughn continued. "And remember, while it's theoretically possible that the Assad regime hid a cache of chemical weapons at that base, the Syrians say they haven't had any WMD in more than a decade. The U.N. inspectors went there. They searched the place, and they certified that there were no chemical weapons. The Syrians claim they gave up all of their stockpiles to the U.N. to be removed from the country and destroyed, and the U.N. weapons inspectors say they feel reasonably confident that the Syrians did exactly that."

"You're going to rest your case on 'reasonably confident'?" I asked.

"You're going to rest *your* case on nothing

but circumstantial evidence that's weak at best?" Vaughn countered.

"Look," I said, "the agency is gun-shy after the blown call in Iraq. I get it. But here you have jihadists seizing a known WMD base in Syria and boasting they have the 'crown jewels' and saying they are going to annihilate the Jews, and you want the *New York Times* to back off the story?"

"You're not listening to me, J. B.," Vaughn protested. "I'm telling you the case is circumstantial at best. Might ISIS have chemical WMD? Yes. I grant you that. And it scares the daylights out of the president and me. Believe me. We can't sleep at night. We're doing everything we can to confirm this story, but so far all we have are a bunch of dots. In my position, I can't connect them based on gut instinct. I have to have ironclad proof. I can't tell the president of the United States that my circumstantial evidence is a slam dunk. And I don't want the American people—or the Israelis and Palestinians—to live in sudden fear that we, or they, are about to get hit by chemical weapons of mass destruction unless I know that for certain. I don't think that's right. I don't think that's moral. And deep down, I don't think you do either. Am I wrong?"

28

* * *

I checked my grandfather's pocket watch again.

The meeting at the White House was finally over. But it was now 7:43 p.m. The former CIA director had already been waiting for thirteen minutes, and I was mortified.

Even in retirement, Robert Khachigian was an important and powerful man. He certainly had a far tighter schedule than mine. He was leaving the country in just a few hours. What's more, he had been a friend of my family's for years, and I had given him my word I would not be late. Twice I had called his mobile phone from the car to tell him what was happening, but he hadn't picked up either time. Now my guilt was spiking along with my heart rate.

A cold late-November drizzle had descended upon Washington. I had neither a warm coat nor an umbrella. I was reminded of meeting Yael in Istanbul just a few nights before, and the very thought made me feel even worse. I wanted to see her again. But how?

The black armored Chevy Suburban I was

riding in pulled to a stop. Four FBI agents newly assigned to me jumped out first, scanned the area, and then gave me the green light. I grabbed my briefcase and dashed into Union Station, the mammoth train depot located just a few blocks from the Capitol building. I raced to the Center Café, a restaurant appropriately positioned in the bull's-eye of the gargantuan Main Hall, and prayed Khachigian was still there.

"Yes, he's waiting for you upstairs," the maître d' said. "Right this way, Mr. Collins."

Every table on the ground level was taken, and there was a line of tourists waiting to be seated as we headed upstairs. One of the agents assigned to me took up a position at the base of the winding staircase. The other three followed me to the second level.

Khachigian was sitting alone at a table for two on the far side of the restaurant. He did not look happy, though as a rule he was a fairly serious guy anyway. As I greeted him, I apologized profusely for my tardiness, but he waved it all off and told me to have a seat.

"You're mad at me," I said.

"No," he demurred.

"You look mad," I insisted.

"I'm not mad, but we don't have much time," he said. "We have a real nightmare developing. But how are you?"

A consummate professional, but always the gentleman.

The graying, bespectacled man before me was the elder statesman of the Washington intelligence community, and he was dressed to the nines. He wore a dark-blue suit, a light-blue monogrammed dress shirt with gold cuff links, suspenders, and a snappy lavender bow tie, which seemed to me a relic of an earlier age. At his feet stood a small suitcase. Clearly he was heading to the airport straight from this meeting.

"I've been better," I said, not sure how much detail he wanted.

"Secret Service?" he asked, referring to the two agents who were now sitting at a table directly behind him and the third standing by the top of the stairs.

"FBI," I replied. "To be honest, I'm not exactly sure if they're protecting me or keeping tabs on me."

"Both," he said without hesitation. "Pain?"

"Sorry?"

"Are you in pain?"

"Oh, well, a little."

"Percocet?"

"A lot."

"Be careful."

"I will."

"I mean it."

"I got it."

"Addictive personality and all."

"Yeah, thanks. Really, I'm fine."

Khachigian and my family went way back, and he'd always seemed to take a liking to me. Almost like a surrogate grandfather, he'd kept an eye on me. In his youth he was a nonofficial cover operative for the Central Intelligence Agency. He was based primarily in Eastern Europe and traveled in and out of the Soviet Union during the Cold War. When he retired from the intelligence business, he returned to Maine, the state where he had been born and raised. He and his wife, Mary, were from Bangor, a bit to the northwest of us in Bar Harbor. They had known my grandparents and later my parents and had become fairly close family friends. After practicing law for a few years, Khachigian ran for office and won the seat serving the Second Congressional District. Later he went on to win a Senate seat and wound up chairman of the Senate Select Committee on Intelligence. Eventually, he was appointed to the top spot at the CIA and served for almost three years before retiring for real.

Over the years, my grandparents—and my mom—contributed to his various political campaigns. In college, I did an internship in his Senate office. During election cycles, my mom often volunteered to put up signs and answer phones and go door to door leafleting for him. She and Mary Khachigian became quite close. They were pen pals and loved to host an annual Christmas tea together for friends and political supporters—that is, until Mary passed away of ovarian cancer three years ago.

Interestingly enough, Robert—called Bob by his friends but always "Mr. Khachigian" by me— had never been a source of mine for all those years. He probably would have agreed if I had asked, but I never had. There was no question he was a treasure trove. He obviously had a great deal of insider details from his various government positions, and I certainly would have benefited from access to all that behind-the-scenes information, especially in the early years when I was building my career. But it never seemed right. I never wanted to cross the line, never wanted to make him think I would trade on a personal relationship. I actually felt uncomfortable even when my mother asked Mary to get me the internship way back when.

I'll never forget the day Khachigian called me out of the blue and asked me to meet him in London, where he was giving a lecture the next evening. At the time I was still a young reporter, and the timing was hardly ideal, and he refused to give me even a hint as to what he was thinking or why he wanted me to come. Nevertheless, I found myself so intrigued that I immediately booked the flight.

Upon my arrival, Khachigian picked me up at Heathrow, alone, and drove me to the Dorchester, one of the swankiest hotels in London. There we had a private, intimate dinner with the up-and-coming leader of the Israeli opposition at the time, a man by the name of Daniel Lavi.

"James, this man is going to be the prime minister of Israel soon," Khachigian told me the moment Lavi and I shook hands. "The polls don't show it. Most analysts don't believe it. But I'm telling you right now it's going to happen. And Daniel here specifically asked me to arrange a meeting with you. He's an admirer of your work. Has read it all. Says you're one of the most trustworthy reporters in the biz. I agree. So I decided to introduce you before Daniel's life gets much busier."

The following morning, Khachigian and I drove to the Ritz in the Piccadilly section of London. There he led me up to the Prince of Wales suite (which I later learned went for a jaw-dropping 4,500 pounds per night) and introduced me to an older gentleman who turned out to be Prince Marwan Talal. At the age of seventy-eight, he was an uncle of Jordan's King Abdullah II and a trusted senior advisor to His Majesty. Khachigian seemed unusually pleased by bringing the two of us together.

"James, His Royal Highness is a dear friend and a most faithful, stalwart ally in the fight against the extremists in the epicenter," he told me as the three of us talked over brunch. "He is not a public man. He lives in the shadows, and he prefers it that way. Few people outside His Majesty's inner circle even know his name. But he knows theirs. He knows where all the bodies are buried. And I mean that literally. He has seen all there is in the region—the good, the bad, and the ugly. Confidentially, I will tell you that Prince Marwan is the king's consigliere when it comes to the peace process. He was an advisor to the late King Hussein, God rest his soul, and upon taking the throne, King Abdullah began leaning on this man—his uncle—for counsel. He's a devout Muslim. He is worried for the future of his country and region. And whenever I find myself growing pessimistic about the prospects for peace in the Middle East, I sit with Marwan and drink coffee and eat hummus and become hopeful once again. I don't know why, but I have a feeling that one day—perhaps not too long from now—you two will find it useful to know each other. This is why I wanted to bring you both together now, before the maelstrom comes."

Khachigian's instincts had been remarkable. Daniel Lavi was now not only the head of Israel's Labor Party; he was also the Jewish State's prime minister. He had recently toppled the right-wing government of his predecessor and cobbled together a center-left coalition most political analysts had believed to be unlikely at best just a few short years earlier.

And now, if my sources were to be believed, Lavi was on the phone almost every day with the prince. Together they were trying to fashion a peace deal that the world said was impossible. I too had thought it impossible. But finally, it seemed, it might actually be coming to pass—unless Abu Khalif and Jamal Ramzy had their way.

I trusted this man implicitly. So what was so important that Khachigian had to tell me tonight or tell the *Post* if I didn't show up in time?

29

* ★ *

"Omar?" Khachigian asked after a long silence.

Every muscle in me tensed. This wasn't a topic I could afford to discuss just then. Too much else was happening. The clock was ticking—for both of us—and I knew if I let myself dwell on the bombing, I wasn't going to make it through the rest of the day. But I didn't want to be rude. Nor did I want to dishonor my friend's memory by brushing off the question or seeming like I didn't care. I did, and it was the very thought of avenging Omar's death somehow that was keeping me going.

"God rest his soul," I managed, though even as the words came out of my mouth, I wasn't sure why I'd put it quite that way. It sounded more like something my mother would say, or more precisely, my brother.

"You two were close?"

"Yeah," I said, though inside I was pleading with him to change the subject. He had to know me better than this.

Then it was quiet again. But instead of spilling

his secrets, the man opened his menu and studied it carefully. I wasn't sure I could wait any longer. He had a plane to catch. I had an editor to meet. Why was he taking so long?

"Can't decide," he finally mumbled.

"On what?" I asked.

"Ordering."

"Really?"

"Yes."

"Get the salmon."

"What?"

"The salmon—it's excellent."

"You're sure?" he asked, the skepticism in his voice palpable.

"Trust me," I said. "It's delicious. You'll love it."

"Cedar plank roasted salmon?" he asked, reading off the menu.

"Right, with the steamed snow peas."

"Really?"

"Positive—I've had it before."

And then it was quiet again.

A waiter filled our glasses with water. My old friend and mentor wasn't talking. I didn't want to think about Omar. I didn't want to think about salmon. I had no appetite. So I just twiddled my thumbs and tried to stay patient. The last thing I needed to do was pressure this man. He would tell me whatever he had to say when he was good and ready.

Finally a waitress came to take our order. Khachigian handed his menu to her, leaned back, and folded his hands. "Lobster ravioli," he said.

I just looked at him and shook my head. Some

things never changed. "Salmon," I told the woman as I handed over my menu.

"So . . . ," he began.

"So," I replied.

Finally this was it. But I was wrong.

"How's Laura?" he asked quietly.

He had to be kidding.

"Listen, I know you're rushed for time," I said. "So maybe the best thing is—"

But Khachigian cut me off midsentence. "How . . . is . . . Laura?"

I just stared at him.

"It's not a trick question," he said calmly, though I wasn't sure I believed him.

"Why would you even ask?"

"Simple," he replied. "I'd like to know."

"Well, I have no idea."

"You haven't talked to her?"

"No."

"Haven't written?"

"Of course not."

"Has she written to you?"

"No."

He paused. He looked at me like he knew something.

"Has . . . she . . . written to you?"

It dawned on me that Khachigian was not only a lawyer by training but also a spook. This wasn't a conversation. It was a deposition, an interrogation, and he already knew the answers.

"I got an e-mail from her the other day."

"When?"

"Sometime after the explosion, I guess."

"You guess?"

"I didn't read it."

"Why not?"

"I deleted it."

"Why?"

"I don't know."

"Of course you do."

"I really don't know, sir."

"Come on, James."

"Look, I don't want to hear from her, okay? I want nothing to do with her. She's a horrible, spiteful, vindictive person, and—with all due respect—I wish you'd never introduced the two of us."

Khachigian leaned forward. "You don't mean that," he said.

"Actually, sir, I do."

"You were in love."

"That was a long time ago."

"Not that long."

"What do you want from me?"

He sighed. "Nothing," he said at last.

There was a long pause. I had nothing to say, and he seemed to be trying to formulate the right words.

"The truth is I haven't seen my niece much since your divorce was finalized," he said at last. "We talk from time to time by phone. We e-mail occasionally. But I want to tell you something I never told you before."

I sat there and waited, my stomach in knots.

"After she left you, after she moved in with . . . Well, anyway, after it all happened, I went to see her on the Upper East Side. I took her out to dinner—just the two of us—and I asked her what went wrong. You two seemed so happy. And she . . ."

The words just trailed away.

"What?" I asked.

"I asked her about that summer when you both interned in my office. If there were still any embers of the love that caught fire that summer."

"And?"

"She said yes."

"I'm not sure I can put into words how much I don't want to have this conversation."

"Well, I thought you should know—she's not with that guy anymore, and she doesn't hate you. I think she feels quite guilty."

"Good."

"And she's moving back to Maine to start her own practice. That's all I wanted to say. Now, tell me about the president."

"You knew I met with him?"

"Of course I knew."

"How?"

"I'm still reasonably well connected in this town, James."

"Did you know Jack was there?"

He nodded.

"So you knew we were talking about the status of the peace process?"

"The peace process is a done deal," Khachigian replied.

"I'd been hearing rumors, but that meeting

confirmed it. Until the last few days, I'd have thought the whole process was going nowhere."

"It's not going nowhere. That's why ISIS is getting ready to strike."

"How much do you know?"

"A lot."

"How much can you tell me?"

"Not much. And you can't print any of this. Not yet. But soon."

"I understand," I replied. "Just cut to the chase."

"I have a good friend, still at the Agency. He left yesterday to visit Jerusalem to do advance for a possible presidential visit."

"Jack said he expected a signing event at the White House just before Christmas."

"I have no doubt," Khachigian said. "But that doesn't preclude a presidential visit to the region. Based on what I'm hearing from old friends here and over there, the White House is planning a surprise trip to Jerusalem in the next week or so. Big photo op. Great optics. Huge international headlines. Signing a 'declaration of principles' or something like that. Then they'll come back and do a big signing ceremony of the final peace treaty in late December, or better yet, in early January as a lead-in to the State of the Union."

"Have you talked to Danny?" I asked, referring to the Israeli premier.

"Among others."

"And he's confirming this?"

"You can't write this," Khachigian said. "That's not why I'm telling you."

"Don't worry; I've got a deal with the president

on an exclusive when they're ready. But as you just said, this is tied into why ISIS is preparing a strike."

"Exactly."

"Which is why you wanted to talk so urgently," I said. "What do you have?"

Khachigian looked around to make sure no one was listening in on our conversation.

"ISIS has loaded sarin nerve agents into artillery shells and missile warheads," he whispered. "My sources say they've moved their men and launchers into position. All they're waiting for now is a final authorization from Abu Khalif."

30

★ ★ ★

"How soon?" I asked.

"That I don't know. But I suspect it's very soon, possibly before this peace deal gets done. That's why you have to finish this story and get it out there fast."

"Jack Vaughn says ISIS doesn't have WMD."

"He told you that?"

"Yes."

"He said those exact words, that ISIS categorically does not have chemical weapons?"

"Well, no," I clarified. "He said it couldn't be confirmed what was in those crates the rebels were taking out of the Aleppo base."

"Jack's wrong."

"You're certain?"

"I am," he replied. "But it doesn't matter what I think. I'm not the director of Central Intelligence. Not anymore. I don't have the ear of this president. And I'm not the *New York Times*. I don't have the ear of the public. But you do. So it's you who has to be sure."

"But how can I be sure?" I asked. "Sure enough to go public with the story?"

"Isn't Ari Shalit going to help you?"

"Maybe. But maybe that's not enough."

"Then talk to the prime minister. Talk to Danny. Ask him to show you what the Mossad has."

"I'm already authorized to see all they have," I said, growing anxious. "Who do you think was with Omar and me in Istanbul? It was a woman from the Mossad. She invited me to Tel Aviv to see what they have. But Jack says that while what I've seen so far is solid, it's also circumstantial. He says it's not proof. He says I need more or I risk panicking a whole lot of people and possibly blowing up the peace process."

"It's spin," Khachigian said. "The president doesn't want you to rain on his signing ceremony."

"I'm sure he doesn't, but that doesn't mean they're wrong. The case *is* circumstantial. Don't get me wrong—it's still a hot story. I can fly to Tel Aviv tonight. I can see what they've got tomorrow afternoon. I can go back to my hotel room and finish my story tomorrow night, and the whole world will read it on Tuesday morning. But it's incomplete. I don't have the whole story. Just because the ISIS rebels captured that base and carted away a bunch of boxes, that doesn't prove they have WMD."

"Then just say that in the story," Khachigian insisted. "You're not writing a book. You're not making a documentary film. You're writing a newspaper story. You have a piece of the puzzle that no one else has. It's important. It's relevant. It's not complete—I grant you that. But what you have *is* news. ISIS rebels under Jamal Ramzy's authority captured a known Syrian chemical-weapons base. They carted away hundreds of crates. They claim to have captured the 'crown jewels' of the Syrian regime. And they're threatening not just to attack but to *annihilate* the United States and Israel with a Third Intifada. Some senior intelligence experts inside the U.S. and two foreign governments believe ISIS now has sarin gas. Ramzy denies it. Senior White House officials downplay the threat. But if ISIS really does now have the very weapons Osama bin Laden only dreamed of obtaining, we are rapidly approaching the most dangerous moment in the history of the War on Terror. There. I just wrote the story for you. That's news, my friend. Game changing. So get it out there, and then go get more."

"More?"

"Go find the source."

"You mean Abu Khalif."

"Absolutely," Khachigian said, leaning toward me. "He's the big story."

"What if Khalif was behind the Istanbul bombing?"

"He wasn't. That was al Qaeda."

"How can you be so sure?"

"I can't," Khachigian admitted. "I'm guessing. But I don't think ISIS is finished with you yet. You're useful to them."

"So you want me to go track him down, even though ISIS is beheading people, crucifying people, blowing them to kingdom come?"

"Look, James, it's a very simple equation," Khachigan said, looking me straight in the eye. "Abu Khalif wants the world to know that ISIS— not al Qaeda—is the most dangerous force on the planet. Now that Zawahiri is dead, he may very well be right. But make no mistake: ISIS doesn't want the world to know they have chemical weapons. Not yet. They want the element of surprise. That's what they have at the moment, and they're going to do everything they can to keep it. That's why you have to get this story out there. You don't work for the president. You don't work for Jack Vaughn or any of the rest of them. You work for the American people. And the American people— not to mention the Israelis, the Palestinians, the Europeans, and the whole world—they all have the right to know just how dangerous this moment is. They have a right to know the president is pushing, pushing, pushing for this deal that is supposed to bring peace but might actually lead to the most catastrophic chemical weapons attack in human history. What people do with that information, what governments do, that's not your business. Your business, like mine, is obtaining intelligence and passing it on to your boss. My boss was the president. Your boss is your readers. Solid, actionable intelligence is worthless unless the people who need it actually have it, know it, and can make decisions based on it. You follow?"

"I do," I said, then paused as the waitress brought out our meals and set them before us. When she had departed again, I said, "But you're not just asking me to publish a story. You're asking me to publish a story Abu Khalif doesn't want out there—a story Jamal Ramzy specifically said he would personally kill me if I published—and then go to Iraq and meet with these guys."

"You think I'm wrong?" Khachigian asked.

"I think you're crazy."

"Maybe, but am I wrong?" Khachigian pressed.

"I don't know."

"Yes, you do. I told you weeks ago the real story wasn't Ramzy. It's Abu Khalif. You agreed. Why?"

"You made a persuasive case—Ramzy is the muscle; Khalif is the brains."

"And what did Sun Tzu say?"

"I know, I know," I said.

"So say it."

Back when Khachigian was the chairman of the Senate intelligence committee, he used to make all of his staff interns learn a few lines from *The Art of War*. He'd made me memorize them too.

"'The reason the enlightened prince and the wise general conquer the enemy whenever they move—and their achievements surpass those of ordinary men—is foreknowledge.'"

"Keep going," he prompted.

Reluctantly I continued. "'What is called fore-knowledge cannot be elicited from spirits, nor by analogy from past events, nor from calculation. It must be obtained from men with knowledge of the enemy situation.'"

"Exactly," Khachigian said. "The only way to really know for sure what ISIS has and what they're going to do with it is to go talk to their leader. That means talking to Abu Khalif."

"Even if he kills me."

"He won't kill you."

"Yeah, well, with all due respect, isn't that easy for you to say?"

"Yeah, well, with all due respect, don't think of yourself more highly than you ought."

"What's that supposed to mean?"

"It means every single one us—this tiny group of us who are trying to get this information out to the American people—we're all in danger. You have friends who have already died because of this story. You of all people should know how very high the stakes are. But, James, many, many more Americans—and Israelis, too—are going to die very soon if Abu Khalif has his way. He needs to be stopped. And the only way he's going to be stopped is if he is exposed. Vaughn isn't going to do it. The president isn't going to do it. The Israelis want to be able to react to the story, not put it out there themselves. So that leaves you . . . or the *Post*. Which is it going to be?"

31

★ ★ ★

Our food was sitting in front of us getting cold.

But I couldn't eat. I just sat there and said nothing. There was no question I wanted to find Abu Khalif and expose him. I'd even been actively pursuing leads as to his whereabouts. I just didn't want to die.

For most of my life—and certainly for most of my career—I'd never really thought much about dying. There was something thrilling, even addictive, about going into dangerous places as a foreign correspondent. I'd always loved taking risks, living on the edge, cheating death, and the exhilaration of coming home alive. But now something was different. Something was changing. *I* was changing. For the first time in my life, I found myself thinking about what was on the other side, about where I was going when I breathed my last, and whether I was really ready for it.

And I knew I wasn't.

I was haunted by the images of Abdel's and Omar's last moments. I was haunted by that soldier dying on the street in Homs, the one who had begged me for help, desperately clinging to life. I couldn't shake the terrified look I had seen in his eyes as the life drained out of him. The sound of his voice was tattooed in my brain.

"James?"

I realized Khachigian was trying to get my attention. I had completely zoned out. "Sorry."

"You okay?" he asked.

"I will be."

"It's okay, son. I know what you're going through. Believe me, I do," Khachigian said, the tone of his voice changing ever so slightly. "You have to do what you think is right. But may I make a suggestion?"

"Uh, yeah, sure," I stammered. "Go right ahead."

"Get on a plane to Israel tonight," he said quietly, almost whispering. "Meet with the Mossad tomorrow. Get that story finished. Get it out there. Make a big international splash with it. And then make a decision about Abu Khalif. But let me suggest that after the *Times* publishes your story on the chemical weapons, there'll be no more reason for Khalif to kill you."

"Why not?"

"Because the reason Jamal Ramzy threatened you was to keep the story from coming out. Once it's out, then the damage is done. Once it's out, I think Khalif would want to talk to you specifically to spin the story, not to deny it. What he wants most is the element of surprise, clearly. But he'll settle for the mystique of being the world's most dangerous terrorist in possession of the world's most dangerous weapons. If anything, publishing that story will be your 'get out of jail free' card."

"That's your theory?" I asked.

"That's my theory," he replied.

I shrugged. Maybe the man was right. I wasn't sure I was ready to find out.

"Aren't you forgetting one thing?" I asked after a few moments.

"What?"

"How exactly am I supposed to hunt down Abu Khalif with five FBI agents connected to my hip?"

"I thought you only had four."

"One is sitting out front in the driver's seat of an armored Chevy Suburban."

Khachigian pulled an envelope out of the breast pocket of his finely tailored suit. He glanced around the restaurant and discreetly slid it across the table.

"What's this?" I asked.

"Don't open it," he said.

"Why not?"

"Just put it in your pocket."

"What is it?"

"Just put it away now," he insisted.

I picked up the envelope and slipped it into my pocket.

"It's a new identity for you," he whispered.

"What?" I asked, completely confused.

"New name," he continued. "New passport. New driver's license. Two new credit cards. And a ticket to Tel Aviv tonight in this new name, not yours."

"Why?" I asked, intrigued.

"Because you're right," he said. "You're going to need to give your new friends from the bureau the slip."

Then he pulled out his smartphone and sent a text. "There."

"There what?" I asked.

"I just told my assistant to book you—the real you—on a series of flights tonight from BWI to Bar Harbor, via Boston and Portland," Khachigian said. "That should provide you with some cover. She's been waiting for my authorization. I just gave it. Now, in a few minutes, I'm going to order dessert. When I do, I want you to go to the restroom—the one over by the Amtrak waiting area near gate A. You know it?"

"Sure."

"Good. Several of your security team, maybe all of them, will follow you. Ask them to check the restroom and make sure it's secure. They will. Then ask them for a moment of privacy and go into the last stall along the far wall. They will step outside and give you some space. That's your moment."

"Why?"

"Because there's a ceiling panel there. Stand on the toilet seat, pop out the panel, pull yourself up, and replace the panel below you."

"You're kidding, right?" I asked.

But Khachigian kept talking, low and fast. "You'll find yourself in an air-conditioning shaft. Go to your left. In about twenty yards, you'll find an opening. Drop down. You'll be in a narrow tunnel that eventually leads to another door. Go through that and you'll end up in an Amtrak storage facility. At this time of night, there won't be anyone there. Exit on the far side, and you'll be on First Street, across from the National Postal Museum. Can you picture that?"

"Yes," I said, a bit mesmerized by the tradecraft and trying to remember every detail.

"It's getting a bit late, but there should still be plenty of cabs. Grab one and head straight for Dulles. By the time the FBI boys figure out you're gone and start to hunt for you, you'll be well on your way. They'll quickly pick up on the reservations from Baltimore back to Maine. Eventually they'll realize it's a ruse, but that should buy you enough time to be on your way to Tel Aviv. And since you'll be using an alias they're completely unaware of, you should make it to Israel with no problems. That ought to give you plenty of time to do your story and make a decision whether to head to Iraq or not."

"You've thought of everything," I said.

"This is what I do," he said. "Well, what I used to do."

I was impressed.

"There's just one thing," he added.

"What's that?"

"You need to turn off your phone right now and remove the battery."

"Okay."

"Don't turn it on for any reason until after you file your story from Tel Aviv."

"Or they'll find me?"

"Exactly."

Then he took a smartphone out of the pocket of his trousers, slid it across the table, and told me to quickly slip it into my pocket.

"What's this for?" I asked, putting it in my pocket.

"You're going to need a phone."

"But they'll know it's yours."

"No, it's totally new. It's not connected to me. It's not even connected to your alias. But it does have all your contact information on it."

"How . . . ?"

"Don't ask," he said. "Use it sparingly, only for emergencies. And whatever you do, don't call your mother."

I nodded, though somewhat reluctantly. This was not a plan I felt comfortable with. I wasn't even sure it was going to work. Still, I was grateful for all the thought and planning he had put into this, and I certainly didn't have a better idea. It wasn't clear to me at that moment that the men from the bureau would prevent me from flying to Tel Aviv that evening if I just decided to head to Dulles and try to book a ticket. But they might. The president didn't want the story out there. Neither did Vaughn. Who knew what excuse they might come up with to keep me in the country. It was not a risk I was willing to take.

Khachigian began to eat his lobster ravioli. I, on the other hand, had no appetite whatsoever.

"Listen," I said, gathering my thoughts, "you said earlier that your sources are telling you that ISIS has mixed the precursors, that they've loaded sarin nerve agents into artillery shells and missile warheads, that they've moved their men into position, and all they are waiting for now is authorization. Right?"

Khachigian nodded as he washed down his pasta with a sip of water.

"So where do your sources say ISIS is going to strike?" I asked. "Here in D.C.? New York? Tel Aviv? Where, and how soon?"

That's when the first gunshot rang out.

32

★ ★ ★

More gunfire came in rapid succession.

It sounded like it was coming from below us, but with the explosions echoing throughout the main hall of Union Station, I couldn't be certain. People began screaming and running in all directions. Under different circumstances, I might have assumed a random shooting spree was under way. But I knew instantly someone was coming for me, and for a moment I was paralyzed with fear.

The first line of defense was the FBI agent standing post at the bottom of the stairs. Had he been hit? Was he returning fire? The agents at the top of the stairs and the table next to us had already drawn their weapons and were preparing for the possibility of a gunman—or several—charging up those stairs. But as I watched, each of them—one by one—was shot in the back before any of them realized what was happening. Someone was now firing from a position above us.

Khachigian reacted instantly. *"Get down, get down!"* he shouted, reaching across the table and trying to pull me to the floor.

But it was too late. Just then, Khachigian was hit directly in the forehead, right in front of me. His whole upper body snapped backward. The back of his head exploded. It all seemed to happen in slow motion. And yet, somehow, rather than remain frozen in horror, my brain and nervous system reacted to his last words. I immediately dove to the floor, knocking over chairs and crashing into other patrons who were doing the same thing, all of us scrambling for cover.

There had to be at least two shooters, I concluded—one on the main level, creating a distraction, and a sniper firing from the floor above me.

Crack, crack, crack.

Each shot echoed through the hall. I could hear wineglasses and china shattering all around me. People were being hit. They were writhing on the floor, covered in blood, screaming in pain, but there was nothing I could do to help them. Not yet. Not now. Not while I was so exposed.

The sniper, I realized, had to be in one of the arched alcoves ringing the upper level. I desperately scrambled past several tables, trying to get behind the bar, which I hoped might keep me safe. But then I saw one of the agents, a pool of blood all around him. To my astonishment he was still alive, though he wouldn't be for long. His face was a ghostly white, but there was still fire in his eyes.

"Get down!" he yelled, then aimed his government-issued sidearm at one of the alcoves over my right shoulder and unloaded an entire magazine.

My instinct was to flatten myself to the ground

and cover my head, but I was still too exposed. The only chance I had to make it through this was to use this agent's covering fire to get to a safer position. So as he pulled the trigger again and again, I climbed over broken glass and bleeding bodies to one of the other agents lying motionless next to the bar. As I reached him, I heard more gunfire erupt from the alcove behind me. A split second later, the agent I had just left was dead. But I kept moving.

Lunging forward, I grabbed the Glock handgun lying beside the nearest agent and quickly found his spare clip. Then I rolled behind the bar just as the shooter in the alcove turned his fire on me. I could hear bullets whizzing over my head. I could hear more bottles exploding and the wood counters being shredded. I was pinned down, and I was terrified. I knew full well the FBI agents and tourists sprawled all around me were not the targets. Khachigian had been, and so was I. This was not another mass shooting event like the ones Americans were becoming all too used to in schools and movie theaters and churches all across the country. It might seem that way. It might even get reported that way at first. But this wasn't random. The shooters weren't going to turn out to be a few drugged-out high school kids overly influenced by violent video games. This was terrorism. This was a professional hit. This was al Qaeda—or more likely ISIS—and Khachigian was right; they weren't going to stop until anyone trying to break the story about the chemical weapons was dead.

Pressing myself as far under the counter as I

could, out of the line of sight of the shooter in the alcove, I aimed the gun at the end of the bar, fearing that the second shooter—if there really was a second shooter—would be coming around the corner at any moment. In all the chaos and confusion, I couldn't be sure exactly what was happening. Nor did I see any way out. If there were multiple assailants, what exactly was I supposed to do? Even if I could take out one of them, how could I stop the rest of them from sending me to the afterlife?

In that moment, I suddenly thought of my brother. Of the two of us, it was Matt who had become religious. It was Matt who had married the daughter of an Anglican priest and then become a seminary professor. Though I'd ridiculed and mocked him for it all through high school and college, it was he who was always talking about the Bible and urging me to "get right with God." What if he was right and I was wrong? What if he was going to heaven and I was about to go to hell?

I felt my fear shift to rage. I wasn't ready to die. But if I did, it wouldn't be cowering under a counter. I determined I would fight back. I was not going to surrender to these bloodthirsty barbarians. I was going to do everything in my power to expose them to the world.

A surge of adrenaline shot through my body. All my senses seemed to go to a higher level of alertness. I began to move, crawling over the lifeless body of the bartender until I came around the corner and saw an opening to the stairs.

This was the only way out. I had no other choice. The shooter behind me knew it, and he had the advantage. But I knew I could not wait. If I didn't go now, I might never get out. Above all the screaming and cacophony down below, I could hear sirens coming from all directions. Within moments, the place was going to be swarming with D.C. Metro police, SWAT teams, and the FBI. They would find the shooters. They would kill them, and then they'd lock the place down. I'd be a witness to yet another crime scene. They'd never let me out of the country.

I checked the pistol to make sure it was ready to fire. It was. I waited for the shooter above me to fire more rounds. When he paused to reload, I popped my head up, aimed for the alcove, and fired off three rounds. Then I jumped to my feet and ran for the stairwell.

As I did, though, I heard more gunfire erupt from down below. I saw a policewoman drop to the floor, blood spraying from her neck. I'd been right. There *were* two shooters. One was firing from above. The second was on the main level, and he was firing at police now arriving on the scene. It was a suicide mission. Both shooters would be dead within minutes. They certainly weren't going to outlast all the layers of police on Capitol Hill. But obviously they knew that, and obviously they didn't care.

My heart was pounding. My adrenaline was surging. I was going on instinct, and my instinct was to move. I raced down the curved stairway— my white knuckles gripping the pistol in front of me for dear life—even as both shooters kept firing on everyone in their path.

As I neared the bottom, I was surprised to see that the first shooter was a woman. She was dressed in dark-blue sportswear as if she'd just come from a gym. She was wearing a black ski mask, holding an AK-47, and spraying anyone and everyone she could. At the moment, her back was to me. But as she started to turn, I pulled the trigger. Again and again I fired. Though several shots went wild, I hit her once in the shoulder and once in the neck. She went sprawling across the blood-spattered marble floor. Then I aimed up to the alcove, emptied the rest of the magazine, and began to sprint.

I couldn't tell for sure if I had killed the first shooter, but I thought I had. I couldn't allow myself to think about it now. I'd never killed anyone before, but for now I just had to keep going.

I had no illusions that I had taken out the upstairs shooter, but I figured I'd at least bought a few precious seconds of cover, and I wasted none of them. I ran across the main terminal and deeper into the station, past the Amtrak ticket counter, past shops and boutiques, and headed for the men's room in the back by gate A. I was following Khachigian's plan. I would use the utility door and the escape tunnel, just as he'd told me to. But when I got there, I found the door barricaded shut by people huddled inside, desperate to protect themselves. I pounded and yelled and begged for them to let me in, but all I got was an earful of curses in return.

I froze with panic. I hadn't anticipated this, and I had no idea what to do next. I couldn't just stand there, vulnerable and exposed. No one was left in this section. It was completely deserted. But it wouldn't take long. Someone would see me. Someone would find me, either the second shooter or someone in law enforcement, and I didn't dare be caught by either.

I glanced to my right and saw glass doors. Beyond them were row upon row of railroad tracks. There were no trains coming or going at the moment—it was clear this was my only way out. Hopping over a barricade, I tried to burst through the doors, but they were locked. I moved right and tried to exit through gates B and C, but they were locked as well. Perhaps they had been automatically locked once the shooting started. I had no idea. But I had a pistol in my hands and didn't think twice. Backing up, I ejected the empty magazine and loaded the spare. Then I fired away until the glass shattered and I could crawl through. Ditching the pistol in a nearby trash can, I sprinted down the tracks. I ran as fast as I could until the sounds of the sirens began to fade. Only then did I dare leave the tracks.

As I climbed up an embankment, I spotted a gas station. I ran to it, found the men's room, and locked myself inside for a few minutes to wash up and catch my breath.

I could still hear sirens screaming toward Union Station. I knew I had to keep moving. I slipped out of the men's room and jogged several more blocks to the north. There I found a cab. I thrust a wad of cash in the driver's face. Fifteen minutes later, I was back at my apartment.

I took a quick shower, changed clothes, packed a bag, and drove my own car to Dulles airport. I was going to Tel Aviv and then on to Iraq. I was going to finish this story. I'd come this far. I couldn't stop now.

TOP SECRET

PART
FIVE

33

★ ★ ★

TEL AVIV, ISRAEL

I landed at Ben Gurion International Airport just after 4 p.m. local time.

Fortunately, I'd fallen sound asleep even before taking off from Washington. I'd woken up only on hearing the pilot say we were on final approach into Tel Aviv. But I hardly felt rested, and I was starving. I'd missed both meals and the snacks.

Then again, I'd missed the chance to buy alcohol too.

Low blood sugar was not helping me. The challenges ahead were daunting. I was about to go through Israeli passport control using a fake passport. For all I knew, I would then be arrested for traveling with false papers. I'd never done this before. I wasn't a trained CIA operative. I had no idea whether I could bluff my way through Israeli security. Even if I could, I still had to get myself to Mossad headquarters, where I had no idea if Ari Shalit would receive me. But I didn't dare contact him yet, lest the FBI pick up my trail.

And these were just my immediate problems. The next set—getting to Iraq and tracking down Abu Khalif—was more daunting by far. Yet I didn't feel scared. At the moment, I just felt numb.

The lines to go through passport control were crazy long. Four international flights had arrived within minutes of each other, and the arrival hall was mobbed. The good news was that the Israeli border control officials were in a hurry to get people processed and through. When it was my turn, I handed over my fake passport and tried to act natural. I waited for the questions, but they didn't come. I waited to be pulled aside, but it didn't happen. Moments later, I was through without a problem. But I was hardly relieved. I was still battling shock.

I headed out into the chilly winter rains to grab a cab when someone suddenly came up behind me. I turned, and to my astonishment, it was Yael Katzir.

"James, thank God you're safe," she said, giving me a hug. "Welcome to Israel."

She had scrapes and contusions all over her face and neck. She had burns and bandages on her hands and arms. But she was alive and holding me.

"Yael," I stammered, "how . . . ? What . . . ? I don't understand."

"Didn't you come to Israel to see me?" she asked.

"Well, I . . ."

"You didn't really think we'd be fooled by your new passport, did you?" she said with a wink.

I just stared at her blankly as a jet-black, four-door BMW pulled up. Yael opened the back door for me.

"Come on; we can talk on the way," she said, her eyes sober but warm.

Rattled by all that had happened in the last twenty-four hours but grateful to see her, I said nothing, just got into the car. Yael got in the other side and gave the driver orders in Hebrew. Then we were off, presumably to Mossad headquarters in Tel Aviv.

"I'm so sorry about Omar," she said, taking my left hand and squeezing it gently. "I know you two were close."

I nodded, still numb.

"And I'm sorry for taking off after the explosion," she continued as we got onto Highway 1, headed west through the increasing rain. "I wanted to see you. I wanted to make sure you were okay. But I was under orders not to draw the attention of the Turks under any circumstances. I hope you understand."

I nodded again. "But you're okay?" I asked.

"I'll live," she replied.

It was a professional answer, polite and succinct and completely expected, but it wasn't enough. I wanted more. I wanted the truth. I wanted to know how she was really doing. Yet what was I supposed to do? I wasn't entitled to anything. She didn't owe me anything. We weren't a couple. We weren't even friends. Not really. After all, we had only just met.

Yael, I was certain, could see the struggle in my eyes. So she changed the subject and offered her condolences for the death of Robert Khachigian. She said she and her colleagues had known Khachigian quite well and had admired him greatly over the years. "We worked together on several operations," she confided. "He was a class act."

"He was," I said, wanting to say more and embarrassed that the words would not form.

The car was silent for several miles. It was awkward, but not just for me. Yael seemed uncomfortable as well. She turned away and looked out the rain-streaked window. I turned and looked out mine. A hundred questions rushed through my mind, but I didn't ask a one.

"Can you tell me what happened in Union Station?" she said after several kilometers. "Ari's going to want details."

It was hardly a topic I wanted to discuss. I still hadn't fully processed the fact that I had very probably killed someone during my escape. Nevertheless, I shared as much about the attack as I could remember, though I left out the details of Khachigian's and my conversation. Some things were private. But there was no good reason not to tell her the rest, and in the end it was helpful to have someone I could talk to, someone who understood the enormous trauma I was going through.

"The media in the States are reporting this as a 'mass-casualty event,'" she said, handing me several printouts of articles off the websites of my own paper and the *Washington Post*. "The FBI is telling the media that one suspect was shot dead at the scene. That's the female shooter you brought down. But a second suspect is on the run. They're not releasing any names or descriptions or any details at all. There are just a few leaks from 'unnamed senior law enforcement sources' hinting that right-wing white supremacists may be responsible."

"Tell me you're kidding."

"I'm not," Yael said. "And the FBI hasn't released the names of the dead. The director is saying not all of the next of kin have been notified."

"You don't believe him," I said. It was an observation, not a question.

Yael shook her head. "Do you?"

I turned and looked out the window again. Why weren't they officially releasing the names, at least some of them? At the very least, why hadn't someone leaked Khachigian's name to the media?

"It's political," I said, almost to myself, as I stared out the increasingly fogged-up window and the driving rains pelting Israel's second-largest city. "They don't want to say a former CIA director was assassinated in broad daylight. They don't want to say it's an act of Middle Eastern terrorism, in the heart of Washington, on the eve of announcing a Middle East peace deal."

"You may be right," Yael said. "But I think there's more."

"What do you mean?" I asked, turning back to her.

"It's not just Khachigian," she said. "I think they don't want your name out there either. They don't know what's happened to you. They don't know why you left the scene. Maybe you were kidnapped. Maybe you were complicit. Either way, they don't want the media to report that you were there."

"Because that would put focus on the threat ISIS just issued."

"That would be my guess," she agreed. "You're a big deal now. You broke the story on how serious a threat ISIS really is and that they are planning a series of imminent attacks on Israel and allies of Israel. But you're also a big deal because you were just nearly killed in Turkey. Can you imagine how big a story it would be if people knew you were almost assassinated in D.C. as well?"

"You don't think they really believe I'm involved, do you?" I asked. The thought hadn't even crossed my mind. Nor had the implications.

"No, but I think you need to contact the FBI immediately. Have you even touched base with your editor yet?"

"No, but I have to get this WMD story done first—tonight," I said, now looking her in the eye. "People need to know about the ISIS attack on that base in Syria. They need to know it's possible that ISIS now has chemical weapons, and that they may be planning an attack on the U.S. or Israel at any moment. I can't do anything else until I get that done."

"I agree, and so does Ari," she assured me. "And as I told you before, the prime minister has given us full authorization to help you, so long as you don't quote us or cite any Israeli sources. Deal?"

"Deal."

"You understand that means you can't have a dateline on your story tomorrow from Tel Aviv or Jerusalem or anywhere in Israel, right?"

"I can live with that," I said.

It wasn't ideal, but it was certainly a small price to pay for a scoop like this.

"Good," Yael said. "We're only about ten minutes out. When we get to HQ, I will take you into the vault, as we call it, and show you everything about the ISIS offensive near Aleppo. But there's something else you should know."

She set the latest edition of the *Jerusalem Post* in my lap. The Union Station attacks in Washington had made the front page. But the lead headline read, **ISIS Forces Continue in Race toward Baghdad.**

I quickly scanned the first few paragraphs. A few thousand Sunni jihadists had already captured control of Mosul, Iraq's second-largest city, and driven off two U.S.-trained Iraqi army divisions. Now the *Post* was reporting that ISIS forces had seized the central bank of Mosul, making off with the equivalent of nearly a half-billion dollars in cash, and were continuing to threaten the capital.

"So Baghdad is about to be attacked by what is now the richest terror group on the planet," I said.

"There's more."

"What?"

"The Iraqi government is in full panic mode. Their army is in retreat. Their capital is in jeopardy. The top Shia cleric is calling on fellow Shias to wage jihad against the Sunnis. Tehran—of all places—is offering to help, even offering to send in Iranian military and paramilitary forces to fight ISIS. But President Taylor is doing nothing. The Iraqis are asking for U.S. air strikes, but the president says no. They're asking for a massive new infusion of military aid. The president says he'll think about it. *Think about it?* We could lose Iraq to a bloodthirsty jihadi force. Do you realize what that means? You guys lost four thousand soldiers and Marines fighting to liberate Iraq, and now you're going to effectively hand it over to ISIS? A group so crazy they were thrown out of al Qaeda for being too extreme? A group that now has chemical weapons and is getting ready to use them at any moment? This isn't leadership, James. It's surrender. But your president doesn't seem to get it. Or maybe he just doesn't care. Instead of taking action in Iraq, he's obsessed with carving up the Holy Land. He's offering all kinds of incentives to my country to sign a deeply flawed peace treaty with the Palestinians, and my prime minister is buying it hook, line, and sinker. It's absolute lunacy."

"I'm guessing that's off the record?" I quipped as we slowed to a crawl and wove through late-afternoon rush-hour traffic.

She didn't respond.

Changing topics, I asked if she thought the military offensive Jamal Ramzy had promised in his interview with me might actually be against Iraq.

"No, I don't think so," Yael said. "Iraq isn't the third target. It's the primary target. Syria is second. I'm guessing Israel is third, though it could be you guys. Khalif and Ramzy aren't idiots. They see the U.S. retreating from the region. They've seen their successes in Syria. And they obviously saw an opening, a growing weakness in the heart of the Iraqi regime, and they decided to strike and exploit it for all it's worth."

"Heck of a gamble."

"They don't call themselves the Islamic State of Iraq and al-Sham for nothing. Controlling Iraq, imposing full-blown Sharia law there, and establishing a caliphate in Baghdad is the ultimate objective. It's the main course. Everything else is dessert."

"Could Baghdad really fall to ISIS?" I asked. "Are they that strong?"

"I don't know if they could seize the capital, but they are definitely getting stronger, especially now that they have WMD," she replied. "And I'm sorry; they're not just an extra-radical faction of al Qaeda, as you wrote in your profile on Ramzy. They're actually becoming a very sophisticated army—highly motivated, well-trained, increasingly experienced, incredibly rich, and very, very dangerous. Imagine what would happen if they truly gained control of all of Iraq. They'd create a base camp from which they could export terrorism, attack American citizens, destabilize moderate Arab nations, terrorize the Iraqi people, drive up the price of oil, and seriously harm the global economy."

"And attack Israel," I added.

"And attack Israel," she agreed. "Wouldn't that be the ultimate irony?"

"What?" I asked.

"If the U.S. invaded Iraq to protect itself and Israel from weapons of mass destruction—which it turned out the Iraqis didn't really have or have many of—only to set into motion the conditions that would leave the rulers of Iraq in a position to threaten both of us . . . with weapons of mass destruction."

Irony didn't begin to describe it.

34

★ ★ ★

The next twenty-four hours were a whirlwind.

Yael and Ari were true to their word. They gave me everything I needed and then some.

As I was preparing to leave, Ari explained why he hadn't personally come to meet me in Turkey. He told me— completely off the record, of course—that the prime minister had sent him on a secret mission to Jordan.

"Lavi is determined to be remembered by history as the leader who nailed down a final peace accord with the Palestinians," he whispered. "I told him the timing was wrong. I'm not opposed to a two-state solution. Not at all. But to make a deal right when ISIS is about to hit us with chemical weapons? It's foolish. But he doesn't agree, and he's the boss. So I went. I'm sorry I wasn't with you."

I thanked him for his candor and all his help and Yael's. I apologized for putting Yael in harm's way, but he wouldn't hear of it.

"That's what I pay her for," the Mossad chief said.

"It can't possibly be enough," I said.

Yael sighed. "You've got that right."

Ari and I shook hands. Then Yael drove me to a private airfield. On the way, she gave me her real mobile number and asked me to call her when I arrived in Amman. Then she put me on a Learjet and instructed the pilot to fly me to Cairo. She said I could write my story there in peace and quiet and have it datelined from an Arab capital, not from Israel.

It was a good idea, and I was grateful. I would be safe there. No one would suspect me of being in Egypt. I didn't want to leave Tel Aviv. I wanted to spend more time with Yael. But the clock was ticking. She wished me well, shook my hand, and said good-bye, and with that, she was gone.

Once on the ground in Cairo, I took a cab downtown. I used the phone Khachigian had given me to scan through the headlines back in the States. The nation was riveted on the events at Union Station. The president had called it a tragedy. The mayor of D.C. called it another senseless slaughter. The head of the FBI called it a cold-blooded homicide without rhyme or reason. But that was all spin. The FBI knew there was a reason for the attack. They knew it was terrorism, and they had to suspect it was either al Qaeda or ISIS. But they were still treating the case like another Columbine massacre or the shootings at Sandy Hook, not like a national security emergency.

What's more, the bureau was keeping what cards it had closer than usual. They still weren't releasing the names of any of those who had been killed. Nor were they releasing the name of the female shooter who had been pronounced dead at the scene. At least they were no longer sticking to the "right-wing white supremacist" nonsense.

The Feds had now confirmed there had been a second shooter. MSNBC was running grainy video footage from someone's smartphone showing a sniper on the second floor, back in the corner. An intrepid *Washington Post* reporter had even gotten a detailed description of the sniper and his weapon from an off-duty D.C. police officer who happened to be eating at the Pizzeria Uno on the second floor at the time of the shooting. The officer had tried to chase the sniper but had been shot twice and was now in guarded condition at a local hospital. The Associated Press, meanwhile, was quoting several witnesses who said there was a third shooter as well. That, I assumed, was me, and I knew I would have to talk to the FBI soon lest I become an active suspect.

I directed the cab to a Hilton I had once stayed in near the American embassy. There were few tourists, few business guests, and plenty of rooms available. I took a spacious suite overlooking the Nile, pulled out my laptop and notes, and set to work.

The process didn't take long, given that I had already written several drafts over the past few weeks. Essentially, all I needed to do now was add in the new material I had gathered over the past forty-eight hours, including several quotes from Khachigian. I decided to break the story of how deeply involved in this process Khachigian had been, along with the fact that he'd been killed at

Union Station. I didn't connect all the dots about why he'd been killed. I didn't need to. I just wanted to stick to the facts that I could prove, and I had plenty.

When I was finished, I debated calling Allen and personally updating him on all that had happened. In the end, however, I opted against it. I simply sent him the story by e-mail with a single sentence that I was safe and coming home soon. I didn't want an argument. I didn't want a dressing-down. I just wanted to file and keep moving. If he was going to fire me, so be it. I wasn't going to fight for my job. I was just going to keep doing it until I was either broke or dead.

The moment the e-mail went through, I jumped in a cab, raced back to the airport, and bought the last seat on the last flight to Amman, Jordan, that night. I didn't want to be in Cairo when my story hit the newsstands. Besides, from Amman I could get a direct flight to Baghdad.

In the meantime, now that my story had been filed, it was time to put the battery back in my iPhone and go to work. I e-mailed and texted every contact I knew in the Iraqi government. Yet again I pleaded for their help to locate and then secure an interview with Abu Khalif. I also said I was coming to Baghdad in the next twenty-four to forty-eight hours and would be deeply grateful for their assistance. It was an enormous risk, especially after filing a story about chemical weapons and ISIS. Jamal Ramzy had been crystal clear that I was to go nowhere near that story. But I was going anyway. I had to.

Live or die, I was going to hunt down this story to the end.

★　★　★

The next morning, I woke up at Le Méridien, an upscale hotel in downtown Amman.

I glanced at the alarm clock on the nightstand beside me. It was 7:23 a.m. I got out of bed, rubbed the sleep from my eyes, and powered up my laptop. As I ordered room service for breakfast, I wondered what Allen had done with the story I'd sent him. Had he run it or buried it? I didn't dare guess. I'd defied his direct orders. He had insisted that I come meet with him in Washington, and I'd planned to, of course. But events had taken a turn I could never have expected. In any case, I had gotten him the third source he'd insisted upon with regard to the WMD story. The final draft I'd sent him was written with significantly more care and precision than the previous versions. But it was still an explosive piece.

If Allen had signed off on it and it was really going to be published soon, it was going to create an international firestorm. Just a few months earlier, few people outside the intelligence community had ever even heard of ISIS. Now the jihadist movement had captured half of Iraq and much of Syria and could very well be in possession of large amounts of sarin gas. Not only that, they were threatening to hit a third target beyond Iraq and Syria. The implications for U.S. and Israeli national security were chilling, to say the least. But would Allen really run with it? I hoped so, but I didn't know.

I pulled up the *New York Times* home page and held my breath.

There it was, on the front page.

ISIS Forces Seize Syrian Base Where Chemical Weapons Stored, read the enormous banner headline, with a subhead that read, *"Intelligence experts warn al Qaeda faction, now signaling new terror attacks, may have WMD."*

My body tensed. I thought I'd be excited. But as I scanned the story, I actually felt full of dread. The weight of what this all meant began to come down on me. I read through it quickly. It was all there. Allen had made only minor edits. Now the story was available for the whole world to see. There was no turning back. The president was going to wake up to it. So was the director of the CIA. And Prime Minister Lavi. And Jamal Ramzy. And, I had to assume, Abu Khalif. What would they say? What would they do?

I had included all the caveats the president and CIA director had warned me about—though not citing them, of course. I had carefully noted that while three different intelligence agencies had clear proof of ISIS seizing the base and carrying off hundreds of crates, none of them could give definitive evidence that ISIS now actually possessed WMD. The *Times* didn't want to get burned on another bogus Mideast WMD story. Neither did I. It was my reputation on the line, and I guarded it jealously.

I had woken up hungry. Now I had lost all interest in food. Instead, I pulled up airline schedules online and considered my meager options. I was going to Baghdad. ISIS could kill me, but they couldn't stop me from letting the world know what they were up to. I had Ramzy's interview. I had the WMD angle. Now I wanted Abu Khalif, and the only way to get him was to get to the Iraqi capital and hunt him down.

I booked a seat on Royal Jordanian Airlines flight 810, departing at 5:30 that evening and landing at about 8 p.m. local time. From the airport, I would head straight for a hotel in the Green Zone where I had stayed in the past.

It would be a return to familiar but dangerous territory: the hotel had a well-trafficked bar. During the second Iraq war, I'd spent countless nights there. I'm guessing that's where I officially became an alcoholic. Everyone who was anyone hung out there in the evenings, after the Western submission deadlines had passed. It was the kind of place I could pick up leads and get the lay of the land. But it was all done over whiskey and bourbon and an occasional bottle of vodka. For that reason alone, it was probably suicide to go back. But that's where the sources were, so that's where I had to be too.

I opened the door to the hallway, picked up my complimentary copy of the *Jordan Times* from the carpet, and brought it into the room. Pulling back the drapes to let in some light, I looked out over the sprawling skyline of the Jordanian capital and thought about Yael. I debated calling her, but what

was there to say? We couldn't have a personal conversation on the phone. She had work to do, and
so did I. She had probably given me her real number in case I had a follow-up question. She was a
professional. She was a spy. She hadn't suggested I
ask her out. Even if I did, when was I going to be
back in Israel? The whole thing suddenly seemed
ridiculous and awkward. Here I was, a grown man.
Divorced. Single. Not seeing anyone. Yet I felt like
a boy trying to get up the nerve to ask a girl to the
junior high dance.

I grabbed my phone off the desk. It had finished charging overnight. Yet instead of calling
Yael or even texting her, I found myself sending an
SMS message to my brother. He was in Amman.
Maybe I should say hi. Seemed like the decent
thing to do. I couldn't avoid him forever, and it
would make my mom happy.

**Matt—hey, in town for a few hours. You
free?—JB**

I debated calling Hadiya, Omar's wife, but I
wasn't sure she would be happy to hear from me.
Instead I sent her an e-mail telling her how much
her husband had meant to me and how sorry I
was for her loss. Perhaps in time I could express
my sorrow and regret to her in person. For now,
I decided, she probably needed some space.

With no one else to contact at the moment,
I scanned the local headlines. None were what I
expected.

**King Says 'Historic Breakthrough'
Possible in Palestinian Peace Talks
with Israel**

**Prime Minister Says 'Peace to
Our West' Would Help Calm
'Storm to Our East'**

**Palestinian President Mansour to
Meet with King in Aqaba**

**Gas Prices Climb, but Food Prices
Stable in November**

To my astonishment, there was nothing about ISIS on the front page, only an allusion to the implosion of Jordan's next-door neighbor. I knew the palace kept a pretty tight grip on news coverage, but were they really going to try to act like ISIS wasn't on the move? I quickly flipped through the pages, but there was little mention of the Islamic State inside the paper either. One story focused on a new refugee camp Jordan and the U.N. were building in the north. Another noted that the U.S. had just authorized the sale of new Hellfire missiles and other arms to the Iraqi government. Only deep inside did I find this headline: **Jordan Does Not Fear ISIS Rebels, Says Interior Minister**. But the accompanying article was only six paragraphs long.

Why?

This was Jordan's largest English-language daily newspaper. The palace was clearly using it to lay the groundwork for the peace talks "to the west," but why were they not making it clear how serious was the "storm to the east"?

I did a quick Google search to see how much coverage of ISIS this and other Jordanian papers had published in recent weeks. Some, but not much. Again, why? To be sure, well over half of Jordan's population was of Palestinian origin. Some said the number was as high as 70 percent. Most held Jordanian citizenship. They were certainly deeply concerned about the future of their Arab brothers and sisters on the west side of the Jordan River. They strongly supported the creation of a Palestinian state. Most believed it was a terrible injustice of the West not to have helped create a Palestinian state sooner. But ISIS posed a clear and present danger to the region.

The Hashemite Kingdom of Jordan sat wedged between Iraq, Syria, the Palestinians, and Israel.

A threat to the others surely posed a threat to Jordan, too.

35

* * *

The phone rang.

Not the room phone but my mobile. I glanced at the caller ID to see who in the world it could be. The screen read simply, *Unknown caller*.

My pulse quickened. Maybe it was Yael. Then again, maybe it was my brother.

"Hello?"

"Mr. Collins?" asked the voice at the other end. "Is that you?"

"Who's asking?" I replied, now somewhat guarded.

"Good, it is you," he said. "I've been worried about you. Are you all right?"

"I'm sorry; who is this?" I asked.

"Come now, my friend, you don't recognize my voice?"

"No, I'm sorry. I don't."

"It's Marwan. Are you dressed?"

Startled, I suddenly found myself rising to my feet. I had not expected a call from Prince Marwan Talal.

"Your Royal Highness, forgive me," I said. "No, I'm sorry. I just woke up."

"I have sent you a car and driver—they are waiting in front of your hotel," he said. "Take a quick shower. Get dressed. And meet the driver in ten minutes. We need to talk."

★ ★ ★

I had met with Marwan Talal many times over the years, but never at his home.

But the farther we drove from the hotel and veered away from any of the main government buildings with which I was familiar, the more I became convinced that's where I was being taken.

Though we e-mailed occasionally, it had been quite some time since I had actually seen the king's eldest uncle. He was now in his eighties, and I'd heard rumors his health was not so good. But as the Mercedes pulled through the security gates of a palatial home on the outskirts of Amman—past the Humvee out front with the soldier manning a .50-caliber machine gun, past at least a dozen other heavily armed guards, and up the long, winding palm tree–lined driveway—I was not prepared for the man who awaited me.

The prince was confined to a wheelchair now. His gray hair had thinned considerably. His face looked gaunt, and I wondered if I was detecting a bit of jaundice as well. But when I stepped out of the car and came over to him, he greeted me with the same warm smile and twinkle in his eye for which I had come to know him. And though his hands trembled slightly as he took both of mine, and though his voice was somewhat raspier than I remembered, there was also an indescribable air of confidence about him that gave me the sense he was still in command of his faculties. That was reassuring, I thought. But that was pretty much the only thing about our time together that was.

We gave each other a traditional Arab kiss on both cheeks, and then I followed as a steward wheeled the prince through the handsomely appointed entry hall to a veranda overlooking the capital. Soon we were served the best Turkish coffee I think I've ever had, and then we were left alone to chat.

"You are a survivor, Mr. Collins," Marwan said to begin our conversation.

"I've been lucky."

"No," he said, wagging his finger at me. "Your protection is Allah's doing. Your enemies have tried to kill you twice. But clearly Allah is not done with you."

"Not yet," I quipped.

"Indeed," he said. "Not yet. Are you okay?"

"I'm fine."

"You look terrible."

"Thanks a lot."

"I just mean all the cuts and bruises and bandages. And you're as pale as a ghost."

"Yet I'm sitting in Amman with an old friend."

"That you are. But you were sitting with an old friend at Union Station when all the shooting broke out."

"Are you saying I'm in danger here?"

"I'm saying one never knows where danger lurks."

"True," I said. "One never knows."

The prince did not touch his coffee. He just sat there and looked at me as if he were studying me, as if he were trying to make sense of who I was despite the many years we had known each other.

"Mr. Collins . . . ," the prince began, and then his voice trailed off for a moment.

He was not the only prince in the royal family. Indeed, there were many, and some of them were very close to the king. But Marwan Talal was the most senior of the princes. Perhaps it was because of his age and insistence on tradition and protocol that he persisted in calling me Mr. Collins. I had long since given up on persuading him to call me James—much less J. B.

"Yes, Your Royal Highness?" I prompted.

"Mr. Collins, are you ready to become a follower of the Prophet, peace be upon him?"

I wasn't sure what to say to that. He knew I wasn't a religious man. But then again, there were few if any Muslims in the royal court as devout as Marwan Talal. He was a direct descendant of the prophet Muhammad. He had been trained as a Sunni cleric and for years had taught Sharia law in Jordan's most prestigious seminary. And honestly, I think he'd been trying to convert me—at least to deism, if not Islam—since the day I'd met him. I appreciated the gesture, but this question still made me uncomfortable.

I briefly considered telling him that my days of atheism and agnosticism had apparently passed.

I did, in fact, believe in God. I just didn't know how to find him, though I was becoming increasingly convinced I had to try. But not here. Not today. And with all respect to Marwan and his impressive family, I was not about to become a Muslim. I'd been raised in a Christian home by a very devout mother. I wasn't exactly ready to embrace my mother's beliefs. I wasn't really sure where I stood with Jesus at this point in my life. But I certainly wasn't about to give my mother a stroke by asking her to come down to the local mosque to pray with me five times a day.

"I am still finding my way, my friend," I said.

"There is only one Prophet," he replied. "There is only one path. There is only one guide, the Qur'an."

"You're starting to sound like a member of the Brotherhood," I said, trying to lighten the mood.

"Why would you say such a thing?" he asked, sounding a bit defensive.

"Didn't you just recite the slogan of the Muslim Brotherhood?"

"Certainly not," he replied. "The Muslim Brotherhood's mantra is: 'Allah is our objective. The Prophet is our leader. Qur'an is our law. Jihad is our way. Dying in the way of Allah is our highest hope.'"

"Close."

"A man can be a faithful Muslim and not be a member of the Brotherhood, can he not?"

"Of course."

"Then I believe you're trying to change the subject, Mr. Collins. Have you ever read the Qur'an?"

"Yes, I have."

"And?"

"Again, let's just say I'm finding my way," I replied, trying to be as diplomatic as I could.

"If I may be direct, Mr. Collins, you are a young man in great need of Islam. You are, I am sad to say, all alone in this world. You have no wife. You have no children. No faith. No community. That is no way to live, my friend. Why not join us? I would be happy to teach you the path of Islam myself."

"Thank you," I said politely. "I will consider your gracious offer. But I suspect this is not why you have brought me here today."

"Not the only reason, no," he said.

"Then how can I help you?"

"Your most recent article in the *Times*. It bothered me very much."

I took another sip of coffee and braced myself. "I'm sorry to hear that, Your Highness. What bothered you in particular?"

"Among many things, your timing," the prince said. "Didn't President Taylor specifically ask you not to publish a story of this sort at this time?"

I was stunned that he knew such a thing, but then again he and his king were in very close contact with the White House, especially now.

"I believe I made the administration's concerns abundantly clear in the story," I responded.

"Nevertheless, the president and His Majesty are in the very delicate final stages of being midwives to an extraordinary peace treaty," he explained. "His Majesty has been working quietly, behind the scenes, with President Mansour and Prime Minister Lavi and their closest advisors for months, along with your president and his administration."

"For how long exactly?"

"Eight months, maybe nine."

Suddenly the prince began a coughing spell that was so bad I worried he might have a heart attack. I poured him a glass of water. He drank it all, and soon he was quiet again.

"How involved is His Majesty?"

"His Majesty is overseeing the entire process."

"Not the Americans?"

"Everything is done under the auspices of the Taylor administration, of course," he said with a theatrical flair, spreading out his arms expansively. "The president does the talk-talk-talk in public. The Americans take all the credit. But His Majesty is doing the heavy lifting."

"Right here in Amman?"

"Some of it, yes," he confirmed. "But mostly at the palace in Aqaba. It's quieter there. It's off the media's radar. King Hussein used to hold many such secret contacts there. His Majesty learned from his father, peace be upon him."

"And the deal is almost finished?"

"Young man, it *is* finished," the prince said. "His Majesty got an agreement on the final language yesterday. I can't give you any of the details, of course. Not yet. But I can tell you both Lavi and Mansour have signed off. Now they are planning the announcement to the media, which will take place in the region in a matter of days. Indeed, your president is coming soon. It's all very hush-hush, but it could happen by the end of the week."

"This week?" I asked.

"It will be a shock to everyone," he said.

"I'll say."

"Until the last twenty-four to forty-eight hours, the media has been filled with stories that the parties were far from a deal. Now, as you can see, carefully timed leaks are beginning to raise people's expectations. When the announcement is made, your president and secretary of state have made it clear they want lots of pomp and ceremony. A big show for the Arab and Israeli and American media. Then the four principals will fly back to Washington, brief members of the House and Senate, and hold a signing ceremony in the East Room of the White House."

"President Taylor, Prime Minister Lavi, President Mansour, and King Abdullah?"

"Of course, but why do you put His Majesty at the end of the list?" he asked. I could not tell by his tone or expression if he was serious.

Then he began coughing violently again.

"And then comes my article," I said when he had taken another sip of water.

"It was, shall we say, a 'monkey wrench.'"

"Not good news."

"Not good at all."

"But it's all accurate."

"So you say."

"You just didn't want it made public on the eve of the big peace announcement," I said.

"Look, Mr. Collins, this is old news," he said,

his expression becoming more somber now. "The ISIS attack on the base near Aleppo happened weeks ago. No one is certain what they found. Your own reporting says as much. But you and the *Times* have sensationalized the story, made it sound worse than it is, and injected fear into the hearts of millions at a moment when His Majesty is trying to bring quiet and calm."

"With all due respect, Your Highness, fewer than a hundred people on the planet knew about the ISIS attack on that Syrian base until this story. Now the whole world knows. It's very much news, and it should be, especially given recent threats by Jamal Ramzy that ISIS is about to hit a third target."

"But my point is that it's all circumstantial and hearsay," the elderly prince shot back. "If ISIS really had chemical weapons, wouldn't we all know by now? But they've neither used them nor admitted to having them; nor do you have any scrap of credible intelligence that Khalif and Ramzy and their people really have these weapons of mass destruction. You seem to be interested in nothing but selling newspapers and making a name for yourself. I expected more from you. I thought we were friends."

I was stung by the personal nature of his criticism. But for now I ignored his last comments and stuck to the central issue.

"Aren't you worried about the threat ISIS poses to the peace of the region? Don't you think it's possible that ISIS is just holding back these weapons, waiting for the right moment to strike?"

"I am not in the intelligence game, Mr. Collins. I am not a military man. I am a simple follower of Allah, and my time in this world is growing short. My eyes are growing dim. My strength is fading. But I intend to give whatever energy I have left in faithful service to Islam. I may not have much influence, but I intend to do my part for as long as I can. The world is changing very rapidly. Forces have been set into motion beyond the West's control, beyond the media's control. Muslims are looking for hope. Arabs are looking for direction, for a clear sense of mission. My colleagues are doing what they can. In the end, I have no doubt we will prevail. We *will* make this a better world. But frankly, your article is a weapon of mass distraction. And I must say I am disappointed. I had hoped that you would have known better."

Just then my phone started buzzing. A text was coming in. Apologizing, I took a moment to silence my mobile when I noticed who the text was from: Hassan Karbouli, the Iraqi minister of the interior.

I got you your interview, he wrote. **Hope you know what you're doing. Will meet you when you land.**

36

★ ★ ★

All the way back to the hotel, my mind was reeling.

How did the prince not see the seriousness of the ISIS threat? He had been around practically forever. He had seen the region engulfed in war time and time again. Now Syria was collapsing. Iraq was collapsing. How could he not see that the forces of Radical Islam were on the move and threatening to undo all the years King Hussein and King Abdullah had poured into peacemaking and moderation? I couldn't fault him for his loyalty to the king in pursuit of a peace treaty between the Israelis and Palestinians. But calling my article a "weapon of mass distraction"? Saying he was disappointed in me? It wasn't the first time a person of influence had dressed me down for publishing something he didn't want to read. But it seemed awfully reactionary from a man I'd never considered prone to such a response.

Nevertheless, the prince's views were not foremost in my thoughts. Hassan Karbouli's text message was. Was it true? Was it really possible that before this day was over, I could be sitting face-to-face with Abu Khalif, the most dangerous terrorist leader on the planet?

What would I say to him? What would I ask him? He had killed my friends. He had very likely tried to have me killed twice. Was I going to confront him? Could I maintain a professional composure? Could I actually conduct an on-the-record interview? Could I really get him to talk about who he was and what he wanted? How?

At the moment I had no idea. For that matter, I had no idea what Abu Khalif even looked like. Almost no one in the world did. Indeed, most people were only just becoming aware of his name and of the inner workings of ISIS. The profile of Jamal Ramzy I had written had helped, but mostly people were learning about ISIS because of the terrorist regime's blitzkrieg through northern Iraq and its extraordinary success in capturing major cities and small towns and thousands of square miles of Iraqi territory in the face of limited Iraqi military resistance.

Rare was the occasion before a major interview that I would ever find myself nervous. I didn't get stage fright. But this was different. This was a big get. Huge.

Finally alone, and suddenly quiet, I toyed with the idea of having a good stiff drink when I got back to the hotel. I knew it was wrong, and I immediately thought of Omar doing his best to keep me sober, one day at a time. A flash of guilt rippled through my system. But what would it really hurt? I'd have a bourbon or two, maybe smoke a fat Cuban cigar, and start jotting down the questions I wanted to ask Khalif. I needed something to take the edge off my nerves. I wouldn't go crazy, I told myself. I'd be careful.

When the prince's driver pulled up in front of Le Méridien, I thanked him in Arabic, grabbed my leather satchel, and entered the hotel. I put my things through the X-ray machine in the lobby, as required by every hotel in Jordan after a series of horrific hotel bombings in the days of Abu Zarqawi, the first leader of al Qaeda in Iraq. When I had cleared the metal detectors, I headed to the bar toward the rear of the ornate main lobby.

But to my astonishment, the first person I saw as I strode past the main desk was my brother.

"Matt?" I said, having a hard time believing it was really him. "What in the world are you doing here?"

"I got your text," he said. "I wrote back but didn't hear from you."

"But how did you . . . ? I mean, how in the world . . . ?"

I was floored and not a little peeved that he'd found me. I'd taken every precaution to make sure no one knew I was here. It was one thing for His Royal Highness to track me down. He had all the intelligence resources of the kingdom at his disposal. But my brother was an academic on a sabbatical. If he could find me, maybe anybody could.

"It's not rocket science," he whispered, seeing my anxiety. "I called your editor—Allen, right?"

"But Allen doesn't know I'm in Amman," I said, my confusion growing. "I didn't tell him."

"No, you didn't. And he's furious with you. But

he figured you weren't going to hang around in Cairo. He thinks you're probably headed for Iraq, so he guessed you'd route through here. When I told him about your text, he wasn't surprised."

Maybe I hadn't covered my tracks as carefully as I'd thought.

"But how did you find this hotel?"

"I explained to Allen who I was. I told him Mom was terribly worried about you. I said I was trying to track you down and would be grateful for his help."

"And he believed you?"

"Of course he believed me, J. B. It's true. You need to call her. She's worried sick. Anyway, he mentioned a handful of hotels you tended to use when you came through town. I did a little homework and wound up here. Anyway, it's good to see you. Thanks for your note. I was surprised to hear from you. Grateful, but surprised."

Struggling to contain a surge of conflicting emotions, I asked him how he was and how Annie and the kids were.

"We're fine, J. B.," he said. "But really, how are you? We're worried about you."

"Well, thanks," I mumbled. "I appreciate it. But I'll be fine."

"Fine? Are you kidding? Look at you. You look awful."

"I'm getting that a lot lately," I said.

"Come on, let's have a seat," Matt replied. "Let me buy you a cup of coffee. What time's your flight to Baghdad?"

I hesitated but saw little point in being coy. "Five thirty."

"Good, so we have some time," he said. "And look, I'll even drive you to the airport."

"No, that's okay, Matt. I really—"

"No, come on; I insist," he said. "I'm glad to see you. It's been too long."

I shrugged and said thank you, and we found a couple of comfortable chairs in a quiet corner of the lounge. A waiter came over and took our coffee orders, and then we were alone.

My brother asked me what had happened back in Washington and how I'd managed to survive. I basically shared with him what I'd shared with Yael. Again I skipped the private details of my conversation with Khachigian, though I did share more with Matt than I had with Yael, in part because Matt had known the man as long as I had, and perhaps better. After all, he had actually worked for Khachigian for nearly two years as a legislative aide in D.C. when Khachigian was serving in the Senate, before Matt decided to leave the Hill and go to graduate school at Gordon-Conwell Theological Seminary in Massachusetts. When Matt became an ordained pastor and was called to serve at a church in Bangor, Maine, Khachigian and his wife, Mary, actually began attending the congregation. And when Mary passed away, it was Matt who performed the memorial service and delivered the eulogy. But then Matt and Annie had moved back to the Boston area so Matt could teach at his alma mater, and as far as I knew, he hadn't had anything but occasional e-mail contact with our old family friend.

"I'm going to miss him," Matt said as the waiter delivered our coffees. "He was always so encouraging to me. When I started as a pastor, it felt like I was making every mistake in the book. I had a hard time getting my sea legs, learning how to preach, how to manage a church, how to really care for people. But I could always count on the senator for a kind word."

Matt was the only one in our family who still called Khachigian "senator."

I could see how hard this was on him. In many ways, Khachigian had become the surrogate father Matt had desperately needed when our father left home. Matt and I had gone our separate ways, but he and Khachigian had become quite close.

"Mary was always the more devout of the two," Matt said softly, staring into his coffee. "But after she died, the senator really began to take his own faith much more seriously. He used to come by my office a couple times a week. We'd chat. We'd read the Bible together. We'd pray together. I loved those times. I'd forgotten how much I'd missed them."

He didn't even seem to be talking to me, just thinking aloud. But after taking a sip of coffee, he looked up at me. "The senator grew up in the church—literally," Matt told me. "Did you know his father was an Episcopal priest?"

"Can't say I did," I replied, adding a little cream to my coffee.

"He was, but it didn't seem to take with his

son," Matt said. "After Mary's funeral, the senator told me he'd always been too busy, too proud, too ambitious to focus much on the things of God. But then he admitted he was suddenly afraid of death. How do you like that? All his years in the military, and all those years as a spy for the CIA in really dangerous places, and he'd never been scared of death. But after his wife died, he told me he had no idea if he was going to heaven when he passed on. He was sure Mary would be there, and he wanted to make sure he'd be with her for eternity. So at one point, I just asked if he was ready to pray to receive Christ as his Savior. He said yes. So we both got down on our knees, right in my office, and we prayed. From that point forward, he was truly a new man."

It was a nice story, as far as it went. It certainly spoke to the sincere affection the Khachigians had had as a couple and Matt's sincerity as a pastor. But the trajectory of this story was beginning to make me very uncomfortable. I wasn't Robert Khachigian. And Matt wasn't my pastor. He was my older brother, and he was about to cross a line.

"You know, I really ought to call Mom and let her know I'm okay," I said, setting down my cup and leaning forward in my chair.

"Are you ready, J. B.?" Matt asked.

The question seemed to come out of left field.

"For what?" I asked.

"Death," he said calmly.

The word just hung in the air for a moment as I hesitated to answer. I was about to tell Matt this was too personal. Instead I heard myself saying, "No, I'm not."

Matt said nothing. We just sat there in awkward silence. After a moment, I glanced at my pocket watch. I really was running out of time. I needed to go up to my room and pack and then head to the airport. I had an interview to prepare for—the most important of my career.

I knew Matt believed he had the answer. But I'll give him credit for not being pushy or preachy. He knew me well enough not to overreach. He'd made his point. And he let it sit.

In that way, he wasn't that different from the prince. One was trying to convert me to Christ, the other to Islam. Both were absolutely convinced they had truth on their side, that they'd found the best way to God. Maybe one of them was right. But at that moment I couldn't say which, and I didn't have the time to figure it out.

37

★ ★ ★

I excused myself and headed up to my room.

I called my mother, but she didn't answer. I left a voice message letting her know I was safe and telling her I'd just had coffee with Matt. Then I packed and headed back down to the lobby.

Matt was waiting for me in a beat-up old Toyota SUV filled with car seats and all manner of kids' toys and not a few fast-food wrappers. He was certainly leading a vastly different life from mine, and though I didn't dare admit it, I envied what he had. A good marriage. Two adorable kids. A measly paycheck but a satisfying profession. Close friends. And a faith that seemed to sustain him and always had.

I threw my bags in the backseat, and we departed for the airport in silence.

What I really wanted to do was ask if I could just go back to their house and crash for the next few days or weeks or months. I had never felt so lost or in so much pain. It seemed almost everyone I knew was dead. I had watched them die. It was killing me inside. I was afraid if I stopped and thought about it too much, I'd lose it—I mean really lose it. So I kept going, kept pushing, trying simultaneously not to think about any of it and yet redeem it as well, make their deaths worthwhile, make them mean something. But sitting here beside Matt, I could feel the tremors of a coming volcano. Raging, volatile, superheated emotions I had long been suppressing were forcing their way to the surface, and it made me want to jump off the grid and hide.

I needed a room to myself. I needed to shut the door and lock it and turn off the lights and crawl into bed and curl up into a fetal position. I needed to weep for my friends and keep weeping and weeping until there were no more tears in me. I couldn't take any more. I felt so alone. I wanted to have it all out with God until he either spoke to me or killed me. The thought of getting on that flight in a few hours and going into Iraq and meeting with the leader of ISIS literally made me want to vomit. I couldn't bear it. It was all too much.

What I needed most of all was time—time to mourn, time to think, time to talk to Matt and Annie. I was sick of eating restaurant food. I was sick of hotels and airports and deadlines and datelines in city after city after city after freaking city. I wanted to eat simple foods cooked by a wife and a mom. I wanted to hear the laughter of little children and sit by the water and lie down in a field and stare at the blue sky and smell freshly cut grass and hear lawn mowers running. I needed time to read Matt's Bible, time to ask a million questions and wrestle through it all and figure out some answers for myself before it was too late.

"Come on, J. B.; it's time," Matt said finally. "Let's pray together. Right now. You and me. Give your heart to Jesus. Let him forgive you and start to heal you and lift all those burdens off your shoulders."

"I'm sorry, Matt. I'm just not there."

"Then don't go to Baghdad."

"I wish it were that easy," I heard myself say in an inexplicable contradiction of everything I'd just told myself. "But I have to go."

"Actually, you don't," he pushed back. "And you shouldn't—maybe not ever, but certainly not until you've gotten yourself right with God."

"It's my job."

"This is not about your job, J. B.," he said. "It's about your soul. Look, you're a great reporter. One of the best in the world. Everyone knows that. I see it, and I'm very proud of you. You meet with presidents and prime ministers and kings and princes. Your articles are read by millions of people, and countless thousands make life-changing decisions because of what they learn from you. But Jesus warned successful people just like you, 'What does it profit a man to gain the whole world and forfeit his soul?' Your soul is at stake here. Please listen to me. I beg you. Don't make another move until you get right with Christ."

I wanted to say yes. I really did. But I just wasn't ready. So I thanked Matt for his concern. I would worry about God later. Right now I had to get ready for Abu Khalif.

38

★ ★ ★

BAGHDAD, IRAQ

Royal Jordanian flight 810 touched down in Baghdad at precisely 8 p.m.

Peering out the window of my first-class seat as we taxied to the main terminal, I could see a squadron of Iraqi military vehicles racing across the tarmac and flanking the jet on either side. I could also see snipers posted on the roofs of the terminal, and tanks on the perimeter of the airfield and surrounding the control tower. Security had been tight ever since the liberation of Iraq by U.S. and allied forces in 2003, but it appeared to have been ramped up significantly in light of the rapidly growing threat ISIS forces now posed to Baghdad and the central government.

I powered up my phone and checked the latest headlines. My story on ISIS had been picked up by media outlets all over the world. Agence France-Presse was quoting an e-mail purportedly from Jamal Ramzy "emphatically denying" that his forces had captured or had possession of chemical weapons. Reuters was citing the Russian foreign minister and an unnamed senior U.N. official saying it "seemed unlikely" and "close to preposterous" that ISIS had WMD, given their joint operation to remove all of the Assad regime's stockpiles of sarin precursors and other chemical weapons compounds.

Still, a *Washington Post* editorial, while expressing caution until more facts were known, nevertheless noted, "The assassination of an esteemed former CIA director who was a prime source in the WMD report adds a significant degree of credibility to the *Times* story." The editorial added, "U.S. officials should work to confirm the precise nature of ISIS's capabilities as quickly as possible, given the high stakes. If ISIS really does now have chemical weapons, the next terrorist attack in Washington or elsewhere in the U.S. could result in the deaths of hundreds—perhaps thousands."

Meanwhile, quite aside from the WMD angle, news of Khachigian's murder at Union Station was creating a feeding frenzy in Washington. With two more critically wounded victims succumbing to their injuries in the past twenty-four hours, the death toll had risen to thirty-nine. The White House press secretary was being hounded with questions as to whether there was an ISIS sleeper cell—or several—operating in the U.S. He declined to speculate. The FBI was under fire for not releasing such vital information to the public immediately. The director cut short a press conference after saying, "We're looking into the matter" to twenty-three separate questions. Several members of Congress were calling the administration's refusal to come clean on the foreign terrorist angle a potential cover-up. Meanwhile, an investigative reporter for ABC News had two sources inside the CIA saying the woman shooter was a Jordanian-American who had traveled to Syria twice in the last eighteen months and had suspected ties to al Qaeda.

As I disembarked the plane and headed into the terminal, I heard someone calling my name.

"Mr. Collins, Mr. Collins, over here."

The voice was unmistakably that of Hassan Karbouli. I approached the tall man in an ill-fitting suit. The minister of the interior was surrounded by several very nervous-looking bodyguards who, I guessed, didn't typically do airport pickups. At his side was Ismail Tikriti, the deputy director of Iraqi intelligence.

"Welcome to hell," Karbouli laughed, vigorously shaking my hand.

No one else laughed, and neither did I.

"Thank you for receiving me, gentlemen," I replied, acknowledging Ismail as well. "I appreciate your willingness to help me."

"I hope you'll forgive us for not giving you an answer sooner," Karbouli said. "As you no doubt know, we've been battling ISIS night and day. I haven't slept more than three or four hours a night. Ismail here is probably getting less. I think we're making progress, pushing them back. But I have to tell you, it's been brutal, especially in Ismail's hometown."

The security detail was getting increasingly nervous with us being out among all the other deplaning passengers. At a sign from Karbouli, they quickly whisked us away and led us through a locked door, down several flights of stairs, and along a series of corridors until we reached the airport's operations center. There they directed us to a small conference room. Karbouli, Ismail, and I entered with a single bodyguard. The rest of the security detail waited outside.

"I'm afraid I cannot stay long," the interior minister began. "I have a meeting with the prime minister in less than an hour. But I have asked Ismail to take you to see Abu Khalif. Ismail did most of the initial interrogations of Khalif himself. He'll be a great asset for you. I'm afraid you won't have much time with Khalif, but it's the best I can do."

"How much time?"

"Thirty minutes," he said.

I wanted more, but I was grateful for whatever I could get and I said so.

"How is the new prime minister?" I asked, knowing that there had been a significant political shakeup in Baghdad since I'd last been in the country.

"Off the record?" Karbouli asked.

"Of course," I said. I wasn't planning to write about anything but Abu Khalif on this trip.

"He's in a bit over his head," the interior minister replied. "And I say that with all respect for him. I don't envy the challenges he's facing."

"Fending off ISIS?"

"Yes, of course, but it's more than that. There is a tremendous division inside the cabinet. Some insist the Americans must be invited to come back and help us defend Baghdad and retake the north. Others—including some of the prominent Shias in the government—want to invite Iranian forces to come in to help us."

"And where are you?"

Karbouli shrugged. "I don't want to see the Iranians here. But I don't think your president has the inclination to send forces back here or—to be candid—the stomach to see the battle through even if he did send troops."

"So what's your solution?"

"Well, I tell you one thing for certain: the Shias have really fouled things up. They have no idea how to run the country. They have so marginalized us—politically, economically, socially, you name it—that Sunnis all across the country are absolutely furious with the government. I'm furious. So are my fellow Sunnis in the government. All four of us. We have no say, no voice. The Shias have created the perfect conditions for this ISIS surge. There is tremendous sympathy for ISIS right now. Not in Baghdad, of course. And not among the Kurds or the Christians. But in the north, in Anbar to the west, and in certain areas in the south. People are demanding change, and so far the prime minister and his people aren't listening."

"I've never see you so upset, Hassan," I said.

"You have no idea," he replied.

I looked at Ismail. I was dying to know his take. I was certain it was different from Karbouli's. Ismail, after all, was a Chaldean and a Christian.

But he remained expressionless. Whatever his views were, he was an intelligence officer, not a politician. It wasn't his place to speak his mind—certainly not here and now.

"I'm sorry, but I really need to leave you," Karbouli said, standing. "But tell me one thing. I'm hearing rumors that the Israelis and the Palestinians are about to sign a final peace treaty. Is this true?"

I was taken aback by the question. I'd thought all this was still a closely guarded secret.

"Wow . . . that would be something," I demurred. "What else have you heard?"

"I've heard from several contacts today," he said. "They say it's a done deal, that they're going to be doing a signing ceremony in Jerusalem. And I hear the Jordanians are the architects of the whole thing. You're not hearing this as well?"

"I've heard some rumors," I said carefully, not willing to burn my sources. "But I'd say that's all it is at this moment—just rumors. I guess we'll just have to wait and see."

"Perhaps," he said somewhat cryptically, and then he bid me farewell.

39

★ ★ ★

"Come, we must go too," Ismail said. "We don't have much time."

I followed him out into the hall, where we joined up with the security officers. We exited through a side door into chilly night air. But we were not getting into an armored motorcade. Ismail led me instead to a military helicopter that was already powered up and ready to lift off. Following his lead, I climbed into the back of the Black Hawk, fastened my seat belt, and put on a headset.

"So where are you taking me, Ismail?" I asked over the roar of the rotors as the rest of the detail climbed aboard.

"I'm afraid that's classified," he said. "But you'll see when we get there."

As we lifted off the ground, the head of security pulled shades down over all the windows. I was facing the rear of the chopper, so I couldn't even see through the front windshield. Then again, it was well past sundown and the pilots were flying with night-vision gear, so I wouldn't have seen much anyway.

"May I ask you some questions before we get there?" I asked.

"Ask anything you want," Ismail said, nodding.

I fished a notepad and pen out of my satchel and got to work. "How long have you had Abu Khalif in custody?" I began.

"Sorry, that's classified," he replied.

"Where did you catch him?"

"Classified."

"What was he charged with?"

"I'm afraid I can't tell you that."

"How many ISIS fighters are being held in Iraqi prisons at the moment?"

Tikriti shook his head.

"That's classified too?" I asked.

"I'm afraid so," he said.

"Okay, fine; Karbouli said you did all the initial interrogations of Khalif," I said, scrounging for something usable. "What can you tell me about him?"

"I'm sorry, J. B. I really can't say anything."

"Are you kidding?"

"No, I'm not."

My irritation was beginning to rise. "I thought you said I could ask you anything."

"I never said I was cleared to give you answers," he said.

That was even more irritating. But Ismail wouldn't budge.

He looked nervous. I wanted to know why. I was sure he wanted to tell me something. But he couldn't. Perhaps if we were alone, but not now—not with the pilots and security detail listening in.

I was beginning to wonder whether the only person I was going to get on the record tonight was Abu Khalif himself.

"So how's your family?" I asked, desperately searching for something we could talk about. "I hear ISIS forces seized Tikrit. Were your people able to get out all right?"

There was a long, awkward silence. At first I thought he was going to quip, "That's classified." But the longer he remained silent, the more worried I became.

"Please tell me they're okay," I said.

There was another long pause.

"I'm afraid not," he finally replied. "They were all wiped out."

"All of them?" I asked, aghast.

"Only one of my nephews survived. My mother was raped by ISIS terrorists. Then they shot her in the face. My father and three brothers were crucified. ISIS posted their pictures on the Internet along with photos of hundreds of others they had crucified as well."

I didn't know what to say, so I said nothing.

"These people are animals, J. B., savages—driven by Satan himself."

I was sickened and speechless, barely able to process what he was saying. I had met Ismail's family years earlier. Ismail had taken me to Tikrit to have lunch with them one day, not long after the liberation of Iraq, and what a sumptuous and festive meal it had been. It was Easter. They were all Chaldean Christians, and this was the first time in their entire lives that they had been able to truly celebrate the death and resurrection of Christ openly and without fear of retribution. They were lovely, joyful people.

Ismail's father had grown up with Saddam Hussein and had become a high-ranking general in Saddam's Republican Guard. Because of his connections, the family had been largely immune from the regime's brutality, and Ismail himself had risen to the rank of colonel in an elite unit that provided protection to Saddam's family. But when the American mechanized forces rolled into Iraq in the spring of 2003, Ismail and his father defected and began secretly helping the CIA bring down the Butcher of Baghdad. Now Ismail was one of the highest-ranking Christians in the modern Iraqi security forces. He was also one of the most committed to Iraq's democratization. To think of the price he was having to pay was almost more than I could bear.

"I am so very sorry, Ismail," I said after a few moments.

The words sounded so lame and so hollow, but I didn't know what else to say. He nodded but did not respond.

★ ★ ★

A few minutes later, we began to descend, and my stomach began to churn.

When we finally touched down, the shades went up and the doors on both sides of the Black Hawk whooshed open. Waiting for us were several dozen members of Iraq's most elite special forces unit in full battle gear. Had they been assigned to guard Khalif 24-7, or were they just here to protect us? There was clearly no point in asking, but I couldn't help but be curious.

I exited the chopper amid the glare of enormous stadium lights, but once my eyes adjusted, a chill ran down my spine. I knew exactly where I was, for I'd been here before.

We were in the central courtyard of Iraq's most notorious prison: Abu Ghraib.

It was a sprawling facility covering the better part of an acre on the outskirts of Baghdad. It had once housed more than fifteen thousand inmates, from murderers and rapists to full-fledged jihadists. Until April 2004, most Americans had never heard of Abu Ghraib, nor had most people in the world. Then *60 Minutes* broke the story of the terrible abuses taking place at the prison and revealed the most horrific pictures of American soldiers smiling beside piles of naked Arab prisoners. There were photos of U.S. soldiers beating—or pretending to beat—prisoners, and photos of our troops engaging in all manner of other terrible and offensive behaviors, effectively torturing and humiliating the prisoners in complete dereliction of their military codes of conduct, the Geneva Convention, and common moral sense.

It was a story I should have broken to the world myself, but I admit I was late to understand the gravity of the rumors I'd been hearing for months. The American public was indignant, and rightfully so, when they saw and heard the reports. So was the rest of the world. But the Islamic world—and especially the Iraqi people, many of whom had initially seen the Americans as liberators—were enraged. As news of the atrocities spread, only the jihadists were overjoyed. A handful of American traitors—that's how I saw them, anyway—had given extremists like al Qaeda and later ISIS the ultimate recruiting and fund-raising tool.

"I thought you closed this place," I shouted, since the chopper was only just winding down.

"For a while, we did," Ismail replied. "But we needed the space, so we opened it again not long ago, but only for the most dangerous of prisoners."

"How many is that?"

"I'm sorry, J. B.; that's classified."

"Come on, just give me a hint so I'm not too far off the mark in my story."

"Absolutely not," Ismail responded. "Please don't ask me again. You can say in your article that you interviewed Khalif in a prison in Iraq, but you cannot provide any other details. Are we clear?"

I shrugged, but he grabbed me by the shoulders and looked straight into my eyes. "Are we clear?" he repeated. "If not, we can power the chopper up and get you back to Baghdad right now."

"Yeah," I quickly conceded. "We're clear."

There was no point blowing the interview over details.

40

★ ★ ★

Ismail led me into the prison.

He introduced me to the warden, and together the three of us walked down one long filthy corridor after another until they ushered me through a steel door into an interrogation room.

The room wasn't small, but it wasn't large, either—maybe thirty feet by twenty feet. It was made of concrete, with a second steel door directly across from the one I had entered through. There was a two-way mirror in the wall to my right, a steel table in the middle that was bolted to the floor, and two steel chairs, also bolted to the floor, neither with any padding or cushion, facing each other across the table. Two soldiers bearing submachine guns entered behind me and took up positions in the two corners of the room at my back. Then Ismail and the warden brought in metal folding chairs, which they set beside me.

My heart began to pound. I was about to be face-to-face with a psychopathic killer. This was the most important interview of my life, but suddenly I wasn't sure I wanted to be there at all.

"Remember, you have only thirty minutes," Ismail said. "Not a second more."

I turned and glanced at the wall behind me, where I could see two small video cameras mounted high above the door, each with a red light on to indicate that they were live and recording everything we said and did here.

Just then, the steel door across the room opened, and four guards brought in a man in handcuffs and leg irons and wearing an orange prison jumpsuit. He looked like a cross between Khalid Sheikh Mohammed and Charles Manson. He had a long face and an angular nose that looked like it had been broken several times, and he sported a bushy gray mustache and a wild, unkempt black-and-gray beard. He had the beginnings of male pattern baldness that spread from his forehead to the top of his scalp, but behind that he had rather long hair, a dirty brownish gray, tied in a ponytail held together by a pale-red rubber band. His arms were clean of any tattoos, but I immediately noticed that there were large, jagged scars on his hands and forearms. That said, it was his dark-brown eyes that any normal person would notice first, for they were sunken with rings around them as if he got very little sleep, and the moment they locked onto mine, the hair on the back of my neck literally stood erect.

I had with me a digital recorder, a Nikon digital camera, and a reporter's notebook and pen, and I set them all on the table, along with my grandfather's pocket watch so I could keep careful time. When the prisoner sat down in front of me and was chained to the metal chair, Ismail nodded his assent.

I turned on the recorder and began immediately.

"You are Abu Khalif?"

Ismail repeated my question in Arabic.

"I am," Khalif replied in English, catching both of us completely off guard.

"You speak English?" I asked. "I had no idea."

He nodded and glared at me, never once looking at the Iraqi officials.

"My name is J. B. Collins," I continued.

"I know who you are."

"I'm a foreign correspondent for the *New York Times*."

"While you're still alive," he replied in a monotone.

That stopped me cold. In chains, in prison, in the middle of Iraq's most secure facility, this man was threatening to kill me. I fought to keep my composure.

"May I take some pictures?"

He nodded, and I snapped twenty or so photos from several different angles. They bore none of the quality or artistry of Abdel's work, but they would suffice.

"Now, recently I interviewed your deputy in Syria, your cousin Jamal Ramzy."

"Yes, he told me."

"You spoke with him? How?"

"That is none of your concern," he said, leaning forward in his chair. "Or yours, Mr. Tikriti," he added while still looking at me.

I looked at Ismail and the warden, both of

whom were clearly flabbergasted. It was all I could do not to get up from the table, but I was determined not to show fear, though it was rapidly welling within me.

"Very well," I said. "Let's begin this interview so you can make your case to the world. First, a few background questions. You are the spiritual leader and supreme commander of the Islamic State of Iraq and al-Sham?"

"Yes."

"And your name, Khalif, essentially means a political and religious leader of a Muslim state, 'the representative of Allah on earth,' does it not?"

"It does."

"But that is your nom de guerre."

"Yes."

"Your real name is Abdel Diab."

"Yes."

"Diab, the wolf?"

He nodded.

"What year were you born?"

"1969," he said.

"Month?"

"January."

"What day?"

"The fifth."

"Your father was Palestinian, from Ramallah?"

"Yes, peace be upon him."

"And your mother's family escaped from Nablus in 1948 and settled in Zarqā, in Jordan?"

"Yes."

"Who was your great-grandfather?"

"Mohammed Amin al-Husseini, the Grand

Mufti of Jerusalem," he said, straightening his posture.

"The Grand Mufti who allied himself with Hitler."

"Yes."

"Would you align yourself with Adolf Hitler if you could?"

"No," he said without hesitation.

"Why not?" I asked.

Again Khalif did not hesitate. "He would align himself with me."

"Why is that?" I asked.

"Because, Mr. Collins, in the end, I will kill more Jews than Adolf Hitler ever dreamed."

41

★ ★ ★

There were still more biographical details I wanted to confirm.

Jordanian intelligence officials had told Omar that Khalif's father was killed during the Black September events of 1970—the Palestinian revolt led by Yasser Arafat that attempted to overthrow the Hashemite Kingdom of Jordan. They also said that after Black September, Khalif's mother had escaped with all six children to the United Arab Emirates, where her uncle was living. She never remarried.

Ari Shalit, meanwhile, had told me Khalif himself had been born in Zarqā and raised in Dubai. He returned to Jordan in his teen years and was reportedly arrested numerous times for theft, drug smuggling, and even rape but was repeatedly released from Jordanian jails in a series of prisoner amnesty programs.

Jamal Ramzy, of course, had told me—or confirmed to me—other details of the story: about recruiting his cousin into al Qaeda to fight in Afghanistan and later in Iraq. But how exactly had Khalif risen to power after the death of Zarqawi? What were the specific events that led to his formal break with al Qaeda? What difference if any did the recent death of Zawahiri at the hands of the U.S. government make to the equation?

I wanted answers to these and a hundred other questions. But there simply wasn't time. I wasn't writing a book on Abu Khalif; I was writing a newspaper profile. I had only twenty-two minutes left, and I had to get him on the record on several current and critical issues.

"What has been the biggest ISIS victory so far?" I asked for starters.

"Being disavowed by al Qaeda," he said calmly.

This guy never ceased to catch me by surprise.

"You're saying of all your successes on the battlefield, you consider Zawahiri publicly disavowing you the greatest ISIS victory?"

"Yes."

"Why?"

"It showed the world how weak Zawahiri was. It confirmed that al Qaeda died with Usama bin Laden, peace be upon him. ISIS is the rightful heir to bin Laden's legacy, and we will build the caliphate without the infidels."

I was taking notes as fast as I could. "You consider al Qaeda leaders *infidels*?"

"Of course, and we call on all their jihadis to abandon them and come join us for victory."

"Okay, what was your second-greatest victory?"

"Driving the Americans out of Iraq and cleansing the holy soil of their filthy, arrogant presence."

"You're speaking of the American military withdrawal from Iraq at the end of 2011?"

"Yes."

"What was your strategy to accomplish this?"

"It had four parts," he replied matter-of-factly. "First, we aimed to target and kill as many of America's allies in Iraq as possible."

"Why?"

"To persuade them to leave and thus isolate the United States."

"Which allies?"

"All of them, but especially the British and the U.N."

"What was the second part of the strategy?"

"To target, kill, damage, and destroy as many Iraqi government officials and facilities as possible to exhaust and demoralize the Iraqi government and persuade them to want U.S. forces to leave."

"Third?"

"We aimed to target and kill as many NGO aid workers and government contractors as possible, to exhaust and demoralize them as well and drive them out of Iraq."

"And fourth?"

"To target and kill Shias, destroy Shia mosques, and bait the Americans into the middle of a Sunni–Shia civil war. Zawahiri was opposed to this most of all. He said it would never work. But as you well know, it did. The last American soldier left the seat of our caliphate in December 2011, and then we turned our attention to Syria."

"Why Syria?"

"Bashar al-Assad is an infidel. He had to be taken down."

"Your gains in Syria have captured the attention of the world."

"Our gains in Syria have been a serious strategic failure, though we recovered in time and recalibrated."

"Failure?" I asked. "What do you mean?"

"One of my major objectives was to penetrate the suburbs of Damascus," Khalif explained without emotion. "I believed that if ISIS forces could breach the perimeter of the capital, we could force the criminal Assad to use chemical weapons against us."

"Which he did," I said.

"Yes, and thereby crossed the Americans' famous 'red line.' At that point, I was certain we had won. I was certain that the Americans would unleash their military might against the Assad regime and either bring it down or so weaken it that we could finish the job. Then ISIS would have filled the vacuum and seized Damascus and the rest of the country. But to my astonishment, your president surrendered. He did nothing. He did not launch air strikes. He did not bring down Assad, and consequently it's taken us much longer than we planned to finish the job. That was a serious failure on my part. I vastly overestimated the fortitude of American leadership."

I was surprised but pleased by how responsive Khalif was being. He was talking, on the record. And he wasn't giving me pablum; he was giving me real insights to his worldview and quotes that would make news.

"Zooming out for a moment to look at the big picture, why is ISIS necessary?" I asked. "I mean, you've talked about your disappointments with al Qaeda, but what about Hezbollah, Hamas, and Islamic Jihad? Why is another jihadist group necessary?"

"Was the caliphate established before we emerged?" Khalif asked. "Has Palestine been liberated? Have the infidels been exterminated from the holy lands, from Mecca and Medina to Jerusalem? No. Why not? Because too many leaders who say they are committed to jihad are really businessmen. They are not true warriors for Allah. They are not true revolutionaries. They are running big corporations, large bureaucracies. They are not true believers. They are infidels. They are *kuffär*. If they were faithful warriors, then the hand of Allah would be with them. They would have gotten the job done by now. They would have established the caliphate and restored the glory that once belonged to Islam."

"Do you believe the hand of Allah is with you?"

"Of course. The evidence is clear."

"Ten more minutes," Ismail Tikriti said behind me.

I glanced at my pocket watch. The time was going far too fast.

"So what are your objectives now?" I asked.

"We have many," Khalif said. "We must finish our work here and in Syria. But as my cousin Jamal told you, we are about to open a new front. We are focused on a third target."

"Where?"

"Wasn't Jamal clear?"

"I think the world needs to hear from you directly."

"It is not a secret—we will ignite a Third Intifada in Palestine," he replied. "We will launch a full-scale, all-out jihad against the Zionists, and we will hunt down and destroy anyone who aids or abets them in their criminal occupation of Muslim lands and their enslavement of the Arab people."

"That's rather ambitious, is it not?"

"We submit to the will of Allah."

"Can you be more specific? What are your tactical objectives in the year ahead?"

"We have ten," he said.

"Ten objectives you want to achieve in the next twelve months?"

"They may take a few years to achieve, but I hope to do it in just one—inshallah."

"Will you share them with our readers?"

"Of course," he said. "We aim to capture and behead the president of the United States and to raise the flag of ISIS over the White House. We aim to assassinate the prime minister of Israel. In due course, we will unleash a wave of suicide bombers and other attacks against the Great Satan and the Little Satan and rid the world of these cancerous tumors. But our highest priorities are to rid the region of apostate Arab leaders who have betrayed the Muslim people and the Prophet himself. We will target the leaders of Jordan and the Palestinian Authority and Saudi Arabia, as well as Syria and Iraq—we will find them, kill them, and topple their governments one by one. In the time of our choosing, we will deal with the Egyptians, too. We will unify these liberated lands and people under a single command and reestablish the true caliphate, with me as the emir, beginning in the heart of the Levant but eventually extending throughout the region and soon the globe."

I was writing as fast as I possibly could. I was struck that Khalif was not animated. He spoke without any real emotion. Indeed, it was mostly in a monotone. He looked like a serial killer—creepy, sadistic—but there was an almost-supernatural aura of authority about him, as if he were truly in complete command of not only his own destiny but that of millions of others as well.

"Suicide bombers against the U.S. and Israel—when, how?" I asked.

"You will see soon enough, Mr. Collins."

"Does ISIS have sleeper cells in the U.S.?"

"I will not go into operational details," he said. "You asked for our goals. That's what I've given you. But I will say that we have recruited many Americans, Canadians, and Europeans to the cause of jihad. These warriors have gained real combat experience in Syria and here in Iraq. They are well trained. They look like you. They will blend in easily. And they carry valid American, Canadian, and E.U. passports. They will not be detected by your Homeland Security. I guarantee you that."

I absorbed this for a moment, then changed course. "Why do you hate the United States so much?"

He started to go on a lengthy riff about America's rejection of God and exportation of pornography and Washington's funding of the Israelis (whom he called "criminal Zionists") and lack of support for the Palestinians. Each sentence was a headline unto itself, and I now realized I might need to break up the interview into a series of articles. But when Ismail said we had just three minutes left, I had to cut Khalif off. There was one more topic I had to ask him about and this was it. It was now or never.

"So, Mr. Khalif, I must ask you: did ISIS capture chemical weapons in Syria?"

There was a long silence. Indeed, it was so long and so quiet that I could actually hear my pocket watch ticking over the hum of the fluorescent lights above us. And all the while he just stared at me, without blinking, and I stared back. It was weird—eerie. I'd heard people say they'd been in the presence of evil and it had made their skin crawl. I'd never known what they meant. But now I did. This guy was sheer evil. I'm not saying he wasn't human. But if I had ever been in the presence of someone who was demon-possessed, it had to have been right then.

I could feel the fear rising in me, but I resolved not to give in. This man was a killer. His people weren't just conquering Arab lands; they were slaughtering everyone who got in their way. But I was not going to let him intimidate me. He was the one in chains. I was walking out of here a free man in a few minutes. He'd already given me a huge story. It was going to be the lead story in tomorrow's paper and front-page news around the globe—the world's first interview with the world's most dangerous terrorist. I had what I needed. If he didn't want to talk about the WMD, that was fine. I'd given him his chance, but I wasn't going to beg.

Finally he opened his mouth and stunned me again.

"Yes."

"Yes, what?" I asked, not sure I could have possibly understood him correctly.

"Yes, ISIS forces captured chemical weapons in Syria," he said clearly and directly. "They were precursors, actually, to produce sarin gas. I don't have the exact figures, but my men drove off with hundreds and hundreds of crates."

"Where?"

"At the base near Aleppo, as you reported."

"You're aware of my report?"

"I am aware of and have read all your recent articles."

"You have access to the *New York Times* in Abu Ghraib?"

"I'm in prison, Mr. Collins, not a cave. We are not, let us say, without certain amenities."

I was insatiably curious about how he got his information and how he could continue to run ISIS and stay in touch with Ramzy and his other commanders from behind bars and walls that were eight feet thick. But there was no point asking him in front of the deputy director of Iraqi intelligence. There were certain questions I knew Khalif would not answer.

"We need to wrap up," Ismail said, tapping his wristwatch.

"Just one more question," I said.

"Make it quick," Ismail replied.

He was on a tight timetable, and I could see the security guys getting antsy. They were clearly not happy having a high-level Iraqi cabinet official outside the Green Zone, especially in the presence of the head of ISIS, who apparently had direct communication with his commanders outside.

I was about to ask my final question when suddenly the lights flickered and the table shook.

The warden barked a question or perhaps an order to one of his aides, who immediately radioed someone else, presumably at the prison's security command post we had passed on our way inside.

I turned back to Khalif to pose my question when the steel door behind me flew open and a guard shouted something in Arabic.

"We need to go," the warden said. "Right now."

42

★ ★ ★

The moment the door opened, I heard the explosions.

I knew immediately the prison was under attack, and I knew it had to be ISIS forces. But what worried me most was the sudden realization that Abu Khalif had likely been aware the attack was coming and might have even planned its timing.

Ismail Tikriti grabbed me by the arm and shouted, "We must go—now!"

I turned to gather my camera, digital recorder, and pocket watch and threw them into my satchel as the guards were dragging Abu Khalif out the other door, but I will never forget the twisted smile on his face or his cry at the top of his lungs: *"Allahu akbar!"*

Surrounded by soldiers, Ismail, the warden, and I raced through the corridors of the dilapidated prison complex amid the sounds of massive explosions, intense machine-gun fire, and the raucous cheers of hundreds of inmates. We quickly linked up with other heavily armed soldiers who guided us back toward the main courtyard.

I could hear the Black Hawk powering up and was eager to board and get as far from this nightmare scenario as possible. But just as the doors to the courtyard were electronically unlocked for us, I heard the high-pitched whistle of an inbound mortar shell coming from the southwest. It missed the chopper's rotors by maybe twenty or thirty feet but created an explosion that literally lifted me off my feet and sent me flying through the air. I lammed against a cement wall and landed hard. A terrible pain shot through my back and right leg. I felt blood on my head and was afraid I'd broken something.

A split second later, another shell came from behind us and scored nearly a direct hit. The helicopter erupted into a massive fireball. I covered my head and shielded my eyes, but it hardly did any good. The searing heat was more than anyone could bear. Scraps of molten metal were falling from the sky. The wretched stench of burning jet fuel and human flesh was overwhelming. And the mortars kept coming.

"Let's go, let's go," shouted the warden and the head of the security detail, grabbing Ismail and me by the collars and hauling us to our feet.

I was limping. I was in pain. But I was moving.

Then I saw Ismail. His face was covered in blood. He had shrapnel wounds all over his body. I could see the fear in his eyes, and I knew we were both in a fight for our lives.

We followed the warden back into the building and soon were moving through the corridors as fast as we could, though to where I had no idea.

Were the guards taking us to a safe room to ride out the attack? Or to the motor pool to grab some Humvees and make a break for it? There were no air options at the moment. But Ismail wasn't talking, and the warden was ashen.

We soon reached the security command center. The warden and his men assessed their options while I helped Ismail sit down. I took off my jacket and draped it over him to keep him warm.

Though I'd had several years of Arabic and was conversational in most situations, these guys were talking too fast for me to follow. But amid the fog of war, one thing was clear: our options were limited and rapidly closing.

Though my vantage point wasn't ideal, I had a partial view of a bank of video feeds from dozens of security cameras positioned all over the enormous labyrinth of prison facilities. I could see what appeared to be the remains of a truck—an 18-wheeler or perhaps an oil tanker—sticking out of the main gates of the prison, engulfed in flames. I guessed that an ISIS loyalist might have stolen the truck and used it for a suicide mission to crash the gates and create an opening for jihadists to pour through.

It wasn't just the main gates, however. On the video monitors I could see multiple car and truck bombers had hit all the prison gates, maybe even simultaneously. That, and the never-ending barrage of mortars, had pinned down the security forces inside the prison and created a breach in the outer perimeter for the hundreds of ISIS forces I could now see making their way inside.

That was when I began to get scared. The initial shock of the attack and its magnitude was rapidly giving way to the realization that these soldiers and guards assigned to us might not be able to stave off this onslaught. A prison doctor rushed over to Ismail and began administering first aid. The warden, meanwhile, was on the phone. I couldn't get much of the conversation, but the words *reinforcements* and *air support* cut through the noise. As soon as he hung up, he turned back to me.

"We need to get you men to a safe room," he said calmly.

"Where's that?"

"Directly below us, two flights down. These men will take you there."

I was about to thank him, but the head of the detail spoke first in rapid-fire Arabic. I didn't get much of it but it was obvious he was insisting that the warden go to the safe room as well. There was a brief argument, but when a series of mortars struck no more than a hundred meters from our position, the warden accepted the counsel of his men.

With a dozen soldiers creating a phalanx of security around us, we started moving down the corridor toward a bank of elevators located around the corner to our right. But at that moment we saw a grenade go skittering across the floor of the hallway directly ahead of us.

We dove for cover as it exploded.

Then someone threw two more grenades, which detonated one after the other, shaking the building and filling the corridor with smoke and debris.

The jihadists were in the building.

I told myself not to panic. I was in good hands. The men guarding us were trained professionals.

But then a group of masked men burst through the exit doors in front of us, firing automatic weapons. The soldiers in front of us never had a chance. Four of them fell immediately, dead or dying fast. I hit the deck as the rest of the detail returned fire. I heard an explosion at the other end of the corridor. Turning to look, I saw that an exit door had just been blown to smithereens. Another group of masked rebels was storming toward us.

One by one, the members of our security team dropped to the ground. Most were dead, but some were writhing on the floor in agony. That didn't last long. The commander of the attacking group, wearing a black hood and a flak jacket with an ISIS patch sewn on the front, drew a pistol and shot each of them dead, one by one. And then he turned to Ismail, the warden, and me.

We were all unarmed. There was no way out and no hope of mercy.

Ismail was already badly wounded, but he was a rock. He showed no fear, only a steely determination I found remarkable. But the warden was shaking. His entire body was quivering uncontrollably.

I was just as scared but forced myself to lie completely still. I kept my eyes open, though. I'm not sure why. Instinct. Fear. Shock. I really don't know. But there was no point playing dead. I wasn't going to fool any of these men. They were going to shoot me anyway.

With mortars still landing and one explosion

after another shaking the building to its core, the warden started to beg for his life. But the hooded ISIS commander would have none of it. He ordered his men, who were surrounding us now, to tie up the warden's hands and feet and put duct tape over his mouth to shut him up. They did the same with Ismail. Next someone opened a backpack and pulled out a tripod and video camera. Another fighter opened his backpack and set up two stands of movie lights. Instinctively, I tried to back away until I felt a boot on my neck and the barrel of an AK-47 pressed against my temple.

When I looked over and saw a bloodstained machete in the commander's hands, I shut my eyes and waited for the end. I wish I could tell you that I prayed, that I cried out to God for mercy. But the honest truth is my mind went blank. I was too terrified to think or speak or pray or beg.

Someone kicked me hard in the stomach. I bit my tongue, trying not to cry out, but I doubled up in pain. Then I heard someone shouting at me.

"Collins! Are you Collins?"

I opened my eyes. What else was I supposed to do? The commander was standing over me, a .45 pistol at my forehead. This was it.

Again the commander shouted at me. *"Are you Collins?"* he demanded in a thick Syrian accent but nevertheless speaking in English.

Someone pulled the duct tape off my mouth. I tried to speak. I tried to say yes. But I couldn't. So I just nodded and said nothing.

"Get up!"

Why? What were they going to do? Legs shaking, I struggled to get to my feet.

"Take this!" he said, putting the video camera in my hands. *"Put it on the tripod. The world must know what we've done."*

This couldn't be happening. They weren't just going to make me watch them do it; they were going to make me film it.

I had no choice. I took the video camera and walked a few steps over to the tripod. I set up the camera, turned it on, and waited, but not for long. A moment later, Abu Khalif came around the corner, dressed in his orange jumpsuit.

Khalif walked over to Ismail and the warden and stopped. The terrorists were binding the Iraqi officials' torsos and extremities with ropes and cords of some kind, making it impossible for them to move their arms and legs. The warden's mouth was taped shut, but his eyes told me everything he was thinking and feeling. The only time I'd ever seen someone as terrified was when I watched that Syrian soldier die in front of me in Homs. Ismail, however, remained resolute. He too was bound and gagged. But he wasn't going to beg for his life, not even with his eyes.

Khalif turned and looked at me.

"Start the recording, Mr. Collins," he ordered.

My hands trembling, I did as I was told. What other choice did I have?

Khalif spoke directly to the camera. He wasn't wearing a mask or a hood. He wasn't trying to disguise his voice or conceal his identity. He simply spoke in the same eerie monotone with which he had spoken to me just minutes before.

"I am Abu Khalif, the emir of the Islamic State of Iraq and al-Sham," he began. "In the name of Allah, the Most Gracious and the Most Compassionate, I declare today that the next phase of the liberation of Iraq has begun. We will establish a true Islamic caliphate, governed by Sharia law. We will care for the poor and set the prisoners free. We will drive out the infidels and restore the justice of the sword to those who commit treason against Allah and against the Prophet, peace be upon him."

Someone handed him the machete.

"Today, the faithful and brave forces of ISIS have captured two of Iraq's most vile traitors," he continued. "As Iraq's deputy director of intelligence, Ismail Tikriti is a criminal. He is responsible for the torture and execution of many loyal servants of Allah. He is a betrayer of all that is good and pure and righteous in the world. The warden of Abu Ghraib is equally complicit in these crimes against Allah and against the true Muslim people. These men are the epitome of corruption and arrogance, and today they will face the sword of true justice."

I couldn't bear to watch but was not allowed to look away.

And I knew I was next.

43

* * *

MOSUL, IRAQ

I will never be able to erase the memory of seeing a man beheaded.

It was the most revolting sight one can possibly imagine.

In the end, only Ismail Tikriti had been murdered on camera; the warden had been dragged away screaming. At some point, after vomiting so many times that I was dry heaving and gasping for air, apparently I finally blacked out. And when I woke up, I had no idea where I was or how I'd gotten there or how long I'd been unconscious. I was stunned that Abu Khalif had let me live, and I was emotionally traumatized in a way that defies description.

I found myself chained to a wall in a small, dank, chilly room. As my eyes adjusted to the dim light, I realized I was surrounded by filthy concrete walls and men with machine guns—men in hoods, men who began to chatter in Arabic the moment they saw me lifting my head off the wooden planks that served as my bed. Before I understood what was happening, I was hauled to my feet, which were bound in leg irons, and led—handcuffed, with duct tape over my mouth—down a dark hallway. We headed up a stairwell, through a door, and into what appeared to be a modestly appointed living room. There I was told to sit on a tattered, faded-red couch, which I did immediately. It was only then that I realized I had been stripped to my boxer shorts and a T-shirt. But the air in the room was not nearly as cold as it had been below.

As I looked around, I saw that we were on the ground floor of an apartment building. My first impression was that an old retired couple had once lived here. Perhaps we were in the flat of the parents or grandparents of one of the ISIS rebels. But this apartment clearly no longer served as anyone's real home. There were basic accommodations and family pictures on the walls and knickknacks of various kinds here and there and even an old upright piano in the corner. But to my right, the table and chairs had been removed from the dining room. In their place were stacks of wooden crates, stamped with shipping instructions in Russian. I wondered if they were full of weapons. To my left was a cramped kitchen, but whatever appliances and cabinetry had once been there had been removed. The space was filled, instead, with rather sophisticated-looking communications equipment, computers, and hard drives.

This was a safe house.

There were no movie lights here in the living room, no tripods, and no video cameras. There were no plastic tarps on the floors or any sign of a sword or machete so far as I could see. I knew full well that could change at any moment. But since I was still alive, ISIS must want something. What that was, however, I had no idea.

A few minutes later, Abu Khalif strode into the room and sat in an old recliner. No longer wearing an orange jumpsuit, he was now wearing a traditional white robe and black- and white-checked kaffiyeh and looking very much like the Arab emir he presented himself to be, perhaps even a Palestinian one, given the color and design of this particular headdress.

"*As-salamu alaykum,*" he began, the standard Arabic greeting. *Peace be upon you.*

I did not respond, "*Wa 'alaykum-as-salam,*" the standard Arabic reply. Even if I had wanted to—and I did not—my mouth was still taped shut. Several of the guards did it, though, and then Khalif ordered one of them to remove the tape.

I could speak again. I just had nothing to say.

"Welcome to Mosul," Khalif began, taking a seat directly across from me. "Though you too are an infidel, Mr. Collins, I chose to spare your life for one very simple reason—you are still useful to me."

He did not emphasize the word *still*, but it stood out to me all the same.

"I did not want the world to know ISIS had seized those chemical weapons," he continued. "I believe Jamal Ramzy made my wishes very clear, did he not?"

He paused for me to reply.

"He did," I said quietly.

There was no point denying it now.

"There are very few people in this world who defy a direct order from me and live," Khalif went on. "But after your article, I realized there was no point in denying it. I realized I should be proud of our accomplishment, embrace it. We have done what Usama bin Laden and his lackey, Zawahiri, were never able to do—become an army that actually possesses weapons of mass destruction."

I could tell he had more to say, so I remained silent.

"Here is what you are going to do," he said. "You are going to serve the Islamic State and prove your ongoing usefulness by writing the story of my escape from captivity at the hands of the traitors to Islam. The story will be datelined from Abu Ghraib. In addition, I will permit you to write the profile of me that brought you to Iraq. That story will be datelined from Baghdad. Under no circumstances will you mention Mosul. Disobedience of any kind will be punished swiftly and severely."

I knew what that meant. I remembered all too well the way Ismail Tikriti had died.

"You will be given a notebook computer and a quiet place to write," Khalif went on. "When you are finished, you will be given a thumb drive to save the articles. I will personally e-mail the stories to your editor in Washington. You will have no direct contact with the outside world by e-mail, phone, or any other means for twenty-four hours."

Against my will, my stomach suddenly growled, and I realized I was starving.

Khalif noticed. "When you are finished writing, you will be given hot lentil soup, bread, and coffee. Until then you will do nothing but write. Do you understand?"

I was offered no choice; nor did I need one. Khalif knew I would say yes. I had no desire to die in the gruesome manner I had witnessed earlier. Besides, this was precisely the story I'd come to Iraq to get.

The second story, at least. Certainly not the first.

I still said nothing. This was clearly not a dialogue or an interview. He was giving me orders. I was expected to obey, pure and simple. I nodded, and once I did, I was quickly led away by several guards. They took me to a windowless room where I found the computer Khalif had assigned to me. Then they left and locked the door behind them.

I checked but the computer had no Internet connection. Either there was no wireless network in the house, or the computer's ability to connect with it had been disabled. I'm not sure which, and since I'm not particularly tech savvy, all I was left with was the stark realization that I was utterly alone with my thoughts.

Then I noticed my briefcase sitting in the corner. Rummaging through it, I saw that most of my things had been removed. But my notepad was still there, as was the digital recorder. So was the gift from my grandfather, still ticking. I concluded that the sooner I was finished, the sooner I would be able to eat and get out of these claustrophobic surroundings. So I got to work.

For the next several hours, I worked without a

break—without coffee, water, or even the opportunity to use a restroom. I wrote the story of the prison break first, as this was the freshest in my mind. It was a first-person account and included the beheading of Ismail Tikriti, though I did not include the most graphic details. Only then did I set to work transcribing the half-hour interview with the ISIS leader and writing an accompanying profile.

When I was finished proofreading the two pieces and making some minor corrections, I knocked on the door. Two guards led me back to Khalif. He read my work and agreed to transmit it.

"You are a first-rate journalist, Mr. Collins," he said.

I wasn't sure how to receive a compliment from a mass murderer.

He asked me for the e-mail address of my editor in Washington, and I gave it to him. He said he would transmit the article and several of the photographs from my Nikon to Allen along with a note written in my name explaining that I was safe for the moment and writing from a "secure and undisclosed location." Then he said that I should go have some bread and soup and get some rest.

"You will need it," he told me. "You have a big day tomorrow."

I didn't ask him what he meant. I didn't want to know.

44

* * *

The guards woke me up before dawn.

They gave me back my clothes and my toiletries and told me to follow them. They locked me in the bathroom and told me to take a shower. The water was freezing cold, so I essentially took a sponge bath instead. When I had dressed and brushed my teeth, I knocked on the door.

They let me out and took me back to the living room. The shades were shut, but I could tell it was still dark outside. As I sat down—once again in handcuffs and leg irons—a deep sense of dread and foreboding came upon me. Whatever Khalif had meant by the "big day" ahead of me had arrived.

I sat there for a while—maybe fifteen or twenty minutes, maybe longer. None of the guards said a word, and I said nothing either. They gave me nothing to do, and with every minute that passed, my anxieties intensified. My mind raced through a thousand what-if scenarios, each more chilling than the last. Finally Abu Khalif entered the room and took his seat across from me while his bodyguards took up positions around the room.

"Now, Mr. Collins, it is time for me to ask you some questions," he began, still without a hint of emotion in his voice. "How is your mother doing? Maggie, yes? What a lovely home she has there in Bar Harbor—Waldron Street, isn't it?"

My stomach clenched. Why was this monster bringing up my mother? And how did he know what street she lived on? I said nothing.

"And your brother—Matt, I believe; and his wife, Annie—how are they? And those precious little children. Is everything well with them? A healthy family is so important. Don't you agree?"

Now it was clear. This was a warning. A direct threat, in fact: play ball or sentence those closest to me to death.

"Feeling a little quiet today, are we?"

I clenched my jaw and said nothing.

"I'm afraid I don't have the time for your resistance, Mr. Collins," Khalif continued. "There are certain things I want to know from you, and I will get answers. To begin with, are the rumors I'm hearing from my sources in Jerusalem and Ramallah true? Is the criminal Zionist Lavi about to sign a treaty with that Palestinian traitor Salim Mansour?"

The question startled me. I'd braced myself for more questions about my family, but it seemed that was just the sadistic preamble to what he really wanted to discuss.

"Why do you ask that?" I inquired.

"No, Mr. Collins, you're not asking the questions today—*I am*," he shot back, his eyes glaring, his voice thick with emotion for the first time.

My pulse began to quicken. It was not wise to make this lunatic angry, but what was the right answer? What did he want to hear?

"Yes, they're true," I replied, concluding if I was going to die anyway, it wasn't going to be for telling foolish lies.

Yet rather than make him angrier, my answer seemed to calm him considerably. He eased back in his seat. The emotions in his face and in his voice seemed to drain away.

"You're saying Lavi and Mansour have hammered out a treaty?"

"I believe they have."

"And it's done, final, complete?"

"That's what I've been told."

"Why haven't you reported it yet?"

"That's not my beat, and I was coming here instead."

"To Iraq?"

"Yes."

"Direct from Israel?"

"No."

"From Jordan?"

I hesitated for a moment but then nodded.

He seemed to chew on that for a moment, then asked, "How soon will the treaty be signed?"

"I don't know."

"What *do* you know?"

"I hear there's going to be a signing at the White House sometime later this month," I said, avoiding any reference to the announcement ceremony that was going to be held within days, presumably in Jerusalem.

"And they will all be there—at the White House—Mansour, Lavi, and President Taylor?"

"Yes."

"And King Abdullah, as well?"

"I believe so."

"That would make sense, would it not, as he has been a key broker of the deal, correct?"

"I'm not sure how the king would characterize his involvement," I said, which was technically true and yet the closest thing to a lie I had uttered so far in this bizarre conversation.

"You don't think the king sees himself as the true author of this treaty?" Khalif pressed. "After all the private meetings he had with the Zionists like Lavi and with a *kafir* like Mansour and with sheer infidels like your president, over and over again for the last few months, you really don't think Abdullah—the betrayer of the Prophet and all that he stood for—not only sees himself but prides himself as the godfather of this so-called peace deal?"

"I really can't say," I replied.

"You can't say, or you won't say?" he asked. "There is a difference, Mr. Collins."

"I can't," I replied. "I have not spoken to the king about this or about anything else. He and I don't know each other. I've never met or interviewed him."

"Your grandfather interviewed his great-grandfather, did he not?"

I found myself both intrigued and unnerved by the intelligence Khalif had on this most top secret of Mideast initiatives, not to mention my own family history. So far as I was aware, not a single reporter in the region, the U.S., or the rest of the world knew the peace deal was done or that the Jordanian monarch was its broker, except me. If some other reporter in any news organization, including my own, had the information, they certainly would have published it. Yet nobody had—not yet, anyway. The *Jordan Times* was furthest out front, giving hints that a deal was in the making. But even they had not been definitive.

How, then, had Khalif gotten such insider information? If it wasn't coming from a reporter, could it be coming from a mole inside one of the four governments involved—American, Israeli, Palestinian, or Jordanian? And how was this lunatic going to use the information?

"Actually, my grandfather never got the—"

But before I could finish my thought, Khalif cut me off. "Oh yes, how could I forget? Fate stepped in. The king was murdered. How sad . . . for your grandfather."

Just then I heard a phone ring several times. An aide entered the living room from a doorway to my right and handed Khalif a satellite phone.

He took it and spoke into it in Arabic, slowly and deliberately. "Not yet. . . . But your preparations are proceeding? . . . Do you foresee any obstacles? . . . And you've briefed the others? . . . Very well, call me again in two hours."

Khalif gave the satphone back to the aide, who now handed over several pieces of paper.

He read them carefully and then passed them

to me. They were printouts off the *Times* website. My articles were both lead stories.

"The news is breaking, Mr. Collins," Khalif said with a slight smile. "But there is so much more to come."

Then he changed directions. "I want to ask you about your profile of me," he said calmly. "Something about it is bothering me a great deal."

I tensed immediately.

"You stated that I 'claimed' to have possession of chemical weapons 'allegedly' captured from a Syrian military base near Aleppo several weeks ago. Why did you use the words *claimed* and *allegedly*?"

"I'm not sure I understand the question," I replied as diplomatically as I could.

"Of course you do," he said. "It's a very straightforward question. Why did you use these words to describe my statements?"

I was still not following but tried to answer nonetheless. "When I asked you about the chemical weapons back at the prison, you did claim to have them, and you did say your forces captured them from that base."

"Exactly."

"So that's what I wrote."

"No, it's not."

"I'm afraid I don't understand," I countered. "That is what I wrote."

"No, you qualified what I said," Khalif replied. "You made it seem like I merely *said* that I had WMD—as if I were making up a story—when the fact is we do have these weapons, and we will use them when the time is right."

"I was only reporting what you said."

"I get the impression you don't believe me."

"It's not a matter of what I believe," I said. "I was just trying to be a careful reporter of the actual facts."

"ISIS has chemical weapons—*that* is a fact, Mr. Collins."

"So you say."

"Yes, I do say, and that makes it a fact."

"Not in my world."

"My confirming the story doesn't make it true?"

"Not without proof."

"I see."

"I don't know what you want from me," I said. "I reported what you said. I showed it to you ahead of time. You e-mailed it to my editor as is. How can you now be upset?"

"I'm not upset," Khalif said. "I just want a story that makes it clear to the infidels that we are not talk, not spin doctors. We don't simply issue press releases and audiotapes and videos on YouTube. I am not Zawahiri. This is not hype. We are the true mujahideen for Allah, and we want the world to know this clearly."

With this, he stood. "Come, Mr. Collins; I have something to show you."

Two guards pulled me to my feet. They blindfolded me and reapplied duct tape over my mouth, and before I knew it I was being shoved into the back of a car. When we began to drive, someone turned on the radio full blast so I couldn't hear anything but some wretched music the others in the car all seemed to love. I couldn't hear street noises or birds or construction equipment or anything that might give away our route or destination. I couldn't even hear what the others were saying.

I would estimate that we drove for fifteen or twenty minutes, though without any points of reference it was difficult to maintain an accurate sense of time. Finally, however, we came to a stop. The music stopped. I heard doors open. I heard Khalif giving orders in Arabic, and then I was pulled from the car.

When the blindfold was removed from my eyes, I found myself inside a dark garage. By the time my eyes adjusted, I saw a hulk of a man in the shadows and realized Jamal Ramzy was standing in front of me, at Abu Khalif's side.

"Welcome to Mosul, Mr. Collins," Ramzy said. "What an honor. You're the first infidel ever to be permitted inside not just one ISIS base but two."

I nodded slightly but said nothing.

"Now, put this on," Ramzy said, handing me a gas mask.

"Why?" I asked.

"So you don't die—at least not prematurely," he said, and I complied.

Ramzy, too, put on a gas mask, as did Khalif and the dozen armed guards around us. Then Ramzy led the group through a dark corridor and down several flights of stairs to the basement of whatever facility we had come to. We headed through one set of doors that were nothing special, but we quickly came to another set of doors that obviously served as an air lock into some sort of research laboratory. Though my gas mask was fogging up a bit, I could see lots of scientific equipment of various kinds and at least a half-dozen men wearing white lab coats and masks.

Ramzy ushered Khalif and me and one armed guard into a separate room. There was nothing in there—no chairs, no tables, no furniture of any kind—but in front of us on the far wall was a rectangular window with glass that appeared several inches thick. On the other side of the glass was a concrete bunker of sorts. It too was empty, but as I watched, someone with a lab coat entered from a side door to our right. He was carrying a wooden chair. He set it down and went to retrieve another and another and then finally a fourth chair. Working quickly and methodically, he lined up the chairs in a row facing us. Then he was gone.

My heart was racing. Sweat was beginning to drip down the back of my neck. I was feeling claustrophobic in this mask and struggling to breathe. But there was no way out. Abu Khalif was standing immediately to my left. Jamal Ramzy was immediately to my right. And an ISIS thug was standing behind me, in front of the door, holding an AK-47.

Through the window—which I assumed was a two-way mirror—I saw three prison guards from Abu Ghraib appear, along with the prison's warden, whom I recognized immediately. They were all handcuffed and shackled together. When they had been led into the room on the other side of this window, they were unchained and ordered to strip. It was clear that each of them had been tortured severely. They were bloodied and bruised. Their faces were swollen. Two of them had broken noses.

Once they were naked, they were ordered to sit down on the chairs, which they did, each of them trembling. Abu Khalif rapped his knuckles on the glass, apparently giving an order to the man in the gas mask and lab coat, who nodded and quickly left the room.

A moment later, a canister dropped into the room from somewhere above the ceiling. It was emitting something that looked like tear gas, but it quickly became apparent that this was not tear gas. As I watched the men behind the glass, I suddenly realized it was sarin gas. Khalif was going to murder these men just to prove to me that ISIS really did have the Syrian weapons.

Before long the prison guards and the warden were on the ground. They were writhing in pain. They were foaming at the mouth, convulsing violently. The chamber they were in was soundproof, so I couldn't hear their screaming. But when I tried to look away, Ramzy grabbed my gas mask and smashed it against the window, forcing me to watch these men suffer a grisly, painful, horrible death. I wanted to close my eyes, but I couldn't. I was there to witness these murders, to be able to tell the world what had happened and how. This was my job. This was why I was here. As much as I didn't want it to be true, I now had proof that ISIS had chemical weapons, and I had to be a faithful witness. Who else would do it?

These men deserved it. And the world had to know the truth.

I stood there, my bloodless face pressed to the window, for what seemed like hours, horrified as I watched these men die a slow, agonizing, excruciatingly painful death. And I must admit that as much as I didn't want any of them to perish, for me they couldn't die soon enough. That seemed a terribly selfish thought, but I couldn't bear to watch them grasp for life any longer.

Eventually it ended. Only then did Ramzy let me leave the observation room and step back into the larger laboratory. I repeatedly felt like I was going to be sick, but I think the fear of vomiting in my mask and suffocating as a result kept down all that was trying to force its way through my esophagus.

Finally Ramzy took me by the arm and led me back through the air lock. Only then was I permitted to remove my mask. Everyone else removed theirs as well.

No one said a thing, not even Khalif. But perhaps that was because Ramzy was not finished. He led the group to a large warehouse next door. To my astonishment, the rectangular building was filled with artillery shells and missile warheads, most of which were neatly and carefully stacked in crates bearing Syrian military markings, sitting on pallets. Some of the pallets were being loaded onto nondescript trucks.

"This is just a small portion of the chemical weapons and delivery systems we captured near Aleppo," Ramzy told me. "These are awaiting the emir's orders. The rest are being pre-positioned to strategic locations, even as we speak."

When Ramzy was finished speaking, Khalif turned to me and, standing less than a foot from my face, gave me a simple order.

"Write *this* story, Mr. Collins," he said. "Write that we're coming after the infidels. Write that we have the motive. We have the means. All we're waiting for now is the opportunity, and I am supremely confident it will show itself soon. Write that, and then I will decide what happens to you."

PART SIX

45

* * *

My flight from Erbīl landed in Amman.

I still couldn't believe they had let me go.

I had tried to sleep on the flight but couldn't even close my eyes. Every time I did, my thoughts were filled with the most ghastly images. The flight attendants had served me a snack, but I couldn't eat. They'd offered me water and soda, but I couldn't drink. My hands were shaking and I couldn't make them stop.

I powered up my phone and checked texts and e-mails. I saw none that looked urgent. But as we taxied to the terminal, I sent three messages of my own. The first was to my mom, letting her know that whatever else she might read, I was safely out of Iraq and out of the hands of ISIS. The second was to Allen MacDonald, essentially saying the same thing and asking him to coordinate a conference call between him, me, and the chief counsel for the *Times*. I was ready to go to the FBI, to do anything I could to put these monsters behind bars, but I wanted to know if my actions had put me in any legal jeopardy. The third text was to my brother, saying I'd just landed back in Amman and asking if he would come pick me up at the airport as soon as possible.

Then I sent a fourth, to Yael.

Grabbing my things from the overhead bin, I made my way off the plane as I scanned the latest headlines on my phone. My two articles—the first on Abu Khalif and his escape from Abu Ghraib and the butchery of a prominent Iraqi government official, the second on the murder of Abu Ghraib's warden and several staff members during an ISIS demonstration of its sarin gas stockpiles—were the lead stories on the *Times* website.

The other major story on the front page was by Alex Brunnell, the *Times* bureau chief in Jerusalem. Its headline read, **Peace Deal 'Close but Not Yet Done' between Israelis and Palestinians, Says Senior U.S. Official**.

The lead story in the *Washington Post* was by their chief White House correspondent: **President Taylor Announces Surprise Summit on Mideast Peace**.

A *Haaretz* headline out of Jerusalem announced, **Israelis Roll out Red Carpet, Prepare to Welcome Air Force One**.

Meanwhile a *Jerusalem Post* headline was more negative: **Right-Wing Cabinet Members Furious with Lavi over Rumors of Secret Negotiations with Palestinians**.

A tweet from Al Arabiya claimed, **Sources close to PA President Mansour say they are "cautiously optimistic" a deal for a Palestinian state could be closed this week.**

Finally, the *Jordan Times* was reporting, **Aides to**

King Say He Is 'Cautiously Optimistic' about Peace Process, Open to Attending Peace Summit in Jerusalem, if Needed.

Clearly events were moving rapidly. I had missed my window for an exclusive on the peace deal, but I didn't care. I was just glad to be out of Iraq, alive and safe and free. The question was for how long? For the moment, I was useful to Khalif and Ramzy. But that calculus could change any minute. What's more, I was terrified for Matt and his family. They had to get out of Jordan as fast as possible.

As I entered the terminal, I was struck by the much-heavier-than-usual presence of armed Jordanian soldiers and border police. Each passenger coming off the flight was thoroughly checked for weapons and explosives. All luggage was put through X-ray machines, subjected to bomb-sniffing dogs, and then hand-searched. In addition, Jordanian officials were asking questions of all passengers to determine why they had been in Iraq and why they were coming to Jordan. The whole process took more than an hour. But when it was finally over and I headed through the main hall outside to get a taxi, I suddenly ran into Matt, who greeted me with a relieved bear hug.

"Are you all right?" he asked, looking me over.

"I'm fine," I said, truly glad to see him again but wishing he wasn't making a scene. "Thanks for coming to get me."

It wasn't true, of course. I wasn't fine. But I couldn't say anything more, not in public.

"We were worried sick," Matt said. "Annie and

I thought we'd never see you again. And don't even ask about Mom."

"But you let her know I'm out, right?" I asked, guilty for all I was putting her through.

"Of course," he said. "As soon as I got your text that you were here, I called her right away. She said she'd just gotten a note from you as well."

"How is she?"

"She's pretty shaken up. I mean, she's been reading all of your articles, and those were hard enough, but she can read between the lines. She knows it was even worse than you wrote."

"It was," I told him. "Worse than you can imagine."

We headed straight out of the airport to his car. As we got in, he asked me how in the world I had gotten back to Jordan in one piece.

"It was bizarre," I told him. "Late last night, Jamal Ramzy and some soldiers came down to the basement where I was chained up. They blindfolded me and carried me upstairs. I was sure this was it, that they were going to behead me right then. Instead, they threw me, bound, into the trunk of a car and started driving. After fifteen or twenty minutes, they stopped the car, pulled me out of the trunk, and removed the blindfold and shackles. It was night, but there was a full moon. So I could see that we were in the middle of nowhere. That's when I thought they were going to shoot me. But instead, Ramzy handed me the keys to the car and a map. He told me to follow the map out of the province of Nineveh until I got to the border of Kurdistan. Then he told me to explain to the *peshmerga* that I was a journalist who had been covering the war and needed to get to Erbīl to catch a flight to Amman."

"They just gave you the keys?" he asked.

"I know. It was crazy."

"So then what?"

"Ramzy and his men got into an SUV that had apparently been following us, and they drove off into the night."

"Just leaving you standing there."

"Yeah."

"And it worked? The Kurds let you in?"

"I'm sitting here with you, aren't I?"

"Why do you think they let you go?"

"I don't know for sure," I said as we worked our way through the neighborhoods of Amman. "I think they changed their focus. Yes, Khalif and Ramzy would have loved to send my head to the president of the United States via FedEx. But I think they decided they liked the WMD story out there. Maybe they think it makes them look tough. I don't know. But I don't think they're content just having the story published. They want me out there doing radio and television shows, telling people what I saw, that they really do have chemical weapons."

"It's so sickening."

"You don't know the half of it," I told him. "I've never seen anything like Abu Khalif. He rarely shows emotion. He talks in a monotone. But you should have seen the sheer twisted joy on his face when he sawed off Ismail Tikriti's head and when he was watching that sarin gas kill the warden and those three guards. It was sick, Matt, worse than any horror film you could possibly imagine."

"You didn't write any of that in your articles, of course," he noted. "I could tell you were trying to be very careful with your words, and I figured he was watching you write."

"It was the most horrible experience of my life."

"Thank God you're out."

"Thanks again for picking me up. It really means a lot to me."

"Of course. What are brothers for? I'm just glad it's over."

"But it's not."

"What do you mean?"

"It's not over," I said. "I think ISIS is going to strike soon."

"In Israel or back in the States?" Matt asked.

"Actually, I think he's going to strike here."

Matt looked stunned. "Here, where? Jordan? Amman?"

"Yes."

"You think Jordan is the third target?"

"I'm starting to, yes."

"Why? What do you mean? I've seen all the stuff you've written in the last few days. Khalif told you point-blank he was gunning for Israel and the U.S. If I were him, I'd be planning to hit the peace summit in Jerusalem, wouldn't you? It's one-stop shopping."

"I have no doubt Khalif would love to strike the summit in Jerusalem, but I don't think he'd ever get that far," I said. "There's too much security. I think he's coming here first. He's just in Mosul. That's practically right down the road."

"But why here?" Matt asked. "Isn't Khalif Jordanian, from Zarqā?"

"Absolutely, and that's all the more reason," I said. "He hates the king. He believes His Majesty is an infidel. He said as much when I interviewed him."

"Sure, but he gave a laundry list of leaders he wants to kill," Matt replied. "Don't you think he was just talking trash, listing everyone he could?"

"No, I don't."

"Why not?"

"Several reasons," I said as Matt wove through traffic. "First, yes, he gave quite a hit list. But look who's not on it— the prime minister of Lebanon, the emirs in the Gulf, the mullahs in Iran."

"So what?"

"So he wasn't just giving me a laundry list," I explained. "I think he was giving me his list of priorities in order."

"Okay, fine, but that still proves my point," Matt replied. "He said specifically he's going to attack the U.S. and Israel with suicide bombers and chemical weapons. That was the first thing he mentioned."

With that, Matt pulled into his neighborhood and we were at his apartment building, a modest complex in a rather run-down section on the outer eastern edges of Amman. The street was crowded, but we soon found a parking space around the corner.

"Go back and reread the transcript," I said when he had turned off the engine. "I can't believe I didn't see this earlier. Khalif told me exactly what he was going to do."

Matt pulled out his smartphone and brought up the *Times* website. A moment later, he had the transcript.

"Okay, now find the section where Khalif vows to capture and behead the American and Israeli leaders," I said.

Matt quickly scanned through the interview and found the section.

"Got it."

"Good, now read exactly what he says there."

So Matt did.

"KHALIF: We aim to capture and behead the president of the United States. . . . We aim to assassinate the prime minister of Israel. In due course, we will unleash a wave of suicide bombers and other attacks against the Great Satan and the Little Satan and rid the world of these cancerous tumors.

"See?" Matt said. "He couldn't be clearer—he's coming after the U.S. and Israel."

"I know, I know, but keep reading," I insisted.

"KHALIF: But our highest priorities are to rid the region of apostate Arab leaders who have betrayed the Muslim people and the Prophet himself. We will target the leaders of Jordan and the Palestinian Authority and Saudi Arabia, as well as Syria and Iraq—we will find them, kill them, and topple their governments one by one."

"There it is," I said. "Khalif says his highest priority is taking out apostate Arab leaders who have betrayed the Muslim people and the Prophet."

"He's coming after the king of Jordan," Matt said.

"Exactly."

"So you think Iraq and Syria were ISIS's first two targets, and Jordan is the third?" he asked.

"I think so," I said. "And what if it is? Imagine if ISIS attacks Amman with chemical weapons, kills the king, destroys most of the government, and establishes an Islamic state right on the border of Israel?"

"That's terrifying."

"Especially if ISIS ends up in control of all of Iraq and Syria too."

We sat for a moment, trying to make sense of all that. Then Matt said, "I have to admit, I never really thought much about Jordan or its importance until we came here for my sabbatical."

"You're not alone," I said.

"But it's actually quite nice here," Matt continued. "I mean, the king seems pretty moderate. And the country is peaceful, friendly, stable. They've got a peace treaty with Israel. They're probably the best Arab ally America has."

"Absolutely," I agreed. "Plus Jordan is the quiet cornerstone of any peace deal with the Israelis and Palestinians."

"What do you mean?"

"Well, think about it," I said. "The president's entire strategic concept of persuading Israel to give up the West Bank for a final peace deal with the Palestinians is predicated on the Hashemite Kingdom being just what you said—a stable and secure friend and ally on the east side of the Jordan River. But what if the king falls? What if jihadists take over? The entire peace process goes up in smoke, right?"

"I guess so. Hadn't really thought about it that way."

"Sure. A strong Jordan is Israel's buffer against any ground invasion from the east. If the jihadists take Amman, Israel's entire security architecture falls apart. If the kingdom falls and ISIS takes over, the whole West Bank could become radicalized and go up in flames. Suddenly Israel isn't facing a jihadi storm way out in the western provinces of Iraq. Suddenly they've got ISIS forces on the outskirts of Jerusalem. At that point, the U.S. and Israel would be facing a radical Islamic caliphate encompassing all of Syria, all of Jordan, most if not all of Iraq, and very likely allied with Iran, which could soon become a nuclear power."

Matt looked through the windshield, thinking. "Okay, that's a horrifying scenario, I grant you that," he said. "But is that really possible? I mean, Jordan's got a great military. They've got American weapons. The king used to be the commander of the special forces here. Do you really think it's possible ISIS could take over this country?"

"Did you think Mubarak would fall in Egypt?

Ghaddafi in Libya? The guy in Tunisia? Now Assad's on the brink. And I'm telling you, the king is next."

"Maybe you're right." Matt sighed. "Maybe the king's days are numbered. Maybe that's how it's going to happen."

I looked at him. "How what's going to happen?"

"The prophecies."

"What prophecies?"

"You know, what I came here to research."

"I'm not following."

"My sabbatical—the whole reason I came here. Don't you remember?"

"Did you ever tell me?"

"Of course I did," Matt said. "I sent you a long e-mail last year explaining the research I was going to do here and suggesting you might do a story on it at some point."

"I don't remember ever getting that."

"Well, that figures. You never reply to any of my e-mails."

I didn't know what to say to that, so I just asked, "What's your research on?"

"Jordan in biblical eschatology."

"Escha-what?"

"Eschatology—End Times theology."

"What about it?"

"Bad times are coming for Jordan."

"Meaning what?"

"Meaning that aside from Israel, few modern nations are mentioned more in the Bible—and especially in Bible prophecy—than Jordan."

46

* * *

"Jordan is mentioned in the Bible?" I asked.

"Well, not per se," Matt replied. "*Jordan* is a recent name. But the nation we call the Hashemite Kingdom of Jordan today is actually comprised of territory once held by three biblical nations: Ammon, Moab, and Edom. And the Bible says a terrible judgment is coming against the people who live in these places in the last days before the return of Christ."

"So?"

"So many people—myself included—believe we're living in the last days. Which means the prophecies that describe the epic destruction of Jordan's cities and the apocalyptic devastation of the Jordanian people could come to pass soon. After all, we've already seen so many other End Times prophecies come true."

This was all news to me. "Like what?"

"Like the miraculous rebirth of the State of Israel. Like the dramatic return of the Jewish people to the Promised Land. Like the Jews rebuilding the ancient ruins of Israel. The ancient Hebrew prophets said all these things would happen in the last days. And one by one, they're happening."

"And you're saying the judgment and destruction of Jordan is next?"

"I can't say it's next, but according to the Bible, it's coming. Maybe what you're describing with ISIS will set the prophecies into motion."

"Hold on a minute. What prophecies are you referring to? What kind of 'terrible judgment' does the Bible actually say is coming? How bad are we talking?"

"Catastrophic."

My first instinct was to dismiss this as crazy talk from my crazy brother. A few days before, I would have. But something in me was changing. I had seen too much horror to be able to discount the possibility that more horror could be coming. Besides, I figured, if anyone knew about this stuff, it was Matt. "Keep talking," I said.

"Okay, well, first of all, there are a number of other ancient sites, cities, or regions mentioned in the Bible that are located in the modern-day nation of Jordan."

"Such as?"

"One would be what the Scriptures call 'Mount Seir' or the 'hill country of Seir.'"

"And where's that?" I asked.

"The term *Seir* is actually used to describe a specific mountain, a whole mountain range, and the entire nation or territory of Edom, which is the ancient name for the southern region of Jordan," Matt explained. "Seir was first mentioned in Genesis 14:6 and then again in Genesis 32:3, among other places."

"So Seir is essentially synonymous with Jordan?" I clarified.

"Southern Jordan, at least, yes," Matt said.

"Okay, what else?"

"Well, there's Bozrah," he continued. "Bozrah was an ancient city located in Edom. For a time it was actually the capital of Edom."

"Any others?"

"Yes, there's Sela, which is also thought to have been a capital or stronghold of Edom. In 2 Kings 14:7, we learn that Sela, whose name was changed by King Amaziah to Joktheel, was located in Edom."

"So that's in southern Jordan as well?"

"Right. And here's something interesting: Sela may actually be the biblical name for the city of Petra, the ancient capital city of the Nabataeans. Have you ever been there?"

"No, can't say I have."

"You would love it. Petra was carved out of solid rock inside a narrow canyon, so it was very difficult for foreign armies to penetrate. And it's one of the biggest tourist attractions in Jordan today."

"Okay, fine, the Bible has all these names for Jordan," I said. "But what about these judgments you're talking about?"

"Great question," Matt said. "Should we finish this inside?"

"No, let's talk here," I said.

"But Annie and the kids can't wait to see you."

"And I can't wait to see them," I said. "But that's why I want to finish this now. The moment we go inside, we're going to get caught up in everything else."

"All right, if you insist," he said.

"I do."

Matt paused a moment, then continued. "Okay, one place where the Bible talks quite a bit about Jordan is in the book of Jeremiah, specifically in chapter 49. In verse 2, God says, 'Behold, the days are coming . . . that I will cause a trumpet blast of war to be heard against Rabbah of the sons of Ammon; and it will become a desolate heap, and her towns will be set on fire.'"

"Pretty dark," I said.

"Yeah, but that's not all. In verse 13, the Lord says, 'I have sworn by Myself . . . that Bozrah will become an object of horror, a reproach, a ruin and a curse; and all its cities will become perpetual ruins.' And then, in verse 17, he says, 'Edom will become an object of horror; everyone who passes by it will be horrified and will hiss at all its wounds.' And these are just a few examples of what the Bible says will happen to areas that are within modern Jordan."

"How do you know all this stuff?" I said, not wanting to offend my brother but not sure what to make of any of it either.

"I've been studying this for the past eight months, remember? You have to admit, it does kind of catch your attention—especially when you're living here."

"It's attention-getting, all right," I said. "But

how does all this relate to what could be going on with ISIS?"

"I'm getting to that," he said. "If you do a careful study of this section of Jeremiah, you'll see that the prophecies are eschatological; that is, they concern the End Times. Jeremiah 48 is a prophecy against Moab, which is central Jordan. Most of chapter 49 is made up of prophecies against Ammon, which is north-central Jordan, and Edom, which is southern Jordan. If you look at these two chapters, you see a lot of language like 'days are coming' and 'in that day' and even 'it will come about in the last days.' Still with me?"

I nodded.

"So it's these phrases, which are consistent with other End Times prophecies throughout the Bible, that let us know Jeremiah was not writing—in this section, at least—about prophecies that would take place in his lifetime but rather about things that would be fulfilled in the days leading up to the return of Christ. Does that make sense?"

"Yes, I think so," I said.

"Now, Jeremiah gave many prophecies that did come true in his lifetime or soon thereafter," Matt said. "Most famous, of course, were his prophecies that God was going to punish his people for their disobedience by sending the Babylonians—led by the evil King Nebuchadnezzar—to conquer Jerusalem and destroy the Temple and carry off the Jewish people into exile in Babylon. And these terrible things happened, just as Jeremiah said. Fortunately, Jeremiah also prophesied that the exile of the Jews in Babylon would only last for seventy years, and then God would have mercy on them and restore their fortunes and bring them back to the land and reestablish Jerusalem as their capital. And that's exactly what happened. The Babylonians were conquered by the Persians, and seventy years after the Jews were judged and exiled, the king of Media-Persia set them free and helped them return to the land and rebuild their Temple."

"Jeremiah wrote all that?" I asked, genuinely intrigued.

"Yes," Matt said, "and this is what gives us confidence that Jeremiah was a true prophet from the Lord and that his End Times prophecies will come to pass at the proper time as well. We don't have time to go through an in-depth analysis right now, but just focus for a second on the places I've already mentioned—Ammon, Edom, and Bozrah. We've established that Jeremiah is speaking about the End Times and that he's giving prophecies from the Lord about the future of places we now call the kingdom of Jordan. Right?"

I nodded again.

"Okay," Matt continued. "Jeremiah clearly describes an apocalyptic, catastrophic judgment that falls on the people and cities of Edom in the last days. I already mentioned some of the verses from chapter 49, but there are others. In verse 18, talking about Edom, it says, 'Like the overthrow of Sodom and Gomorrah with its neighbors . . . no one will live there, nor will a son of man reside in it.' And in verses 20 and 21, the text describes enemies dragging off 'even the little ones of the flock.' It says, 'The earth has quaked at the noise of their downfall. There is an outcry! The noise of it has been heard at the Red Sea.'"

Matt was quiet for a moment, presumably to let me absorb what I'd just heard. I was beginning to understand what he had said about bad things being in store for Jordan. But was any of it actually true?

"Look," Matt finally said, "a person can and should study these passages very, very carefully, and use all the tools and resources available to a modern Bible scholar. But it doesn't take a PhD in theology to understand the meaning of the text. The preponderance of the evidence is clear. These biblical prophecies indicate that God has decreed judgment on the people living in Ammon, Moab, and Edom. These are facts. They're not comfortable ones, especially in this modern age. But judgments *are* coming. And if you look at this text, and the many other prophecies about the future of Jordan found in Isaiah, Jeremiah, Ezekiel, Obadiah, Daniel, and elsewhere, you'll find that God gives numerous reasons for such judgments. Because he can see the future, God has declared the people who live in these places in the last days guilty of arrogance, pride, hatred, violence, cruelty, injustice, worshiping false gods, and a profound lack of compassion toward women, royalty, neighbors, and particularly toward Judah, Jerusalem, and Israel."

"And none of these judgments have already come to pass in history?" I asked.

"Some have, sure," Matt said. "But not all."

"How do you know for sure?"

"Well, for one thing, there are still people living and working and prospering in southern Jordan," Matt replied. "But the text clearly indicates that the End Times judgment that is coming on Edom will be utter, final, and irreversible. Verse 13 says, 'All its cities will become perpetual ruins.' Verse 18 says, 'No one will live there.' And of course, the text likens the future destruction to the judgments of Sodom and Gomorrah. Guess where those two cities were located?"

"Jordan?"

"Southern Jordan."

"Ouch."

"Exactly," Matt said. "So while Edom has been conquered in the past, it hasn't experienced the absolute cataclysmic judgment that Jeremiah foretold in this chapter."

"In other words, according to the Bible, this is all coming in the future?" I asked.

"Right—in the future, in the lead-up to the return of Christ," Matt confirmed. "And that's why this is weighing heavily on me. I have come to love this country, and I love its king. I mean, he's not perfect; what leader is? But His Majesty really is one of the good guys. So was his father, King Hussein. These men made peace with Israel. They chose to be close allies with the U.S. and the British. King Abdullah has emerged as arguably the leading Reformer in the Arab world. He actively promotes a moderate, tolerant, peaceful model of Islam. He's reached out to Christian leaders all over the world, Protestant and Catholic. For the most part, Jordanian Christians are treated kindly and with respect. Did you know a few years ago the king created a national park along the east bank of the Jordan River to protect it for Christian baptisms?"

"No, I didn't."

"And that's not all," Matt continued. "The king actually gave land to thirteen different Christian denominations to build churches and baptismal sites along the Jordan River. I've been there, J. B. I've seen hundreds of Christians baptized there since I came to study here."

"Your point?" I asked, not wanting to be rude but not totally following some of his jargon.

"My point is that this king doesn't strike me as a candidate for divine judgment," Matt said. "Now, Isaiah tells us that God's thoughts are higher than our thoughts, and his ways are higher than our ways, and I believe that. So in his sovereignty, God can bring righteous judgment on a nation that isn't following him at any time. And Jordan, by and large, isn't following him. But . . ."

"But what?" I asked, curious why he was suddenly hesitating.

"I don't know," he said, clearly searching for the right words. "After everything you've told me about ISIS, combined with what the Bible says about Jordan, I'm just wondering if this king is going to be toppled. Don't get me wrong; I don't want it to happen. He's a good man, and he's doing a great job in many ways. But I wonder if his days are numbered. What if the Arab Spring erupts here in Jordan? What if the king and his family are brought down and replaced by tyrants who lead the people to war against Israel, to war against the Christians, to the kind of social dynamic that is consistent with these Scriptures? I can't say that's what's going to happen. I don't know that for sure. But what if the return of Christ is sooner than most people think? And what if ISIS is the tool Satan uses to take Jordan down a long, dark path?"

47

★ ★ ★

We finally got out of the car and headed into Matt's building.

As Matt pressed the button for the elevator, I realized I couldn't procrastinate any longer. "Listen, Matt, there's something else."

"What?"

"You guys need to leave Jordan."

The elevator door opened, and Matt shot me a look. "What are you talking about?"

"You're not safe here. You need to go back to the States—immediately."

"Immediately?"

"Tonight," I said as we stepped into the elevator and the door slid shut behind us.

"J. B., are you crazy? I'm on a yearlong sabbatical. I've still got four months to go."

"No, you and Annie have to take the kids and leave. Don't worry about the cost. I'll cover your tickets."

"Because you think ISIS is going to attack Amman?"

"No, it's not just that."

"Then what?"

"It's Abu Khalif."

"What about him?"

"He mentioned you guys by name. He knows you're here in Amman. He knows where you live. You're not safe here, any of you. Mom's not safe either. Abu Khalif made it clear that when he's good and ready, he's coming after all of us."

The bell rang and the door opened. We stepped out into the hall, but Matt stopped me before we went any farther. "You're serious about this?"

"I'm afraid so. And you've got to move fast."

"But why us? What does Khalif want with any of us?"

"I don't know," I said. "I told you, the guy is a psychopath, a Hannibal Lecter with sarin. I'm just telling you what I saw and heard. What kind of brother would I be if I didn't?"

Matt stood there in the hallway for a moment. I could see him trying to process all that I'd told him and what it meant for him and his precious family.

"Katie turned four last week," he said softly.

"Already?" I said. I desperately wanted to make sure nothing happened to her.

"She's in a Sunday school class at the church we're going to," Matt continued. "She loves it. Can't wait to get there every week. And there's a competition. For every Bible verse she memorizes, she gets a point. Whichever kid gets the most points by the end of the semester gets a prize. Right now, she's in second place."

I nodded but said nothing, not quite sure where this was headed.

"Do you know what her verses were for last week?"

"No," I said. "What?"

"1 John 5:11-12."

"Okay . . . ?"

"Do you remember that from when we were kids?"

"Can't say I do; why?"

"'And the testimony is this, that God has given us eternal life, and this life is in His Son. He who has the Son has the life; he who does not have the Son of God does not have the life.'"

"All right," I said. "I guess I remember something like that, vaguely."

"I'm not worried about us, J. B. The four of us know where we're going. But what about you?"

"What do you mean?"

"I mean Annie and the kids and I have trusted Christ as our Savior," he replied, lowering his voice to almost a whisper. "We have the Son. We've been forgiven our sins and adopted into the family of God—by grace, not because of anything good we did. Have you? We've been praying for you for years. And we were praying for you from the moment you left for Baghdad—for your safety, but more importantly for your soul. So I have to ask you: where are you with Christ right now?"

I tensed. "I appreciate your concern for me, Matt, I really do, but I—"

I suddenly had no idea how to finish that sentence, so I just stopped midflight.

"Look, this isn't some game. Everywhere you go, people around you—people close to you—are dying. Someone's gunning for you. And sooner than later, they may get you. I hope to God they don't. I pray every day and every night they don't, and I won't stop. But the odds are against you, and they're slipping fast. You need to make a choice—heaven or hell, in or out. What are you going to do with Jesus? You're running out of time to decide."

It was a valid question. Especially now. I just didn't want to answer it.

"I don't know," I said, looking away.

"Why didn't you ask Christ to save you while you were in Iraq? Don't you realize how close you came to death?"

"Of course I do, but what do you want me to say? That I had a foxhole conversion? That I saw my life passing before my eyes and decided to accept Christ as fire insurance, just in case?"

"No, of course not. I'm not telling you to make some superficial leap into religion. Certainly not for my sake or Annie's or Mom's. What I'm saying is you need to make a serious decision, on your own, in your heart and in your head, based on the facts. Is Jesus the Messiah or isn't he? Is he the only way to eternal life or not? The stakes couldn't be higher. It's not just life or death; it's your eternity we're talking about. And it's time to choose, J. B. Before it's too late."

"Matt, for crying out loud, why are you pushing me on this?"

"I'm not pushing you."

"Of course you are."

"Okay, fine, I'm pushing you. But what else am I supposed to do? I love you. So do Annie and the kids. We care about you."

"And you're worried for me."

"Of course we are. Aren't you?"

I sighed and looked away. "Yeah, guess I am. But I'm not there, Matt. I'm sorry. I'm just not."

It was quiet in the cluttered, narrow hallway. The only sound was the low hum of the fluorescent lights above us. The whole place was filled with kids' bicycles and balls and dolls and empty soda bottles and various other kinds of family-related litter. It was a long way from the adorable little three-bedroom bungalow Matt and Annie used to live in near Boston before they had kids. A long way from my luxury penthouse apartment in Arlington, Virginia, too. We had very different lives, Matt and I. And now here we were in Amman of all places.

"Okay," he said after a moment. "But I'm not going to stop."

"Fine."

"I'm going to keep praying for you."

"I appreciate it."

"And I'm going to keep asking you. Because at the end of the day, when it's all said and done, the simple truth is I want to be with you and Mom and the whole family in heaven, and I'd never be able to forgive myself if I didn't do everything I could to get you there. What kind of brother would I be if I didn't?"

I sighed. He hadn't changed a bit. I shrugged

and nodded. He put his arm around me and walked me to his front door.

"Come on," he said. "I'm starved, and Annie's making her famous lasagna."

We stepped around all the clutter, and Matt unlocked the door. As we entered the apartment, I expected a warm and enthusiastic greeting from Annie and the kids.

But that's not what happened.

48

* * *

Greeting us were two plainclothes agents from the Jordanian secret police.

With them were two soldiers in full combat gear, sporting automatic weapons. Annie and the kids stood behind them, looking frightened.

"What's the meaning of this?" Matt demanded.

"Are you Matthew Collins?" the lead agent asked.

"Of course. What do you want?"

"I am Ali Sa'id, chief of security for the Royal Court," said the lead agent, who then turned to me. "And are you James Collins?"

"Why are you asking?"

"Are you or are you not James Collins?" the agent repeated.

"Yes, I am."

"Then I need you to come with me."

"Where? What in the world is going on?"

"You'll understand soon enough."

I protested, but it didn't make any difference. These men clearly had their orders and weren't taking no for an answer.

Matt gave me a hug and whispered in my ear, "We'll be on the first flight out tonight."

I said nothing but rather turned and hugged Annie, Katie, and Josh as tightly as I could. I didn't want to let go. I so wanted to spend time with them. I wanted to play with the kids and hear their laughter. I wanted this family to help me get my mind off the terrible things I had seen and heard. After so many years of avoiding my brother, now I wanted to spend real time with him, see his life up close, and ask him a thousand questions. But right now I just hoped they would get out of the country before Khalif's men hunted them down and butchered them like cattle.

The agents led me downstairs and put me in the backseat of a black, bulletproof Mercedes. We peeled away from Matt's neighborhood with an urgency that only heightened my anxiety.

"Where are you taking me?" I asked, but the lead agent didn't answer.

"Am I under arrest?"

Nothing.

"Am I being deported?"

Still nothing.

"Look, I'm an American citizen and an accredited member of the press," I reminded them. "I have a right to know what's happening."

But my pleas fell on deaf ears.

We were heading back into the heart of Amman, I could see, and dense traffic slowed the journey. Given the route, I initially suspected they were taking me to the Interior Ministry. Omar and I had been there numerous times over the

years to talk to high-ranking officials, including the minister. Then again, perhaps we might
be going to see General Kamal Jeddeh, the head
of the General Intelligence Directorate, another
occasional source. But soon it became clear that
both of these guesses were off the mark.

When we passed through the center of the city
and began zigzagging through a series of side streets
heading to the city's northwest quadrant, my mind
started racing. Was it possible? Were we really heading to Al-Hummar? I'd never been there before,
and a visit there now of all times seemed unlikely
in the extreme. Yet after a somewhat-lengthy and
circuitous drive through the city, we eventually did
arrive in the heavily guarded section of the capital
where the Royal Court was located. The agents
radioed ahead, and before I knew it, enormous
steel gates were opening to us and the Mercedes
pulled up in front of a huge building I'd seen
countless times on television but never in person.

"Welcome to the palace, Mr. Collins," Sa'id
remarked before jumping out of the car and opening the door for me. "His Majesty is expecting you."

I stepped out of the car. Baffled yet intrigued
by this turn of events, I found myself staring up at
a mammoth structure made of beautifully carved
limestone with a slightly pinkish hue. I'd always
thought of this building material as "Jerusalem
stone," but apparently it was common to the
entire region. I saw five huge exterior archways,
each leading to an equally huge interior archway.
Framing the center archway were two flagpoles,
one on each side, upon which the distinctive

black, red, white, and green flag of the Hashemite
Kingdom snapped smartly in the brisk December
winds.

At least a dozen soldiers stood guard in front of
the palace. I saw several others patrolling the roof-
top. Then a half-dozen large trucks—resembling
moving vans but unmarked—pulled through
the gates, drove past us, and parked to my left.
Moments later, a group of workers, presumably
employed by the Royal Court, came through a side
door and began unloading a series of boxes from
the trucks.

Several additional security guards approached
and surrounded us as Ali Sa'id asked me to follow
him. He led me through one of the archways and
two large wooden doors and then we were inside
the Al-Hummar Palace.

Under the circumstances, I expected to
be thoroughly searched. Certainly I would be
directed to pass through a metal detector and have
my briefcase and camera bag run through X-ray
machines. But no. All the equipment was there,
but we passed straight by it. I wasn't even asked to
show my driver's license or passport or any other
form of ID.

The agent took me down one hallway after
another lined with framed portraits of the
Hashemite monarchs. The lovely Queen Rania
smiled out from one frame, and I saw another
featuring Crown Prince Hussein, the king's eldest
son. There were also a number of photographs of
significant dignitaries meeting with the late King
Hussein as well as the current King Abdullah II,

including American presidents and secretaries of state and various European and Asian heads of state and foreign ministers, as well as the Saudi king and other Arab presidents, monarchs, and emirs. There was even a recent picture of the king greeting the new pope. It was, in many ways, a monarchy museum, complete with oblong glass cases containing various ancient vases, a gleaming silver saber that looked several centuries old, and other archaeological and historical artifacts from the age of the Ottomans, Roman times, and even biblical times.

On a normal day I might have been interested in some of it or perhaps even all of it. But this was no ordinary day. I was about to meet the king of Jordan for the first time, and I could only imagine why. My stomach was in knots. I hadn't eaten anything substantive in hours. I was suddenly parched, as well, and still battling shock from all that had happened in the last few days. But at that moment, I could only think about one thing: Was this meeting going to be on the record or off?

As I came around a corner, I found Prince Marwan waiting for me in his wheelchair. He was dressed in his traditional white-and-beige robes and wore his traditional red- and white-checkered kaffiyeh like a true Jordanian royal. He was not smiling. Indeed, he not only looked tired and ill but deeply troubled as well. However, he greeted me politely and asked me to follow him. As Sa'id and the rest of the security detail took up their positions around us, two ceremonial guards wearing ornate bedouin military uniforms opened two large doors.

We entered a room I recognized from photos as the king's official receiving room. This was where he typically held meetings with heads of state and dignitaries from all over the world. The walls were covered with rich, dark mahogany paneling. There were two beautiful ivory-and-beige couches straight ahead, one close to the door and the other facing it on the far side of the room.

In the center of the room was a low, modern, rather sleek-looking coffee table upon which were small vases of white flowers and various wooden bowls containing several small archaeological artifacts. There were two small end tables beside the couch at the back of the room. The one on the right side bore a lamp and a large ceramic ashtray, while the one on the left bore a framed eight-by-ten black-and-white photograph of the late King Hussein wearing a Western business suit and his signature kaffiyeh. Behind the couch near the back wall was an end table with what appeared to be several priceless vases and pieces of ancient pottery, as well as another framed photo of King Hussein.

As I looked around, I saw Kamal Jeddeh, Jordan's intelligence director, a fit, barrel-chested man in his midfifties, rise from one of the couches. We greeted one another, but only for a moment. The prince seemed to be in a bit of a hurry, and he immediately asked me to take a seat on another couch on the left side of the room. I did as he asked, then admired the photographs and other details of the room while we waited several minutes in silence. Jeddeh struck me as uncharacteristically anxious, toying with a pen and glancing repeatedly at his watch.

The prince was not his typically warm self. I wanted to ask why, but at the moment it did not seem appropriate, so I held my tongue. To be honest, I was actually grateful that no one was talking quite yet. The silence gave me a chance to get my bearings, settle my heart rate somewhat, and start thinking about why His Majesty had summoned me and what I wanted to ask him if he gave me the chance.

Suddenly my phone vibrated. I quickly checked. Yael had responded to my text.

James—thank G-d you're safe! Thnx 4 the note. Have been worried sick. We need to talk. Dangerous new developments. Call me ASAP.—Y

Just then a door opened in the back of the room. Several more security men entered. Then the king entered as well, followed by the crown prince. In that moment it occurred to me that I was about to experience something my grandfather never had; I was about to meet a king.

His Majesty wore a finely tailored dark-blue suit, a light-blue shirt, and a red power tie. He was handsome and clean-shaven, and the thought struck me that he could have easily passed for the CEO of a high-tech company or perhaps a university president rather than a sovereign and one of the West's most important allies in the entire Arab world. He was somewhat shorter than me but obviously in excellent physical shape—no doubt the result of discipline gained from his many years in the military—and was clearly in command with a broad smile and warm manner. Although there was no question who was in charge when he entered the room, I didn't detect any arrogance or pomposity as I had when meeting other world leaders.

"Mr. Collins, it is a delight to meet you," he said with an accent that bespoke his years of secondary and university schooling in England, graciously extending his hand. "Thank you for agreeing to meet with me on such short notice."

"It is an honor to meet you, Your Majesty," I replied, not entirely sure of the proper protocol but taking his cue and accepting his firm handshake.

The king introduced me to Crown Prince Hussein as an official photographer snapped several pictures and then stepped out of the room.

"Please have a seat," the king said. "Make yourself comfortable. I have been reading your dispatches. What a harrowing couple of weeks you have had."

"Thank you, Your Majesty," I replied, feeling butterflies in my stomach. "Harrowing, indeed."

The king took a seat on the couch across from me. His son, in his early twenties, wore a black suit with a crisp white shirt and a purple tie and sat on the same couch as his father. Prince Marwan was wheeled into position off to my right, just beyond the coffee table, while Director Jeddeh, in a gray suit and a bland-yellow tie, sat directly to my right, at the other end of the couch. We were served coffee, but as thirsty as I was, I couldn't think about drinking it right now.

The king ignored the coffee as well and motioned for his servants to step out of the room.

"Everything we say here today is off the record. Is that understood?" he began when we were finally alone.

"I would really like to get you on the record," I replied. "No Arab leader has reacted to the Abu Khalif interview. You should be the first."

"Tomorrow," he said. "I will give you exclusive access to me for the day, including a formal sit-down interview. But right now I want to talk with you privately."

I could hardly say no, so I nodded and said thank you.

"I want to start by updating you on the peace process," the king said.

"Not Abu Khalif?" I asked in amazement. "Not ISIS?"

"First things first."

"With all due respect, Your Majesty, I would think ISIS would be your top concern," I responded.

"I am well aware of the risks," he replied.

"Abu Khalif clearly wants to seize control of Iraq and Syria. But he and Jamal Ramzy told me they are now about to strike a third target. And based on everything I have seen and heard, I have come to believe that target may be Jordan."

"We've been dealing with ISIS for a long time, Mr. Collins. We know who they are and what they want. We are ready for them. I am not worried. My focus right now is to help the Palestinians get their state, and I believe that after many tears and much heartache, that time has finally come."

I had tremendous respect for this king, but I wasn't sure this was wisdom. To be sure, His Majesty was highly experienced in surfing the turbulent waves in the region. And of course, he was not only a highly trained soldier, but he had once been commander of Jordan's special forces. Nevertheless, at that moment I was concerned that he and his royal advisors were so focused on the peace process to their west that they might not be sufficiently attentive to the threat rising to their east.

"You are aware that the Israelis and Palestinians are about to announce a final, comprehensive peace agreement that will, after far too many years, finally establish a sovereign Palestinian State in the West Bank and Gaza, correct?" the king continued.

"I've seen mixed reports in the press, Your Majesty," I replied. "But if we are off the record, I will say I have heard the same thing from several trustworthy sources, including President Taylor. I understand you have played a key role."

"Prince Marwan and I have lost a lot of sleep in recent months, but it has all been worth it," he said.

"Every issue has been solved?" I asked.

"Remarkably, yes," he said.

"The borders?"

"The Israelis agreed to relinquish about 94 percent of the West Bank and all of Gaza. There are land swaps. The Israelis will keep all the major settlements but will dismantle and evacuate the smaller ones. In return, the Israelis have carved out sections of the Negev and parts of the Galilee region to give to the Palestinians to compensate for the 6 percent of the land on which the major settlements are located."

"And Jerusalem?"

"The Palestinians will have their capital in East Jerusalem."

"All of it?" I asked.

"Parts of it," the king said. "The Dome of the Rock, the Al-Aqsa Mosque, and the Temple Mount will be managed by a special committee, chaired by Jordan and including the Palestinians, Israel, the U.S., and Saudi Arabia. The Palestinians will have sovereignty over the Muslim Quarter of the Old City."

"What about the Jewish, Christian, and Armenian Quarters?"

"Israel will control those," the king said. "Each side will guarantee access for adherents of all religions to their holy sites. Meanwhile, the Israelis will have sovereignty over Mount Scopus and the Mount of Olives and will control the current tunnel from the West Bank into Jerusalem. The Saudis and Americans will finance the building of a separate tunnel leading from Arab towns into East Jerusalem. And the Palestinians will establish government offices near the Damascus Gate."

"Prime Minister Lavi agreed to all that?"

"Mr. Collins, my good friend Daniel *proposed* all that," the king replied.

I wondered if I looked as surprised as I felt.

"It wasn't such a stretch for him," the king added. "Daniel was on the negotiating teams with

Ehud Barak at Camp David in 2000. He was a key aide in helping Ariel Sharon with the disengagement in 2005. And he was a senior advisor to Olmert in 2008. He's been working on these issues for a long time."

"President Mansour wanted more, no doubt," I said.

"He did."

"But you persuaded him to take the deal?"

"Salim and I had many long talks," the king said. "He is not Yasser Arafat. Nor is he Mahmoud Abbas. They weren't ready for peace. Salim is. The Palestinians are ready. It's time."

"What about refugees?"

"Palestinian refugees will have the right to return to the Palestinian State—as many as want to," the king replied. "But Daniel conceded East Jerusalem as the Palestinian capital on the condition that Salim not insist on the right of Palestinian refugees to return to Israel en masse. In the end, the Israelis agreed to accept fifty thousand refugees—five thousand per year for ten years—so long as each one is vetted by their security services and does not pose a security threat. This was actually the most contentious part of the negotiations and certainly took the longest. The formula is very close to what Olmert proposed in 2008, but Olmert was only offering visas for a total of five thousand Palestinians to enter Israel. This is ten times as many."

"Water rights?"

"It's a complicated formula. It divides the water between the Palestinians, the Israelis, and us, but it's consistent with the treaty my father signed with the Israelis in 1994."

"And what about security arrangements?" I asked.

"The short version is this," King Abdullah replied. "The Palestinian State will be demilitarized. They will have police and border security forces, of course, but no army, no air force—except a specified number of helicopters for surveillance and medical rescue purposes—and no significant navy except patrol boats to protect the Gaza coast. No rockets or missiles are permitted on Palestinian territory. No launchers. No new tunnels. We and the Israelis are responsible for security in the Jordan River Valley. The Israelis will have seven manned outposts in the valley, but they will rent the land from the Palestinians. The Israeli Air Force will maintain security over all airspace west of the Jordan. We'll do the same on the east side. The rest of the security in the corridor will be highly coordinated between all three sovereign governments."

"This sounds a lot like a confederation," I said.

"In some ways it is, yes," the king conceded. "But everyone has specifically agreed not to call it a confederation."

"Why not?"

"Because Salim says that the very word infuriates Palestinians, dishonors them, makes them feel like they don't have true sovereignty."

"And you?" I asked.

"I want to honor our neighbors," the king replied. "If they don't like the term, I'm happy not to use it."

"But you're satisfied the security arrangements will protect your kingdom?"

"I am," he said. "Look, no one has been more supportive of a sovereign Palestinian State than my father and me. My father made a terrible gamble in 1967. He listened to Nasser's lies, and in so doing he lost Jerusalem and nearly half his kingdom. We learned a great deal from that disaster. One lesson was that it was not the will of Allah for Jordan to control the West Bank. That was painful to accept. Very painful. But accept it we have. What we cannot accept, however, is creating a security vacuum on the west side of the river. We want the Palestinians to have a strong security force. We are happy to help fund their training and equip them with whatever they need. But we need to make sure all security issues in the corridor are carefully coordinated. These were not the most contentious elements of the negotiations, but they were among the most time-consuming. In the end, I was and am satisfied."

"So everything is set?" I asked.

"It is," the king said. "In fact, President Taylor called me not ten minutes ago to go over the final details and to review the rollout plan. I told him I was about to meet with you. He asked me to tell you he's glad you are safe and that he looks forward to discussing Abu Khalif with you directly."

"That's very kind," I said. "When does he touch down in Israel? And are you going to Jerusalem for the big announcement?"

"The president is not going to Jerusalem, and neither am I, Mr. Collins."

"Why not?" I asked, wondering what I had just missed.

"The 'big announcement,' as you call it, will be held tomorrow afternoon," the king said. "But it will not be held in Israel. It will be right here, at the palace."

49

★ ★ ★

"Here? Tomorrow? How is that possible?" I asked.

The king smiled. "It's going to take a lot of work, but my team will be ready."

The large trucks and all the workers out in front of the palace now made sense. The staff of the Royal Court was going to be working through the night to prepare for the arrival of the president of the United States, the Israeli prime minister, the Palestinian president—and all the staff, security, and media that were coming with them.

"Does anyone have this story yet?" I asked.

"That everyone's coming here?"

"Right."

"No, not at all," the king said. "Each leader has gone to great lengths to keep any details from the media. In part, that's to create the biggest media impact. It's also for security purposes. But again, tomorrow's events aren't what worry me."

"Why not?" I pressed. "All four leaders here at the same time present a tempting target, do they not, especially to ISIS?"

"Look, Mr. Collins, Jordan's security services

are first-rate. The U.S. Secret Service is helping us. So are the Israeli and Palestinian security services. We'll be fine. What worries me more—and this is absolutely off the record—is that this weekend I am flying to Baghdad for a series of meetings with the prime minister on the ISIS threat and the future of Iraq. Frankly, if ISIS is looking for a window of vulnerability, that is it."

"Can I go with you?" I asked.

"You really want to?"

"Absolutely."

For the first time, the king turned to Prince Marwan and his intelligence director. I couldn't read the signals, but the king didn't say no. Rather he asked for a day to think about it, which I took as a positive sign.

Returning to the issue at hand, I asked why all the media leaks were indicating that the peace treaty ceremony was going to be held in Jerusalem.

"Jerusalem was the original plan—that's why you've seen these leaks in the last twenty-four hours," he explained. "But Salim and Daniel couldn't agree over exactly where to hold it, and in the end, Salim called me and asked if I would host the whole thing here."

"Meanwhile, the Israelis are literally rolling out the red carpet," I said. "But it's all a head fake?"

"It didn't start that way, but now, yes, I guess it is," the king agreed. "We will have a wonderful crowd at the peace ceremony, but none of them know that's what they're coming for."

"Then what do they think they're coming for?"

"There is an awards ceremony beginning at

2 p.m. with about five hundred high school students from all over Jordan and the West Bank. There is even a delegation of Israeli students coming, about fifty, I believe. The brightest students in their schools are supposed to meet with my son and various ministers. Then I am scheduled to deliver the keynote address. All the students arrived in Amman this morning. They're touring the city all day. When they arrive here tomorrow, they will go through security and then learn that they are participating in the most important event of this millennium."

"And the awards ceremony?"

The king smiled again. "Everything has been thought of, Mr. Collins. It will be held at the performing arts center downtown the following day."

"What time do the various government delegations arrive?" I asked.

The king turned to Kamal Jeddeh.

"President Mansour and the Palestinians arrive late tonight," the intelligence director explained. "As a matter of fact, the entire Palestinian delegation is staying at your hotel, Le Méridien. If it is all right with His Majesty, perhaps we can arrange for Mr. Collins and President Mansour to have breakfast in the morning and do an interview."

"Absolutely," the king said. "That's a good idea."

"I'd like that, Your Majesty; thank you," I replied. "And the Israelis?"

The head of the Mukhabarat addressed that question as well; clearly it was his responsibility to keep all these delegations safe.

"As you can imagine, it's difficult for Prime

Minister Lavi to travel without the press noticing. But he'll depart Ben Gurion at 10 a.m., touch down here in Amman around ten thirty, and be brought by helicopter to the palace no later than eleven. His advance team is already here, and most of his security detail arrives less than an hour from now."

I turned to the king. "Could we arrange for me to have lunch with Danny Lavi?" I asked.

"I'm afraid not," the king replied. "He and Salim and I are having an early working lunch. But we'll make sure you get a meeting with him at some point."

"And what about President Taylor?"

"Air Force One touches down at one," Jeddeh said. "President Mansour, Prime Minister Lavi, His Majesty, the crown prince, and Prince Marwan will greet him at the airport, do a photo op, and then all come back here for the official ceremony. I'll make sure we get you a final, detailed schedule in the morning."

"Thank you," I said. "But with all due respect, Your Majesty, what good is the exclusive you're giving me tomorrow if hundreds of reporters will be here from all over the world as well?"

"None of them will have backstage access to the principals except you," the king said. "You'll be in the limousine when we pick up President Taylor. You'll be sitting directly behind me during the ceremony. You'll be privy to conversations and details that no one else will have."

"Why me?"

"Why not?" He smiled. "If you would prefer, I can certainly give this to one of your competitors."

"No, no, don't get me wrong," I replied. "I'm very grateful. Just curious why I've been granted such a favor."

"It is simple, really," the king replied. "You're the only reporter in the world to have actually met and interviewed Abu Khalif. We want to send him a message."

"And what message would that be?"

"That he cannot win," the king said. "That peace and moderation and tolerance will prevail."

Sitting back for a moment, I carefully considered what he was telling me. I was intrigued and impressed with Abdullah bin al-Hussein, both as a monarch and as a Reformer. He was actively trying to lead his small, oil-less, but vitally important nation toward progress and freedom, toward tolerance and modernity. He was keeping close ties with the Arab world. But he was also working hard to maintain a close friendship with the United States and the European Union. On top of all that, he was maintaining his nation's courageous peace treaty with Israel despite all manner of trials. Now he was trying to help the Palestinians and Israelis make peace, even while standing strong against the radical forces in the region. It was not an easy task.

The Radicals—al Qaeda, ISIS, the Muslim Brotherhood, and the mullahs in Iran, to name a few—desperately wanted to topple the king and seize Jordan for themselves. In the last few years, the Radicals had seized Tunisia, Libya, and Egypt, albeit briefly, and they were presently fighting to grab Syria and Iraq too. Would Jordan be next? I hoped the answer was no. But Abu Khalif had told me he planned to strike again soon. And common sense suggested the king was a prime target. Did he not see it this way? I needed to persuade him to go on the record—immediately, for tomorrow's paper. But how?

"Your Majesty, may I ask you a question?" I said finally, leaning forward.

"By all means," he said. The man was nothing if not gracious. The bedouin tradition of hospitality was deeply ingrained in him.

"I realize there is much you don't want to say until all the principals initial the comprehensive peace treaty tomorrow, and I respect that enormously," I began. "But there are two facts I need to address. The first is that my editor expects me to file a story from the region by midnight tonight so it can make it into tomorrow's newspaper. The second is that given the events of the last few days and the threats made specifically against you and your kingdom, I would think that it is important for everyone in Jordan—but especially everyone in Israel—to hear from you directly on how seriously you're taking ISIS and what security measures you're implementing to ensure not only that tomorrow goes well but that Jordan remains the vital cornerstone of security in this corridor over the long haul. So my question, Your Majesty, is simply this: Would you be willing to do a short interview with me right now to explain why you are so confident that Jordan will play a major role in securing this peace, no matter what Abu Khalif is saying?"

50

★ ★ ★

To my surprise, the king agreed.

I looked at Prince Marwan and Kamal Jeddeh. They, of course, deferred to their monarch. So I fished my digital recorder out of my briefcase, turned it on, and set it on the table. Then I pulled out a pad of paper and pen, and we began.

"Your Majesty, thank you for agreeing to sit down to talk with the readers of the *New York Times*," I began.

"Always a pleasure," he replied, taking a sip of coffee for the first time since entering the room.

"To begin with, how would you characterize this moment in the broad sweep of Middle Eastern history?"

"I would restate the central case I made in my 2011 book, *Our Last Best Chance: The Pursuit of Peace in a Time of Peril*," he replied. "I believe we still have one last chance to achieve peace. But the window is rapidly closing. If we do not seize the opportunity presented by the now almost-unanimous international consensus of the solution, I am certain we will see another war in our region—most likely worse than those that have gone before and with more disastrous consequences."

"You don't consider the carnage inside Syria and Iraq to be regional wars?"

"The situation in Syria is a civil war, and it is very serious indeed," the king said. "Our brothers and sisters in Iraq are fighting a terrorist movement. This too is quite serious. But what I was referring to in my book, and what I am warning of now, is the danger of another full-scale war between Arabs and Israelis. This would be catastrophic, which is why we are working so hard to help the Palestinians and Israelis make peace."

"Is peace at hand?"

"Inshallah," he said. *God willing.*

"You have been deeply involved in behind-the-scenes negotiations between the Israelis and Palestinians, correct?"

"The Palestinians and the Israelis have done all the work," he said modestly. "I have been particularly impressed with President Mansour. He has worked tirelessly to secure a fair and just result for his people. We have played a minor role, tried to encourage him and Prime Minister Lavi as best we could, based on lessons King Hussein learned while making peace with the Israelis back in the 1990s."

"What tangible benefits do you see from the Israelis and Palestinians signing a comprehensive peace agreement?"

"As you know, Jordan has been the region's strongest and most consistent supporter of the creation of a sovereign Palestinian State with its capital in Jerusalem," the king replied. "If this could truly be achieved—and I do say *if*, though we are closer than ever before—then it would be the most important geopolitical development of the millennium. This would be the fulfillment of a dream that eluded my father, Yasser Arafat, Mahmoud Abbas, and one Israeli prime minister after another. It would be a tremendous blessing for the Palestinian people, who have suffered too much for too long."

"And for Jordan?"

"My dream, as I have stated on countless occasions, is to link the economies of Israel, Palestine, and Jordan in a common market—similar to Benelux in Western Europe. Imagine if we could combine the technical know-how and entrepreneurial drive of all three nations to create an economic and business hub in the Levant? The potential for joint tourism is massive, as is the potential for foreign investment."

I was about to shift the conversation to Abu Khalif, but the king was not finished.

"And let me say another word about tourism," he added. "Jordan is a leader in encouraging Islamic tourism not only throughout our own nation but to Mecca and Medina and Jerusalem. But we also know that there are some two billion Christians in the world. Imagine if there was truly peace between Jordan, Palestine, and Israel. Imagine if Christian pilgrims could come and visit the Holy Land— on *both* sides of the Jordan River. What a blessing that would be for Christians, as well as for all the people of the region. It is not widely known in the West, but we have in Jordan a small but thriving Christian community that is perhaps the oldest in the world. The place where Jesus was baptized is Jordan's most important Christian site. It is here on the east bank of the Jordan River. This is where Jesus' mission started. This is where Christianity began. Jordan is also where Moses lived and died. This is where Elijah the prophet was taken up to heaven in a chariot of fire. There is so much rich history here, and pilgrims could not only come to see it all, but then cross the Jordan River and visit Jericho and Bethlehem and Jerusalem. They could behold the wonders of ancient and modern Jordan, Palestine, and Israel in ways never before possible.

"On my trips abroad I have met with priests, preachers, rabbis, and imams," he continued. "We have been working hard to build relationships with Christians, the Jewish community, and of course Muslims. We want everyone who shares our heart for peace to come and walk where Jesus and the prophets walked. We are not just *talking* about peace. We are not just *dreaming* about it. We are working very hard each and every day to make peace a reality."

It was time to pivot.

"Have you read the interview Abu Khalif gave to the *Times* the other day?"

"I have."

"How would you respond to the ISIS leader's threats not only to annihilate Israel but to take out any Arab leader who makes peace with the Israelis, yourself and President Salim Mansour included, all to establish a true Islamic caliphate?"

"I am pained by the twisting of my religion by a small band of misguided fanatics," the king replied. "Such people embrace a deviant form of Islam. While claiming to act in its name, they are in reality just murderers and thugs. They constitute an unrepresentative minority of the 1.57 billion Muslims in the world, but they have had a disproportionate impact on how the faith is perceived. These people are *takfiris*, which in Arabic means 'those who accuse others of being heretics.' They rely on ignorance, resentment, and a distorted promise of achieving martyrdom to spread their ideology, turning their backs on over a thousand years of Qur'anic scholarship in the name of what they presume to be the authentic ways of seventh-century Arabia. But the actions of the *takfiris* have nothing to do with Islam and its message. True Islam stands for justice, equality, fairness, and the opportunity to live a meaningful and good life. They seek to destroy these things. In doing so they have turned their backs on the ancient traditions of clemency and compassion.

"My advisors and I have been working for several years to build a broad-based consensus among Islamic scholars and clerics of all stripes regarding the true nature of Islam and the many reasons the *takfiris* are both theologically and historically wrong in their interpretations of the Qur'an. The scholars have produced a document called the Amman Message, which sets out what

Islam is, what it is not, and what types of actions are and are not Islamic."

From memory, he then recited for me a brief passage from the document.

"Today the magnanimous message of Islam faces a vicious attack from some who claim affiliation with Islam and commit irresponsible acts in its name. We denounce and condemn extremism, radicalism, and fanaticism today, just as our forefathers tirelessly denounced and opposed them throughout Islamic history. On religious and moral grounds, we denounce the contemporary concept of terrorism that is associated with wrongful practices. Such acts are represented by aggression against human life in an oppressive form that transgresses the rulings of God."

I was writing as fast as I could. I glanced up to make sure my digital recorder was still working. Fortunately it was.

"One more question, if I may?"

"Please."

"Thank you, Your Majesty. I read your book when it was released in 2011, and I have also read your father's memoir published in 1962, *Uneasy Lies the Head*," I said. "One of the common threads of both books is how often the extremists have tried to assassinate you and overthrow your kingdom. As you know, my grandfather, A. B. Collins, witnessed the tragic assassination of King Abdullah I. Now Abu Khalif, the commander of ISIS, is personally threatening to behead you and destroy the peace process into which you and your family have invested so much. My question is, how can you assure the American people, the Jordanian people, the Palestinians, and the Israelis—along with all those in the region and throughout the world who care about peace—that Jordan will remain a strong and stable cornerstone of regional security, especially in light of the ISIS threat?"

"I would simply say this," the king replied. "The Hashemite Kingdom is the longest-reigning regime in all the Middle East and North Africa. I am not going anywhere. Jordan is not going anywhere. We are here to stay, and we will remain a beacon of peace and moderation in troubled times."

I wrote down his words verbatim. They certainly sounded good. And the king was nothing if not sincere. This wasn't spin. He was saying this from his heart.

I just feared he was dead wrong.

51

* * *

Just before three in the morning, I sat bolt upright in bed.

Shaking and so covered in perspiration that my pillow and sheets felt damp, I got out of bed, turned on the bedside lamp, and made my way across my hotel room to the bathroom to get a glass of water. When I glanced in the mirror, I saw my eyes were bloodshot, but I didn't have a fever. As far as I could tell, I wasn't really sick. I was terrified.

ISIS had threatened to wipe out my entire family. I'd just learned that four of the world leaders Abu Khalif most wanted to kill—the president of the United States, the Israeli prime minister, the Palestinian president, and the king of Jordan— were all gathering under one roof, here in Amman, in a few short hours. The question wasn't "Why had I woken up so early?" but "How had I actually slept at all?"

Death surrounded me.

Matt was right. Everywhere I went, people I cared about wound up dead. I kept telling myself

I was strong and able to keep going in spite of it all. But I was no longer sure that was true. I'd just had the most vivid dream of Matt and his family being killed with sarin gas. I'd seen them writhing and gasping for breath and couldn't do anything to save them. It was all I could do to convince myself it wasn't real. It was a nightmare; that's all. Yet who was to say it wouldn't soon come true?

If there really were five stages of grief—denial, anger, bargaining, depression, and acceptance—I couldn't honestly say I'd even begun. I hadn't even started into denial. I was somewhere between shock and primordial fear. For most of my life, I hadn't been afraid of death because I'd never really taken it seriously. I'd never even thought about it in any depth. I hadn't believed in an afterlife. But now everything had changed.

I was now certain there was an afterlife. I was now certain that heaven and hell were real places that real people went. I couldn't explain how. I just knew. What I didn't know was how to get to heaven. Matt said Jesus was the only way. I wasn't so sure. Which meant he was right about another thing—I was in danger. If I didn't have a route to heaven, didn't that mean I was on the road to hell?

I turned off the lamp, unplugged my mobile phone from its charger, and used the glow of its screen to find my way to the darkened window. I turned on the air-conditioning and then lay down on top of the comforter. I checked the *Times* home page. My interview with the king had just been posted. Allen and I were still communicating only through e-mails and text messages. But he was no longer telling me to come home. I was in the epicenter of the story, and he wanted me to stay put and send him everything I could. That suited me just fine. I had no intention to run from Abu Khalif, even if I had told my brother to.

I checked my e-mails. There were nine, all from various U.S., European, and Israeli reporters. They were all asking for interviews describing my personal take on Abu Khalif. I didn't have time for that. But I did take the next ten minutes or so sending a few quotes to each of them, giving them some tidbits. Most important, I verified that I'd seen ISIS use chemical weapons in Mosul. After all, the only reason Khalif hadn't killed me yet was so I could keep telling the world he had weapons of mass destruction. And that was a story I was determined to tell anyway.

I checked my text messages. There were three from my mom, telling me she was praying for me, asking me to come home, and asking me to read the Twenty-third Psalm. There was a smattering of others from various sources and colleagues, checking on me and asking me to call them. There were no new messages from Yael. I'd called her twice the previous evening—once immediately after my interview with the king, on the drive back to Le Méridien; the other right before I went to bed. I'd texted her too. I was eager to talk to her, to hear her voice, to learn more about the "dangerous developments" she had referred to. But so far, nothing.

There was, however, a text from Matt.

Just touched down in a faraway city, it read simply. **Won't say where for now, but wanted you to know we're safe. Don't worry about us. Kids don't understand what's happening. Think it's an adventure. Annie's fine. Sends her love.**

Two minutes later, another came in.

Annie says read Psalm 3. Thought you might be encouraged by it too. Praying for you. Love you.—Matt

A moment later, another SMS message arrived, this one with a link to Psalm 3 on some online Bible. With nothing else to do at the moment, I clicked on the link and read it aloud in my room.

"O Lord, so many are against me. So many seek to harm me. I have so many enemies. So many say that God will never help me. But Lord, you are my shield, my glory, and my only hope. You alone can lift my head, now bowed in shame. I cried out to the Lord, and he heard me from his Temple in Jerusalem. Then I lay down and slept in peace and woke up safely, for the Lord was watching over me. And now, although ten thousand enemies surround me on every side, I am not afraid. I will cry to him, 'Arise, O Lord! Save me, O my God!' And he will slap them in the face, insulting them and breaking off their teeth. For salvation comes from God. What joys he gives to all his people."

The heading above the psalm noted that its author was the ancient King David. I wondered how David could lie down and sleep peacefully when ten thousand enemies were hunting him down to kill him the first chance they got. I didn't get it and wasn't sure I ever would.

I got up again and opened my laptop. While I was waiting for the computer to boot up, I thought about the king's upcoming trip to Baghdad and whether I really wanted to go along after all. Professionally, it was probably the right thing to do. But I wasn't sure I could pull it off. How much more of this could I really take? I was emotionally and physically exhausted. My nerves were shot, and truth be told, I had no idea if I could make it through the day. Maybe I should follow my own advice, I thought. Maybe it was time to get out of Jordan—get off the grid and lie low until this whole thing blew over.

It was tempting, but I couldn't just ditch my job now. People were counting on me, and I had to deliver. I had a huge day ahead of me—interviews with the leaders of Palestine, Israel, and Jordan, and perhaps one with the president of the United States as well. I had to ask them about the ISIS threat, but how could I engage them and get them to really make news, not just spit out prepackaged talking points?

My thoughts shifted back to Abu Khalif. How had he known the peace treaty was a done deal? How had he known King Abdullah had been its broker? How had he known Ismail Tikriti was going to be at the Abu Ghraib prison that night, or that I would be there as well? There wasn't a reporter on the planet who had known any of these facts in advance, except me. But clearly someone was feeding Khalif insider information. And if it wasn't coming from the media, it could only be coming from a mole inside one of the four governments involved. Which meant I had to consider the possibility that Abu Khalif not only knew about the king's upcoming trip to Baghdad but might know exactly what was happening later today. If there was ever a time for ISIS to strike and strike hard, it was now. It was here.

I shifted my attention again, this time to scanning more of the latest headlines.

**Daily Mail—Another Day,
Another ISIS Crucifixion:
Man Accused of Joining Syrian
Regime Found Hanging from a
Cross in Busy Market Town with
Cryptic Note Pinned to His Chest**

**CNN—Death and Desecration in Syria:
Jihadist Group Crucifies
Bodies to Send Message**

**The Washington Post—ISIS,
Beheadings, and the Success
of Horrifying Violence**

**The Wall Street Journal—Militants Claim
Photos Show Mass Execution in Iraq**

The *Daily Express*—The New Dark Ages:
The Chilling Medieval Society ISIS
Extremists Seek to Impose in Iraq

The *Guardian*—British PM Warns ISIS
Is Planning to Attack UK

On top of all this were stories about the continuing spike in oil prices that was sending new shock waves through an already-battered and fragile global economy.

I shut down the computer and collapsed on the bed, staring at the ceiling in the darkness.

All the lights in the room were off. Only the red numbers on the digital clock were visible. It was 3:46 in the morning. And that's the last thing I remembered until my alarm went off two hours later.

52

* * *

I had never seen Salim Mansour happy.

Not "so happy." Not "this happy." I'm saying I had never seen him happy.

Ever. Period. End of sentence. New paragraph.

An economist by training, with a doctorate from the University of Chicago, the Palestinian president was not someone I would naturally characterize as an optimist. Once, over a meal of hummus and lamb at a restaurant in Jericho overlooking the Jordan Valley, he had told me—off the record, of course—how despondent he had become by Yasser Arafat's "congenital incapacity to say yes" to any proposal the Israelis offered.

"The U.N. offered Ben-Gurion a fraction of what he wanted in '47, but he took it," Mansour had said, referring to David Ben-Gurion, the founder of the Jewish State. "He didn't demand the whole loaf, even though he wanted it. He took what he could get and he started building. And look where Israel is now. Their per capita GDP is over $32,000. Ours is not even a tenth of that. Their unemployment rate is under 7 percent a year. Ours is almost four times that number. They're becoming a high-tech capital of the world. At times it feels like we're stuck in the Stone Age. We have so much potential. But we've let ourselves get trapped in a cycle of violence and envy and resentment, and where has it gotten us?"

Over dessert, he'd continued his diatribe. "Don't get me wrong. The Israelis have done everything they could to slow us down and keep us back. I'm not absolving them of anything. Every charge Arafat makes against them is true. But when Barak offered him a serious, substantive deal at Camp David in 2000, Arafat rejected it out of hand. Why? How has that helped us? I'm not saying the deal was everything we wanted. Of course not. But think of it—Palestine could have been an independent, sovereign state since 2000. We could have been building. We could have been growing. Instead, we remain in the mire while the Israelis continue to prosper."

Less than a year later, in another off-the-record lunch, Mansour extended his complaints to include Mahmoud Abbas, aka Abu Mazen.

"Arafat was a revolutionary—I get it," he'd said over stuffed grape leaves and grilled chicken. "Arafat aimed for the sky. Abu Mazen's job was to turn the dream into a reality. Ehud Olmert gave him that chance in '08, but he wouldn't say yes. He was too much a disciple of Arafat. Too weak. No creativity. Imagine if he'd said yes—we could have been sitting in a bona fide State of Palestine since 2008. Yet here we are, stuck as ever."

What made him even more despondent, he

said, was the "endemic corruption" and "bureaucratic incompetence" that he felt had characterized the Palestinian Authority for so long.

"The world is not just going to hand us a state on a silver platter if we can't tie our shoes and pay our bills on time," he had insisted. "Maybe we can't stop the Israelis from occupying us, oppressing us, imposing apartheid on us. Not yet. But we can make sure we are building a solid, functioning, serious economy and democracy. And the sooner we do it, the more credibility we will gain in the eyes of world leaders who can then ratchet up the pressure on the Israelis to acknowledge our God-given right of self-determination."

But this meeting was different. Mansour was smiling.

Born in Jenin but raised in Dubai, Mansour had stayed away from the West Bank and Gaza for decades. In 2010, however, he reluctantly accepted then-President Abbas's request that he serve as the Palestinian Authority's finance minister. Facing enormous odds and bureaucratic infighting, Mansour had set about to make the very reforms for which he had been advocating so long. It wasn't easy. Indeed, it was often painful. But it began to work. The Palestinian economy began to grow. The bureaucracy began to function—not great, certainly not perfect, but better than before. The U.S. State Department took notice. So did the European Union. Jordan certainly did. And so did Mansour's fellow Palestinians. As their fortunes began to improve bit by bit, Mansour's stock began to rise as well. Then came Hamas's repeated rocket wars against Israel and the resultant destruction of Gaza. That had been an enormous setback. Yet in the end, Hamas was humbled and internationally isolated. The rocket wars, as devastating as they'd been, had given the Palestinian Authority—not Hamas—a new lease on life. And when Abbas finally announced he was retiring and calling new elections, there was a groundswell of support for Salim Mansour, the balding, bespectacled economics professor who was offering a serious vision of growth and opportunity for a people long bereft of either.

"It's happening," he now told me over a plate of fruit he wasn't touching and a cup of Turkish coffee that was getting cold. "After all this time, the dream is really becoming a reality."

We were on the record. My digital recorder was on. And despite a deep sense of foreboding I couldn't seem to shake, even I had to smile at Mansour's self-evident joy. "Honestly, Mr. President, I have never seen you happy."

"You weren't at my wedding," he said.

"True."

"Or the births of my four daughters."

"Fair enough."

"Or their weddings or the births of my nine grandchildren."

"My apologies."

"I can be happy, Mr. Collins. I am happy when I have hope, when I see love and fruit and growth and dreams coming true. That's what makes me happy."

"So you're satisfied with this process?"

"Of course not," he said. "It was a circus."

"But you're satisfied with the outcome."

"Hardly," he said defiantly, the smile beginning to fade somewhat. "My people deserve so much more than this. But at the risk of sounding trite, I refused to let the perfect be the enemy of the good. The Palestinian people want a state. They deserve a state. They have fought for one. They have worked for one. They have suffered without one. My job is not to think of a thousand reasons why they cannot have one. My job is to deliver one, and today I have. This is a historic day, one we will not forget for a long time."

"Are you worried about the ISIS threat?"

"No."

"You're not worried that Abu Khalif has threatened to assassinate you and anyone else who makes peace with the 'criminal Zionists'?"

"I am not wasting my time with the mad ravings of a sociopath."

"You know he is calling for a Third Intifada."

"There is no appetite among the Palestinians for another uprising," Mansour said. "Why would there be? We are about to get a state of our own, a true and legitimate state. And once we have it, I believe we will take away the central argument of the *takfiris*, that only through violence will the Palestinian people be liberated. We have been oppressed. And we do need to be liberated. But not through violence. Not through jihad. Today we begin our own liberation. We don't need the help of a rapist and a murderer. We're not seeking a killing ground for jihadists. We're building a real state here, one based on the rule of law and the principles of economic growth, democratic values, and respect for Islam and all religions."

"Do you fear an attack by ISIS using chemical weapons?"

"Of course not."

"Why not?"

"Maybe they don't really have them."

"They do," I said. "I've seen them."

"Then that's what our security forces are for, and Jordan's and Israel's," he replied, a hint of exasperation now rising in his voice. "We have professional security forces, and I have every confidence they will do their job. But this is not our focus today. This is a day of celebration, a day for great joy and optimism, not fear and doubt. Don't spoil this for us with your tales of imminent doom. We have had enough pain to last a thousand lifetimes. We have had enough stormy days. Let us, just this once, have our moment in the sun."

53

* * *

I called Yael again but got voice mail and didn't leave a message.

Then I went to back to my room, wrote up the interview with Mansour, and filed it with Allen.

I pulled out my grandfather's pocket watch and saw it was almost 12:30 p.m. The limo that was supposed to pick me up on the way to the airport to meet President Taylor was late. I was about to call Yael again when my mobile phone rang. But it wasn't her. It was Kamal Jeddeh.

"There's been a change of plans," the Jordanian intelligence director said.

"Is there a problem?" I asked.

"No, just a change," he said. "I have a car waiting for you downstairs. It will take you to the airport. The foreign minister will meet Air Force One and greet the president when he arrives, and the president has requested that you join him for the drive to the palace."

"The king isn't going?" I asked.

"No."

"What about President Mansour and Prime Minister Lavi?"

"They are not going either."

"Why not?"

"Their meeting with His Majesty is running long. That's all I know. But time is short. We must get you to the airport. Please head downstairs immediately."

Something was wrong. The protocol, the timing, every minute of this trip had been mapped out in excruciating detail. I rechecked the official schedule some envoy had slipped under my door earlier that morning. All three Middle Eastern leaders were supposed to greet the American president at Queen Alia International Airport. Why the sudden change—especially one as significant as this? The arrival of the president in Amman under such circumstances would be worldwide news. It would likely be broadcast on live television throughout the region and around the globe. Shouldn't the king be there to greet him? The only thing I could think of that would warrant such a serious deviation from the itinerary was that a last-minute snag had occurred in the peace plan. Was it possible Lavi or Mansour were having second thoughts or reopening some final-status issue that was supposedly already, well, final?

I grabbed my briefcase and camera bag and headed down the hallway. Waiting for the elevator, I quickly sent individual text messages to each of the principals, as well as separate texts to each of their top advisors. On the elevator, I called

Prince Marwan but didn't get him. I called Youssef Kuttab, the Palestinian president's most trusted advisor, as well, but he wasn't picking up either.

Ali Sa'id, on the other hand, was waiting for me in the lobby.

"Ali, my friend, how kind of you to fetch me," I said.

"Of course. Please, come; we must hurry."

We left the front entrance of the hotel and got into the back of Sa'id's government-issue Mercedes. Up front were a driver and a bodyguard. But what really caught my attention was the black Chevy Suburban behind us, filled with a half-dozen additional well armed men.

"Expecting company?" I asked as Sa'id donned his sunglasses and we started moving through traffic.

"You can never be too careful," he replied.

"Ali, how many Syrians are in Jordan at the moment?" I asked.

"Around 1.3 million," he replied.

That was more than double the number I'd heard. "I thought it was between five hundred thousand and six hundred thousand," I said.

"That's *registered* refugees," he explained. "There are just over six hundred thousand refugees living in the camps we've set up with the U.N. But there are another seven hundred thousand who are not officially registered with the Jordanian government."

"How do you know the number then?"

"They came before the civil war—to work, to visit family, to take a vacation, to study, whatever.

But they were already here when the civil war in Syria got so bad they couldn't go back."

"So they got stuck here?" I asked.

"You could say that."

"So the total number is 1.3 million?"

"Give or take."

"Do you know who those people really are?"

"What do you mean?" he asked.

"You know what I mean," I replied. "Have they been vetted? Are they all safe? Or are there jihadists among them?"

"The honest answer?" he asked.

"Of course."

"You can't print this."

"I understand. I'm just curious."

"Well . . ." He glanced nervously at the other agents in the car.

"You can tell me," I said. "I promise I won't tell anyone."

There was a long pause, and then he finally said, "The truth is we have no idea who they all are."

"You mean there could be extremists among them?"

"Yes."

"A few?"

"At least."

"Many?"

"Perhaps."

"Could there be ISIS rebels among them?"

"Yes."

"Sleeper cells?"

"Probably."

"You just don't know."

"Not precise numbers, no," Sa'id told me. "But even if it's just one percent of the total number of Syrians who have entered the country, that could be more than thirteen thousand *jihadis*."

I winced. "Ready to strike?"

"Perhaps," he said again.

"When?"

"Who knows? Whenever Abu Khalif gives the order."

"Have you captured any ISIS members so far?"

"Just between us?"

"Yes."

"Not for publication?"

"Yes."

"Then yes," he said. "The answer is yes."

"How many?"

"In the last eighteen months, we've captured twenty-four ISIS and al-Nusra cells. We've also captured more than four tons of weapons."

"Four tons?" I asked, incredulous.

"I'm afraid so."

"What kinds?"

"Light arms and ammunition, mostly," he told me. "But also mortars, rocket launchers, and IEDs. Look, Mr. Collins, we know Syrians loyal to ISIS and other radical groups have penetrated the country. But as bad as that is, that's not even our biggest concern."

"What is?"

"Jordanian nationals."

"What do you mean?"

"I mean, think of Abu Khalif himself," he explained as we sped southward along Highway 15 toward the airport. "He's a Jordanian. Obviously he's on a watch list because we know about him. And his predecessor, Zarqawi—also a Jordanian national. Again, we knew about him. We kept a vigilant eye out for him. And in the end, we helped the Iraqis and the Americans find him and bring him to justice. But how many other Khalifs and Zarqawis are out there that we don't know about? How many Jordanian nationals, with Jordanian passports and Jordanian driver's licenses and Jordanian ID cards work directly for ISIS or one of the other extremist groups, and we don't know who they are? That's the X factor, Mr. Collins. And these traitors could be anywhere."

"Sprinkled throughout the government bureaucracy?" I asked.

"Maybe."

"The police force?"

"It's possible."

"What about the army?"

"Less likely, but I wouldn't rule it out."

"Why not?"

"Look—all of us who have served in the military or the security services love the king," he said. "We're very loyal to him. He's an extraordinary man and a great leader. In some ways, he's even more impressive than his father, may God give his soul rest. Some were worried when King Hussein died in 1999. They were expecting Prince Hassan to take his place. But just a few days before his death, the king changed the laws of succession. He made his eldest son the crown prince. And when Hussein died, Abdullah took the throne.

I know the royal family very well. My father and grandfather were personal bodyguards for them. We would give our lives for them. But when the changeover happened, many were nervous. They didn't say it out loud, mind you. But they weren't sure the young new monarch was up for the challenge. He proved them wrong."

"But . . ."

"Unemployment among the youth is hovering around 30 percent," he said as we passed through the last of several military checkpoints and then turned at the airport. "And that's just the official number. The real number may very well be even higher. And then there are army veterans."

"What about them?"

"Their pensions are not that much, and it's hard to find a good job, even when you come out as a high-ranking officer. You're not that old—maybe in your mid- to late forties or early fifties. You still have many years of productive service left in you, but the army doesn't need you. So what are you supposed to do? How are you supposed to provide for your family? I'm not talking about food and clothing. But how do you help your son put together money to get married, to buy an apartment, to buy a decent car? For that matter, how do you help your daughter pay for college? This is not a wealthy kingdom, Mr. Collins. This is not Arabia. This is not the Gulf. The government does the best it can. But guess where most of the benefits go?"

"To the refugees from Syria and Iraq?"

"No, no—that's a new problem," he said. "They

go to the Palestinians—that is, to Jordanian citizens of Palestinian origin."

"Which is about how many people?"

"Some say up to 70 percent of the population," Sa'id said. "Some say it's only 50 percent. Does it really matter? The point is the Palestinians—whom some call the 'West Bankers'—get a lot of the government's time, attention, and resources."

"And the East Bankers?"

"Well, we're the ones who built the country," he said. "We're the ones who run the government and fight in the army and are loyal to Jordan first and foremost, not to Palestine."

"But the West Bankers are getting most of the perks."

"That's how some people feel."

"Enough to join ISIS, enough to actually overthrow the king?"

"I hope not, Mr. Collins," he said as we pulled up to the main terminal and a sea of heavily armed soldiers and secret police. "But these are crazy times. If you'd asked me a few years ago whether the Egyptians would try to overthrow Mubarak, and Mubarak would let them, I'd have said you were crazy. If you'd asked me if the Syrians would rise up against Assad, and Assad would have such a hard time stopping them, I'd have said you were out of your mind. But the world is changing very, very fast. I have no idea what will happen next. And that's what scares me."

54

* * *

Air Force One was on approach.

I was standing ten steps away from Jordan's foreign minister, right beside Agent Sa'id, with a front-row, all-access pass to President Harrison Taylor's arrival.

But as impressive as the sight was, I had seen the gleaming blue-and-white Boeing 747 land at foreign airports before. To the enormous crowd of at least ten thousand Jordanians, I'm sure there was electricity in the air as the leader of the free world prepared to land in the country they loved so dearly. For many—indeed, probably for most—all the pomp and circumstance of a state visit was exciting. The bedouin honor guard. The military band. The freshly vacuumed red carpet. The reviewing stand and the camera platform and the klieg lights and the rest of the hoopla.

But all that barely registered for me. My eyes were trained on the United States Secret Service agents and their Jordanian counterparts scanning the crowd for trouble. I was watching the sharp-shooters on the roof and the spotters at their sides with their high-powered binoculars. What interested me was the enormous military presence on the perimeter of the airport, the tanks and armored personnel carriers and hundreds upon hundreds of Jordanian soldiers at the ready, as well as the squadron of Jordanian F-16 Fighting Falcons that were streaking through the sky flying CAP—combat air patrol—in airspace that had been closed the entire day except for official travel. Was the king right? Was his upcoming trip to Baghdad more vulnerable than this? Or were the traitors among us, ready to strike when and how it was least expected?

Every face in the cheering crowd looked, to me at least, genuinely excited. News of a final deal had been leaking out all morning. There was a buzz in the air. Peace was at hand. A sovereign if largely demilitarized Palestinian State, fashioned in a confederation with the Hashemite Kingdom of Jordan, was about to be established once and for all. Why wouldn't this nation so filled with West Bankers be overjoyed for their brothers and sisters across the river and even for themselves?

Yet every face on the security personnel, the vast majority of whom were East Bankers, looked worried and grim. They knew everyone here had been screened by metal detectors and X-ray machines. They knew these observers had been patted down and their purses and handbags and briefcases and backpacks thoroughly searched hours ago. But they still had to be vigilant for the unexpected. That was their job. Was there a killer among them?

And if so, were they looking for a lone gunman or a highly trained, carefully coordinated movement?

Sa'id's words on the drive to the airport were bothering me enormously. I had been through Jordan numerous times. I had developed friends and sources among senior government officials. But I was not an expert on Jordan. Like most reporters, indeed like most Americans, I had never carefully studied the nuances of this country. To me, Jordan was a lovely, safe, friendly country, and I rarely gave it another thought. But after Iraq and Syria, was Jordan the third target of the ISIS terrorists? Was this the crown jewel they wanted to help them build their Islamic caliphate?

And what of my brother Matt's words? Was it possible that the future of Jordan was as dark as the Bible seemed to foretell? Could ISIS really be some kind of instrument about to unleash hell on earth? Was today the day?

If so, would a mere assassination or two—even today—satisfy them? How could it? ISIS hadn't simply tried to take Assad out. They were trying to bring his entire government down. They were trying to seize full control of Damascus and the rest of Syria. The same was true in Iraq. For a Sunni extremist like Abu Khalif, merely beheading Ismail Tikriti or any Iraqi official, even the prime minister, who was a devout Shia, couldn't possibly be enough. Khalif was looking for a way to bring down the democratically elected government of Iraq and establish a Sharia-governed state with himself as the emir. So, too, Khalif wouldn't just want to kill the king of Jordan. He would want to obliterate the royal family and the entire government as well. He would want to create the conditions upon which he and his forces could seize full and complete power. Could that be accomplished on the upcoming royal trip to Baghdad? Not nearly as well as it could be if ISIS struck today, I concluded. But when? How? Who?

As Air Force One touched down to the surprising cheers of the crowd—a crowd that obviously now believed the American president was bearing the gift of a Palestinian State—someone tapped me on the shoulder. I turned, expecting to see Sa'id or perhaps a colleague from the *Times*. Instead, it was Yael Katzir.

"Hey, stranger," she said with a gracious smile and a warm hug.

"Yael . . . what are you doing here?" I asked, as baffled as I was pleased.

"Ari sent me with the PM's delegation," she said. "But I also came to see you. I was so worried about you."

"Thanks. That means a lot."

"You don't look so bad, considering."

"I'll take that as a compliment."

"You should."

"I tried to reach you."

"I know. I'm sorry. It's been crazy. Nonstop. I've hardly eaten a thing. And don't ask me the last time I slept."

"Well, you don't look so bad," I said. "Considering."

"Aren't you sweet."

"Where are you staying?" I asked, hoping that didn't sound too forward.

"Grand Hyatt, and you?"

"Le Méridien."

"Nice."

"Beats a safe house in Mosul."

"I bet," she said, then lowered her voice to a whisper. "Speaking of which, we need to talk."

"Dangerous developments?" I whispered back.

"I'm afraid so."

"You're worried there's going to be an ISIS attack today."

Yael raised an eyebrow. "I see we're thinking the same thing. How did you know?"

"Just a hunch, but one I tried to share with the king yesterday," I said.

"What did he say?"

"Told me not to worry—they've got the city sealed up like a drum."

"Same with my PM," she said. "Ari won't rule it out, but we don't have proof. Just the interviews Khalif did with you. Seems to me Khalif made it about as clear as he could he was coming after the king. And if he could take out my PM, Mansour, and your president all in one shot, it seems kind of irresistible, doesn't it?"

"It does to me," I said. "The question is, does Khalif have the means to launch such a massive attack?"

"The PM doesn't think so," Yael said, scanning the crowd from behind designer sunglasses. "And Ari could hardly stop him from coming without solid evidence of an imminent attack.

Lavi insists Amman is the safest city in the world today, between the Jordanian police, the army, the Mukhabarat, the Palestinian security services, the U.S. Secret Service, the Mossad, and Shin Bet. The PM says ISIS would be crazy to launch an attack today."

"Unless they had someone on the inside," I said.

"You mean a mole?"

"Maybe, or maybe more than that."

"What do you mean?"

"Look, there's no question Khalif has someone inside one of the four governments here today. He has to. He knew about the treaty before anyone else. He knew it was a done deal. He knew the Jordanians were involved. He knew the king was the broker. No one could have known all that several days ago unless they had inside access to at least one of the principals."

"But just that knowledge wouldn't be enough."

"No, which means ISIS would have to have a force already on the ground inside Jordan, inside Amman."

"Inside the palace?" Yael asked.

"That's what worries me," I said. "But how?"

A military band was now playing "Hail to the Chief" as the door of the 747 opened and the president of the United States stepped out and waved to the roaring crowd.

"What about al-Hirak?" she asked.

"What's that?"

"You've never heard of it?"

"No."

"What kind of foreign correspondent are you?"

"The kind that has never heard of al-Hirak. What is it?"

"It means 'the movement,'" she said. "It's a secret underground network of Islamists throughout Jordan made up of disaffected East Bankers. They're devout Muslims, over-the-top, and they think the king has gone soft on Islam. They say the royal family and the government are riddled with corruption. They say the king gives too much money and attention to the West Bankers. They think he doesn't care about the East Bankers or about Islam. They want him to govern like a true Muslim. They want Sharia law."

Again I thought about Sa'id's words in the car. It seemed Yael's intel was correct. "So I'm guessing the king is too pro-Western, too pro-American, and too close to Israel for their tastes?" I said.

"Absolutely. They're Salafists. They want to annihilate the Jews, not have a peace treaty with us. And don't get them started on the queen."

"Why? What's wrong with her?"

"Doesn't wear the veil, wears the latest fashions from London and Paris, likes to hobnob with the rich and famous in Davos and Monte Carlo. They say she dishonors Islam and must be humbled."

"So basically they're just like the Muslim Brotherhood?" I asked.

"No, no, much worse. They loathe the Brotherhood, say they're a bunch of sellouts. And the Brotherhood isn't so strong here anymore. They used to be. But they've made some missteps in recent years. Plus, the Brotherhood isn't illegal in

Jordan like they were and now are again in Egypt. They're aboveground here. That's made it easier for the king and the secret service to keep tabs on them."

"So how big is this Salafist movement, this al-Hirak?"

"We don't have any hard numbers, but the analysts that track this stuff back in Tel Aviv, the ones I've talked to at least, say it's metastasizing quickly."

"And these guys are jihadists?" I asked. "They're violent?"

"Hard to say," she said. "They haven't launched any type of operation yet. But our guys are picking up evidence that some of them seem inspired by the message and methods and success ISIS is having."

"You think they're getting ready to launch a coup?"

"That's exactly what I'm afraid of. Alone, I'm not sure ISIS could pull off here what they're doing in Iraq and Syria. But remember, Khalif is Jordanian. He has a lifetime of contacts here. He knows Jordan better than either of the other two countries. He very likely has thousands of warriors stashed around the country using the Syrian refugee crisis as cover. And if he could activate the al-Hirak network . . ."

She didn't finish the sentence, but she didn't need to.

"Could al-Hirak have loyalists inside the police?"

"Probably."

"The military?"

"Possibly."

"The palace?"

"I don't know," Yael told me as the president descended the steps of Air Force One and prepared to address the crowd.

"But that's why you're here."

"Right," she said, "me and the IDF's most elite NBC unit, hoping to God we're not needed."

NBC unit. She wasn't talking about the National Broadcasting Company.

She was talking about a team of specialists trained in handling nuclear, biological, and chemical warfare.

55

* * *

Ali Sa'id turned to me when the arrival ceremony was nearly finished.

"We need to go," he said.

"Where?"

"Just come quickly."

"What about my friend Yael?"

I introduced her as part of Prime Minister Lavi's delegation, though I said nothing about her expertise in chemical warfare. But Sa'id had his orders, and they didn't include an Israeli.

"It's okay," she said, putting a hand on my arm. "I've got my own orders. But I'll see you at the ceremony."

"Great—and what are you doing afterward?"

"Hopefully nothing."

"Maybe we can think of something."

"Maybe."

I turned back to Sa'id. Neither President Taylor nor the foreign minister was saying anything particularly memorable or newsworthy. The military band was about to strike up the music again. It was all pomp and circumstance and precious little substance, and there was no reason to stay. So as discreetly as possible, I followed Sa'id out of the VIP section with our security detail spread out around us.

A moment later, we reached two golf carts. Sa'id and I boarded one along with two other agents while the rest of the detail boarded the other. It struck me how much security had suddenly been assigned to me. I don't think I'd ever had a single bodyguard in my entire life. Now I had nine, including the chief of security for the royal palace. Why? What did they know that I didn't?

I assumed we were going to the motorcade to link up with the president for the ride to the palace. But when we passed the long line of presidential limousines, Chevy Suburbans, military vehicles, and police cars, I was a little concerned.

"Why aren't we stopping?" I asked a bit more forcefully than I had intended. "His Majesty promised I would be traveling with the president."

"And you will be, Mr. Collins," Sa'id replied. "Please be patient."

No sooner had we passed the idling motorcade than we drove through a hangar and came out onto a secure tarmac that could not be seen by the general public. Waiting there were three of the famous green-and-white VH-3D Sea King helicopters. One of them would serve as Marine One and carry the president. The others would serve as decoys to confuse any enemy that might be lying in wait to shoot the president down.

"You're not using the motorcade," I said, more an observation than a question.

"No," Sa'id replied. "The president is going by air. You'll be in the seat right beside him."

★   ★   ★

Ten minutes later, the president greeted me, but he did not look happy.

"You've really made a mess of things, Collins," he shouted over the roar of the chopper as he saluted a Marine guard and boarded the aircraft.

"I'm afraid I don't see it that way, Mr. President," I shouted back, climbing in behind him.

The White House chief of staff and national security advisor boarded after us, along with Ali Sa'id and two Secret Service agents. I took my assigned seat beside the commander in chief and buckled up. I guessed the rest of Sa'id's men would meet us at the palace. Two minutes later we were airborne.

It was the first time I had ever been on Marine One, and it was hard not to be impressed by the sleek design, classy interior, and high-tech wizardry. It was also one of the quietest helicopters I had ever been on, so while we couldn't exactly talk in a whisper, we weren't shouting at one another either.

"Your articles have rattled the Israelis," the president told me, his body language and tone suggesting any delay in the peace process would be my fault. "They've been raising concerns and asking for changes on the documentation all night."

I refused to take the bait. "What are their specific concerns?"

"You'll have to get that from Daniel, not from
me," the president said. "The details aren't important. What matters is that the Israelis were locked
and loaded, and then your interview with Khalif
comes out and then one story after another about
chemical weapons and . . ."

"And what?"

"And you've got them spooked."

I had to smile. "Because of *my* stories?"

"You think this is funny?" the president asked,
quickly becoming agitated.

"No, of course not," I replied. "I just think
it's a bit—I don't know . . . ridiculous to say
the Israelis are getting spooked by me. I'm not
making this stuff up. ISIS is a real threat. The
Israelis have plenty of reasons to be concerned
about getting a final status agreement with the
Palestinians just right regardless of what I put
into my stories."

"Obviously," the president said. "But Daniel
Lavi called me yesterday and specifically said all
this talk about Abu Khalif was creating enormous
pushback from the members of his coalition."

"Does that really surprise you?" I asked.

"No one would be talking about Abu Khalif if
it wasn't for you, Collins," the president shot back.

Was he serious? How could he say that?

"Look, Mr. President, I'm sorry you're upset
with me. I really am. I'm not trying to rain on your
parade. But I truly believe ISIS could be planning
an attack today."

"On this event?"

"Yes, sir."

"Based on what?"

"Based on my interview with Khalif. He made it clear he wants to bring down the king, you, and Daniel Lavi and Salim Mansour as well. Suddenly you're all in one place, in a country he knows like the back of his hand. He's got chemical weapons. He's got the systems to launch them. I'm worried, and honestly, I'm surprised you're not."

"Well, I'm not. The Secret Service is well aware of your interview *and* the risks, and so am I. But there's no way I'm going to let Abu Khalif, of all people, stop a peace treaty of historic proportions."

"I understand, sir, but I have to ask you a question," I began, trying to quickly compose my thoughts. "How serious a threat do you think Abu Khalif and ISIS really pose?"

"To whom?"

"To the U.S., to Israel, to our Arab allies in the region."

"They're a threat, sure," he said.

"How serious?"

"I don't know—they're one of many."

"The main threat?"

"No."

"You don't think they'd like to take you all out today?"

"I'm sure they would. But that's not possible."

"Not possible?"

"No."

"So what would you say *is* the main threat in the Middle East, if you don't mind me asking?"

"The lack of peace between the Israelis and Palestinians, of course," he replied. "That's the holy grail, Collins. That's the missing piece. If we can get that right, everything else falls into place."

Marine One began to bank to the left, and then we were heading north. I had always wanted to see Amman from the air, but this conversation was too important to play the tourist.

"And you believe this treaty will bring lasting, comprehensive peace to the Middle East?"

"Of course," the president said. "Why do you think we've worked so hard and for so long to create a two-state solution? And not just my administration but all those who went before me."

"Are you saying you believe the region will become quiet once this treaty is signed?"

"Not immediately, but in time, yes."

"The Iranians will stop pursuing nuclear weapons?"

"Once we conclude our negotiations with them, yes, I believe they will. Why would they need nuclear weapons if the Palestinians have made peace with Israel?"

"What about their vow to 'wipe Israel off the map'?"

"That's rhetoric, not policy," the president said.

"And ISIS—do you believe they will lay down their arms and give up their goal of establishing an Islamic caliphate if the Israelis and Palestinians make peace?"

"Eventually, yes, I do."

"Isn't it possible that the peace deal you've

helped bring about today could actually trigger more war, more violence?"

"How?"

"By enraging Abu Khalif and other militants who have sworn they will stop at nothing to destroy Israel and anyone who tries to make peace with her."

"Are you saying we should stop trying to make peace because some lunatics like Abu Khalif are going to get mad? That's ridiculous."

"I'm not saying you shouldn't try to make peace," I clarified. "I'm just saying a signing ceremony isn't going to stop the jihadists from trying to kill. It is more likely to inflame them. I mean, Anwar Sadat made peace with Israel in '79, and the Radicals killed him for it."

"And King Hussein made peace with Israel in '94 and lived a long and happy life," the president responded. "Look, Collins, I want peace. The Israelis want peace. The Palestinians want peace. The Jordanians want peace. It's what we all want, and a two-state solution is what's going to make it happen. That's what everyone has been demanding for decades, and that's what I'm delivering, beginning today. You guys in the press can snipe and carp and give all kinds of reasons why it won't work and why it's not worth it. But you're wrong. Dead wrong. You're on the wrong side of history."

I couldn't believe how personally he was taking this. "Mr. President, I'm not trying to be cynical or critical. I'm just asking the questions, trying to understand your thinking about this whole process."

"Well, now you know."

"Yes, I do; thank you," I said, taking a deep breath and pulling my digital recorder out of my jacket pocket to turn it off.

"Whoa, whoa, wait a minute—this is all off the record," the president suddenly said.

"What are you talking about?" I replied, genuinely confused. "No, it isn't."

"Of course it is," he shot back.

"You never said that," I responded. "I was told I had an exclusive interview with you. I thought it was going to be in the limousine, but clearly we're doing it here instead."

"No, no, no—absolutely not. I'd be happy to do an interview with you when the ceremony is over, but this is just a friendly off-the-record discussion, nothing more."

"You can't just say that after the discussion is over, Mr. President. That's not how the game is played."

"It's not a game," he replied, incensed. "These are highly sensitive background discussions, not for public consumption."

"Well, I'm sorry, but that's not how it's done," I said, holding my ground. "I'm sorry you think I'm complicating your life. But with all due respect, sir, I'm just doing my job."

"By playing gotcha? By undermining the entire peace process in its final hours?"

"I'm not playing gotcha, and if anyone undermines this peace it will be ISIS, not me. I know these people, Mr. President. I've talked with them face-to-face. I've seen who they are. I've seen what they do. And I'm telling you, ISIS and the rest of these radical Salafist jihadists pose a clear and present danger to the national security of the United States, Israel, Jordan, and everyone who loves peace in this region. And anyone who thinks Abu Khalif is going away after this treaty gets signed ought to have his head examined. He's not going to stop. He's going to redouble his efforts until he wreaks havoc and creates mass carnage throughout this region or until he is hunted down and killed."

"This conversation is over," the president said. "And off the record. If you print it, I swear to you the *New York Times* isn't going to have access to me or my administration in any way, shape, or form ever again. You're playing a game, Collins, but you just went too far."

"I could give a flying leap whether the *Times* has access to you or not, sir. Abu Khalif is a serial killer. He's murdered my friends. He's tried to murder me. He's threatened my family. And he's coming after you and every single leader who signs this treaty. I'm not saying don't sign it. I'm saying you'd better be ready for what comes next. Maybe ISIS won't strike today or this week. Maybe you're right and all the security in place will suffice. But every day ISIS is recruiting more foreign fighters into their movement. And they're not just coming from Arab and Islamic countries. They're coming from Europe. They're coming from Asia. They're coming from America, Mr. President. Americans are signing up for jihad. They're fighting in Syria and Iraq for Abu Khalif

and Jamal Ramzy. They carry American passports. If you don't get serious about stopping
them, they're coming home to unleash jihad on
American soil. And when it happens, it won't be
the fault of the *New York Times.* I'm just the mes-
senger. The buck stops with you."

56

* * *

It was deadly quiet in the chopper for the next five minutes.

Then Marine One touched down inside the royal compound. As soon as the engines shut down and the rotors came to a stop, the side door opened and the president was immediately greeted by the king and the crown prince. The three of them chatted for a few minutes, out of my earshot, and then headed inside the palace.

I was now persona non grata, at least as far as the president was concerned.

When it was all clear, Sa'id exited the chopper and I followed him. He gave me a special pin to wear on my lapel and a lanyard attached to a laminated press pass with my photo and media credentials. He explained the combination of these two would give me nearly complete backstage access for the remainder of the day. I put them on and followed him inside.

We entered through a back portico, then turned right and walked down a long hallway to a wing on the northeast side of the building. We stepped into a large, ornate hall. It had enormous crystal chandeliers and original paintings in gold-leafed frames and a massive antique table of polished wood with matching chairs. I couldn't tell at first if it was supposed to serve as a cabinet room or a formal dining room, but it didn't really matter at the moment, for there was no food set out and no drinks were available. Rather, I saw President Mansour chatting with Prime Minister Lavi. I didn't see Prince Marwan, but I did see my old friend Youssef Kuttab talking with some of Lavi's men. I nodded to him, and he nodded back. But I decided now might not be the best time to approach him. He was deep in conversation, and at the moment I wasn't quite sure what was wanted or expected of me, especially after the dustup I'd just had with President Taylor.

To be candid, though, I was excited about the exclusive he had given me. Despite his protestations, his remarks had been on the record, and they provided a fascinating picture into the thinking of a president with whom the American people already had serious and growing concerns. Taylor's approval ratings were dropping steadily. They were lower than those of Presidents Bush and Obama, and it wasn't due solely to the weak economy. Americans were souring on his handling of foreign policy. The latest CBS News/*New York Times* poll found that most people saw the president as "disengaged" and "aloof" on national security matters. They specifically believed he was "on the wrong track" when it came to handling the Middle East, particularly vis-à-vis the dual crises in Syria and Iraq. Those numbers could change quickly, of course, if the new peace treaty was popular. But the rapid ISIS takeover of large sections of Iraq—and now the clear and convincing proof that this al Qaeda breakaway faction actually had acquired, on the president's watch, the very weapons of mass destruction the country had gone into two wars to keep al Qaeda and Saddam Hussein from having—were weighing heavily on the public's mind.

I looked carefully to see if there were any visible signs of discord or disunity between Lavi and Mansour. From my angle, I couldn't see any. They actually seemed quite jovial and relaxed. Whatever concerns had been voiced earlier in the day—assuming the president wasn't spinning me—had apparently been worked out. From all evidence, the ceremony was on.

Ali Sa'id came over and whispered in my ear. "Mr. Collins, we're about to begin. His Majesty would like to get you in place."

"Thanks, Ali," I said. "By the way, where are the king's younger children? I don't see them anywhere."

"The queen sent them to spend a few days with their cousins," Sa'id replied.

That made sense, I guessed, given all that was happening, though I would have liked to meet them. At some point it might make sense to do a story on the entire royal family and how unique they were in the region for being so committed to peace.

For now, I followed Sa'id out a back exit. As chief of security for the Royal Court, he was certainly a senior official in the General Intelligence Directorate in addition to being very close to the king and the royal family. Yet he had been assigned to take care of me in every way, and I was touched by His Majesty's kindness. This was not standard operating procedure. This was special. I couldn't let it skew my coverage, I knew. That had to be straightforward and as objective as humanly possible. But given that the king and I had never met until the previous day, I was certainly grateful on a personal level. I was still anxious something terrible was coming. But honestly I didn't see how. And I did feel safer with Sa'id at my side.

We walked down a series of hallways, and Sa'id was clearly in his element. This was a palace he knew and loved dearly. He gave me a little history lesson along the way, making comments about various paintings and artifacts as well as about some of the interesting leaders he had met over the years.

He also briefed me on various security protocols that were in place, including escape routes if there was a fire or some other incident. He made very clear from the beginning that this information was not for publication, a lesson I thought he might want to share with the president of the United States. Sa'id wasn't giving me any classified or proprietary information. He was just making sure I knew what to do in case of emergency, and he stressed that no matter what, I should stick close to him.

In his own way, he also seemed to be expressing a sense of deep professional pride. I realized that in many ways this palace was as much his home as it was the king's. Sa'id cared deeply about making sure everyone here was secure and cared for. He shared His Majesty's tradition of warm Arab hospitality, and everything he said and did showed it.

It was a much longer walk from that formal dining room to the main entrance of the palace than I had expected. But finally we arrived, and I could hear another military band playing. Then we stepped through a side door into the courtyard where I had been dropped off the day before.

The Mercedes was gone, and so were the large moving trucks and all the workers. I saw the crowd and the cameras and the television lights. I saw the stage and the red carpets and all the Jordanian, Palestinian, Israeli, and American flags, snapping in the crisp breeze. I saw the bleachers filled with five hundred or more smiling, excited, fascinated high school students—Arabs and Israelis, Muslims, Christians, and Jews—and for the first time, I have to say, I was moved by it all.

I can't explain it really, but all my hardbitten professional cynicism began to melt away for a few moments. This was really happening. This was no longer talk. This was no longer a "backgrounder briefing" about how the parties were going to talk about the ground rules for the discussions about the negotiations. This was the real thing. The Israelis and Palestinians were really going to sign a final, comprehensive peace treaty.

And people were excited. Not just the students but the palace staff and hundreds of other government workers who apparently had been invited to see it all unfold.

I had no idea exactly how it was all going to play out. Nor did anyone else. But this was history in the making, and I was here at the center of it all, and I couldn't really believe it. I can't say I felt pride at that moment. To the contrary, I felt humbled. My grandfather would have loved this, and he would have done an amazing job covering it all. But I was just a kid from Bar Harbor, Maine. Who was I to be a witness to a moment in history as profound as the birth of the Palestinian State? Who was I to become a friend and confidant to presidents and prime ministers, much less a king? I was nobody. But at that moment I felt like God was looking down at me with pleasure. I didn't deserve it. I still wasn't even sure I really believed it. But God did seem to have saved my life countless times and was now opening these doors and seemed to be putting me exactly where he wanted me. And I have to say I felt grateful. I couldn't escape the feeling this was a special moment. I only wished Omar and Abdel could have been here to see it too.

Sa'id walked me to my seat at the end of a riser situated immediately behind the main stage, the signing table, and the speaker's podium, then took a seat directly behind me.

It was an excellent spot. From this vantage

point, while I wouldn't be able to see the faces of the various leaders as they addressed the crowd and the cameras, I still had a commanding view of the environment. I could see what the king would be seeing and how the crowd reacted. It was certainly a much better position than any of my colleagues in the media enjoyed. Plus, seated near me in this VIP section were a number of Jordanian ministers, members of Parliament, judges, and generals, along with their many aides. In part, I'm sure, this was simply because there was no other place to put these dignitaries. The courtyard wasn't small, but there were limitations. I suspected, however, that the royals' media advisors wanted to project TV images around the world of Jordan's government fully behind this treaty, literally as well as figuratively.

The one person I didn't see was Prince Marwan. I wanted to congratulate him on all his hard work. He had a great deal to be proud of, and I wanted to get his thoughts for my next story.

Scanning the crowd, I found the media pool in the back of the large courtyard. They were at least half a football field away, and there were a lot of them, but I was fairly sure I could pick out Alex Brunnell, our Jerusalem bureau chief, standing with the *Times* White House correspondent and chief diplomatic correspondent. At Allen's direction, the Gray Lady was covering this event from all angles, and rightly so.

I realized at that moment that I had absolutely no idea what else was happening on the planet. Surely there were floods and droughts, elections and resignations, weddings and babies being born, and every manner of news being made—"all the news that's fit to print, and quite a bit that isn't," as my colleagues and I liked to joke—but I'd had neither the time nor the capacity to pay attention to any of it. Since entering Homs, I hadn't been able to think about anything but the ISIS threat. But now, finally, I breathed a sigh of relief.

I pulled out my grandfather's pocket watch. It was two minutes before two o'clock. Almost showtime. And then Yael Katzir sidled up beside me.

"Is that seat taken?" she asked, pointing to the empty chair to my left.

"As a matter of fact it isn't," I replied, standing and pretending to doff my cap. "Would you care to join me, young lady?"

"I would be honored, kind sir. Thank you."

We sat down and she scanned the crowd.

"Impressive," she said.

"It is."

"Maybe we're overreacting a little," she added.

"Maybe," I said. "I was half-expecting to see you next in a chem-bio suit."

"It's in the trunk." She smiled, but I couldn't quite tell if she was kidding.

I looked up at the F-16s flying their missions, though they were way out in the distance, not close enough for the roar of their jet engines to disrupt the moment. I looked at the soldiers and Secret Service agents on the roof and tried to pick out the plainclothes agents intermingled in the crowds. Generally, it wasn't hard. Everyone else was smiling. The security guys were not. Plus they had those little squiggly earpieces, of course, a dead giveaway. Still, I was very glad they were there.

Five minutes passed, then ten, but there was still no sign yet of the principals or the prince. Aides continued scurrying around on the platform, making last-minute tweaks. They were setting out fountain pens, pouring glasses of water, checking the microphones, and resetting audio levels. A newcomer to state events would naturally assume all these things would have been taken care of already, but I knew from years of covering such functions how many details there were to be handled, and how rarely such events began on time.

Still, the schoolkids were clearly becoming a bit restless. They had already been sitting there for the better part of an hour, and their chairs couldn't be the most comfortable in the world.

At least it was December, so the sun wasn't blazing down on us all. Rather, there was a blanket of dark-gray clouds overhead and a slight breeze that made it chillier than some might have wanted but also made the flags flutter perfectly for the cameras.

"Everything okay?" I said to Sa'id.

"Of course," he said. "But you know how these things go. I'm sure they'll be out soon."

"Where is Prince Marwan?" I asked. "And where will he be sitting?"

"I don't know where he is—that's a good question," Sa'id replied. "He should be here by now. He must be conferring with His Majesty. He'll be sitting directly behind the king. Should I radio my men to find him?"

"No, no, they've got enough to do. I'm sure he'll be here soon."

I turned to Yael. "So I guess we have a little time to kill," I said, trying to come up with some small talk that didn't sound completely ridiculous.

"We try not to say 'kill' in this part of the world," she replied. "But yes, I guess we do. Got something on your mind?"

I certainly did. I wanted to ask her out, but I was hesitant to go too quickly. "Well, I'm realizing I hardly know you."

"That's true."

"Where were you born?"

"Up in the Galilee."

"Where?"

"It's a little town called Rosh Pinna. It's up in the hills. It's adorable. You should come sometime."

"Sounds fun. Do you still have family there?"

"My parents are there. They run a restaurant—amazing—best food in Israel. And a stunning view, especially at night."

"Even better. Do you have siblings?"

"I had an older brother."

"Had?"

"He was in a special forces unit. Killed in Lebanon in '06."

"I'm sorry."

"Yeah, well, what can you do?"

We were quiet for a moment, and then she asked, "How about you?"

"What about me?"

"All I know about you is what Ari told me."

"Well, you already know about my parents," I said. "My mom is in Bar Harbor, where I grew up. My dad is gone. But I didn't know him much anyway. He left the family when I was a kid."

"I'm sorry."

"Yeah, well, what can you do?"

"Have you had any contact with your brother since Istanbul? He's here in Amman, isn't he?"

"He was, but he left with his family when Abu Khalif threatened to use them against me."

"So you talked with him?"

"Yeah, we actually had a nice visit. It had been a while."

"And Laura?"

"Oh, well, let's not go there."

"No longer the marrying type?"

"Couldn't we talk about something else?"

"Like what, sarin gas?"

"That would be less painful."

"Ouch."

"Exactly."

She paused for a moment, then asked, "Did she leave you?"

"No, but she cheated on me. A lot. So I left her."

"I'm sorry."

It was quiet again for a bit, and then Yael said, "Let's pick something happier to talk about."

"That would be good. Thanks."

Just then the spokesman for the Royal Court went up to the main podium, tapped on the windscreens for the two microphones. The band stopped playing. Cameras started clicking, and the aide cleared his throat.

"This is the two-minute warning," he said. "I repeat, the ceremony will begin in two minutes."

A newfound surge of electricity rippled through the crowd, myself included.

It was time to get this thing done.

57

★　★　★

I checked my pocket watch—it was 2:28 p.m.

I pulled my digital recorder out of my pocket, double-checked the batteries, put it back, and then grabbed my notepad and scribbled down a few observations and a few questions I wanted to ask President Mansour and Prince Marwan after the ceremony.

Again I scanned the crowd. People were actually leaning forward now in anticipation. I noticed a side door open off to my right—the same door Sa'id and I had come through earlier—and a half-dozen agents from the Shin Bet, the Israeli secret service, and another half-dozen agents from President Taylor's protective detail entered the courtyard and took up their positions. I saw one of the agents say something into his wrist-mounted radio and watched to see other agents react. One by one, they seemed to stand up a bit straighter. They were on their toes, ready to prevent anything from going wrong. But what really could?

The king was right. This was essentially a hermetically sealed environment. If there was going to be an attack, it might happen in Baghdad, but it wasn't going to be here. Every person in the courtyard had already been carefully, meticulously screened. The only people who had weapons were Sa'id's team, responsible for the security of the palace and its grounds, and the most trusted agents protecting each of the leaders. What's more, the Jordanian army and police forces were on full alert. Several thousand troops were patrolling the streets of Amman. Security checkpoints were everywhere. The police were stopping cars and trucks and vehicles of all sorts, checking IDs, asking questions, on the lookout for anything suspicious. I told myself to take deep, long breaths and relax.

The words of FDR echoed through my brain: *"The only thing we have to fear is fear itself."*

"Yael," I said after a moment.

"Yes?"

"If you're free this evening, would you like to have dinner with me? You could ask me more painful questions and I could spend the evening dodging them and trying not to look pathetic."

"That's quite an offer."

"I thought so."

She looked at me and smiled. "Sure. That would be nice."

"Eight o'clock?"

"Better make it nine," she said. "The PM has an early state dinner with the other principals and then flies out around eight. I should be clear by nine."

"Then it's a date?"

"It is. Thank you, Mr. Collins."

"My pleasure, Miss Katzir."

I started breathing again. But my heart was racing.

It was ridiculous. I think I was actually blushing. The back of my neck felt hot.

I looked away. It was showtime. I needed to focus. But for the first time in a long time, I actually felt happy. It was a strange sensation, almost surreal, in fact, but nice. I needed a little happiness in my life just now.

I looked up into the cloudy gray sky. A flock of birds flew past and the breeze picked up. It occurred to me that I hadn't been given any prepared remarks for any of the leaders, typically standard operating procedure for an event like this, and I suspected this could be accounting for the delay. They were all probably making last-minute tweaks to their remarks. Then again, I would hear them soon enough. Did I really need a sneak preview?

At that moment, however, two Jordanian F-16s caught my eye. They were flying their combat air patrol, keeping any stray aircraft—Jordanian or otherwise—out of this corridor, which was now restricted airspace. Both were quite a ways off in the distance, but what seemed odd was that while they had been flying from left to right across the horizon, heading from south to north, one of them was now turning right and banking toward the palace. Was that normal? It didn't seem so. Several pairs of fighter jets had been crisscrossing the distant skies for the last half hour or so in the same predictable manner. So why the deviation?

I leaned over to Yael. "What do you make of that, twelve o'clock high?" I whispered, discreetly nodding toward the western sky.

She looked up. "I don't know," she replied. "Ask Ali."

The jet was still several miles away, but there was no question it was headed in our direction. The question was why. I turned and whispered to Sa'id.

"What's going on with that F-16?" I asked. "He's broken off from his wingman."

Sa'id had clearly been scanning the crowd, not the skies, because he didn't immediately respond. But a moment later, he said something in Arabic over his wrist-mounted radio.

"Stay calm, but come with me, both of you," he whispered back a few seconds later.

Startled, I had a hard time taking my eyes off the plane, but when I saw him discreetly get up and walk back toward the doorway from which we had come, I followed his lead.

Yael was right behind me. The band was playing again. Just then, I got a text from Allen back in D.C. **This is exciting.**

He didn't know the half of it.

"Where are we going?" I asked Sa'id.

"The command center."

"What do you think's going on?"

"I'm not sure," he conceded. "But I'm not bringing His Majesty out here until I know."

As he said this, I turned and took one last look at the F-16 before going inside. And at that very moment I saw a flash of light and a contrail.

"He just fired a missile!" Yael said, now motionless.

"Code red! Code red! Everybody down!" Sa'id yelled at the top of his lungs to his fellow agents and the rest of the crowd.

But he didn't dive to the floor or take cover in the courtyard. Instead, he grabbed Yael and me and shoved us through the door. *"To the stairwell—move!"* he said. *"Quickly!"*

He started running and so did I.

As we came around a corner, we nearly ran into the king and the other world leaders who were coming down the hall toward us.

"Through this door, Your Majesty!" Sa'id yelled, pushing open an emergency door and nearly throwing King Abdullah and the others through it. *"Run, Your Majesty! To the safe room! Go, go, go! There's no time to waste!"*

The king's instincts were exceptional. His special forces training kicked in instantly. He grabbed Presidents Taylor and Mansour, the closest men to him, and began pulling them down the cement stairwell toward the basement. The rest of us followed hard on their heels, including Prime Minister Lavi and all the various security agents. A moment later we felt the explosion and then heard its roar.

The force of the blast knocked everyone off their feet. Some went tumbling down the metal stairs. Yael and I were thrown against a concrete wall.

The king was the first back on his feet, and he started shouting commands. *"We can't stay here! Follow me!"*

The security details found their principals and got them moving. In the confusion, Yael and I were shoved to the back. But soon we were racing down two more flights of stairs, trying not to be left behind.

Then a second explosion hit, again knocking us off our feet.

Jordanian soldiers in full combat gear now burst into the stairwell. They grabbed the king and took off. The rest of us scrambled to our feet and hustled to keep up. We raced down one hallway, then another. We were now apparently heading toward a bunker of some kind, something akin to the Presidential Emergency Operations Center located deep underneath the White House.

We passed what appeared to be a command center, not unlike the one I'd seen in Abu Ghraib, though far more modern and sophisticated. Sa'id stopped me there and pulled me inside.

The king and the others didn't stop. They kept moving and passed into what looked from my angle like an enormous bank vault. The moment they were inside, a massive, three-foot-thick steel door was quickly shut and sealed behind them as Jordanian soldiers brandishing automatic weapons rushed to take up positions in front of the door.

Yael, trailing the leaders and agents, tried to join them, but she was too late. The soldiers wouldn't let her in. She protested that she was part of Lavi's team, but they wouldn't budge. The door was locked.

At least the king and the others were safe. That was all that mattered for the moment.

"Where is that?" I shouted. "Where did they just go?"

Sa'id was about to explain, but the explosions just kept coming.

I looked at the bank of security monitors inside the command center, and all the blood drained from my face. I could see the flames and the smoke and the burning, screaming, dying children above us.

But as horrific as those images were, they paled in comparison to the image now on the main large flat-screen on the far wall. It was a live shot of the F-16 screaming inbound. Whoever was flying that plane was on a kamikaze mission into the palace. There was no one to stop him, and all I could think of was Abu Khalif and ISIS.

58

* * *

With Yael and Sa'id at my side, I stared at the video monitors.

Unable to move and with nowhere to go, we watched as the pilot of the second Jordanian F-16 swooped in behind his rogue wingman and began firing on it. The lead fighter jet bobbed and weaved, dived and rolled, trying to outmaneuver his colleague. But despite the aerial acrobatics, he was still coming in hard and fast.

Though some of the cameras were obscured by fire and billowing smoke, I could see the people who hadn't already been incinerated by the air-to-ground missiles screaming and running in all directions. Then we and the four duty officers in the command post erupted in cheers as one of the second F-16's Sidewinder missiles actually clipped the right wing of the inbound fighter jet.

But it was too little, too late. At the last moment, I instinctively turned away and covered my head as the flaming jet crashed headlong into the Al-Hummar complex, but that didn't stop me from being thrown off my feet by the tremendous force of the blast several stories overhead. The whole complex shuddered and groaned. And I smelled it. The thick, acrid smoke was seeping even into the climate-controlled environment below the palace. Yael and several of the men began choking.

Sa'id took control and threw several switches, presumably activating an air-purification system because some machinery rumbled to life and began to exchange the air quite rapidly.

The video monitors flickered and then went dark. A moment later, all the lights on our level flickered as well, and before we knew it, all power was lost and we were standing in the bunker in complete darkness.

Then came a series of deafening booms, one after another, as the rest of the jet's munitions cooked and exploded in the raging fires above. Framed pictures of the king and crown prince fell to the floor and smashed into pieces.

Down the hall, a pipe burst. I heard water gushing out.

When the explosions ended, we still heard people screaming and dying up above us, their chilling shrieks making their way through the heating and air-conditioning ducts.

Soon we heard emergency generators roaring to life, and low-level emergency lighting kicked in. Some of the video monitors flicked back on as well. Not all of them did, but there were enough to give us a terrifying glimpse of what was happening above us.

I turned to check on Yael. She had a large gash on her forehead and was bleeding profusely.

I called for a first aid kit, and one of the watch commanders rushed to my side with one. As I bandaged her up, though, Yael gasped. At first I thought I had hurt her somehow. But when I saw her eyes grow wide, I turned to see what she was looking at.

In a scene eerily similar to what I had witnessed at Abu Ghraib, I could now see dump trucks and cement trucks loaded with explosives making speed dashes for the outer gates of the royal compound. I watched as soldiers fired automatic weapons at them, but one by one the trucks were hitting their targets and erupting in massive explosions.

Huge gaps appeared in the perimeter fences, and hundreds of fighters in black hoods and ski masks rushed through to engage in brutal gun battles with Jordanian soldiers fighting desperately to save themselves and their beloved king.

"Ali, we can't stay here," I said, turning to Sa'id. "We need to get these men out of here while we still can."

"No, we are safe here," one of the duty officers replied. "We must wait until reinforcements arrive."

"It could be too late by then," I argued. "Look, the rebels are pouring in from the north and the east. But there—screen eight—there are three armor-plated Suburbans parked in the south parking lot. That's just a few hundred yards away. If we can get to them, we can get these men out of this kill zone."

"These men?" the officer asked, incredulous. "You mean His Majesty?"

"And the presidents and the prime minister— all of them."

"No, we have a protocol; we stay here until the army arrives," he insisted.

"You have a protocol for *this*?" I asked, now incredulous myself. "For a catastrophic attack on the palace with the leader of the free world trapped amid an onslaught of ISIS jihadists?"

"I have my orders," the officer shot back. "We wait for the army."

"The army is here, and the ISIS forces are still getting through. We have a chance to get the principals out, but only if we move now. If we wait here, we all die."

Just then we were all startled by the vault door opening behind us. Suddenly King Abdullah was coming out of the safe room and directly toward us.

"Ali, we need to go now," he ordered. "How many men do you have?"

Sa'id stood there for a moment, dumbfounded. Not only was the king standing before him, but Queen Rania, the crown prince, the three other heads of state, and their bodyguards were all waiting in the hallway.

"How many?" the king pressed, white-hot with urgency.

"At the moment, Your Majesty, there are just four duty officers besides me, plus Mr. Collins and Miss Katzir."

"Who is she?"

"She's with me," Prime Minister Lavi said, stepping forward. "Mossad."

"Very well," the king said. "Do you all have weapons training?"

"Yes, Your Majesty," most of them said.

"Good," he said, stripping off his jacket and tie. Then he addressed the duty officer who had been arguing with me. "Get weapons, flak jackets, and helmets for everyone out of the vault. Move, go!"

The man did as he was ordered, and Sa'id and the other officers went with him.

The king turned to me. "Have you ever used a gun, Mr. Collins?"

"Uh, sure. I grew up in Maine, Your Majesty."

"Do a lot of hunting and fishing?"

"Yes, sir."

"Ever use an MP5?" he asked.

"Can't say I have, sir."

"Piece of cake," he said as Sa'id and his colleagues rushed back with weapons and protective gear for everyone.

To my astonishment, the king of Jordan gave me a crash course on how to use a submachine gun. Then he strapped on a bulletproof vest and an ammo belt as everyone else, including the Secret Service and Shin Bet agents and of course the agents of the Royal Court who were directly assigned to protect the king, did the same.

Scanning the video monitors, the king quickly assessed the situation and came to the same conclusion I just had. "We're going to head for those three Suburbans," he said. "Are the keys inside?" he asked.

"No, sir," the head of President Taylor's detail said.

"Where are they?"

"The doors should be unlocked, but the keys will be in the pockets of those dead agents lying on the pavement."

"What's the chance they're using chemical weapons out there?" President Mansour asked. I had been thinking the same thing.

"Don't worry; they're not," the king said.

"How do you know?" President Taylor asked.

"Look at the video monitors," the king replied. "The rebels don't have gas masks on. They're not wearing protective suits. We should be fine."

"With all due respect, Your Majesty," Yael interjected, "the rebels who have penetrated the palace compound may not be planning a chemical attack, but their commanders still might be."

"Miss Katzir is right, Your Majesty," Sa'id confirmed. "We have backpacks in the vault with chem-bio suits, gas masks, gloves—everything you need. I would advise that each person take one."

"Fine, go get them," the king ordered.

Once again Sa'id and his colleagues moved quickly to comply.

"Now, Your Majesty, assuming we get out of the compound alive, where do you suggest we go?" asked the Israeli prime minister, himself a former special forces commando, as he popped a fresh magazine into an MP5.

"The airport," the king said. "My brother is the head of the air force. I'll call him on a secure phone in a moment. I'll tell him to bomb the day-lights out of the palace. I'll also tell him to give us air cover and have the army prepare to meet us at the airport."

"Good," President Taylor said. "I'll order Air Force One to be ready for immediate takeoff when we arrive. I'll take you all out with me. Once we get out of Jordanian airspace and get a U.S. fighter squadron to provide security for us, you can direct a counterstrike from the communications deck."

Everyone nodded.

"Very good," the king said. "There's just one catch."

"What's that?" President Mansour asked.

"There are checkpoints everywhere. Don't stop."

"At which ones?"

"Any of them."

"Why not?" I asked.

"Because right now, Mr. Collins, we have no idea who's on our side and who isn't," the king replied. "If we stop, we die. Clear enough?"

I nodded. So did everyone else. It was ugly, but it was clear.

"Ali, I need a secure satphone," the king said.

Sa'id set down his weapons and immediately unlocked a safe in the command post. He pulled out five satphones and gave one to the king. He gave three to the other leaders and kept one for himself. "These were specially built by the Jordanian military for the Royal Court," he explained. He handed out three-by-five laminated cards with each of the satphone numbers and passcodes on one side and simple instructions in both

Arabic and English for using the phones on the other. Meanwhile, the duty officers handed out the backpacks filled with chem-bio equipment, and we suited up.

"Okay," the king said at last, switching off the safety on his weapon. "Follow me."

59

* * *

That's when we heard the muffled sounds of automatic gunfire above us.

"They're inside the palace," the king said. "We need to go now."

The king's bodyguards absolutely refused to let him take the lead. They didn't care how long he had served in the army. Nor did they care that he was a direct descendant of Muhammad. Not right now. They had taken an oath to lay down their lives to protect the monarch and keep him alive at all costs, and that's what they intended to do. Thus, four of the king's six protectors moved ahead of him to the front of the pack, while two others covered his back. The rest of the assembled agents and duty officers formed a protective ring around President Taylor and President Mansour and Prime Minister Lavi, as well as the queen and the crown prince. Yael and I brought up the rear, with Sa'id in the very back.

The lead agents decided not to take either of the stairwells back up to the top, assessing them as too risky. Instead, they unlocked an emergency escape hatch on the far side of the bunker and ordered us all to climb up what looked like the inside of a missile silo to the main level. The king went after the lead agents and the rest of us followed quickly behind.

"Where does this lead?" I whispered to Sa'id while I waited anxiously for my turn.

"It opens in a service garage on the south side of the compound," he whispered back. "It won't get us any closer to the Suburbans, but there are only a few people beyond those gathered with us who even know this route exists."

The climb up the metal ladder drilled into the side of the concrete silo, three stories high, was all the more difficult with the bulky and heavy backpacks we were carrying. As we worked our way upward, the sound of the gun battle above us reached a fevered pitch. What worried me, aside from whether Queen Rania had the arm strength to make the climb, was how vulnerable we now were. If an enemy was waiting for us at the top, we'd all be dead before any of us could turn around and get back into the bunker. And what if ISIS rebels got into the bunker behind us?

But that wasn't the only problem. The closer we got to the top, the more intensely hot it became. Within minutes I completed the climb and found out why. The burning remains of the F-16 and the resulting explosions from its suicide mission had created a scorching inferno. The service garage that was supposed to shield us and give us some initial cover was gone. Obliterated. Wiped out in the crash.

The scene at the top of the silo was surreal. I had never witnessed anything like it. It was an image of the apocalypse. Fire was everywhere. Whatever structures had not yet been destroyed were completely ablaze. The flames soared twenty, thirty, forty feet or more into the air. I was immediately drenched in sweat. I could feel the searing heat cooking my skin.

From my right, I suddenly heard screaming. When I turned, I saw one of the king's bodyguards engulfed in fire. And then I heard a burst of automatic-weapons fire and saw three agents fall to the ground.

"Hit the deck!" the king yelled in English.

We all instantly dropped to our stomachs. Yael and a Secret Service agent to my left were the first to return fire. Soon everyone around me with a weapon was firing. Through the leaping flames and the thick, black, nearly blinding smoke, I could make out hazy figures moving here and there. They were wearing black ski masks. They were ISIS, and they couldn't be more than fifty yards away. I aimed my MP5, flicked off the safety, and fired two bursts, then two more.

The masked men ran off, and I heard a Shin Bet agent yell, *"Clear! We're clear on this side! Let's go! Let's go!"*

Turning toward him, I realized four of the agents near me were KIA—two Americans, a Jordanian, and an Israeli. The protective team around the principals was dwindling fast. We were outmanned, outgunned, and running out of time. Our only hope was making it to those armor-plated SUVs before the enemy did or before they captured us and cut off our heads.

I was about to jump up to join them when I saw the flaming wreckage of Marine One at two o'clock. It looked like it had taken a direct hit from an antitank missile. There was almost nothing left.

Then I saw someone creeping behind the burning Sea King. I fired two bursts and was about to fire again, but then Yael was on her feet. She dropped her backpack and ran toward the flames, firing as she went. *What was she doing? Was she mad?* She had no idea who was back there or how many more were hidden by the smoke.

As she disappeared from view, I heard an enormous firefight erupt behind the chopper. She was in trouble. I looked behind me. The principals and their details were racing for the SUVs. Sa'id was with them, flanking the royal family and yelling for me to join them. I looked back toward the chopper as the gunfire intensified. But there was no question—I had to go find Yael. I couldn't just leave her to fight alone.

Scrambling to my feet, I shrugged off my own backpack and ran headlong into the flames and around the front side of the Sea King. For the moment, I held my fire. I couldn't see an enemy, and I'd never forgive myself if I killed or wounded Yael. Amid the billows of smoke, my eyes were watering. I could barely breathe. I was starting to choke. But as I came all the way around to the other side of the inferno, I stopped dead in my tracks.

Yael was not more than thirty or forty feet

ahead of me. But she was no longer armed. She had her hands up over her head and was surrounded by three hooded men. Each was pointing a Kalashnikov at her. Why they hadn't killed her yet I had no idea. But they were screaming something at her in Arabic. She began lowering herself to the ground. Soon she was on her knees, her back to me. The men were still screaming something, but she didn't seem to be responding.

I quickly checked behind me and to both of my flanks. I hadn't been spotted yet. And most of the action was well behind me, likely converging against the principals. But I had no idea what to do next. It was clear Yael's only hope was for me to kill these three—and fast—before more terrorists arrived. But I wasn't a trained soldier. I wasn't a sniper or a sharpshooter. The chance of my hitting any of them, much less killing all three of them, without killing her too seemed minuscule at best.

I just stood there frozen. Then one of the terrorists put the barrel of his machine gun on the back of her neck. He barked something at her. She didn't respond at first, so another one drove his boot into her stomach. She cried out and doubled over in pain but he forced her back up to her knees. She tried to raise her hands over her head again but was clearly having a hard time doing it. I could see now that she was bleeding from her left shoulder. And then one of them ripped her shirt halfway off.

Something in me snapped. I yelled at the top of my lungs and charged them as fast as I could run. I started firing—short bursts, one after another.

I might very well kill her, I knew, but it was a chance I had to take. There was no other choice. If I did nothing, she'd be dead for certain. Raped first, probably, and then beheaded. Or crucified. Possibly dismembered. But she wasn't getting out alive unless I did something fast.

Two of the terrorists heard me coming and began to turn, aiming their weapons at me. I pulled the trigger. One of them took a full burst of machine-gun fire to the face and went sprawling. The other took three shots to the chest and collapsed to the ground as well. Yael hit the deck, flattening herself against the ground, facedown. As she did, I was afraid the third terrorist would pull the trigger and finish her off. Instead, when he saw his friends go down, he pivoted toward me. I was coming at him full bore. He was about to open fire. I unleashed all the ammo I had left. His gun did fire but the shots went wild, and he went crashing to the pavement as one of my bullets struck home. The next instant I reached the four of them. Throwing down my MP5, I grabbed the third terrorist's Kalashnikov and unloaded a full burst into his chest.

That's when I heard Yael scream, *"James, look out!"*

I turned but it was too late. Another terrorist was coming around the corner. He had a pistol, not a machine gun, but he got off at least three rounds before I could return fire. One hit me in the left arm, just above the elbow. I spun around and dropped to the ground. The guy kept coming at me and firing, but as he closed the distance, Yael sprang to her feet and tackled him in midstride. They struggled furiously. Yael took two hard punches to the face and then the guy was on top of her. I watched in helpless amazement as she drove her right knee into his groin. I'd never seen a man double over like he did. She added a sharp crack to his neck, then pushed him off her and dove for his pistol. A split second later, she wheeled around and double-tapped him to the chest. He collapsed.

Adrenaline surging, I grabbed my MP5, ejected the spent magazine, reloaded, and scrambled to my feet.

"Come on," I yelled. *"They're leaving without us."*

60

★ ★ ★

Yael began running flat out, and I followed.

We retraced our route around what was left of Marine One. On the way, Yael dropped two more terrorists. But to our horror, when we got past the flaming wreckage and back to the silo opening, we saw the rest of our team. They were under withering fire from our right, pinned down in a grove of trees about halfway to the Suburbans.

Yael didn't hesitate. Without making a sound, she pointed for me to head right. She would go left. I nodded and bolted to the cover of a half-destroyed cement wall on the back side of the palace remains. Drawing no fire, I inched my way forward. Ahead of me was an inferno, the burning shell of a three-story wing of the palace. There were no doors where a double set should have been. I moved closer, pointing my machine gun inside, searching desperately for any signs of movement as my skin baked and my eyes filled with smoke.

Thirty yards to my left, I could see Yael doing the same thing, moving into the other side of the building as the firefight between our team and the

ISIS rebels raged another fifty yards to her left. As best I could tell, the rebels were shooting from the cover of this section of the palace. If we could find them, perhaps we could distract them and give our guys a chance to make a break for the armored vehicles.

Yael pointed to me and then to a stairway ahead and to my right. Then she signaled that she would work her way through the ground floor. A flash of fear rippled through me. That gave me two floors to clear and very little time to do it.

Seeing no one yet, I cautiously worked my way up the stairs. I could hear machine-gun fire coming from above, but I couldn't tell from where exactly. The stairs were creaking. I was making too much noise. Anyone waiting for me would cut me down in an instant. So it hardly made sense to go slow.

Abandoning all caution, I bounded up the steps, legs aching, lungs sucking in as much air as they could. I reached the top and swept the MP5 from side to side. But no one was there. Then I heard more machine-gun fire, clearer now, coming from the third floor, almost directly above me.

This time I moved more carefully up the stairs, placing my feet on the extreme edge of each step, hoping they would creak less or not at all. Inch by inch I moved my way upward while all around I could hear nonstop gunfire and men suffering horrible, ghastly deaths. The only good thing was that all the cacophony covered up whatever sounds I was making.

As I reached the top step, the gunfire stopped. I froze in place, my heart pounding through my chest. I heard a clatter. Someone was reloading. But in which room? How many were there?

For a moment I hesitated, trying to map out my next action, when gunfire erupted on the first floor. Yael was all in now. I needed to move as well.

Sliding off my dress shoes, I crept down the smoke- and rubble-filled hallways in my socks. Then the shooting began again. It was coming from one of the last rooms at the end of the hall, the rooms overlooking the courtyard, the grove of trees, and what was left of our team. I wasn't sure if it was the room on the left or the room on the right. Maybe it was both.

Under the cover of the gunfire, I bolted forward as fast as I could and made my bet. Sliding to a halt, I pivoted and burst through the door on the left and started shooting. An instant later, two snipers had collapsed to the ground. I put another two bullets into each to be sure and then turned around.

Was that it? Was it over?

No. I heard more gunfire coming from the other side of the hall. And now I had lost the element of surprise.

Moving carefully, I made my way to the door just as it began to swing open. I aimed at the center of the doorframe and pulled the trigger. A hooded figure dropped to the floor in front of me.

I quickly reloaded and moved into the hallway. Then I burst into the room across the hall only to find that a sniper had just been shot down by someone out in the courtyard. He was rolling around in pain. I switched to single shot, fired two rounds, and it was over.

Switching back to automatic, I returned to the hallway. It looked clear. I started running, desperate to get back to our team. But then I heard Yael yell, *"James, duck!"*

Without thinking, I dove to the floor, just as Yael—crouching in the stairwell—fired a long burst down the hallway over my head. Terrified, I let go of my weapon and covered my head with my hands. Yael fired again. And then all was quiet—in this wing of the building, at least.

"You okay?" she asked, coming up quickly to check on me.

"You nearly killed me!" I said, breathing hard.

"Sorry," she said. "I wasn't aiming at you."

I got up, picked up my gun, and turned to find another ISIS rebel on the floor at the end of the hallway, bleeding out. I had no idea where he'd come from—one of the other side rooms, apparently. I was just glad it was over.

But it wasn't over. The man was lying facedown as the pool of crimson around him grew. Cautiously, my gun aimed at his head, I walked over to him. Yael warned me not to get too close, and she wasn't wrong. I could now see that he was still moving, still breathing. Yael came over and was about to finish him off, but something made me stop her. Perhaps it was his enormous size. Perhaps it was the fact that he wasn't wearing a hood like all the others. But for whatever reason, I drove my foot into his ribs and ordered him in Arabic to turn over. Maybe he couldn't. Maybe he wouldn't. But I told Yael to cover me, and I rolled him over myself.

He was a bloody mess, but there was no mistaking who it was.

This was Jamal Ramzy.

In a blinding rage, I moved in and stuck the barrel of my MP5 in his face.

"Where is Abu Khalif?" I yelled.

He was fading fast, but he could hear me.

I drove my foot down on his right knee and he shrieked in agony. In my peripheral vision, I could see Yael growing edgy, her finger itching toward her trigger.

"Where . . . is . . . Abu . . . Khalif?" I repeated.

"You'll never find him," he replied through gritted teeth.

"Did you bring the sarin?" I demanded. "Are you going to use poison gas?"

Yael was now the frantic one. "Come on. It's over. He's not going to talk. Let's go."

"He'll talk," I said and fired a single round through his left arm, just above the elbow.

Ramzy's eyes rolled back in his head. They closed, then briefly opened again and readjusted. Blood was gurgling up from his stomach and dripping down his chin. I didn't have much time.

"Who's the mole?" I shouted.

But Ramzy refused to speak.

"Who's working for you inside the palace?" I shouted again.

"Burn in hell, kafir!" he screamed as he spat blood in my face. Then he fell back, and his eyes closed for the last time.

"After you," I said as I stood.

61

* * *

I just stared at the corpse, not quite believing my eyes.

Jamal Ramzy was dead.

"We need to go," Yael said, turning and heading back up the hall.

But I wasn't through. I reached down and checked his pulse. Sure enough. Ramzy was gone. Then I checked his front pockets. I found nothing. I checked his back pockets. They were empty as well. I patted him down, top to bottom. There had to be something. A wallet. An ID. A plan of some kind. But Ramzy was clean. I pulled out my cell phone and snapped several pictures. This was a huge story, and I needed proof. And as I did, I noticed that Ramzy's enormous left hand was closed tight.

"James, come on," Yael shouted, already at the stairs. *"We've got to move."*

Instead, I set down my weapon and got onto my hands and knees. I pried open Ramzy's thick, bloody fingers, one by one. And there it was. A small cell phone. I quickly flipped it open.

There was nothing in the contacts section. But the call log showed nine calls that had been made and three that had been received. I had numbers, dates, and times.

Pay dirt, I thought.

Yael was frantic. I grabbed my gun and ran. Together, we raced down both sets of stairs and a moment later we burst out the same side door where I had entered this wing. We could see Ali Sa'id beginning to rally what was left of our group and move them from the grove of trees toward the SUVs.

"Let's go, you two! Move!" he yelled when he spotted us.

We retrieved our backpacks and raced to catch up. But suddenly there was another burst of gunfire from our right. I saw two gunmen emerging from the smoke near Marine One. I pivoted and fired three bursts on the run. One of the terrorists fell to the ground, his AK-47 skittering across the pavement.

The other kept running. He wasn't shooting at us, though. He was shooting at the royal family and screaming something in Arabic. The others ahead of me were running hard, but at the rate this guy was coming, I feared none of them would make it in time. So I dove to the ground, rolled to a stop, took a deep breath, tried to steady my aim, and fired two bursts, then three more. Yael was running, but she was firing too, and a moment later the rebel fell to the ground.

"Clear!" she yelled.

I jumped back to my feet. But then Yael yelled

that rebels were coming over the wall about thirty yards to our left. I turned and saw three. One by one, they dropped to the lawn below and started racing for us, raising their weapons and preparing to shoot.

Prime Minister Lavi reacted first. Shooting from the hip, on the run, the former Israeli special forces commando must have emptied an entire magazine. It was a sight to behold, and it worked. Each of the attackers was riddled with bullets and fell to the ground, writhing in pain. They weren't dead. But they weren't coming at us anymore, and for now, that was all that mattered.

"Come on!" the king yelled. "We have to keep moving!"

I quickly ejected a spent magazine and reloaded and kept running. I could see the crown prince helping his mother while Sa'id—and now Yael and I—came in behind them. We were all running as fast as we could, but the weight of the backpacks slowed us down. Yael and I were bleeding, too—both quite seriously—but there was no time to do anything about it.

As we approached the SUVs, however, it was a kill box. Rebels were shooting at us from all directions. One agent just ahead of me, providing cover for the queen, dropped to the ground. He'd been shot four times in the face and legs. Two more agents to my right were killed a moment later.

Terrified, yet propelled by a surge of adrenaline, I looked to my right and saw the remains of another garage. I could see one of the king's limos ablaze, but at the moment I didn't see any rebels.

I checked with Yael and Sa'id. They didn't see any either. But it didn't matter, we decided. Rebels or no rebels, we had to get to the SUVs.

Sa'id suggested I fan out to the right. He would go left. Yael would go straight. I nodded and began running. Each of us opened fire and kept shooting until we reached the first SUV. While Sa'id dug through the pockets of the dead driver and retrieved the key, I reloaded, with Yael providing covering fire. Sa'id found the key a moment later, opened the front door to use as some cover, and got the queen and the crown prince safely in the backseat.

The ISIS rebels continued firing back. Agents were dropping all around me. We weren't going to make it. Not like this. I finished reloading and saw several terrorists moving through the flames of the garage. I opened fire. A split second later, Sa'id was at my side, firing back as well. But when he asked me where the king was, I realized I had no idea. The last time I'd seen him, he was on the other side of this SUV. Was he already inside? And for that matter, where was President Taylor? Where were Lavi and Mansour?

"Ali, go find them!" I shouted.

Yael and I kept returning fire. I certainly wasn't the most accurate shot of the group, or what was left of it, but all I was trying to do was buy time until everyone could get safely into the vehicles and we could get out of there.

Suddenly I heard Ali yelling for me to get over to him right away. I fired two more bursts, emptying my magazine, reloaded, and quickly worked my way around the back of the truck while Yael covered me. I could hear bullets whizzing over my head. I could hear them smashing into the side of the armor-plated trucks. I could see round after round hitting the bulletproof windows, though fortunately they refused to shatter. But as I came around the far side of the Suburban, I froze in my tracks. Prime Minister Lavi and President Mansour were lying side by side, surrounded by several more dead agents.

The king was crouched over them. I couldn't see what he was doing. Was he trying in vain to revive them or just mourning over them? Either way, it was no use. They were gone. Nothing was going to bring them back. We had to go. We couldn't stay out in the open like this.

At that moment, I went numb. I could feel myself beginning to slip into shock, and I couldn't help it, couldn't stop it.

And then, as if through a tunnel, I thought I heard the sound of someone calling my name.

"Collins, they're alive!" the king yelled. *"They're unconscious, but they're still breathing. They both have a pulse. But we need to get them into the Suburban. Cover us!"*

I couldn't believe it. They weren't dead? They looked dead. They weren't moving. But at the very thought, I snapped to.

Sa'id opened the back of the truck and put down the rear seat to make space while Yael covered his right flank. Then Sa'id helped the king lift Prime Minister Lavi and gently set him inside the SUV.

Reengaged, I pivoted hard to my left and followed my orders. Firing short bursts in multiple directions, I had no illusions I was going to kill many rebels. But I was determined not to let them get to the king or his family or these other leaders. All I had to do was buy time. The question was whether it would possibly be enough.

As the king and Sa'id put President Mansour in the back, I continued firing. Then I heard one of the other SUVs roar to life. For a moment I stopped shooting. I looked to my right and saw two American agents peeling off without us.

"That's President Taylor!" the king yelled as he covered the limp body of the Palestinian leader with a blanket.

He was right. It was Taylor in the other truck. It had to be. The Secret Service wasn't waiting. They'd gotten their man into a bulletproof vehicle and now they were getting him to the airport.

We had to move too, and fast.

"Ali, you drive," the king ordered as he closed up the back. "Yael, you ride shotgun. I'll sit behind you and work the phones. Collins, get in the back with Lavi and Mansour and cover my family."

It was a good plan, and I was prepared to follow it. But as the king disappeared around the other side of the truck to get in behind the front passenger seat, Sa'id was shot multiple times. He cried out in pain. I turned and saw two masked rebels running at us through the smoke. I ducked, aimed, and unloaded everything I had.

Both men dropped to the ground.

"Go, Collins!" Sa'id shouted with the last breath

in him, stumbling backward. *"Don't wait. Take the king and go!"*

I hesitated. I couldn't leave Sa'id behind. He'd already saved my life countless times, starting with getting me out of the courtyard before the missiles hit and the F-16's kamikaze attack. But he wasn't long for this world—he knew it, and he was right. I had to go. I had to save the king's life.

Sa'id fell. I went to my knees to reload. When I was done, I checked his pulse, but Sa'id was gone.

Yael was now climbing into the passenger seat. She was yelling at me to hurry. As quickly as I could, I pushed Sa'id's body out of the way of the truck. I grabbed the keys and satphone from his hands, and his MP5 as well. It felt cruel. It felt callous. But I had no choice and no time.

I opened the truck door, but before I could jump into the driver's seat, I lurched forward. I'd been hit—not once but multiple times. I couldn't believe it. I'd felt the impacts, but I wasn't in pain. Not yet. But that had to be the adrenaline. I'd feel it soon, and then what? Was this it? Was I dying?

"Get in, get in!" the king yelled.

Dazed and confused, it took me a moment to get my bearings. I thought briefly of just slumping back to the ground. I didn't want to hold the king and his family back. He could drive this thing better than I could. But Yael was screaming at me to stay focused and get in. And somehow—I'm really not sure how—I managed to climb into the driver's seat and pull the door shut behind me.

The king then hit a button and locked all the doors.

"Where is Ali?" he asked.

"I'm afraid he didn't make it, Your Majesty," I said.

The king just looked at me for a moment, a thousand emotions in his eyes.

"You've been hit too?" he asked.

"I think so," I said.

But as Yael helped me remove my backpack, handing it to the king to get it out of my way, she noticed something. "Look," she said.

I looked where she was pointing and saw that five rounds had hit the pack, but none of them had penetrated. Yael told me to turn so she could check my back. She looked me over quickly, as did the king, but they found nothing.

"You're okay," she said.

"It's a miracle," the queen said.

I couldn't believe it. "Really? You're sure?"

"I'm sure, Collins," the king said. "But you need to floor it, or none of us is going to make it out of here alive."

62

⋆ ⋆ ⋆

I turned the ignition.

The engine sputtered but wouldn't catch. I tried again, but still nothing.

"*Hurry,*" Yael cried.

"*I'm trying—it won't start,*" I said as I tried again and again.

"*Collins, let's move; they're coming,*" the king shouted.

But nothing was working.

Through the smoke I could see rebels running from all parts of the compound. They were firing everything they had at us. We could hear and feel the rounds hitting the truck. We could see the windows splintering. They had not yet shattered, but it was only a matter of time.

Over and over I turned the key but to no avail. I began to panic. Once more I could feel myself slipping into shock. My hands were shaking and my body felt numb. My throat was dry. My eyes were getting heavy and everything was blurring. I could hear the king shouting at me, but it was as if he were far away. Everything seemed to be happening in slow motion. I tried to say something. I tried to explain what was happening. But my brain couldn't quite send the proper signals to my mouth.

Then finally the engine roared to life. I didn't know why or how but I didn't care either. I hit the gas, and we were moving.

I'd never driven an armor-plated SUV. But two things became instantly apparent. First, because the engine was powerful, I had all the horsepower I needed. But second, because it was so incredibly heavy, it didn't handle like a normal truck. I flicked on the lights to find my way through all the smoke. I hit the windshield wipers to clear away at least some of the soot and ash. I was terrified of hitting someone. I knew they were enemies. I knew it was either them or us. But I still didn't want to plow anyone over.

The king was my navigator. He gave me directions, guiding me around obstacles even as he powered up the satellite phone and dialed his brother. A moment later, he was shouting in Arabic. I didn't understand more than a few words. I heard *safe* and *family* and something like *the palace is gone*. I was pretty sure I heard the names Lavi and Mansour mentioned too, but he was talking too fast for me to get much else, and I had to stay focused.

We hit a speed bump—I hoped it was a speed bump—going almost fifty miles an hour and suddenly we were airborne. I struggled to maintain control as the heavy vehicle crashed back down.

"There, through that hole!" Yael shouted.

"Where? Where?" I shouted back.

"There—on the right!" she yelled.

Finally I saw it. There was a massive breach in one of the concrete walls that surrounded the perimeter of the compound. It didn't have a road leading to it. It was in the middle of a large lawn at the bottom of an incline. But I could see the tracks of another vehicle. I had to assume President Taylor and his team had gone this way as well. The only problem was the hole was guarded by at least a dozen rebels, and they trained all their fire on us now. But there was no other way out.

I gunned the engine and made for the hole, gripping the steering wheel so tightly my fingers and knuckles were white. I forced myself not to duck, not to cover my eyes. We couldn't stop. We couldn't go back. We couldn't look for another way out. There might not be one, and we didn't have time to try. The moment the Secret Service got the president to the airport, Air Force One was going to take off, with or without us. The only chance we had was to catch up.

At the last moment, the rebels dove out of the way. *So much for being martyrs for Allah,* I thought. They'd had a chance to save their own skin, and they'd taken it.

We barreled through the hole and spilled out onto a side street. I slammed on the brakes, but not in time. We smashed into two parked cars on the other side of the street, sending all of us lurching forward. The steering wheel stopped me. But Yael slammed into the front windshield. The gash over her left eye reopened and blood poured down her face.

"I'm fine," she said quickly, seeing the distress in my eyes. "Just get us out of here."

"Which way?"

"Right," the king said. "Go right."

I jammed the truck into reverse, did an awkward K-turn, and hit the gas. We were moving again.

"Left at the light!" he ordered.

I made the turn, barely, though for a split second I thought we were going to spin out or roll over. I glanced in my rearview mirror to see if the king and his family were okay. He ordered me to keep my eyes on the road and not worry about them—they'd be fine—so that's what I did.

For the next few blocks, we barreled down empty streets, cleared by security for the peace summit. Soon, however, we reentered the crush of daily life in Amman. I was weaving through traffic at forty and sometimes fifty miles an hour. The king insisted I not stop for anything, so I blew through traffic lights praying we wouldn't be broadsided.

For a man who probably hadn't driven himself through the streets of Amman in twenty years, if ever, the king seemed to know the roads like a taxi driver. When we hit traffic, he started telling me to take this side street or that, apparently determined to keep us off the main boulevards and thorough-fares. It worked for a while, but all good things come to an end.

"Uh, Your Majesty, we've got a problem," I said, glancing in my rearview mirror.

Yael looked in her side mirror. The king and his family craned their necks to see what was happening.

We had company. A pickup truck filled with masked rebels had picked up our scent and was following us. Not just following—gaining on us. With all the bullet marks, I couldn't see out the back window too clearly, but I was pretty sure at least one of the rebels had a shoulder-mounted RPG launcher.

Yael unbuckled her seat belt, rolled down her window, took her MP5, and began firing at our pursuers, but they immediately moved to their left and out of her view.

"Climb into the backseat," the king told her. "Collins is going to let these guys catch up a bit. Then we'll lower the rear window ever so slightly, and you're going to fire everything you've got at the driver. Got it?"

"Absolutely," Yael said.

Careful not to disturb the Israeli and Palestinian leaders lying bleeding and unconscious in the back, Yael got herself into position, on her knees—her back leaning against the middle row of seats to provide a measure of stability, however small.

"Ready," she said.

I eased up on the gas. The pickup truck surged closer.

"Wait for it," the king said.

I glanced back and could see the rebels closing the gap. This had better work, I realized. And then I saw one of the jihadists raise the RPG and prepare to fire.

"Lower the window, Collins!" the king ordered. I did.

The king gave the order to fire.

Yael obeyed. She unleashed an entire magazine into the front windshield of the pickup. I tried to keep my eyes on the road ahead of us, but I couldn't help but glance back several times. I could see the driver behind us being riddled with bullets, and then the truck swerved wildly out of control until it finally careened off the road and plowed into a petrol station.

The explosion was enormous and deafening. I could feel the heat on the back of my neck. I quickly raised the rear window as the king directed me onto Route 40—the Al Kodos Highway—heading southwest out of Amman.

We were now going nearly a hundred miles an hour, and we had a new problem. The king was back on the satphone with his brother, who informed us that there was a police checkpoint at the upcoming interchange with Route 35, the Queen Alia Highway. The checkpoint itself wasn't the issue. The problem, the king said, was that it had apparently been overrun by ISIS rebels, and they were waiting for us with RPGs and .50-caliber machine guns.

"How long to the interchange?" I asked.

"At this rate, two minutes, no more," the king replied.

"What do you recommend, Your Majesty?" I asked, not sure if I should try to go any faster or slow down.

"Do you believe in prayer, Collins?" he said. "Because now would be a good time to start."

63

"I'm out of ammunition," Yael said. "Does anyone have more?"

"There's a full mag in my weapon," I replied.

"Where's that?" she asked.

"Here," the crown prince said from the backseat. He picked up my machine gun from the floor, removed the magazine, and handed it to Yael.

"We need to get off this road," the queen insisted, her voice quaking. "It's not safe."

I glanced back and saw the fear in her eyes.

"No, we have to keep going," the king replied.

"But we're out in the open," she countered. "The rebels know we're coming. We're sitting ducks. Let's just pull off. Let's hide somewhere until the army comes to get us."

The queen had a point, but it was not my place to say. I just kept driving. We needed a decision, and fast. In the distance, I could see the interchange approaching. I desperately wanted to know what the king was going to say. Would he accept his wife's counsel, or were we going to try to blow

503

through this checkpoint? That, it seemed, was a suicide mission. And I wasn't ready to die.

A second later the issue was moot. Rising over a ridge off to our right were two Apache helicopter gunships coming low and fast. Yael noticed them first and pointed them out to the rest of us. Now we were all riveted on them, and one question loomed over everything, though no one spoke it aloud: which side were they on?

They very well could be loyal to the king. His brother, after all, was the head of the air force, and we had no doubts about his loyalty. But there were no guarantees. Who were these pilots? How carefully had they been vetted? Did their families have ties to ISIS or al-Hirak? A few hours ago, such a thought would have seemed ridiculous. But that was before a Jordanian air force pilot had attacked the palace.

The checkpoint was fast approaching. So were the Apaches.

"What do you want me to do, Your Majesty?" I asked, easing imperceptibly off the gas to give us a bit more time.

"There's one more exit before the checkpoint," Yael said, her window down, her weapon at the ready. "Let's take it. The queen is right, sir. We need to get off this road before it's too late."

"No," the king said. "Keep moving."

"But, Your Majesty—"

"Salim and Daniel need a hospital," he insisted. "They need massive blood transfusions. We can't stop to save ourselves. We need to think of them first."

"We're not trying to be selfish," the queen interjected. "But if we die at this checkpoint, they die too. If we live, even for another hour, we might have a chance at saving them."

We were quickly running out of time. The checkpoint was dead ahead. So was the exit. If I pulled off, we might all have a shot. What was the king going to do, kill me for disobeying him? I glanced back at the queen. She looked away. She clearly didn't want to disrespect her husband, but it was just as clear she was not happy. I looked at the crown prince, but he was fixed on the Apaches. They had banked to their left and then swooped around and were now coming straight at us from behind.

This was it. At more than a hundred miles an hour, I had only seconds to decide. And then in my mirror I saw the 30mm open up.

"They're shooting at us!" I shouted.

I saw a flash. I knew what it was. I'd seen it a hundred times or more, from Fallujah to Kabul. Someone had just fired an RPG. I could see the contrail streaking down the highway behind us. It was coming straight for us. The queen screamed. I hit the gas and swerved to the right just in time. The RPG knocked off my side mirror and sliced past. It hadn't killed us.

But the next one might.

That was it, I decided. I was taking the exit.

But at that moment I saw another flash, this one from the lead Apache. He too had just fired, and this wasn't a mere RPG. This was a heat-seeking Hellfire missile. There was no swerving or avoiding it. It was coming straight for us, and there was nothing we could do about it. We were about to die in a ball of fire. It was all over.

But to my relief, the missile didn't slam into us. Instead, we watched it strike one of the Humvees at the checkpoint ahead. In the blink of an eye, the entire checkpoint was obliterated in a giant explosion. Stunned—mesmerized by the fireball in front of me—I forgot to exit. I just kept driving. Then we were crashing through the burning remains of the checkpoint, racing through the interchange, and getting on Route 35, bound for the airport.

None of us cheered. We were relieved beyond words, but we all knew this was not of our doing. Forces beyond us were keeping us alive and clearing the way for us. And it wasn't just the chopper pilots.

The Apaches banked hard and came up beside us. One after another, they kept launching Hellfire missiles, clearing checkpoints and allowing us to keep moving undeterred. By now I was topping 120 miles per hour, but there was no way we were going to get to the airport before the president took off. The queen and crown prince had climbed into the back of the SUV. They had found a first aid kit and were doing the best they could to care for Mansour and Lavi. Yael watched for new threats while the king worked the satphone again. He was getting updates from his brother and from other generals. He was organizing a massive counter-strike on the ISIS jihadists.

Soon we saw one squadron after another of

Jordanian F-16s and F-15s streaking across the sky. I had to believe they were headed to Amman to bomb the palace and crush the rebellion. I couldn't imagine how difficult a decision that must have been for the king, but I also knew he had no choice. He was the last of the Hashemite monarchs, and he seemed determined not to go down like those before him.

Somewhere along the way, I had ceased to be a journalist. I was no mere observer of history; I was a participant. I could no longer claim to be objective. Yes, this king had his flaws, and so did his government. No, Jordan wasn't a Jeffersonian democracy. But His Majesty had emerged in recent years as the region's leading Arab Reformer. Where once the presidents of Iraq and Afghanistan had looked like promising Reformers—battling hard against the Radicals—they had not proven themselves up to the task. This king was different, and my respect for him had shot up enormously in recent days.

Maybe my brother was right. Maybe the prophecies indicated Jordan was going to take a seriously dark turn in the last days. Maybe that was coming up fast. But I hoped not. I didn't want the Hashemite Kingdom to fall—not yet, not now. I wanted this king to crush his enemies and help fulfill his destiny as a peacemaker in the region. I wanted him to succeed in making Jordan a model of tolerance and modernity.

As we sped along Highway 35, against all odds, strangely enough I actually began to feel a sense of hope again. We were still alive. We were safe for now. And I had the strongest sense that the king was going to prevail. He had been blindsided, to be sure. But he had enormous personal courage. He had an army ready to fight back, and he had the Americans and the Israelis ready to fight with him.

But when we arrived at the airport, those feelings instantly evaporated.

64

As I surveyed the devastation around us, all hope disappeared.

The gorgeous new multimillion-dollar terminal was a smoking crater. The roads and runways were pockmarked with the remains of mortars and artillery shells that apparently had been fired not long before we arrived. Jumbo jets were on fire. Dead and dying bodies lay everywhere. Fuel depots were ablaze. The stench of burning jet fuel was overwhelming.

Air Force One was gone. The president had left without us.

The Apaches above us went to work. They joined other Royal Air Force helicopter gunships and fighter jets in finishing off the remains of the rebel forces, some of which were still fighting at the southern perimeter of the airfield. But the Jordanian army was nowhere to be seen.

To be precise, there was evidence that the army had been here but apparently had retreated. Why?

All around us were burning tanks and armored personnel carriers. We could see slain Jordanian soldiers everywhere. There were bodies of many ISIS terrorists, too. But why wasn't the Royal Army in full offensive mode? This wasn't the Iraqi army. The Jordanians were highly trained, highly motivated, well-led troops. Why had they fallen back?

None of us said a word, not even the king. We were all aghast. It took us several minutes to absorb the magnitude of the disaster.

It was Yael who first realized what had happened.

"They used the sarin," she said.

There was dead silence in the SUV. No one wanted to believe her. Surely it wasn't possible.

"The mortars and artillery shells that were fired here must have all been filled with it," she continued.

I wanted to believe she was wrong. But as I slowly drove through the fire and smoke, it became clear that the Jordanian troops who had fought here had not died of bullet or shrapnel wounds. As we got a closer look at the bodies—hundreds of them—we could see the vacant eyes and twisted, contorted faces. I had seen such horrors before. I had seen them in Mosul just days earlier. This was the work of Abu Khalif.

There were no words. The queen wept quietly in the back. The crown prince was frozen, his hand over his mouth. The king said nothing either. He just stared at the carnage in disbelief.

Finally he pointed to a half-destroyed hangar off to our left. I drove there immediately at his command. Under what meager cover it provided, I pulled to a stop. We all knew what we had to do.

The crown prince handed us each a backpack. We all put on the chem-bio suits, the gloves, and the gas masks as quickly as we could. Then Yael and I helped the queen and the prince put protective suits on Lavi and Mansour, desperately hoping to shield them from whatever trace of the deadly chemical was still in the air.

As we did, I could hear the roar of choppers. I turned and saw two military helicopters approaching from the east. They were preparing to land not far from us.

Just then, two Jordanian F-15s shot right over our heads. A moment later, four more streaked past.

The king's satellite phone rang. He answered it but mostly listened, saying only an occasional "Yes" or "I understand," and then hung up.

"Who was that?" I asked as I finished zipping up President Mansour's chem-bio suit.

"My brother," the king said as if in a daze.

"And?"

"He sent the choppers," he replied, turning to his wife and son. "The first one is for you both, to get you to safety."

The queen and crown prince appeared too numb to speak.

Then the king turned to Yael and me. "The other is to take Salim and Daniel to Jerusalem," he told us. "You two will go with them. IDF medical crews are on standby. Daniel will go to Hadassah. Salim will be transferred to a hospital in Ramallah."

We watched as the two Black Hawks landed

and teams of heavily armed soldiers in full protective suits poured out of both. The king held his wife briefly. Then he hugged his eldest son and walked them both to the first chopper. I watched as the door was shut and the Black Hawk lifted off while the king waved good-bye to his family.

Then I realized there wasn't a chopper for the monarch. I turned to him and asked, "But, sir, what about you?"

"I'm not leaving," the king said. "My brother is on his way. He's bringing a team of specialists."

"You can't stay here, Your Majesty," I said. "We need to get you someplace secure."

"No," he said. "I need to figure out exactly what happened here and why my men failed to stop it."

"And then?"

"Then we're going to unleash the wrath of Jordan on ISIS," he told me.

"But, sir, James is right—it's not safe here," Yael protested. "Please, we need to get you out of here."

"No," the king said. "This is my home. And these are my people. We're not going to surrender. We're going to fight back. These demons are not going to win. I promise you that."

The king gave us no opportunity for rebuttal. He immediately opened the back of the SUV and with the help of his troops began carrying President Mansour to the second chopper. Yael and I worked with several other soldiers to get Prime Minister Lavi into the remaining Black Hawk as well.

Just then the king's satphone rang again. As he answered it, Yael climbed into the Black Hawk and sat next to her prime minister, checking his vital signs. I was about to get in myself when I saw a strange expression on the king's face. It started off as bewilderment. It turned into horror.

"What is it, Your Majesty?" I asked.

"That was the Pentagon," he said. "Chairman of the Joint Chiefs."

"What did he say?"

"He wants to know where President Taylor is," he replied.

"He's not on Air Force One?"

"No."

"What do you mean?"

"Apparently, when the ISIS attack on the airport began, the president called the pilot of Air Force One and ordered him to get off the ground and into safe airspace until my forces retook the airport and it was safe to come back and get him."

I felt a pain growing in my stomach. "So where was he going to go in the meantime?"

"He didn't say," the king replied. "He just said he and the agents with him would take shelter and hunker down until the coast was clear. Then he'd order Air Force One to come back for them all."

"And?"

"They haven't heard from him since. The chairman says they've been calling every number they have for the president and for every member of his detail. They can't get through to any of them."

"So where is the president?"

"I have no idea."

I just stared at the king. I had no clue what to say.

Then Yael told me to get into the chopper.

They needed to get off the ground and get Lavi and Mansour to safety right away. She was right, of course. But I couldn't go.

"Go without me," I told her.

"Are you crazy?" she shot back.

"No, I'm staying."

"Oh no, you're not. Come on."

"There's no time to argue, Yael. Get this bird off the ground."

Shocked and angry, she turned to the king. "Your Majesty, order him to get on this chopper."

But I shook my head. "I'm staying with you, sir. This is my president. I need to follow this story, wherever it goes and whatever it takes."

The king looked into my eyes but didn't say a word. Then he waved to the pilot, signaling for him to take off. Before Yael could respond, a soldier slammed the side door and the Black Hawk lifted off the ground. It quickly gained altitude and headed west toward Jerusalem with two fighter jets flying escort on either side.

As I stood there and watched them fade into the distance, I became physically ill. I felt hot bile rising in my throat. My body was soaked with sweat. I was suffocating in this suit. The president was missing. Mansour and Lavi were critically injured. Jordan was in flames. ISIS was on the move. And for the life of me, I could see no way out.

Then I remembered Jamal Ramzy's cell phone. I ran back to the Suburban and grabbed it off the dashboard.

"What's this?" the king asked as I put it in his hand.

"A lead, Your Majesty," I replied. "Something you can use. It's Jamal Ramzy's phone."

Then a thought struck me.

I pulled out my own phone and dialed Allen's number in Washington. It rang twice before someone answered.

It was not Allen.

"Hello, Allen MacDonald's office. Can I help you?"

"Where's Allen?" I demanded.

"He's out for the moment. Who's calling, please?"

"It's J. B. Collins calling from Amman with an urgent exclusive. I need Allen right away."

"Hold, please."

The wait that followed felt like an eternity, and the longer it took, the more irritated I became. I was right in the middle of the story of the decade—maybe the century—and Allen was nowhere to be found.

Finally I heard my editor's voice on the line. "J. B., is that you? What on earth is going on over there?"

"What's going on is all hell is breaking loose. Prime Minister Lavi and President Mansour are injured and en route to hospitals via helicopter. The king is furious but resolute and is swearing vengeance against ISIS. But never mind that. Take this down and get it out on the wire, on Twitter, everywhere. The lead is—"

"What?" he asked frantically. "Say again. I can hardly hear you."

"I said, take this down. The president of the United States . . . is missing."

TURN THE PAGE

for an excerpt from the next thrilling novel by

JOEL C. ROSENBERG

New York Times bestselling author

★ ★ ★ THE ★ ★ ★

KREMLIN
CONSPIRACY

A gripping tale ripped from future headlines!

PREORDER NOW!

Available in stores and online March 6, 2018.

★ ★ ★

MOSCOW, RUSSIA

Louisa Sherbatov had just turned six, but she would never turn seven.

The whirling dervish had finally fallen asleep on the couch just before midnight, crashed from a sugar high, still wearing her new magenta dress and matching ribbon in her blonde tresses. Snuggled up on her father's lap, she looked so peaceful, so content as she hugged her favorite stuffed bear and lay surrounded by the dolls and books and sweaters and other gifts she'd received from all her aunts and uncles and grandparents and cousins as well as her friends from the elementary school just down the block at the end of Guryanova Street.

Strewn about her were string and tape and wads of brightly colored wrapping paper. The kitchen sink was stacked high with dirty plates and cups and silverware. The dining room table was still littered with empty bottles of wine and vodka and scraps of leftover birthday pie—strawberry, Louisa's favorite.

The flat was a mess. But the guests were gone and it was Thursday night and the weekend was upon them and honestly, her parents, Feodor and Irina, couldn't have cared less. Their little girl, the only child they had been able to bear after more than a decade and two heartbreaking miscarriages, was happy. Her friends were happy. Their parents were happy. They were happy. Everything else could wait.

Feodor stared down at the two precious women in his life and longed to stay. He had loved planning the party with them both, had loved helping shop for the food, loved helping Irina and her mother make all the preparations, loved seeing the sheer delight on Louisa's face when he'd given her a shiny blue bicycle, her first. But business was business. If he was going to make his flight to Tashkent, he had to leave quickly. So he gently kissed mother and daughter on their foreheads, picked up his suitcase, and slipped out as quietly as he could.

As he stepped out the front door of the apartment building, he was relieved to see the cab he'd ordered waiting for him as planned. He moved briskly to the car, shook hands with the driver, and gave the man his bag. The night air was crisp and fresh. The moon was full, and leaves were beginning to fall and swirl in the light breeze coming from the west. Summer was finally over, thought Feodor as he climbed into the backseat, and not a moment too soon. The sweltering heat. The stifling humidity. The gnawing guilt of not being able to afford even a simple air conditioner, much less a little dacha out in the country where he and Irina and Louisa and maybe his parents or hers could retreat now and again, somewhere in a forest with lots of shade and a sparkling lake for swimming or fishing.

"Thank God, autumn has arrived," he half mumbled to himself as the driver slammed the trunk shut and got back behind the wheel. Growing up, Feodor had always loved the cooler weather. The shorter days. Going back to school. Making new friends. Meeting new teachers. Taking new classes. Fall meant change, and change had always been good to him. Perhaps one day, if he continued to work very hard, he could save enough money to move his family away from 19 Guryanova Street, away from this noisy, dirty, run-down, depressing hovel on the south side of the capital and find some place really lovely and quaint and quiet. Some place worthy of raising a family. Some place with a bit of grass, maybe even a garden where he could till the soil with his own hands and grow his own vegetables.

As the cab began to pull away from the curb, Feodor leaned back in his seat. He closed his eyes and folded his hands on his chest. Yes, autumn had always been a time of new beginnings, and he wondered what this one might bring. He was not rich. He was not successful. But he was content, even hopeful, perhaps for the first time in his life.

He found himself reminiscing about the first time he'd laid eyes on Irina—the first day of middle school, twenty-two years ago. He was so caught up in his memories that he did not notice the car parked just down the street, a white Lada with its headlights off but its engine running. He didn't notice that the front license plate was covered with some sort of masking tape, revealing only the numbers 6 and 2. Nor did he notice the car's driver, nervously smoking a cigarette and tapping on the dashboard, or the two burly men, dressed in black leather jackets and black leather gloves, emerging from the basement of his own building. When the police would later ask about the men and the car, Feodor would be unable to provide any description at all.

What he did remember—what he could never possibly forget—was the deafening explosion behind him. He remembered the searing fireball. He remembered the taxi driver losing control and crashing into a lamppost not fifty meters up the street, and he remembered smashing his head against the plastic screen dividing the front seat from the back. He remembered the ghastly sensation of kicking open the back door of the cab, jumping out into the pavement, blood streaming down his face, heart pounding furiously, and looking up just in time to see his home, the twelve-story apartment building at 19 Guryanova Street, collapse in a blinding flash of fire and ash.

A NOTE FROM
THE AUTHOR

★   ★   ★

When I started writing *The Third Target*, I had never heard of ISIS.

I knew I wanted to write a series about the threat Radical Islam poses not only to the U.S., Israel, and the West but also to our moderate Arab/Muslim allies in the Middle East and to Arab Christians in the region. I knew I wanted my main character to be a *New York Times* foreign correspondent who sees a grave new threat coming up over the horizon. I also knew I wanted to write about a serious and believable enemy. I just didn't know which one it should be.

To determine that, as I began to sketch my outline in early 2013 I posed two sets of "What if?" questions.

First: What if Radical Islamic extremists were able to seize control of a cache of chemical weapons in Syria that were overlooked or not reported to the U.N. disarmament teams? Which terrorist group would be in a position to do that? What would they do with such weapons of mass destruction once they grabbed hold of them? Who might they use such weapons against? And how might the powers in the region and the international community respond?

Second: What if Radical Islamic extremists chose to target the Hashemite Kingdom of Jordan? What if they tried to seize control of her territory and people to establish a violent caliphate on the East Bank of the Jordan River? What would be the implications for the rest of the Middle East? What would be the implications for America, Israel, Europe, and the rest of the world? And again, which Radical group might be inclined to launch such an attack and be in a position to do so?

I knew going into this project that few Americans spend much time—if any—thinking about the Hashemite Kingdom of Jordan. But over the years I have come to regard Jordan as one of the most important Arab allies the West has in the epicenter.

Since ascending to the throne in 1999, Jordan's King Abdullah II has proven himself to be a moderate, peaceful, wise Reformer who has been a true friend of the United States, Great Britain, and NATO. He has also maintained the peace treaty with Israel and a healthy relationship with the Jewish State, a relationship that began with secret contacts between his father, the late King Hussein, and Israeli leaders as far back as the 1960s. The present king has been actively engaged in combatting the terrorist activity of Radicals via his military, police, and intelligence networks. He has also sought to combat the ideology of Radicals by building a global network of Islamic scholars and clerics who reject the takfiris, violent extremists, and heretics, and who are proactively trying to define Islam as a peaceful, tolerant religion.

At the same time, he has worked hard to make Jordan a safe haven for both Muslims and Arab Christians fleeing from war and persecution in the region. What's more, it has become increasingly clear that a safe, secure, and moderate Jordan is the absolutely essential cornerstone of any serious future comprehensive peace agreement between the Israelis and Palestinians.

As I went down the list of Radical states and terrorist organizations in the region that might be able to gain control of WMD in Syria and might choose to attack Jordan, I conferred with a range of Middle East experts, current and former intelligence officials, and retired U.S. and Israeli diplomats and military leaders. I asked who they thought was the next big threat likely to rise in the region. Without exception, they all told me, "ISIS."

At the time, neither I nor my publisher, Tyndale House, had heard of this group. Yet the more I learned, the more convinced I became that in the following five years or so, ISIS could actually become a global threat and a household name. Indeed, the ISIS threat has metastasized even faster. Now the whole world has heard of ISIS (the Islamic State of Iraq and al Sham), which is also known as ISIL (the Islamic State of Iraq and the Levant), or simply the Islamic State.

Indeed, as I write this author's note, events are moving quickly. The president of the United States has declared ISIS a threat to our national security. Several Sunni Muslim Arab countries have joined a military and political coalition to "degrade and defeat" ISIS. All eyes are now on the epicenter, but it remains unclear just how successful the strategies employed against ISIS by the U.S. and our allies will be. I pray the events I have written about here never take place. I fear, however, that some world leaders may still underestimate the threat. If so, the consequences could be devastating. I hope that those who are able to act will do so before it is too late.

This book is obviously a work of fiction, but I tried to set the fictional events in as realistic a framework as possible. To that end, I included references to a number of real-life people and events. Journalist A. B. Collins is a figment of my imagination, but the assassination of King Abdullah I that he witnessed in Jerusalem in 1951 is a real, historical event. Abu Khalif is a fictional terrorist, but you may see some similarities to Abu Bakr al-Baghdadi, the real-life head of ISIS. Ayman al-Zawahiri, the real-life leader of al-Qaeda, has not been assassinated by the U.S. government— yet—but the tension between his terrorist organization and ISIS is real.

Of course, the most obvious real-life character in the book is King Abdullah II, Jordan's current monarch. I considered fictionalizing him, as I did the leaders of the U.S., Israel, and the Palestinian Authority. After all, it is always sensitive to write about a current leader in dangerous times, and I certainly do not want to offend His Majesty or the Royal Court. But in the end I chose to include King Abdullah II as a character in this novel primarily because I thought it would not be as effective to write about the emerging threat to Jordan without including him directly. People need to understand who this king is, and why he is uniquely important in Jordan's past, present, and future. I hope readers will come to appreciate just how dangerous the region and the world would be if this king is toppled or violently overthrown. To help in this process, several of the things the king says in chapter 50 of this book, for example, are actually direct quotes (or close adaptations) from King Abdullah's excellent 2011 book, *Our Last Best Chance: The Pursuit of Peace in a Time of Peril*. I highly recommend that nonfiction work if you are interested in a true insider's perspective on current events in the epicenter.

Other books I used for research include:

Uneasy Lies the Head: The Autobiography of His Majesty King Hussein I of the Hashemite Kingdom of Jordan

Fighting Terrorism: How Democracies Can Defeat Domestic and International Terrorists by Benjamin Netanyahu

Hussein and Abdullah: Inside the Jordanian Royal Family by Randa Habib

Lion of Jordan: The Life of King Hussein in War and Peace by Avi Shlaim

King's Counsel: A Memoir of War, Espionage, and Diplomacy in the Middle East by Jack O'Connell

Son of Hamas: A Gripping Account of Terror, Betrayal, Political Intrigue, and Unthinkable Choices by Mosab Hassan Yousef

Once an Arafat Man: The True Story of How a PLO Sniper Found a New Life by Tass Saada

The Second Arab Awakening and the Battle for Pluralism by Marwan Muasher

Kill Khalid: The Failed Mossad Assassination of Khalid Mishal and the Rise of Hamas by Paul McGeough

From Beirut to Jerusalem by Thomas L. Friedman

The Case for Democracy: The Power of Freedom to Overcome Tyranny and Terror by Natan Sharansky and Ron Dermer

The Fight for Jerusalem: Radical Islam, the West, and the Future of the Holy City by Dore Gold

As part of the research process I undertook for this novel, I had the incredible opportunity to travel to Jordan in the spring of 2014 to meet with several senior officials. While I have traveled to Jordan numerous times over the years, this was a particularly special trip. I have a deep love and respect for the people of Jordan. This has only grown over time, but never more so than on that trip.

Special thanks to everyone who made time for me and shared with me their perspective as I did research for this book, both on that research trip and others. Not everyone I met and spoke with will agree with what I have written here. Nevertheless, I am enormously grateful for their insights, wisdom, and kindness, and I hope the book is richer for what I learned from them. Among those to whom I would like to express my deep gratitude are:

His Excellency Abdullah Ensour, Jordan's prime minister

His Royal Highness Prince Ghazi Bin Muhammad, senior advisor to His Majesty King Abdullah II

H.E. Nasser Judeh, Jordan's foreign minister

H.E. Hussein Hazza' Al-Majali, Jordan's interior minister

H.E. Nidal Qatamin, Jordan's minister of labor and tourism

H.E. Alia Bouran, Jordan's ambassador to the United States

James Woolsey, former director of the Central Intelligence Agency

Porter Goss, former director of the Central Intelligence Agency

Danny Yatom, former director of the Mossad

Hon. Dore Gold, former Israeli ambassador to the United Nations and president of the Jerusalem Center for Public Affairs

Yechiel Horev, former Israeli director of security of the Defense Establishment

Robert Satloff, executive director of the Washington Institute for Near East Policy

I'm also deeply grateful for the aides, advisors, and colleagues of those mentioned above who were so generous with their time and insights. There are others who were enormously helpful that I am not able to mention publicly. To them, as well, I say thank you.

Writing and publishing a novel is a team effort, and I am so grateful for a number of people who have helped me on this project as with so many other books.

Many thanks to:

My wonderful literary agent and good friend, Scott Miller, and his team at Trident Media Group

My first-rate publishing team at Tyndale House Publishers, including Mark Taylor, Jeff Johnson, Ron Beers, Karen Watson, Jan Stob, Cheryl Kerwin, Todd Starowitz,

Dean Renninger, Caleb Sjogren, Erin Smith, Danika King, and the entire sales force—and special thanks to my editor, Jeremy Taylor, who has really done an outstanding job on this one

My blessed parents, Leonard and Mary Rosenberg

My excellent November Communications team, June Meyers and Nancy Pierce

My four wonderful sons—Caleb, Jacob, Jonah, and Noah

My dear, sweet, and amazing wife, Lynn, who has blessed me every moment of every day since we first met in college at Syracuse University and has continued to bless me beyond belief through twenty-five fantastic years of marriage! What an adventure we have been on, Lynnie—may it never end!

Most of all, I am grateful to my Lord and Savior Jesus Christ, who loves so deeply the people of Israel, and Jordan, and Iraq, and Syria, and all the people of the epicenter, and for some unfathomable reason loves me and my family, too.

ABOUT THE AUTHOR

★ ★ ★

Joel C. Rosenberg is a *New York Times* bestselling author with more than three million copies sold among his twelve novels (including *The Last Jihad*, *Damascus Countdown*, and *The Auschwitz Escape*), four nonfiction books (including *Epicenter* and *Inside the Revolution*), and a digital short (*Israel at War*). A front-page Sunday *New York Times* profile called him a "force in the capital." He has also been profiled by the *Washington Times* and the *Jerusalem Post* and has been interviewed on ABC's *Nightline*, CNN *Headline News*, FOX News Channel, The History Channel, MSNBC, *The Rush Limbaugh Show*, and *The Sean Hannity Show*.

You can follow him at www.joelrosenberg.com or on Twitter @joelcrosenberg and Facebook: www.facebook.com/JoelCRosenberg.

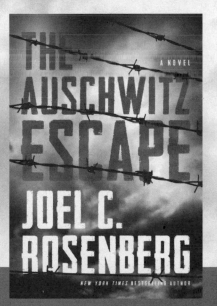